The
LIFE
and
DREAMS
of
EFFIE FARRADAY

L.A. Williams

ALSO IN THE EFFIE FARRADAY TRILOGY...

The Continuing Saga of Effie Farraday

The Loves and Sorrows of Effie Farraday

Available on Amazon

******

Book cover design by Lynn Williams

I dedicate this book to my daughter

INTRODUCTION

It is said that dreams are our release, our salvation from the troubles of life. It seems to me they are all stored away methodically in the library of our minds, and in our subconscious state we choose one at random to re-live whilst we lay sleeping. How welcoming it is as we drift along the twisting pathway of our minds and stumble across a dream. The way ahead maybe clear and will allow us to enter a dream, which has no meaning but is enjoyable all the same, or we may find ourselves being whisked away from that path to an exciting adventure in another world. Occasionally we are transported back to the past where we are reunited with loved ones that have long since departed, and we might have a tiny glimpse of a cherished memory we thought lost in the midst of time. But sometimes, just sometimes, it is too dark to see the path ahead and we become lost along the way by a cold and sinister mist that envelopes us in our deepest darkest fears, and causes us to stumble upon horrors that we would wish buried for all eternity.

I for one, although I'd never claim to be an expert, can honestly say that dreaming can be both a delight and a curse. Why only yesterday I had the strangest dream; it took me back in time across the years to my old childhood home of Rawlings. I hovered over the house like a bird then swooped down through the tiled clay roof and into the building within as if I were a phantom. I floated from room to room like a shadow from the past and gazed in wonder at the beauty of the house, which seemed to be rather grander and more impressive than I remember. For a moment I was elated that my dream allowed me one last tiny glimpse of my beloved home and my heart was filled with joy at how familiar it all still seemed. But then a chill came over me, and Rawlings was shaken by a sudden tremor that reached throughout the foundations. A dark mist seeped down from above like a huge hand shrouding the entire house in darkness, and I found myself standing in the grounds surrounded by ruins, lost and forlorn. It was a cruel dream, a poignant reminder that I can never return to my beloved home. But this isn't the last time I shall mention Rawlings, as it is vital as the blood running through my veins. It *has* to be where my story begins, for its involvement is the only way to give you an accurate account of what happened to me, before I disappeared from the world…

Chapter 1

I suppose my safe and relatively ordinary little life begun turning rather strange near the time of my very first art exhibition. In those days I tended to be consumed with self- doubt which caused me to severely question nearly everything in my life. There was often an aggravating voice inside my head, nagging away at me, denting my confidence. So, in those anxious days leading up to the exhibition, I found myself praying that something would occur to delay the big day, such as a fire in the village hall where the exhibition was to be held, or a thief perhaps – they would break into Rawlings overnight and steal all my paintings for the event. And, of course there was always the chance that we'd got the dates mixed up. All these scenarios of course had very little chance of actually happening, but I rather wished they would. *If* there'd been a way to look into my immediate future, I would swiftly realise how stupid I was acting, that the exhibition was completely insignificant, in comparison with what was coming, and *who* was coming for me…

So, there I was sitting on the edge of the bed with the early morning sun streaming through the window. There was something about my room that brought upon me an air of calmness and in other circumstances I would have been perfectly content, but not on *this* particular day. Today was the day I had come to dread, the day of reckoning, the day when all eyes would be on me, judging me, waiting for me to slip up, in some way shape of form. My only saving grace would be my paintings – people would be more interested in them than me. I would fade away into the background, just like a distant figure in one of my landscapes.

With a sigh, I rose and wearily made my way over to the dressing table, where I sat down and stared at my reflection. My general appearance didn't help boost my mood, as last night I'd slept particularly badly, tossing and turning for hours on end, and the lack of sleep showed in my face: I looked deathly pale and my eyes were rather bloodshot; then there was my dishevelled hair. I started to drag a comb through it, trying desperately to remove the tangles.

There was a gentle tap on the door.

'Effie dear. Are you ready?'

Without waiting for a reply, the door swung slowly open. My Aunt Constance stood in the doorway, smiling apprehensively, but her face soon dropped when she saw me.

'Oh, Effie, you look like you've literally got out of bed.' She said in a concerned voice.

I looked sheepishly at her. 'I overlaid Aunt.' There was little point in lying, as she knew me too well. 'And I ah, well...I'm not sure if I can go through with this today.'

'Oh Effie, everything will be fine, just you wait and see.' She grabbed my arms. 'Come on, be strong. The brave shall conquer the world.' Her eyes narrowed and she looked up at the ceiling. 'Who said that? I'm sure it was someone of importance.'

'It was you Aunt.' I said smiling at her.

She had a tendency to come out with these phrases, and although they didn't always make much sense, I wouldn't dream of telling her. I would've hated to upset her in any way as she was like a mother to me, and I loved her dearly. My actual mother was rather an enigma. Shortly after my birth she left without any explanation whatsoever, leaving Aunt to bring me up, and now there is a dark lingering cloud that shrouds my mother in a veil of mystery.

'So dear, what are you wearing on this fine day?'

'Um, I'm not really sure Aunt.' I murmured. 'The usual I suppose, something casual.'

She tutted. 'You need to dress for the occasion Effie. This is your moment to shine.'

I glanced at her smart tweed suit, knowing how she'd carefully selected it last night from her wardrobe. It was very like my Aunt to be so organised, always prepared for an occasion.

'Well, you know me - I'm not really one to dress up.'

Without answering, she marched over to my wardrobe and began rifling through its contents, grimacing and muttering under her breath. Finally, she pulled out a summer dress that had hardly seen the light of day.

'Here. This will have to do.' She handed it to me and made her way to the door. 'I'll be back in 5 minutes. I expect you dressed and ready to go.' Her hand reached up to smooth over her dark brown, slightly greying hair, which was arranged neatly in its usual bun at the back of her head. 'And please do try and tame that hairs of yours.'

'Oh Aunt, you do fuss so.'

She turned and gazed at me, her green eyes bright and alert as ever. 'When I was your age young lady, I made a point of dressing appropriately for each occasion. People would often remark how exquisitely turned out I was.'

My Aunt was very pretty when she was younger, and would make a point of showing me old photos of when she was my age. Sometimes she'd drift off into a world of her own, lamenting over lost loves and missed opportunities. With a mournful sigh she would turn and tell me how truelove doesn't come knocking on your door, that you have to go out there and find it, and when you do, grasp it with both hands and never let it go, because sometimes it slips away and never returns; it's evident her words of advice are from her experiences of the heart, but she would never tell me what happened in her past, and I would never press the subject, for I fear that somewhere along the way she had her heart badly broken.

'Yes Aunt. I know, you've told me before.' I stared down at the dress. 'I'm sure this will be fine. Besides, no one will notice my attire. They'll come to see my paintings.' I gulped. 'Hopefully, at least, one or two people will turn up.'

She frowned and rolled her eyes.

'Effie, appearance is everything. You really should take more care about the way you dress, rather than looking a mess all of the time?'

I glared at her and sighed. 'Please don't be critical Aunt, not today.'

She threw me a stern look and frowned, shaking her head as if in despair.

'Well, I just want you to look your best Effie, for the big day.'

'Anyone would think it's my wedding day.' I chuckled.

Finding this highly amusing she erupted into laughter.

3

'Well, we would certainly have to postpone that Effie, you'd need far too much work.' She opened the door, smiling bashfully at me. 'Sorry dear, that was rather mean. You just need a *little* work, to allow your natural beauty to shine through. And there's also the question of a man, we couldn't have a wedding without the groom.'

I raised my eyes at her. 'Please Aunt, can we stop discussing my imaginary wedding day.'

Chuckling, she glanced at her watch then looked at me in alarm.

'Oh Lord Effie the time. Quickly get dressed.'

I watched as she scurried out the room.

From a stranger's point of view my Aunt might have seemed rather prim and proper but impressions can be deceiving: When you got to know her, you'd discover she had a rather mischievous sense of humour and strange little quirks that were really most endearing. All of my Aunt's acquaintances and close friends would undoubtedly describe her as extremely kind and loyal, and throughout my younger years she tirelessly endeavoured to make sure I was always courteous to others. 'Treat people with respect and they in turn shall do the same with you Effie.' She would tell me in her direct manner. I admired her frankness and understood it was for my benefit. But her behaviour seemed rather odd of late, and I'd become increasingly concerned for her welfare. It was perfectly natural for her to take an interest in my life, however recently it had been verging on the extreme, and I found myself unable to leave the house without an interrogation. Perhaps she imagined I was going to suddenly vanish in the dead of night, never to return.

I dressed and once again attempted to comb my unruly auburn hair.

'It's an improvement.' I mumbled, tucking a stray curl behind my ear.

This time my Aunt didn't bother to knock but just strolled into the room, looking a little tense. She narrowed her eyes, scrutinising my appearance.

'Mmm, well I suppose you'll have to do.'

I wondered if my Aunt was concerned about what her committee friends would think. There was no doubt they'd all be there today, ready to voice their opinions. I'd met them before and they'd been perfectly lovely. But I couldn't help but picture them huddled around a table with their tea and scones, carefully watching me, noticing every move I made, every mistake. They would comment about my scruffy appearance. And then the talk would turn to my paintings, and how dreadful it was that I hadn't managed to sell any. My name would crop up in their conversations for months to come, until finally they would grow weary of the topic and forget all about it. But on the other hand, why would they talk about me at all...I was totally insignificant.

I bit my lip nervously.

A fleeting thought rushed through my mind – perhaps getting married would be *less* daunting than the exhibition. I had someone in mind for the groom, though sadly I feared he wouldn't be able to attend...

'Effie, Effie please focus.' My Aunt said crossly. It's time to leave.'

I could hear my heart hammering in my chest as a surge of panic hit me.

'Yes, yes of course.'

She smiled gently at me and took my hand. 'Come on dear. Isaiah is patiently waiting for us downstairs.'

I'd almost forgotten Isaiah was driving us to the village hall. It would have been a whole lot pleasanter if it had just been Aunt and I.

'He's so looking forward to it Effie.'

I smiled weakly as we made our way down the stairs. My heart sank as I saw him hovering in the hallway, staring at me.

Isaiah was an old family friend. He first entered our lives many years ago when he'd been the private investigator looking into my mother's strange disappearance, and ever since then he'd been skulking around our home, as if waiting for something. On numerous occasions I'd mention to my Aunt how odd it was that Isaiah was always visiting us, and that he seemed to be gradually worming his way into our home and lives. She would merely shrug her shoulders and tell me I had an overactive imagination. I would lie in bed some nights trying to figure out the motive for his constant presence at Rawlings. Sometimes I wondered if it was solely because of my Aunt -after all, he gave the impression of being very fond of her, and was always showering her with compliments which she lapped up like a naïve young girl. And as for my Aunt – she *totally* adored him and was strangely powerless when it came to resisting his charms. But the strange thing was that it wasn't just Aunt who found him appealing: many of the locals, especially the woman of the community, seemed to flock around him like bees to a honeypot. I suppose he did possess a certain charisma and he certainly knew how to use it to his advantage, to lure people into liking him. To me however it was all an elaborate façade, and behind the mask lay something decidedly unpleasant. My best friend Mace also had his doubts but strangely enough was not very forthcoming when it came to discussing Isaiah.

Despite their age gap, I wondered if my Aunt and Isaiah might marry one day. For some reason I had dreadful thoughts of her perishing shortly after their wedding, by Isaiah's hand. There would be a tragic accident, and Isaiah would appear distraught. Although the police would have their suspicions about him, I was certain he would find a way to wriggle out of any wrongdoing, and then he'd be free to take on full ownership of Rawlings. And the money - perhaps he believed we had a tidy sum in the bank, or wads of notes stuffed under a mattress. I'm sure my Aunt had too much pride to tell him the real state of our finances, for in reality we had very little.

My Aunt stumbled slightly and I tightened my grip on her arm.

'Careful Constance.' Isaiah exclaimed. 'One could easily lose their footing on those stairs.' For a moment he appeared deep in thought before turning his attentions towards me. 'Well finally.' He sniggered. 'The artist has decided to make an appearance.'

My Aunt giggled.

As we reached the foot of the stairs Isaiah took my Aunt's hand and kissed it gently. He whispered something into her ear and she playfully smacked him on the arm. I suspect it was something to do with my dress.

'Well, perhaps we should get going then.' I said, trying to keep calm.

I walked ahead of them and out the front door. Stepping outside I felt a chill in the air. The early morning sun had faded under several ominous looking storm clouds, and it looked like we were in for a downpour. Was this an omen of how the day was going to go.

With his profound limp, Isaiah made his way towards his vintage car, with my Aunt following close behind. Apparently, he'd fallen from a tree as a child and his leg had never been the same again. I suppose some might say he was an imposing looking man, a little on the stocky side perhaps. He was always dressed immaculately with his cropped grey hair always neat and presentable. As he pushed his spectacles further up over his nose, I was reminded of how my Aunt frequently mentioned about the mischievous twinkle in his eye and how it caused his entire face to light up with laughter. I always thought it a mocking type of expression, and there was something in the way he looked at people that wasn't quite right.

'Well come on Effelia, hop in.' He exclaimed, gesturing his hand towards the car door. 'You can't be late for you own exhibition, now, can you?'

Isaiah was the only person I knew that called me Effelia, even though my actual name was just plain old Effie. Over the years I'd tirelessly corrected him but he seemed oblivious to my pleas, and seemed to take great joy in aggravating me.

I smiled half-heartedly at him and clambered in the back. Aunt sat at the front, checking her reflection in the car mirror.

'Do stop it Constance. You can't improve on perfection.'

I tried to ignore the giggle.

As we drove out of the long driveway the motion of the car was rhythmic and steady, which somehow calmed my nerves. I closed my eyes for a moment and tried to direct my mind to pleasanter thoughts. I imagined being in a tranquil forest, where one was safe and hidden from the world, I could lose myself in such a place and never return to reality. With a deep sigh I opened my eyes and looked up to see Isaiah peering at me in the car mirror. I met his gaze for a moment then turned to look out the window.

It seemed a shorter journey than usual to the village hall and I suspected Isaiah had been speeding in his eagerness to get there. What a shame we hadn't taken the slightly longer route that would delay our arrival and allow me a little extra time to calm my nerves, I thought. However, on the flip side perhaps arriving here *this* early would mean avoiding me walking into a room full of staring people.

My Aunt glanced at her watch. 'Bang on time Isaiah, what would we do without you.'

'I aim to please Constance.'

'But, aren't we early?' I asked, beginning to feel anxious.

'No Effie, as I just mentioned to Isaiah we have arrived precisely when we meant to.' She turned and smiled at me. 'Now do try and enjoy it my dear, this is your big moment.'

Chapter 2

My heart sank as the both of them opened the doors and stood there, waiting for me to make my grand entrance. To my horror a huge crowd had already gathered in the building and many of the guests had already spotted me and were staring curiously over. People were standing around in little groups, looking at my paintings. Most of the work I brought along was of landscapes and beach scenes but there were various portraits too. It was surreal seeing all my paintings displayed in the village hall, rather than propped up against the wall in the old garden shed at Rawlings. If I made any money today, I would hand it over to Aunt, to put towards renovating the house.

I felt the familiar heat rising in my cheeks.

'Oh my, what a splendid turn out.' Exclaimed Isaiah in a loud voice.

'It most certainly is.' My Aunt gasped, looking pleasantly surprised. 'How marvellous. See Effie, I told you everyone would come and view your paintings.' Looking suddenly agitated she peered at Isaiah. 'Perhaps we should have got here earlier, so we could have brought out the refreshments before everyone arrived.'

Last night all three of us had organised the hall, arranging the tables and chairs for the guests, and displaying the paintings in prominent positions. We'd also brought the sandwiches and cakes over and placed them in the fridge overnight, ready to put out the following day.

'Oh, tosh Constance, there's no rush.'

'Aunt's right.' I said, narrowing my eyes at Isaiah. 'That would have been sensible thing to do.'

'Well, I don't always do the sensible thing now do I? he snapped angrily at me. I was actually thinking of you Effelia.'

'How so?'

'Well, I thought the lovely Constance and I would make ourselves scarce for a bit and give you some time on your own to greet your guests properly, without us glued to your side.' He

9

smiled at my Aunt. 'We'll toddle off to the kitchen and sort out the refreshments.'

I nodded slowly, suddenly lost for words.

My Aunt patted him lightly on the arm. 'That was very thoughtful of you Isaiah. But firstly, let's show Effie to her seat.'

For a fleeting moment he glared at her, then his face broke into a smile.

'Well of course Constance, that way we can be sure Effelia doesn't lose her nerve and sneak out the front door.'

They both laughed in unison.

'You really don't have much faith in me, do you Isaiah?'

'I have *total* faith in you Effelia. It's just a shame you don't have faith in yourself.'

We stared at one another.

I opened my mouth to speak but nothing came out. Isaiah was right, only I couldn't bring myself to tell him, it was too humiliating, and I couldn't bear to see that smug smile of his.

'Oh, come on now, let's stop dithering.' My Aunt said with a nervous laugh. 'People will start to wonder what's going on.' She grabbed my arm and began leading me across the hall, closely followed by Isaiah.

Taking a deep breath, I tried to compose myself. My plan was to try and portray the persona of a self -assured young lady who was adequately equipped to engage in conversation. As we fought our way through the throng of guests my Aunt and Isaiah exchanged pleasantries with several people, and I smiled fleetingly at people trying not to make too much eye contact with anyone. I was secretly pleased that so many people had turned up, but that also meant more people to talk to.

'Now you sit down Effie, dear. My Aunt said, gesturing for me to take a seat.

'Here?' I asked in a surprised voice.

We'd reached the less crowded part of the building now, but it was considered the most prominent spot-as this is where the head table was situated. Bride and grooms would sit here when they were having wedding receptions in the hall. As long as I'm not expected to make a speech, I thought in amusement.

'Yes dear. Her voice was slow and steady, as if speaking to a child. 'Now Isaiah and I shouldn't be long. You know we have to go and bring out the food and make the tea.'

I could feel panic rising up inside of me, choking me, preventing me from breathing, it would take my voice soon, and then strip me of the tiny shred of confidence I was desperately trying to keep hold of.

Effie. Effie, can you hear me?'

I looked at my Aunt but didn't reply.

Swiftly my eyes swept across the room, searching for a familiar face. My friend Clarice had promised to come along today and support me, but it seemed she hadn't arrived yet. Suddenly I spotted a small group of my Aunt's committee friends; they were all gathered on a corner table busily chatting away amongst themselves. I was sorely inclined to go and join them, at least then I wouldn't stand out like a sore thumb.

'Oh Lord Isaiah, I think she's having a panic attack.'

I gasped for air, wiping my brow.

'No, no, I'm fine.' I uttered rather breathlessly. 'Just give me a moment.' I watched them both peering at me, concern etched across their faces. 'I...I'd quite like to go and sit with your friend's Aunt.'

'Yes, Effie. Perhaps you should.'

Isaiah looked astonished. 'On no Effelia, that certainly won't do. You must remain here where everyone can see you.' He pulled the chair back and waited for me to sit down. 'You don't want to become lost in the crowd now do you?' he smiled slyly at me.

'Well, yes, actually I do.' I felt like saying. But instead, I remained silent.

'Today your Abercrombie's star attraction, Effelia.'

Suddenly I had the urge to thump him.

My Aunt smiled graciously at me. 'Yes, you mustn't be invisible. You are alright though, aren't you dear?'

I was about to reply but Isaiah rudely interrupted.

'Yes, yes, Effelia is fine. Now come along Constance let's make a start on the refreshments.' He said taking her arm. 'I can't wait to try one of your scrumptious homemade scones.'

My Aunt chuckled.

Without another word they walked arm in arm to the small kitchen at the other end of the hall. I stared after them until they'd disappeared out of sight. In dismay I tentatively sat down in the chair at the head table.

I often pondered how many people existed like me, who had to endure the heavy burden of being shy, how many suffered in a terrible silence and weren't capable of escaping their affliction. They would create a wall to hide behind, a solid wall that prevented anyone from seeing the real person, and only by chiselling away would it gradually collapse, and reveal who was really there.

For a few moments I sat there fiddling with my hair, hoping the ground would open up and swallow me whole. People was staring over at me and they probably thought me rude for not mingling. I hated the word *mingling;* it was one of those irksome words that shouldn't be in the vocabulary; I probably only thought this because I wasn't very good at *mingling.* With a sigh I rose from the chair and made my way towards the mass of guests.

As it turned out, I was making a fuss about nothing. Somehow, I managed to get by without saying anything stupid; there were a few awkward silences but that was to be expected. Most of the guests were perfectly amiable, shaking my hand and praising me on my outstanding work. However, at this stage, I wasn't sure if anyone had actually purchased any of the paintings, or whether they were simply curious. I noticed some of the guests had already left. Maybe they wanted to escape Isaiah, who was scurrying around like a headless chicken offering people cakes and endless cups of tea. However, it was so warm in the hall I've no doubt people wanted to get out into the fresh air.

Suddenly there was a loud shatter.

'Oh Mrs Baxter, I'm so dreadfully sorry.' Exclaimed Isaiah.

It seemed Isaiah had accidently knocked into Mrs Baxter, causing her to drop her cup of tea. He was now on his hands and knees picking up pieces of broken crockery, apologising profusely.

I couldn't help but smile.

Suddenly I heard my name being called. I scanned the hall until my eyes rested on my Aunt, who was signalling for me to join her. As I strolled over towards her, I saw she was shaking hands with an elderly lady.

Someone suddenly grabbed my arm.

'Hello Effie.'

A slender young woman with light blond hair was standing there grinning at me.

'Clarice, I'm so glad you're here.' I said, giving her a hug.

'Sorry I'm late, I had an appointment.' She said excitedly. 'I've been here for a while but only just spotted you. 'Wow, I've never seen the hall packed with so many people before.' She pulled a face.

I gave her a warm smile.

I'd known Clarice for years, she was a quiet, unassuming type of person, and I suppose that's the reason we always got along so well, but unlike myself she was always happy and smiling, an eternal optimist who viewed the world with wide-eyed wonder.

'Oh, don't worry Clarice, better late than never.' I said, laughing. 'Yes, it is rather busy, isn't it?' I said, linking my arm with hers.

She giggled. 'Too crowded for you eh Effie?'

'Slightly, you know what I'm like.'

With a rapid nod she smiled at me then began looking across the hall. 'But just think how this exhibition will advertise your talent. It will catapult you to fame and fortune.'

'Yes, well I wouldn't go that far Clarice. I'm not even sure that I've actually sold any yet. I really should go and find out.'

'Effie, I'm certain you will.' She squeezed my hand and carried on looking around the hall as if searching for someone. 'So, where's that peculiar friend of ours?'

I looked cheerfully at her. 'If you're referring to Mace, he couldn't make it, he promised his parents he'd help them with the garden, but he's coming over to Rawlings later.'

Clarice nodded. 'Well, it's nice to see you without him chained to your side.' She said giggling slightly.

'Actually, I was somewhat relieved Mace was absent today, as I was rather worried he may put some of the buyers off with his outspoken manner.' I screwed up my face. 'Is that really mean of me to think that Clarice?'

She gave me a playful slap on the arm. 'Absolutely not, he'd not only frighten everyone off, but he'd eat all the cakes too. You know what greedy-guts he can be; I'm amazed he remains so skinny.'

'I know, I don't think he's human.'

'Ha – that would explain it.' Suddenly she looked pensive. 'Anyway, there was another reason for me coming here today, other than to show my support. I've got something major to discuss with you Effie. Is this a good time to talk?' She stood there, anxiously waiting for me to reply.

I was about to say yes when I caught a glimpse of my Aunt's infuriated face as she glared at us from across the hall. It wasn't hard to deduce she wasn't amused to see me chatting with a friend, rather than the guests.

'Can we talk later, when it's less busy?' I said, glancing fleetingly at Clarice. 'Why don't we go over and see my Aunt.'

I took my friends arm and led her over to where my Aunt was standing, rather stiffly with her arms folded.

'Good morning Clarice, it's so nice of you to finally join us.' said my Aunt with a frown. 'You really should have arrived sooner you know, to support Effie.'

Although Aunt was very fond of Clarice, she couldn't bear it when people were late and was a stickler for reminding me it was rude and showed lack of consideration to others.

Clarice stood staring at her, temporary taken aback by her harsh words. 'I'm...I'm dreadfully sorry Constance.'

'So, you should be.'

'Aunt please.' I retorted angrily. 'Poor Clarice didn't have to come today and I really don't mind that she's late, the main thing is she's here now.'

My Aunt stood there for a moment contemplating her next sentence. And when she spoke again her mood seemed to have lifted. 'Well, anyway Effie, I thought you might like to know that you've sold eight of your paintings, isn't that super?' She embraced me.

'Really?' I exclaimed in a disbelieving voice. I laughed, rather shocked that people had actually purchased some of my work.

My Aunt pulled away and looked at me. 'See, you should have more faith in yourself Effie. Isaiah thinks there will be more purchaser's soon.' She exclaimed, her face beaming.

I glanced over in Isaiah's direction. He caught my eye and smiled at me then winked at Clarice. He then quickly returned his attention to the group of people who were hovering around him, as if he was simply marvellous.

14

'I'm just going to say hello to Isaiah.' Clarice said, staring over at him. 'You'll be ok, won't you?' She said, without turning her gaze away from him. 'Don't forget about our chat.' She threw me a rapid glance and before I had a chance to answer, strolled over to where he was standing.

It seemed even Clarice was under his spell. I watched as he smiled at her, then taking her arm he moved away from the small crowd of people he'd been talking to. I narrowed my eyes in puzzlement as they then stood in deep conversation.

My Aunt tapped my arm. 'Look Effie.'

I glanced over to where she was pointing and saw an elderly man surveying some of my portraits, and my heart sank when I saw him taking an avid interest in one particular painting.

She looked anxiously at me. 'Best go and speak to him Effie. He looks rather keen on buying it.'

'I knew it was a mistake bringing it here.' I exclaimed. 'Why did I have to be so weak and give in so easily?'

I looked at my Aunt, hoping she'd sympathise with me but all she did was pat me on the hand, saying she needed to make more tea. I looked at her for a moment, thinking that perhaps she'd not heard me properly, either that or she chose not to. A cup of tea it seemed was the answer to all life's problems.

I smiled poignantly at her. 'Don't worry Aunt I promise not to sell the painting.'

With a sigh I strolled over towards the man, leaving my Aunt staring after me. I knew it would break her heart if we sold the portrait. I blame Isaiah, as he was the one who persuaded me to bring it along in the first place. 'Just for display purposes only,' he'd told me. 'It will add a welcome addition to the diversity of your work.' He'd then directed his gaze to Aunt. 'Do you not think so Constance? After all, you're such a fine judge on these sorts of matters?' My Aunt, who could be cajoled by him so easily, quite happily agreed and told him what a good idea it would be to bring the portrait along, and I foolishly went along with their decision.

One might be inclined to ask why, what's so special about this specific portrait, and considering the history behind it I'd struggle to give an honest or logical explanation. I suppose it's best described as a moment captured in time; a fleeting glimpse of my mother preserved in oils. Of course, the real story behind the painting is rather a strange one. I was about seven at the time and had been tucked up in my bed, trying to ignore the branches that tapped against the windows like wooden hands. As I was laying there a shadowy figure of a lady suddenly appeared, gazing down upon me. Although I must have been afraid, I couldn't resist reaching out for her, however, just as I did so, she mysteriously faded before my very eyes. I was sure it was my mother, and night after night I yearned for her to appear once more, if only for a moment, but sadly it wasn't to be. Many years passed but my memory of her face had never faded. In fact, it was so vivid and alive that I found a way to preserve the image and store it away in my mind, and when the time was right, I sat down at my easel and painted her portrait.

Just remembering those days of my youth filled me with anguish, when my mother's whereabouts was shrouded in mystery. Many times, I'd questioned my Aunt in a vain attempt to discover at least one tiny clue, only she was always reluctant to talk about it, and would become agitated and upset. All I knew was that my mother had met someone and gone away to be married, returning some years later heavily pregnant with me. However, after giving birth, my mother inexplicably vanished, leaving me with my Aunt. On many a rainy afternoon I would spend my time searching through the endless trunks and boxes in the attic at Rawlings, hoping to discover photos of her, or scraps of information. Strangely, I wasn't able to find a thing, it was almost as if someone had come along and removed all trace of my mother.

There was however one particular occasion that struck me rather odd. My Aunt and I were both in the garden at the time, sitting there reading, when all of a sudden, a haunted looked appeared in her eyes. As she stared vacantly ahead, she began to speak about how my mother was forced to leave after I was born and that someone had come in the night and smuggled her away. When I questioned her about it the following day, she couldn't recall saying such a thing and dismissed it as being the ramblings of a silly old woman. On the last occasion when I asked her, she flared up for no particular reason, scolding me for dredging up the past. I can remember her standing there with her hand over her chest, telling me in a shaky voice how all this talk of my mother was making her feel quite unwell. Some might say it was a convenient way to avoid the subject, but Aunt wasn't a devious type of person at all, in fact it wouldn't enter her head to pretend to be ill. Therefore, I found myself duty bound to keep quiet on the subject, not wishing to fluster her unduly.

So sadly, I found myself in eternal speculation, attempting in vain to conjure up a likely scenario for my dear parents, a delusional past time but necessary at times. If I didn't know the truth, I would make it up, I created a fictional family, a mother, father, brother and a pet cat, and for a while it worked and I was content in my make-believe little world, but a I grew older this fantasy faded and was replaced with a dark oppressive cloud that lingered over me, reminding me of my absent parents.

I went and stood beside the man, who was still staring intently at my mother's portrait.

'Hello, can I help you?' I said in a polite voice.

Deep in thought, he tilted his head slightly to the right, and then with a brief smile he looked into my face. 'Are you Effie?'

'Yes, yes I am sir.'

With a broad smile he held out his hand. 'I'm exceedingly please to meet you, young lady.' As we shook hands, he continued to meet my eye. 'I'm Mr Lombard and I would very much like to purchase this painting.'

The man had such a kindly face that I felt rather bad he couldn't have the painting. I was almost tempted to drag Isaiah over and make him explain why.

I cleared my throat.

'I'm really very sorry but this particular painting isn't for sale. It shouldn't be here really -it should be at my home above the fireplace.'

For a moment he was silent, as if surprised by my words. He turned from me and gazed once more at the painting, scratching his head. 'Oh, what a terrible pity, it's so, so....'

'Endearing? I said, interrupting him in mid-sentence. 'The...the expression on her face is the look a mother would bestow upon her daughter.' I gazed at the portrait, still mesmerised by it even after all these years.

The young woman in the canvas was wearing a pale blue dress embossed with an intricate gold leaf effect and was sitting down with her hands clasped neatly in her lap. Dark auburn hair seemed to flow down her back like waves of shimmering gold, and there was an endearing tenderness emanating from her warm emerald eyes.

A shriek of laughter sounded from across the room immediately bringing me back to reality. I glanced at Mr Lombard, who was staring at me in bewilderment, and laughed nervously.

'That's just my interpretation. I didn't mean to put words in your mouth.' I said, trying to gage his reaction.

'No, no you're right.' He said, looking intently at the portrait and then me. 'Is it a portrait of *your* mother?' he said, eyeing me closely.

'Yes.' I said quietly.

'Well, she's very beautiful. I can see where you get your looks from.'

I smiled shyly, my face burning up. 'Thank you.' I said, suddenly feeling plaintive.

'Is your mother here? I'd love to compare the person in the flesh with the painting.' He looked hopefully at me.

If only that were possible, I thought, how lovely it would be if my mother suddenly walked across the hall and stood beside me, allowing us to see if my brush strokes did her justice.

'I'm sorry but she's not available at present.' I said in a surprisingly calm voice.

Mr Lombard furrowed his brow for a minute before answering. 'Oh well if you change your mind about the painting, please give me a call.' He handed me a card from his coat pocket and stared into my face, his expression a mixture of sadness and concern. 'Do take care of yourself young lady.'

'I will sir.' As he went to leave, I called out to him. 'And thank you for coming here today, Mr Lombard.' We exchanged smiles and I watched as he slowly wondered off towards the exit.

The hall was becoming empty now, and my Aunt had begun to clear away the crockery from the tables. Clarice was *still* having a supposedly deep and meaningful discussion with Isaiah, and as I peered over at the two of them in disbelief, they caught me looking. Isaiah immediately touched Clarice on the shoulder, muttering something in her ear. He then came limping over towards me at a rapid speed. Quite impressive for a man with a bad leg, I thought.

'Did that gentleman want to buy the painting Effelia?' He exclaimed excitedly, slightly out of breath.

'Well yes…'

Before I could finish my sentence, his booming voice came right into my ear.

'Effelia, today's been such a success; we've already sold nine of your paintings. If you sold the painting of your mother, it would be an even ten. Let me run after that gentleman and tell him you've had second thoughts.' He said with a look of anticipation spread across his red face.

'No Isaiah you're well aware that I couldn't possibly part with it.' I snapped at him.

'Oh Effelia, it's just a painting; you can always do another one just like it.' He laughed mockingly at me.

'No.' I shouted, furious with him. 'Why won't you respect my decision.' I heard my voice rising but was unable to stop it. 'God, you're so infuriating.'

There was a sudden deathly silence throughout the hall.

I felt the colour flame into my cheeks as I noticed the remaining guests staring over at us. Feeling embarrassed I lowered my voice. 'I shan't ever sell that painting; do you not understand?' I spoke to him slowly. 'Now, I don't want to hear another word on the subject.'

My Aunt looked over in great concern and came rushing towards us, looking distressed. Folding my arms in defiance I told her what was going on whilst Isaiah glared at me sullenly. I remember thinking how satisfying it felt, to annoy him. Unfortunately, his expression only lasted for a moment and was then replaced with a sarcastic smile.

Bending over he whispered coldly in my ear.

'Mark my words, you'll regret speaking to me in that manner.'

My Aunt's eyes darted to his in shock. 'What did you just say Isaiah?'

'On nothing Constance.' He replied, reverting back to his usual charming manner. 'I was just saying to Effelia, that I hope she doesn't regret not selling the painting.' As he lowered his eyes, he retrieved a handkerchief from his back pocket and dabbed his eyes. 'I'm sorry to have upset you Effelia. I was only trying to help further your career.' Glancing up his pitiful face looked from me to my Aunt.

I gaped at him in disbelief.

'Don't lie Isaiah. You hate the painting of my mother, you always have, and that's why you wanted me to sell it. It had nothing to do with my so-called career.'

My Aunt looked infuriated. 'Effie really, why are you being so spiteful towards Isaiah, he's gone out his way to help you arrange this art exhibition and this is how you repay him?' she huffed. 'I'm extremely disappointed in you, young lady.'

Out of the corner of my eye I could see Isaiah standing there, gloating. With a sigh I averted my gaze to the other side of the hall. Perhaps I should have retaliated, but for my Aunt's sake I remained silent.

I jumped slightly as she briskly clapped her hands together.

'Now come on, let's finish clearing up and then we can pack up the remaining paintings and head home.' She threw me a stern look and then looked sympathetically at Isaiah. 'Would you give me a hand my good man?'

'I will do anything for you, your ladyship.' Isaiah said smiling at her and bowing.

My Aunt giggled like a schoolgirl, eagerly lapping up every word he spoke. He took her arm and together they headed for the kitchen, leaving me standing there. As they walked away, I could hear her mumbling to him about my dreadful behaviour.

'Hi there, friend. Is...everything okay?'

Hearing laughter behind me I turned round to see Clarice standing there with a plate of food in her hand.

'Yes, yes Clarice. I er, just had a little misunderstanding with Isaiah, that's all.'

'You know Effie, perhaps you should appreciate Isaiah a little more. He's so kind and attentive to you and Constance, and such a great listener. He was so interested in what I've been up to.' Her large eyes suddenly looked soulful. 'You're lucky to have him in your life.'

'Am I?'

'Yes. He's very fond of you, you know.'

I looked at her blankly, deciding it would probably be of little use trying to convince her otherwise.

'I suppose he's bearable in small doses.'

Clarice pulled me to one side. 'Anyway, I bet you can't guess where I've been this morning.' She said gleefully.

Slowly I began to gather up the teacups and empty plates from the table next to us. I shrugged my shoulders. 'No, where?' I said only half listening.

'Well, I've just been to see a flat that's for rent, with views across the bay. Mrs Applegate the estate agent has said I can return tomorrow for a second viewing.' She paused to take a bite out her sandwich 'I told her you'd be coming along too as you were very interested.'

'What?' I nearly dropped the tray of crockery on the floor.' Clarice, why did you say that, we've never discussed renting a flat?'

She stared at the floor, unable to meet my eye.

'I know, it's just that I saw the place on a whim and couldn't resist a peek.' She put down her sandwich. 'Please come and see it with me Effie, I know you'll fall in love with it. Wouldn't it be great moving in together?' She looked pleadingly at me.

'Well, yes, but Clarice…'

She interrupted me, shoving a piece of paper in my hand. 'Good, here's the address. I shall meet you tomorrow outside the flat at 10am sharp.' She gave me a hug. 'Don't be late.'

I looked at the huge grin on her face, and although I really had no intention of moving out of Rawlings, I didn't want to disappoint her.

'Oh, ok Clarice, I'll be there at 10am. But I'm not making any promises.'

I was already regretting my answer as Clarice flung her arms around me once more.

'Won't it be wonderful, you and I as flatmates. Oh, and don't go in without me.' She said, putting her coat on. 'I told Isaiah about the flat and he thinks it's a great idea. He agrees that I need to spread my wings, and thinks my mother will understand.' Suddenly she looked forlorn. 'Ever since my father's death she's not been the same.'

Clarice's father had disappeared a few years back and his remains were found recently in the woods in a nearby town. It was a suspected suicide but the inquest was inconclusive.

'But won't she miss you?'

'It's not like I'm moving to another world, now is it, Effie?' She chuckled. 'I shall pop in and see her most days, and make sure she's not…'

'What?'

With a sigh she shrugged her shoulders. 'Oh, it's nothing.' Letting out a high-pitched giggle she waved to Isaiah, who was peering our way.'

'You know Clarice, I really wished you hadn't mentioned this flat thing to Isaiah.' I said, picking up some napkins from the floor. 'He's bound to mention it to my Aunt.'

'Oh Effie, don't worry. He seemed to be genuinely interested, especially when I told him I wanted *you* to share with me. I'm sure your Aunt will have the same reaction.'

'Huh. I severely doubt it.' I glanced into her face. 'Promise not to say anything about this to her, will you Clarice. I shall make sure Isaiah also keeps silent on the subject.'

'Sure, my lips are sealed.' She said, smiling happily at me. 'See you tomorrow, roommate.' She laughed and hurried off towards the exit, saying her goodbyes to my Aunt and Isaiah on the way out. Just as she reached the door, she turned for a second and waved at me, her face looked so happy and carefree.

I shall never forget that particular moment, as this is how I should like to remember her.

As I stood there, I couldn't help but be relieved the ordeal was all over, and I had emerged the other end in one piece. Apart from the incident with Isaiah and my mother's painting I had rather enjoyed the whole experience.

We all said goodbye to the remaining guests, thanking them for coming. Many of them were my Aunt's friends from her committee, and didn't seem in a rush to leave. They stood in the doorway chatting away with Aunt, for what seemed like an eternity. Apparently, from what I could make out, Lydia Davenport, one of the committee members had passed away last night from an overdose. The whole community was understandably deeply shocked by the news, as it was so out of character for her. Poor Miss Davenport, I'd met her a few times and she'd seemed so lovely. What a terrible shame for her sister Agnes, to have to deal with such a thing, I felt so dreadfully sorry for her loss.

Finally, after the hall had been tidied up sufficiently, and my Aunt had said goodbye to all her friends, we were ready to go home. I watched as Isaiah carefully loaded up all of my unsold work in the boot of his car, and cursed underneath my breath as I saw how little care he took over my mother's portrait, crashing it down on top of the others with little thought.

My Aunt of course said nothing to Isaiah, even though she'd clearly seen what he'd done. She turned to me with a smile on her face and hugged me tightly.

'I think today is cause for a celebration, don't you Effie? I'm sure we have a bottle of champagne buried away somewhere in the cellar, and this is the best time as any to open it.'

I raised my eyebrows in surprise. 'Very well, that would be nice.'

My Aunt wasn't really one for drinking and very rarely had alcohol in the house. 'It's the devil's brew.' She would say to me in warning. 'Keep off it my girl or it'll ruin you.'

I smiled endearingly at her. 'You know that Mace is coming over, don't you?'

Isaiah must have overheard us as his bellowing voice came into earshot.

'Effelia, I'm sure your Aunt would prefer just the three of us. It's been a tiring day for her.' he said, opening the car door.

I glanced at him in disbelief, the sheer cheek of the man, I thought. Although Mace wasn't any relation, he was the closest thing I had to a brother; he was my best friend, the sole person I confided in, and he knew *most* of my closely guarded secrets. Isaiah on the other hand, well he was just an odd sort of man who for some strange reason seemed to think he had the right to be part of our family.

'I'm sure Aunt won't mind.'

She looked at me with a slightly pained expression. 'Of course, not dear.' With a nervous laugh she glanced at Isaiah, as if seeking his approval. 'He can stay for a while.'

'Thank you, Aunt.' I said graciously.

I was extremely tempted to aggravate Isaiah by reminding him that he couldn't dictate what visitors we had in our own home, the home that *didn't* belong to him. He practically lived at Rawlings, and no doubt would have loved to stay there permanently, but Aunt had assured me that she would never allow it.

'Mace will enjoy scoffing all the leftover cakes from the exhibition, especially the lemon drizzle cake you made Aunt.'

'Yes, yes he will Effie. I really don't know where that lad puts it all. Anybody would think his parents never feed him.'

By the lack of expression on Isaiah's face I could tell he wasn't impressed with Mace coming over. He said nothing as he clambered in the car, slamming the door after him.

As far back as I could remember Isaiah had always disliked Mace, and I didn't know why. He'd always treated him with contempt, as if he'd wronged or offended him in some way. It struck me peculiar that Isaiah was so good-natured to everyone else, bestowing upon the good people of Abercrombie that sickly sweet charm of his, and yet this one person, my dear friend, he wouldn't give the time of day. But in a strange way I was glad, for it reinforced my belief that this man had a dark side to his character.

'They don't bake cakes like you Aunt.' I said as we sat in the car. 'You know how much Mace loves Rawlings; it's like a second home to him. I'm sure he'd move in if we asked him.'

She began cackling with laughter. 'Well perhaps we should ask him dear.'

'Maybe we should.' I said jubilantly, looking at Isaiah's face in the car mirror. I smiled at him with a smug satisfaction. 'We could easily turn one of the spare rooms into a bedroom.'

I didn't consider myself a nasty person but there was something deliciously tantalising in infuriating him. It reminded me of a painful mouth ulcer that you just couldn't help but aggravate.

Isaiah swung round in the seat and glared at me. 'Let's not be too hasty now shall we. The boy's foster-parents would be deeply hurt to see him leave home.'

Mace's real mother had sadly passed away when he'd been a baby, and for a few years he was placed with foster-parents in a neighbouring town, before settling in Abercrombie with Giles and Marigold, a lovely couple that agreed to foster him for the long term. I think at one stage they were going to adopt him but it had never come to be, nevertheless Mace looked upon them as his very own parents.

'Too true, too true.' Replied my Aunt with a nod. 'We were only joking, weren't we Effie?'

'Of course.' I replied reluctantly.

Most of the journey home was spent in silence, until my Aunt began to talk about poor Lydia Davenport, muttering how she really must visit Lydia's sister, Agnes tomorrow as she was obviously extremely distraught. Her words became a blur as I drifted off into a daydream, a particular bad trait of mine. At school I'd been frequently scolded for not paying attention, choosing instead to gaze out the window, imagining the adventures I would have, adventures in other lands.

Chapter 3

Before I knew it, we were turning into the gravel driveway at Rawlings. Much had faded from my memory over time, but when it came to my old home it was as clear as yesterday. Your eyes would immediately be drawn to the ancient oak trees standing like statues, proud and sturdy along the winding pathway leading up to the house, their wide-spreading branches making dancing shadows on the ground. Once you had passed under the archway of trees, the house would be standing there- the magnificent Rawlings. Some often said it was a mansion but I always thought that sounded rather fancy and much preferred the term large house. Great trees enfolded the red brick building, which was smothered in a tangled mass of ivy that crept dark and uncontrolled to the borders of the property, covering the terrace and sprawling along the paths and under the windows. Various attempts to remove it had been in vain, as it always found a way to return with a vengeance, but in the summer months the ivy was half hidden with a mass of pale purple blossoms from the wisteria, that cleverly adorned the old brickwork, bringing much needed colour to our old home. It's true to say that time had not been kind to Rawlings and it was very slowly decaying with age. Lack of funds had left it sadly neglected, but not unloved, never unloved...

It had been in our family for generations, but I fear that if our ancestors could see it now, they'd probably come back to haunt us, in punishment for not maintaining it. I promised my Aunt I'd restore it one day, to its former glory, and she'd smile plaintively at me.

A vast porch ran along the whole front length of the house, with various mismatched wicker chairs and cracked terracotta plant pots full of weeds. When the weather was too hot for gardening, my Aunt and I would sit there, stretched out lazily in two of the old chairs; she would knit and I would read or sketch, and we would pretend not to notice the work that needed doing around us. Around the rear of the property we had a large back garden, which was mainly laid to lawn, apart from the flower beds which were adorned with a variety of flowers such as rhododendrons, petunias, daisies, all intermingled with dandelions and nettles. The entire perimeter of the garden was sheltered by a tall, grey bricked wall where thistles and brambles grew tall and vigorously. I would tirelessly endeavour to help my Aunt with the weeding, and on many a day we would be out there on our hands and knees pulling up giant thistles and such like, but unfortunately, they had a nasty way of returning, and we could never manage to banish them completely. Down the very back of the garden was a large dilapidated shed, containing much of what you'd expect, a rusty lawn mower, garden tools, plant pots and seedlings. But if you were to look further, you'd see it was also a workshop, my workshop. An array of paints and brushes lay about in boxes and pots, scattered in every available spot, and tucked away in the corner was my easel; various dusty canvases were propped up against the shed wall and forgotten about. Up until my art exhibition I'd stored all of my work in the shed, hidden away safely from sight, but the night before my big day I'd painstakingly chosen a few of my more professional looking work to display in the hall, ready for the exhibition. How strange it felt to think of how many of those paintings wouldn't ever be returning to Rawlings, instead they would be hanging up in someone else's house. I suppose now they could be appreciated rather than discarded in an old garden shed.

At the front entrance stood a solid oak door with two large white pillars standing proudly either side. On entering the house you'd find yourself in an immense hallway with doorways leading to various rooms, many of which lay idle and neglected; it hardly made sense to use more than we required, after all why dust a room you're not going to use. My Aunt always said housework was a chore and was not to be undertaken where it was not necessary, a philosophy I entirely agreed with. So, in these forgotten rooms we had dustsheets covering the furniture. As a child I was sure a demon or a ghost lurked under the sheets, ready to pounce if I came near, needless to say I rarely entered these particular rooms.

The living room was situated to the far left of the hallway, a room of such huge expanse that the sparsely arranged furniture hardly did it justice. The focal point of the room was the wide fireplace, which when alight would immerse the entire room in a warm glow. On many occasions, I would sit there gazing into the mesmerising flames of the fire, drifting off into a dreamlike state. Either side of the fireplace there were two high-backed armchairs, and an old dresser stood on the far side of the room displaying pieces of fine china, which were a little chipped, mostly from over use and the heavy- handed Mace. There was also a tatty old bureau, scattered with an abundance of paperwork that required sorting through. 'It's a job for a rainy day.' My Aunt would say with a chuckle, knowing that it would never get done. The long sash windows had views across the back garden and were framed in red velvet curtains, sweeping down majestically to the floor.

To the right of the hallway was the kitchen, the heart of the house. A huge charcoal range stood on the far side of the wall generating warmth throughout the property, and in the long winter months we were very thankful to have it. Pale blue units lined the room and a large wooden table stood in the middle, and was invariably where we would eat, unless of course we had guests. Pots and pans hung down from the wooden beams on the ceiling and tarnished silverware sat in a tray on a shelf next to the rusty old fridge.

My favourite room by far had to be the library. As you entered you would undoubtedly notice the damp, musty odour that permeated within. Strangely I found this comforting as it reminded me of times gone by. Dark wooden panels covered every wall but could scarcely be seen through the mass of books that stretched to the ceiling. Soft armchairs were situated randomly around the room and a writing desk stood by one of the tall windows. Many blissful hours were spent in this room, curled up on an armchair or the window seat. Quite often I wondered what other long forgotten soul had once sat in that very spot, reading a dusty old book.

Direct your gaze to the very top of the wide sweeping staircase and you would see a large gothic stained-glass window, with a landing leading off either side. Situated on the far left was my room. I called it my haven, because it was my little hideaway from the world. It was a large airy room with wide sash windows looking down across the back garden. Sometimes in the peacefulness of the night I'd creep over and open the windows, and leaning there with my arms upon the sill, I would breathe in the glorious scent from the rose garden, marvelling at the quiet stillness of the night air. The main feature of the room was the four-poster bed, which incidentally was as old as Rawlings itself. However, the object I loved most about my room was the portrait hanging above the bed. I painted it myself and it was of a very honourable looking man, whose kind gentle face was captured so fittingly in the soft oils of the paintwork. Large steady eyes stared out at you and seemed to come alive with the hazel brown flecks of colour within them. Rich, dark curls framed his face so perfectly and his broad mouth displayed a warm welcoming smile that filled your soul with contentment. The man in the painting was named Gideon...dear Gideon. I'd known him for most of my life, but hadn't *truly* met him, not then anyway. You see, we would meet in our dreams, during the night, and in these dreams, we were always in the same forest, an enchanted place where we could remain for hours on end without any time passing in the real world. Looking back, I can't exactly recall when the dreams first started, and why. But one thing was certain – these recurring dreams were happening for a reason – they *must* be of vital importance, otherwise what would be the point of them.

When we were younger being in the forest was one big adventure. Night after night we'd have great fun playing hide and seek and darting between the trees, or we'd sit on the soft ground and make endless daisy chains. We'd laugh together and chase the luminous fireflies that danced around us, their wings glowing brightly in the darkness. There was one special tree, our tree, which was the tallest and oldest oak in the forest, with branches practically reaching the sky; one day we carved our initials deep within its bark, and some years later Gideon made a heart around it. On my birthday he would adorn the tree with the most exquisite looking wild flowers and crown me with a wreath of daisies, then he would present me with a gift; the last one was a heart shaped trinket box made from his very own hands, with the words "*My heart will always belong to you*" carved on the lid. Turning a lovely shade of crimson, I stored it away with gifts from previous birthdays in the hollow trunk of an ancient tree that had fallen to the ground many years ago. On numerous occasions I tried to return home with the gifts but sadly I could not, it seemed they had to remain in the dream. As the years passed, we would spend our nights laughing and chatting together, much like when we were children. However, suddenly we begun holding hands and exchanging long lingering stares all the time, and that's when I realised our relationship was changing, and we could no longer carry on the way we were. But he was someone who existed purely in a dream, not someone you could share your future life with.

'If only we had a way to meet for real.' I said to him one night, laughing nervously. 'Everything would be different then.'

He'd sat there for a moment, deep in thought. 'I know Effie. Believe me I think about it all the time. Unfortunately, where I come from time passes by at a much slower rate, similar to that of our dreams. My father has always told me that because I've spent my entire life in my homeland, if I was then to travel to another world my body would not be able to take the strain and I would most certainly perish.' He shrugged his shoulders. 'Of course, I'm willing to risk the journey if it means being with you.'

I'd stared back at him in disbelief, trying to comprehend how it would even be *possible* to travel across worlds, let alone being dangerous. It was outlandishly ridiculous, wasn't it?

'No Gideon, you mustn't come here if it means you could die. Maybe I should come to see you instead.' I replied with a laugh, not believing for one second he would take me seriously.

'You could Effie, indeed you could.'

'What?'

He gave me an amused smile. 'I know of someone who has already made the journey, and they were perfectly fine.'

'Who?'

With a short laugh he shook his head. 'Just trust me, it's safe. You could come for a visit...if you so wish. Then perhaps you could stay.'

'For good?'

'Yes Effie, you'd like my home, it would suit you.' His face clouded over for a moment. 'However, if you stayed for too many years then changed your mind, travelling back home could then become harmful.' Seeing the look of alarm on my face he came over and placed his hands on my shoulders. 'Look, think about it. If you don't want to make the journey then I shall perfectly understand.'

He glanced around at the trees. 'We've got our own little world here, and there's no reason why anything needs to change.'

I tried to give him a reassuringly smile, knowing in my heart that, sooner or later, *everything* would change, one way or another. We had two options: either we ceased contact altogether – although I'm not sure how this would work in a dream! Or, I would go and see him. I chose the latter.

Suddenly the whole idea of being able to travel across worlds wasn't just utterly ludicrous, but completely enthralling as well. My thoughts became consumed with taking the trip. Gideon seemed sure that the doorway, or gateway, as we liked to call it, was hidden away in the woods somewhere, which didn't really help considering over half the country was covered in woodlands and forests, and therefore it would take my entire life to search them all, and even if I did manage to stumble across it how would I know it was the right one. But then his face looked amused as if he sensed what I was thinking.

'I believe the woods is fairly close to your home and is situated near two large beech trees.'

I gazed into his eyes. 'Well, why didn't you say that in the first place?' I said with a grin. 'At least that's something to work on.' I said with a smile. 'I shall see if my friend will help.'

It could have been a big mistake asking Mace, for he had a tendency to tease me relentlessly for the slightest thing, only despite his behaviour I trusted him more than Clarice. I worried that she might inadvertently blurt it all out to Isaiah. To my utter surprise Mace didn't poke fun at me whatsoever when I told him about the trip. I was however convinced that deep down he feared for my sanity, and I really can't say I blame him, for the sensible side of me still disbelieved that any of this was possible.

There is one more room that *must* be mentioned, but not because it's pleasant or holds fond memories, but because it played a significant part in my life. The attic room contained my deepest darkest fear, and even to this day it occasionally haunts my dreams. To reach it you would have to go along to the landing on the left, and then veer around the corner until you came upon a tiny door. When I was a child, I had this theory that the opening had been specially designed for little people, such as dwarfs and fairies, who would use the attic as their secret hideaway, and if anyone else came near them they would pelt the invader with conkers stored in one of the boxes. Once you'd unlocked the door you would need to crouch down and clamber into the enclosed space that was literally only large enough for the cast iron stairway that twisted its way upwards and led you directly into the ominous attic. My friends were too scared to venture up into this room. Aunt and I came up here only when necessary, and Isaiah had a habit of sneaking up for no apparent reason. I used to wonder if he was hiding stolen property up there, such as mountains of cash or precious gems, either that or he was searching for something, with the intention of robbing us. The room was full to the brim with memories of a bygone time, where the forgotten contents lingered like melancholy ghosts, who felt trapped and neglected. Age-old pieces of furniture, smothered in cobwebs, covered the perimeter of the room, and discarded in front of them were boxes and trunks, scattered haphazardly on top of one another with little regards to their contents. Amongst all that there were paintings, books, photos, china, toys, clothes, shoes, and a scary looking mannequin which my Aunt had stood directly in front of an ornate mirror; sometimes I tormented myself into thinking the mannequin's reflection had suddenly come to life and was out to get me. But there was a far more sinister presence that furtively languished in one of the big old trunks in the far corner of the room; it was a ventriloquist dummy that I purposely stuffed there in the hope it would rot away to nothing. He had large bulbous eyes that protruded from their sockets in a perpetual state of alarm and the painted skin on his face was gradually peeling away in strips, causing a scar like effect. His wooden mouth was fixed in a wide grotesque smile, displaying a toothy grin and a few lonely strands of hair poked out pitifully from his head like spider legs. Once upon a time his attire must have been vibrant and smart but now his little red jumper was faded and threadbare and his green checked breeches were full of holes, the only item that had kept its colour was the dark green cravat around his neck. Do not be fooled into thinking he was a harmless dummy that had seen better days, for I knew only too well he was a vile creature who frequently lurked at the side of the path when I slept, waiting to snatch my dreams away and replace them with terrifying nightmares. His name is Gilbert, and he was the root of all evil.

Chapter 4

We carried all the remaining paintings inside, leaving them in the hallway until later. I carefully hung my mother's portrait in its rightful home, back up above the fireplace and my Aunt brought in the champagne and some of her homemade lemon cake. Exhausted from the stress of the day we all collapsed in front of the fire, and just as we'd got settled the front door slammed and a familiar voice called out.

'Hello?' I didn't bother knocking as the door was open anyway.'

We heard a loud crash.

'Oops sorry, I just knocked over some of your paintings Effie. Why in heaven's name did you leave them lying in the hallway.'

Isaiah groaned then muttered something inaudible under his breath.

'We're all in the living room Mace' I called out, a little concerned at what damage he'd done to my paintings. Automatically, I rose to greet him. 'Are you alright?'

He came bounding into the room, rubbing his leg. 'Yeah, you know me E, as strong as an ox. And don't worry I didn't damage any of your precious paintings.'

I smiled sheepishly at him. 'That's good to hear.'

Over the years I'd lost count of the accidents he'd had. A while back he tripped and fell into a railway track but managed to clamber back up onto the platform just before a train came careering past. Mace was convinced that someone pushed him from behind. And then there was the time he was driving down the road when the steering wheel literally came off in his hands, and his car went veering into the canal. Luckily, he'd managed to jump out beforehand, with only a few minor scrapes, but since the accident he'll not get behind the wheel and has taken to cycling everywhere. He now has this theory that someone wants to bump him off, and because of this he has become rather paranoid.

He threw Isaiah a sideways glance before looking at my Aunt and grinning.

'Hello Connie.'

This was Mace's nickname for her, and although she never moaned, I was certain she disliked him calling her that.

'It's lovely to see you Mace.' My Aunt said looking warmly at him. 'I'm sure you've got taller since I last saw you.'

Mace laughed with amusement. 'But Connie, you only saw me yesterday, maybe you've grown shorter.' He said, dragging a chair near the fire and plonking himself down in the seat.

She chuckled and reached over to the table 'Champagne Mace?' she started to pour him a glass.

'Oh yes please.' He said, rubbing his hands and holding them out towards the fire. 'I'm parched after cycling all the way over here.'

I looked at him and smiled as he stretched his legs out and nearly hit the stone hearth with his foot. Mace was very lanky and had a habit of peering at you from underneath his dark mane of rather dishevelled looking hair, and there was a certain pureness about his large grey eyes as they looked at you; they illuminated the entirety of his face, flooding it with sincerity.

He took the glass from my Aunt and immediately gulped some down.

'Well?' said Mace, studying my face. 'How did it go?'

'Well, it....'

Isaiah interrupted. 'Not that it's any of your business, but it went rather splendidly.' He exclaimed in a loud voice. 'His gaze rested on me. 'And at least *we* were there to give Effelia moral support.'

Mace raised his eyes at him, his mouth slightly ajar. 'Bully for you.' He murmured underneath his breath before bounding over towards me. 'Didn't I say you had nothing to worry about Effie?' He said, hugging me and nearly knocking over the glass of champagne in my hand. 'God, I wished I'd been there, what did I miss?'

I did my best to tell him what I could remember. Isaiah interrupted constantly, adding the bits I'd not mentioned, and failing to glance at Mace once. I thought it wise to omit the part of Clarice and the flat. At one stage I feared Isaiah was going to broach the subject, but then thought better of it. I'm sure he revelled in the knowledge that he knew I had a secret, a secret I was keeping from my Aunt.

'Did you see the look on Mrs Temple's face when she saw your paintings, Effie? For once in her life, she was speechless.' Aunt said jubilantly.

Mrs Temple was on the church committee and was renowned for her constant chatter.

'Yes, I'm not sure she could comprehend that I'd actually painted every single one. I thought at one point she was going to keel over through actual shock.'

A momentarily pang of guilt swept over me as I suddenly recalled how she had praised a particular watercolour of mine, a beach scene. But it rapidly vanished as I remembered how she'd then made a comment about it being far too expensive for the work of an amateur.

My Aunt suddenly looked pensive and stared up at my mother's portrait. 'I just wish your mother could have been there Effie, she'd be so proud.' She reached for my hand.

'Oh Aunt.' I squeezed her hand. 'I wish mother was there too.' I glanced up at the painting, and it almost seemed she was smiling down upon us.

Isaiah grunted. 'Yes, what a shame.'

'And then...' Aunt said starting to sniffle. 'And then we had the terrible news of Lydia Davenport, which rather cast a shadow upon the day.' She reached for her hanky.

Isaiah suddenly rose and began to clear away the glasses. 'Terrible, terrible business.' He said gruffly and went out the room.

Mace went over and put his arm around my Aunt. 'I'm sorry Connie, I know she was your friend.' He looked sympathetically at her. People are saying that it was an accident, as she didn't leave a goodbye note.'

'There's going to be an inquest, hopefully that will explain more.' Aunt said, rising from her chair wearily. 'Please help yourself to cake Mace.' She tottered towards the door.

I got up slowly from the armchair and went to give her a hand to the door.

'Why don't you go to bed Aunt and get some rest. Would you like me to walk you up?'

'Oh no dear, it's far too early. 'I'm off to the kitchen to make some coffee. You sit and chat with Mace.'

I smiled at her. 'Okay, thanks Aunt.'

With a weary sigh I went and sat back down in the armchair and watched as Mace devoured three slices of cake, barely coming up for air. My gaze drifted to the crackling fire and I started going over the events of the day in my mind. Before long I was struggling to keep my eyes open.

I heard Mace calling my name. 'Effie, Effie?'

Waking up with a start I looked up into his face. 'What…. what's wrong?' I said groggily, realising I must have dropped off.

'I'll be going now, sleepy head.' He said, slowly.

Dragging myself up from the chair I called out to him. 'Oh Mace, do you have to?'

'I think someone needs their bed.' He said in a low voice. 'You've had a hectic day E, talking to all those people. I know you find it an effort.'

'Unlike you.' I answered with a smile.

'Too right, no offence E, but if *I'd* been at the exhibition, you probably would have sold more paintings, and those canvases that I tripped over in the hall wouldn't have been there. Those old ladies might have got fed up of hearing the sound of my voice, but you cannot deny my selling skills are sublime.'

'Yes Mace, of course.' I said, stifling a yawn. In my present state I was far too exhausted to contradict him, and just wanted to go upstairs and flop onto the bed.

He made his way to the door and I followed along behind him.

'Meet up tomorrow in Hudson's café, say 11am?'

'Yes, alright then.' I said wearily. 'Thanks for coming over Mace.'

For a second, he looked towards the kitchen then leant forward and whispered in my ear 'I think I've found the answer to our little problem.'

'Sorry?'

He made a huffing noise. 'The woods Effie, the one you're looking for?'

'Oh, I see.' I replied suddenly feeling wide-awake. 'In that case let's go back into the living room and you can tell me all about it.' I said excitedly.

Isaiah had suddenly emerged from the kitchen and was lingering beside us.

'Tell you all about what? He said in a sly voice.

'It doesn't concern you, Isaiah.' Said Mace gruffly.

36

'Keeping secrets, are we?'

'Yes Isaiah, and I bet you're dying to know what it is, aren't you?' Mace voice was dripping with sarcasm. 'Well sorry, we're not telling you.'

Isaiah glared at him. 'Oh, we all have our little secrets, don't we Effelia.' With a snigger he glanced into my face. 'Were you not discussing one with Clarice in the village hall today?'

That silly flat business, I thought glumly. For a while it had totally slipped my mind, probably because it was meaningless, as well as pointless. The kinder thing would've been to tell Clarice the truth there and then, for I wasn't interested in viewing a flat and had no intention of leaving Rawlings, not unless it was for another reason, a reason that completely overshadowed everything else and involved the suspense and intrigue of going on a mysterious journey to another land.

I took a quick peak towards the kitchen door, hoping that Aunt couldn't hear.

'That was hardly a secret Isaiah.' I patted Mace on the arm and gave him a quick reassuring grin. 'I shall tell you all about it tomorrow, I promise.'

'You'd better E.' He said, raising his eyebrows. 'And in that case, I shall keep *my* news from you until tomorrow too.' He kissed the top of my head. 'Besides, you need to get some sleep.' he said, darting towards the door. 'Say bye to Connie for me and thank her for the cake.'

Before I could reply he was gone, slamming the door behind him. I stood there for a moment, wondering if I should run after him to discover would he'd found out about the woods, knowing that it would prey on my mind and stop me from sleeping.

'Oh, what a tangled web we do weave.' Isaiah was laughing as he spoke.

I turned and gave him a steely glare. 'Pardon?'

'Secrets Effelia, secrets, sometimes they have a nasty way of spiralling out of control, and then the person you care about most in the world ends up getting hurt.' He paused and tapped his finger against his lips. 'A person like your Aunt for instance, how do you think the poor woman would feel knowing that you're leaving.'

My eyes widened in alarm. 'I don't know what you mean.'

'The flat?'

'Oh that.' I said suddenly feeling relieved. For one scary moment I thought he knew what Mace and I were planning.

He narrowed his eyes. 'Why, what other reason would you be leaving for?'

As we stood there facing one another I did my best to keep composed, not wishing to make him any more suspicious than he already was. For he knew only too well that my face always gave me away.

I lowered my eyes.

'Don't you think it's time you went home Isaiah?'

The kitchen door swung open and my Aunt stood in the doorway.

'What was that? No, you're not leaving *yet* are you, Isaiah; I've just this minute made a pot of coffee. It would be a shame not share it with us.'

'Well, there's an offer I certainly can't refuse. I would love to stay.' He said smugly, looking at me. 'Are you joining us Effelia?'

'No, no I don't think so.' I said turning to my Aunt. 'Do you mind if I turn in, I'm awfully tired?'

'No of course not Effie.' She gave me a peck on the cheek. 'Sweet dreams dear.'

Isaiah placed his hand upon my shoulder.

'I'm *so* glad it all went so well for you today Effelia.'

As much as it pained me, I knew Isaiah deserved to be thanked, for he was the one responsible for orchestrating the gathering in the village hall and making it into a reality.

I went and stood by the stairs, resting my hand on the banister.

'Thanks, Aunt for all your support today, I couldn't have done it without you.' I had to force out my next words. 'You too Isaiah.' I nodded at him, barely making eye contact. 'I'm grateful for all your help.'

'You're welcome Effelia, what a great day it's been.' He said sounding genuinely happy.

Nodding, I turned and made my way up the stairs, knowing that they were both staring after me.

It *had* been a good day, it had started off a little shaky, however that was just nerves. But from that day forth my normal little world was about to change.

Chapter 5

With a yawn I collapsed wearily onto my bed, exhausted from the strain of the day. I couldn't wait for sleep, and I couldn't wait to see Gideon. Along the pathway of sleep, I went, slowly drifting along until I was in the familiar surroundings of the forest. It was shrouded in a grey mist that evening, which seemed to be thicker than usual and I could only faintly make out the trees. However, gradually it begun to disperse, and there sitting under the great oak was the shadowy figure of Gideon, with his dark curly hair swept across his brow as always. Even though I was used to seeing him, my heart still skipped a beat. He had this certain allure about him, which was so captivating that I wondered if his entire being had been illuminated by the brightness of the sun, making everything else a blur. It was strange to see him already sitting there, for usually it was I who arrived first. I crept over and sat beside him, watching as he busily crafted a figure out of a piece of wood.

'Good evening Gideon.'

He looked up and smiled gently at me, his whole face lighting up. 'Effie I've been waiting for you.

'Well, you're early' I said, leaning my head against his shoulder. 'What are you making?

'It's a surprise' he said, covering the carved wooden shape with a cloth and placing it in the pocket of his waistcoat. His eyes rested on me. 'How did the exhibition go?'

'It was most satisfactory.' I said, smiling at him. 'The only awful part was when Isaiah tried to make me sell the portrait of my mother. There's something very wrong with that man.'

He stared at me for a moment as if in a daze, then bent his head and looked at the ground.

'What is it Gideon, what are you thinking about?'

With a sigh he looked up at me. 'My apologies Effie, my mind seems to be elsewhere tonight.'

'Whatever is wrong?'

'Oh, it's nothing really.' He looked at me and smiled. 'Did you know Effie that some people have the ability to physically transport themselves to another place by using the power of their minds?'

I looked curiously at him. 'Is it similar to how you and I meet in the forest?

'Well, no, not exactly, you and I don't have any control over what happens in our dreams, and how it all works is one of life's little mysteries.' He paused for a moment. 'But this is different, you see if you shut your eyes and shift your consciousness by relaxing, you can allow yourself to drift into a daydream type state. You would then need to focus your thoughts on one particular person or place so it's firmly fixed in your head. And, if you manage to be successful in carrying this out, you'll physically be transported there for a short while. The possibilities are completely endless and it allows us to travel faraway in our world, or any other world.'

'Have you ever tried it yourself?' I asked.

'Only occasionally, it's extremely difficult to maintain that level of concentration for long and it is very draining on the body.'

'Is there a reason you're suddenly telling me all this.' I said looking confused. 'Are you planning on making an appearance at Rawlings?' I grinned. 'That would be lovely.'

His eyes darted to mine. 'No, no I...I just thought you should be aware that such a thing is possible.' With a gulp he reached for my hand. ''Just in case...'

'Just in case of what?' I studied his face closely. 'Gideon you're beginning to scare me.' I snatched my hand from his.

'Effie I'm sorry. It was never my intention to frighten you.' He suddenly rose up from the ground and held out his hand. 'Let's go for a walk.'

As we ambled through the forest, we began discussing the location of the woods, and how we might have found it. Gideon's mood lightened as I told him how I was meeting with Mace tomorrow and we could hopefully put a plan together of when to leave. I did however have serious doubts about the entire situation, as it was too farfetched to be believable, and yet it was my truest wish that it was.

'Do you *really* believe this gateway exists Gideon?'

'Yes, most certainly, if you find the right location, you shall find the gateway. Then once you have travelled through, I shall be there to meet you at the other end.'

'You make it sound so easy.' I bowed my head, suddenly feeling anxious. 'What if something goes wrong, what if I travel through the gateway but become lost along the route, where will I end up?'

He took my face between his hands and stared deep into my eyes. 'Effie, nothing in life is without risk. But I totally understand if you don't wish to make the journey, really I do.' His face suddenly looked grave. 'I was trying to warn you of something earlier, you see Effie there's a...'

I jumped suddenly as I heard a loud tapping noise.

'Gideon, Gideon don't leave.' I cried out, realising I was drifting away from him. 'What was it you were trying to tell me?' I could hear the faint voice of my Aunt in the background, calling my name. In vain I tried to reach him. 'No, not yet.' But as he disappeared amongst the mist, I knew my dream was over for the night. In fact, come to think of it, our time together this evening had been strangely short.

'Good morning Effie' said my Aunt, drawing back the curtains. 'You were mumbling again in your sleep dear, was it a nightmare?'

I blinked, trying to focus. Surely it couldn't be morning already, I thought to myself. Why did the dream had to end so abruptly, just when Gideon was about to warn me about something. If only my Aunt hadn't come an awoken me so early, I would have known.

'No.' I uttered rather coldly. 'I was having a very interesting dream, one that I didn't particularly want to be woken up from just yet Aunt.'

'That's nice dear.'

I could tell by her voice that she wasn't really listening.

'What time is it?'

'Time you were up and about young lady. Isaiah mentioned you had a meeting today, is it with anyone nice?'

I stared at her. 'No, no um.... it's just Mace I'm meeting.'

'Oh. I see. 'She laughed, looking a little perplexed. 'Well, I've made you scrambled eggs and it's ready and waiting on the kitchen table.' She said, going to the door in rather a hurry. 'Don't be too long or it will become cold.'

'Thanks Aunt, I'll be down in a minute.' I said, yawning.

After breakfast I glanced at the clock and panicked, I was supposed to be meeting Clarice soon and I wasn't even dressed. Frantically I got ready and was just about to go out the front door when I realised I'd not said goodbye to my Aunt. She was standing in the hallway putting her coat on, waiting for Isaiah to give her a lift over to the Davenport's house. I gave her a hug and asked her to send my regards to poor Agnes.

Isaiah crept up behind me from outside the front door. 'Why don't you send them in person Effelia, surely that's more important than this meeting you have.'

'Yes dear, can't you re-arrange the time you're seeing Mace?'

Isaiah glared at me with a strange look on his face. 'Yes, your Aunt is right Effelia. Besides, the boy is so unreliable he probably won't even turn up. Come along with us. Or have you somewhere else you need to be?'

I let out a short laugh. 'No, no of course not.' Rather swiftly I reached for my coat. 'I shall call on Agnes Davenport another day.' Averting my eyes from his I hurried towards the front door. 'Bye, Aunt, see you later.

Once I was safely out the house, I retrieved my bike from the garage and cycled towards Bay Street, frozen from the icy winds that were blowing across from the sea. Resting my bike up against the fence by the flats, I stood waiting patiently for Clarice, who appeared to be late. It made me extremely irritated that she wasn't here yet, not when she'd been so eager for me to come and view the flat, and tell *me* not to be late. With a sigh I checked the address she'd given me which confirmed I was at the correct location.

I let out a frustrated groan. 'Come *on* Clarice.'

A lady was fast approaching, looking rather tense. She briefly glanced over me before saying she was the estate agent, Mrs Applegate. After explaining to her that Clarice was late, I apologised and rushed to the phone box at the end of the street to call my absent friend. I rang twice but there was no answer.

'I have another appointment soon.' Shouted a grim looking Mrs Applegate as she hovered near the phone box.

'Let me try once more. I'm sure there's a logical explanation as to why Clarice hasn't arrived yet.' Giving her a nervous smile, I dialled the number once more, muttering under my breath for

Clarice to pick up the phone, and to my relief I finally heard her voice.

'Yes.' Clarice snapped.

'Clarice? Clarice what's happened. I'm waiting for you outside the flat with Mrs Applegate.'

Apart from the slight crackle of the line there was a deathly silence. And when she finally spoke, I didn't recognise her voice, it was quiet and vague.

'Oh, sorry Effie but I've changed my mind.'

I waited for her to elaborate but she said nothing, and for a moment I stood there staring out the tiny window of the phone box. Suddenly I heard a rather loud cough coming from behind me, and turned to see Mrs Applegate glaring at me impatiently from the open door.

'Well?'

I put my hand out towards her. 'Just a minute Mrs Applegate, I won't be long.' With a nervous smile I closed the door, leaving her standing outside looking furious.

'Clarice, Clarice are you still there?'

'Yes.'

'I...I thought you loved the flat.' I murmured, surprised by her clipped tone.

'Yes, well that was yesterday, I'm no longer interested.'

The phone suddenly went dead and I laughed in shear disbelief. Her voice had sounded so cold, not at all like the Clarice I knew and loved. I quickly wracked my brains, trying to think if I'd offended her in some way, but couldn't come up with a reason. In bewilderment I stood there biting my bottom lip, debating what to do next.

Mrs Applegate had yet again opened the door.

'Has Clarice had a change of heart about the flat?'

'Well, I really don't know.' I lied. 'She's not feeling too well and asked me to do the viewing without her.' I could feel the colour rushing to my cheeks as I saw Mrs Applegate studying my face. I'm sure she knew I was lying.

Any other person would have apologised and cancelled the viewing, but no not me, I had to go and say the wrong thing, and now I would have to suffer for it.

She glanced at her watch. 'Well, we shall have to be quick as I'm now running late.' She snapped. 'Come along then, let me show you up.'

I gave her a meek smile and followed behind her up the steep steps. Once we were in the flat Mrs Applegate began to comment on how cosy and sweet all the rooms were; I suppose it sounded more impressive than saying they were small. I nodded and agreed with her without really taking in what she was saying. Dreamily I glanced out of the small window.

'If you look hard enough you can just make out the boats moored in the harbour.' She paused and looked at me. It's a fair price, don't you think? You'll not get better for this area.' She inclined her head towards me and gave me a rather insincere smile.

'No, I'm sure you're right.' I answered, trying to think of what to say next.

For a second, I stood there, wondering what it would be like to live here, and to be away from Rawlings. To be cooped up in the small stark rooms with their tiny windows and distant views of the sea.

Mrs Applegate hovered over me impatiently, tapping the pen against her clipboard. 'Is it slightly over your price range Miss Farraday?' She gave me a smug smile. 'Please don't feel bashful about telling me.'

I stood and faced her, smiling sweetly. 'No, not at all, I can easily afford it. I just think it's a little small. Now that my art business has taken off, I shall be in need of a larger space.'

Mrs Applegate peered at me from underneath her glasses, her face changing to a mixture of amazed puzzlement and surprise. 'Well surely there's plenty of space at Rawlings. That *is* where you live, isn't it?'

'Well yes I...'

She interrupted before I could finish my sentence. 'Strange then that you are looking for alternative accommodation.' She screwed her face up and placed her hand on my arm. 'I imagine it must cost a fortune to run that big old house, so I'm not surprised you're thinking of selling.' She began to laugh. 'Not unless of course you're making an absolute fortune with your art business and can afford more than one property.'

I glared indignantly at her. 'Rawlings is doing perfectly fine thank you and we have no intentions of selling whatsoever. And excuse me, but it's hardly any of your business how much I earn and why I'm looking at this tiny flat.'

Looking suddenly contrite, she took a few steps back. 'I'm dreadfully sorry. You're right, it's not my place to pry.' She cleared her throat. 'Anyway, can I assume both of you are not interested in the property?'

'Not me, but I'm not sure about Clarice, you may have to ask her yourself.'

'When she's feeling better?'

I nodded slowly. 'That's right.'

After a few moments of staring at me she began muttering on about how sought after the flats were and how rare they became available. Her voice became a murmur in the background as the notion of sharing a flat with Mace popped into my head. I imagined how we'd be surrounded by our untidiness, swamped under mounds of books and discarded old socks. Laughing to myself I glanced up at the garish looking clock on the wall, realising I was supposed to meet him in a few minutes. I mumbled his name under my breath and turned to see Mrs Applegate giving me a strange look.

'Well Mrs Applegate I'm so sorry to have wasted your time. But like you say I'm sure it will be snapped up soon'.

'Yes indeed.' Her voice sounded agitated as she swiftly made her way towards the doorway without glancing at me.

The wind blew into my face as we went outside, causing me to shiver. With a sharp goodbye Mrs Applegate trotted over towards her car and was gone.

I thought of Clarice as I cycled over to Hudson's cafe, deciding I should visit her later to find out what was going on. Surely there had to be a logical explanation for her odd behaviour, but I had a strange feeling it was something more serious.

Some moments later I was sitting in Hudson's café, stirring my coffee. Mace and I had become creatures of habit and every time we met up in the cafe we'd sit in the exact same place, in the corner next to the window that looked out onto the hardware store opposite. This specific spot was the best place to sit and chat without people on the next table hearing every word; not that we had anything interesting to discuss, or something astounding that would cause them to gasp in shock. I suppose they might have thrown us a second glance if they heard us talking about magical portals and other worlds, but then they would just think we were mad.

Glancing outside I saw sombre looking clouds hovering in the grey sky, preparing for the coming rain; it was enough to make even the happiest person a little melancholy. Wrapping my cold hands around the mug of coffee, I carried on staring vacantly out of the window in the hope of seeing Mace strolling up the street. He was late as usual.

I cast my mind back to the very first day I'd met Mace when he was six years old. I can picture him now, standing there in the classroom with his shirt hanging out his shorts, looking decidedly nervous. For some peculiar reason he looked directly at me when he said hello to the class, making me feel quite uneasy. It seemed such an odd thing to do but I just put it to the back of my mind. However, from that moment onwards he would constantly follow me around, which was rather annoying at the time, as being so shy I could hardly say two words to a boy. But it seemed all his hard work finally paid off and somehow, we suddenly became friends.

Sensing someone near me I turned my head to see Mrs Worthington, one of the waitresses, standing there with a glorious smile on her face.

'Hello Effie my dear, is that chap of yours late again?'

Mrs Worthington was a large lady with dyed blond hair and a round, kind face. I liked her immensely, and over the years I had never known her to be anything but cheerful. She would invariably come and chat and would sneak us over extra cake when her manager wasn't looking.

'Yes, he is.' I replied. 'Just like always.' I grinned at her.

Despite explaining to her on many occasions that Mace and I were just friends she seemed to have it in her head we were a couple. So, it seemed easier just to go along with it.

'Don't fret, Mace will be here.' She gave me a reassuring pat on the shoulder and chuckled, placing a mug of hot chocolate down on the table where I was sitting. 'Here, have this, I think you'll find it's somewhat better than that murky coffee you're drinking.'

'Thanks, Mrs Worthington.' I gave her a smile and sat forward, gently blowing on the hot chocolate.

She smiled sweetly and headed over towards the kitchen, stopping to chat to some customers on the way.

The rain began to patter lightly on the windowpane and I watched as people outside frantically reached for their raincoats and umbrellas. Just as the bell jingled on the café door, a cold wind blew in through the open window beside me, and with a shiver I reached over and pulled it shut. As the door was flung open it crashed noisily against the wall and several customers turned round to see what all the commotion was about.

The stooping figure of Mace shuffled into the café with a jacket draped over his head. 'Sorry, sorry all.' Looking apologetic he closed the door then casually removed his jacket and threw it over the coat stand, causing several other coats to drop onto the floor. As he strode over towards me, he slipped slightly on the vinyl floor but managed not to fall over. Looking solemn he nodded at me and sat down on the chair opposite. 'What are you doing here Effie, did we arrange to meet?

I narrowed my eyes and glared at him. 'Can't you remember the arrangements we made yesterday Mace?'

'What arrangements?' He was frowning now and stamping his foot, noisily.

'Yesterday, we were going to discuss the woods and so forth.' I said with a whisper.

'Woods, what woods? E, you may be my best friend but you really are extraordinary odd at times.'

Mrs Worthington walked by, trying to catch what we were saying.

I looked at him stony faced. 'I know you're having me on Mace.'

His face relaxed and he laughed. 'I fooled you for a moment though, didn't I Effie?' He said with a mischievous grin.

'Yes, yes you did Mace.' I said looking away from him and staring out of the rain splattered window.

I was just about to comment on how late he was when something caught my eye, something that shouldn't have been there. I gazed in disbelief at the familiar figure standing in front of the hardware store. It was Gideon. As I continued to stare everything seemed to fade into the background, and I rose mechanically from the chair and walked out the cafe. I could hear Mace calling after me but I ignored him, and in a dreamlike state I crossed over the street. The thunder rumbled ominously overhead as I went and stood directly in front of him. There was something wrong with his appearance, for his form looked almost transparent, like a ghost. He looked ill and vulnerable, and his dark eyes were filled with a pain and anxiety I'd not seen before.

'Gideon?' I said in a low voice. I searched his face and waited for him to answer but there was silence. Yet again I muttered his name. 'Gideon, what…what are you doing here?'

There was a deafening clap of thunder and the rain became heavier, lashing down upon us. I looked at his sodden hair and the tiny droplets of water trickling down his pale face.

Without warning he reached out and grabbed my arms extremely tight. Excruciating pain shot through my body and I cried out. Feeling light headed I closed my eyes for a moment and when I opened them again, we were in the forest, surrounded by the thick dark trees, but I could still hear the rumbling of thunder in the background and Mace yelling frantically at me.

Finally, Gideon spoke. 'Listen Effie, I haven't much time.' His voice was barely audible, as if coming from a great distance rather than right by my ear. 'I…I tried to warn you last night. I think she's coming after you.'

'Who's coming after me?'

Although he was still speaking his voice had become hardly a whisper and I couldn't understand what he was saying. I shivered as the thunder raged through the forest and all of a sudden, he began to fade from my vision.

'Gideon, Gideon what's happening?'

His figure was evaporating rapidly, and before I could utter another word his fragile form had completely disappeared and I found myself back by the hardware store, bewildered and alone. Unable to move I stood there in the street, oblivious to the rain that was pelting down upon me. The pressure of Gideon's hands could still be felt on the tops of my arms.

'Effie?' Uttered Mace in a questionable voice.

Shakily I glanced across the street to see Mace standing in the café doorway, his face etched with concern. A feeling of dizziness came over me and I felt myself beginning to fall, but thankfully a strong arm grabbed me just before I stumbled to the ground. In my state of confusion, I thought it was Gideon returning. I leant heavily against him, unable to stand by myself.

'Effie.' Mace exclaimed lifting me up in his arms and carrying me back to the café. With great care he placed me down in my usual seat. 'My god Effie, what's wrong with you?'

I lolled forward slightly over the table, then rested my head in my arms. Although everything was still a little hazy, I realised that it had in fact been Mace coming to my aid and not Gideon. I couldn't help but feel rather sad.

'Effie, are you ok? You're trembling?' Mace said, draping his jacket around my shoulders.

Still in a state of disorientation I groggily mumbled into my arms. 'Give me a minute and I'll be fine.' My voice sounded thick with emotion, and for some reason I wanted to cry. A wave of sickness came over me as I tried to lift my head.

I sensed Mrs Worthington hovering over me.

'Oh my, the poor thing. Whatever do you think is wrong with her?'

'I'm not sure Mrs Worthington. But I'm sure she could do with a strong cup of tea.' Mace said urgently.

'Right away, I'll also bring over some lovely hot soup and a roll.' Mrs Worthington uttered. 'She's probably not eaten for a while and that's what's caused her to faint.'

She bolted off towards the kitchen, muttering that she wouldn't charge us for the food.

Beginning to feel slightly better, I sat up and rubbed my eyes. Nearly all the customers were staring over at us with concerned looks on their faces. I mustered a weak smile in their direction. 'Mace, did you see him, did you see who I was speaking to?' My voice was shaky as I spoke.

He looked puzzled 'Well, yes Effie.' he replied quietly. 'It was some stranger, wasn't it?'

For one silly moment I almost forgot Mace knew nothing about the existence of Gideon, and even if he did, he wouldn't have recognised him. Naturally he knew all about my recurring dreams in the forest, only in my infinite wisdom I had thought it better to keep everything to do with Gideon a secret, believing that to mention him to another would somehow cause the dreams to inexplicably disappear. The strange thing was that although Mace had taken an avid interest in finding the woods and the gateway to another world, he never actually asked me how I came to know about it, which made me wonder if he was humouring me. Putting all of that to one side it now seemed the right time to tell Mace about my forest friend, for if he was coming with me on this trip, he deserved to know the truth.

'No Mace, he's not a stranger, he's a friend of mine. His name is Gideon.'

His eyes widened in surprise as if taken aback and for a moment he just gaped at me.

Mrs Worthington was hurrying back over with a tray.

'Now, you make sure you eat this Effie my love. You don't want to be fainting again.' She placed the steaming hot bowl of soup and a bread roll down beside me on the table. 'Look, are you sure you're all right my sweet. You look like you've seen a ghost.'

Although she sounded concerned, I suspected she wanted to learn all the gory details of what had happened so she could inform all of her friends, some of which belonged to Aunt's little committee. I imagined her taking great joy in jabbering on to them about how poor Effie Farraday had had a total breakdown, collapsing in the street no less, she would then go on to say that it must have been the strain of my recent exhibition, and that I just couldn't cope with the pressure. For as likeable as Mrs Worthington was, she couldn't help but be one for the gossip. The last thing I wanted was for the whole of Abercrombie to learn of my incident in the street. Maybe I should conjure up a tale of woe and heartbreak, providing them with a topic of great discussion. At least then they wouldn't think I'd gone mad; they would just feel sorry for me instead.

'Really, I'm fine Mrs Worthington. Now please, do you mind? You see Mace and I really need to discuss a rather delicate matter. Thank so much for the food.' I said, smiling sweetly at her.

She pursed her lips and nodded her head. 'Certainly dear, I understand. Lover's tiff eh.' She chuckled at both of us. 'I shall leave you two in peace for a while.' Reluctantly she shuffled off to the kitchen.

Mace began to chuckle. 'Mrs Worthington *still* thinks we're a couple?' He sighed, deep in thought.

'Well, Mrs Worthington is a sweet old lady with a very vivid imagination.' I said laughing.

'Maybe you should get a boyfriend E.' he grinned. 'That would really give Mrs Worthington something to talk about. Or have you found one already, is it that strange looking man you just saw in the street?'

I stared at him but said nothing. We sat there in silence whilst I ate my soup. Mrs Worthington returned with the cup of tea she'd forgotten and then scurried off to serve some customers who'd just arrived, moaning under her breath.

'So, how come you've not mentioned this...what's his name before?'

'Gideon, his name is Gideon.' I lowered my eyes and swirled the spoon round in my half-eaten soup, trying to think of the best way to explain. 'Well, you see I wanted to only.... only.' I paused, struggling to explain.

Mace groaned. 'Oh, look don't worry E, tell me another day. I can see you're still a little dopey from your fainting episode.'

I gave him a half-hearted smile, rather relieved that I didn't need to explain the whole story of Gideon, just yet. In my present state I suspect it would come out all muddled.

Mace reached down into his rucksack and pulled out a map.

'Look, I've highlighted the route I think we should take. I'm pretty sure it's located in Browning's Wood. It shouldn't take more than a few hours to get there.' He said, spreading the map out on the table.

In my eagerness I didn't bother to enquire how he'd found it, all I cared about was when we could leave. After Gideon's warning I was more desperate to go than ever.

'Can we leave tomorrow?' I asked anxiously.

Mace screwed up his face and laughed. 'Effie please, what's the rush. Besides, the gateway might not even be there, and we could travel all that way for nothing.'

'Well, there's only one way to find out, isn't there Mace.' I said in a sharp tone. 'And there's no time like the present.'

'Okay E, there's no need to take that tone. I'm only being realistic.'

I suddenly felt wretched. The events of the last half hour had thrown me into disarray, and I just couldn't think straight. Perhaps

I did need a little time to recuperate. 'We could delay the trip for a day. I said, quietly.

Mace looked intently into my eyes.

'Why don't we make it Friday? That'll give us time to pack' He looked at me and grinned. 'What a jolly little holiday we're going to have.' He said jovially.

'Let's hope so eh?' I threw him a sceptical look and wondered if he truly believed in what we were doing, or if he really thought it one big joke.

Mrs Worthington was back again. 'Well, how are you two getting on?'

'All sorted thank you Mrs Worthington.' said Mace nonchalantly, sounding like he was becoming tired of her interference.

'Oh.' she exclaimed, seeming rather disappointed.

I could tell she wasn't going to let us off that easily and was about to open her mouth when, luckily for us, a large group of tourists entered the café, shaking their umbrellas and wet raincoats, a perfect distraction.

Mrs Worthington turned away in a huff, annoyed at the intrusion.

'Oh, not now.' She muttered furiously under her breath.

'Quickly, let's get out of here before she comes over again.' Mace said, drinking the last of his hot chocolate. 'Don't you want that?' he said, pointing at the bread roll I'd left on my plate. Not waiting for a reply, he began to stuff it into his mouth.

'Yes, let's go.' I said wearily.

I had to heave myself up from the chair. Ever since Gideon had grabbed my arms I felt as if all my energy had drained from my body, and now all I wanted to do was go home and slump into bed. Mace and I grabbed our coats and I paid for the drinks. We waved to Mrs Worthington as we reached the door and I mouthed a thank you to her. She smiled sweetly and nodded her head.

Although the rain was still heavy it didn't bother me. I'd become soaked through when I was talking to Gideon and would probably catch a cold anyway; even so I did my coat up. Mace retrieved my bike and began pushing it along beside us. Strangely enough he didn't question me further on the subject of Gideon, for which I was thankful. He wrapped his arm around my shoulders and we walked up the street in silence, dodging puddles as we went. Although we were both comfortable without having to feel the need to make conversation his sudden quiet mood unnerved me. Invariably he would ramble on about something or other and I would find myself drifting off into a daydream, nodding intermittently so as to make it look like I was being attentive. One day he would catch me out and ask me what it was he'd been saying and I would have to own up.

'Can you manage to ride your bike the rest of the way E? He stopped and pushed my hair back off my face. 'I don't want you to keel over again.'

'Mace I'll be fine.' I said as my hair fell back forward over my face.

'I'll come over and see you tomorrow, shall I?' He titled his head slightly, awaiting my reply.

'Very well then, don't forget to pack for Friday?'

'Oh yes, our little trip.' he said, smirking.

With a sudden urge to tell him everything I stared up into his face. 'Mace about what happened today....'

He interrupted me. 'Effie, you really don't need to explain. You bumped into an old friend of yours, that's all. And as for this gateway business...well has it ever occurred to you that it might only exist in the make-believe world of your dreams, in which case we'll never locate it. Have you ever considered that?'

'Yes, yes I have Mace. But you understand how I need to find out, don't you?'

'Yes Effie, I do.' He said in a thoughtful voice. 'I'm glad you're keeping an open mind over this whole thing. I'd hate for you to pin all your hopes on this.' With a nervous laugh he cleared his throat. 'Anyway, I'm more intrigued to know what you and Clarice have been plotting. I know you two are up to something.'

With all that had happened, Clarice and the flat seemed suddenly insignificant.'

'Oh, it's nothing, really. That's the least of my concerns, believe me.' I said with a big sigh.

He looked at me discerningly, and for a moment I thought he was going to disclose a vital piece of information, but then his face softened. 'Poor Effie, you have the world's burdens upon your shoulders. Go home and get some rest.'

I nodded slowly, sensing there was a hint of spitefulness in his tone, rather than mere sarcasm. 'See you tomorrow then?' I said, dubiously.

Mace nodded, giving me a quick hug.

'Watch how you go on that bike and no more bumping into old friends that might make you faint.' He said with a chuckle. 'I'll be over sometime in the morning.'

Mace sprinted off down the street, his feet splattering in the puddles as he went.

Chapter 6

When I'd reached home the rain had become little more than a steady drizzle. Spots fell from the dripping leaves and from the gutters above the windows, and a fresh moist breeze lingered in the air.

I called out to my Aunt when I entered the hallway but there was no answer. I suppose she was still with Agnes Davenport, trying to console her, for the poor lady would almost certainly be beside herself with grief, as she'd been extremely close to her sister Lydia.

Pulling my coat off, I almost had to drag my legs up the stairs. My whole body felt heavy with tiredness, and although it was only early afternoon, I really felt the need to sleep. I assumed Gideon had used the power of the mind method he'd told me about last night to transport himself here, and when he grasped my arms outside Hudson's café, he must have inadvertently taken some of my energy, as well as his own and that would explain why I felt so drained. It was puzzling though, why we were temporarily transported to the forest, only I wasn't sure if it was the same forest from our dreams, for it seemed darker, and more sinister.

I changed out of my wet clothes, put my dressing gown on and flopped onto the bed. Struggling to keep my eyes open I briefly thought over how Gideon had tried to warn me last night before our dream finished, and how he'd come to see me today to forewarn me that I was in danger, that he thought *she* was coming after me, whomever *she* was. Was all this real, should I *really* be scared, I wasn't sure; perhaps Mace was right and all of this was conjured up in my dream world, which would mean seeing Gideon today in the street, soaking wet, had been a mere hallucination of mine, and my best friend hadn't *really* seen me speaking to anyone. This was an exceedingly worrying thought for that would mean there was something seriously wrong with my mind. I remember my Aunt mentioning once about a friend of hers that had become hysterical after claiming she was seeing apparitions in her home, and was carted off to the mental asylum on the outskirts of

Abercrombie, a grim looking building called The Manor. The poor woman never did get better, and spent the remainder of her days locked away in there. I shuddered with the notion that this horrid place could become my new home.

Just before I drifted off another notion came to mind that filled me with an awful sense of foreboding – if I *wasn't* going mad then surely that would mean that this woman coming after me would also be capable of transporting herself to this world, just like Gideon, only unlike him she wasn't going to be in the least bit friendly.

I slept most of that afternoon, it was a dreamless sleep that left me feeling quite refreshed, and for a while all those thoughts of a woman coming to get me and mental institutions got pushed to the back of my mind. Feeling happier I wandered downstairs and got some food and a cup of tea. My Aunt had returned from her visit, and as I thought had spent most of the day with Agnes Davenport, there was going to be an inquest for poor Lydia to establish the cause of death. For some reason my Aunt seemed rather tense and on edge. I put it down to the sad occurrence at the Davenport's, but wasn't entirely sure. When I asked her, she just shook her head and gave a little smile, telling me it was nothing. With a deep sigh she glanced at me from across the table and asked for a full account of my day so far. Unable to meet her in the eye I explained how I'd been to the local library and then had an uneventful meeting with Mace in the café. I told myself it was only half a lie and therefore didn't count, but I could still feel my face burning as I told her. A concerned look crossed over her face when I mentioned my afternoon nap and she informed me how it just wasn't normal for a young woman like myself to fall asleep in the middle of the afternoon, not unless I was ill. I reassured her by saying how it must be the after effects of yesterday's exhibition. To my way of thinking this was perfectly feasible.

For the remainder of the day my Aunt and I busied ourselves doing various jobs around the house, and then we discussed the more urgent renovations that were crying out to be repaired on poor old Rawlings. She wasn't happy for me to use the money from my paintings on the house but I insisted, telling her I wouldn't dream of spending it on anything but our home.

After my Aunt had finally retired to bed, I found myself sitting in the living room on the window seat, gazing out at the early evening sky. It remained rather overcast and the dark clouds were bunching together in readiness for yet another downpour. I had an uneasy, sick feeling in the pit of my stomach that wouldn't go away. It had arrived shortly after Gideon had uttered those fateful words about the woman who wanted to harm me, it was eating away at me like a ferocious beast, and there was nothing I could do to stop it. So, I found myself delaying my bedtime, scared of what might happen in the darkness of the night, fearful of any unknown shadows I might catch a glimpse of out the corner of my eye.

In the end the inevitable call of sleep was too much and I staggered up the stairs, sleepily glancing around just in case there was a figure lurking in the corner ready to pounce. I showered, cleaned my teeth and clambered into bed, dragging the bed covers over my head, as if they had the ability to protect me. Lightning struck intermittently, bathing my room in a luminous glow, and with the soft sound of rain against the windowpane, I was soon lulled to sleep.

In my dream the moon shone down, bathing the forest in a muted blue, never before had I seen it looking so lovely. However, I then noticed a thick mist rolling in from nowhere, covering the place in darkness. As I stared over towards the trees, I could see a figure gradually emerging from the fog. But my happiness soon turned to terror as I realised it wasn't Gideon at all, it was a thing, a horrid thing created especially for the worst of nightmares. Aghast I watched as it slowly shuffled along, its wooden joints creaking. It came nearer and nearer until it was standing directly in front of me, its eyes upon me, frighteningly wide and cold looking. It was Gilbert.

'Greetings Miss Farraday.'

Feeling frozen with fear, I opened my mouth to scream but found myself unable to utter a single word, it almost seemed a muffle had been placed over my mouth.

The dummy glared at me with his dark stony eyes. 'It's been far too long since we last saw one another.'

'Mm, mm.' I moaned.

'It's very gracious of you to remain silent, not that you have a choice. You see in this nightmare I'm the one who can really talk and you're the stupid dummy.' He grinned abnormally wide. 'Don't you just love it?'

As he came nearer, he appeared to be twirling a piece of cloth around in his hands, and I saw it was the old cravat he usually wore round his neck.

'Well, are you not curious to know why I'm here?' he shrieked.

I attempted to move but the whole of my body was completely stiff as wood, and I was literally rooted to the spot like a tree.

'What's that you're trying to say, I can't quite hear you.' His wooden mouth clunked as he spoke, and then he began to chuckle. 'Well, you see Miss Farraday I'm going to kill you. I believe it's strangling you wanted, wasn't it madam?' His toothy grin widened, making his appearance even more hideous.

'Mm, mm.' I murmured in vain.

Still unable to move a muscle I watched in horror as Gilbert stood before me and raised his left arm, clouting me with a blow that came crashing down on my temple. I fell to the ground. He hunched over me and rasped in my ear.

'They'll be no precious Gideon to come and save you now, so you might as well accept it, Miss Farraday.' He growled at me, twisting the cravat around in his cumbersome hands and placing it around my neck.

My head was aching, making it difficult for me to focus but I had to think, I *had* to do something fast. I was sure it was fear keeping me from moving but there had to be a way to overcome it. Taking a deep breathe I closed my eyes and tried to concentrate on being angry instead of frightened, and miraculously as I opened my eyes an unexpected surge of strength coursed through my body and I could suddenly move my hands and arms. Shakily I wrenched his hands from my neck, and with one swift movement I grabbed his spindly body in a firm grip then lifted him up and threw him against one of the nearby trees, amazingly breaking several of the branches in the process. For a moment he lay there, as still as a toy dummy, before suddenly leaping up from the ground.

'That wasn't very nice now, was it?' he shrieked.

Thankfully, I seemed to have regained the movement in my legs too, and heaving myself up I ran over to where Gilbert was now putting his shoulder back into its socket. Wasting no time, I grabbed one of the broken branches, and with one swift swipe I hit him hard across the head; I stared in morbid fascination as it sat at an unnatural angle to the left of his shoulders, an evil grin still spread across his face. I struck him frantically, again and again until his head had become completely dislodged from his body and was rolling down the bank like a ball, it stopped at the bottom and laid there, the eyes and mouth still moving.

'I congratulate you Miss Farraday, on your triumph. But others may not be so easy to defeat.'

What *others*? I wanted to ask, but still, I couldn't speak.

'Your efforts tonight have been futile. Surely you must know you cannot destroy me, when you next see me, I shall be completely intact once more.' A cruel laugh escaped from his mouth, becoming louder with every second that passed.

I wanted to laugh hysterically as I saw his headless body stumbling about in confusion, with his arms stretched out in front of him precariously, searching for his decapitated head.

'I'm over here you fool of a dummies body.' His head shrieked.

I sprinted down the bank as fast as I could, picked up his head and quickly kicked it into the nearby stream. It made an almighty splash then floated off, carried along with the current of the stream.

'Noooooo. I shall return before you know it, Miss Farraday.' He wailed, his voice gradually petering out.

I stood there for a moment and watched as his head disappeared out of sight. Feeling relieved I relaxed a little, believing it all to be over, but then something grabbed my ankle in a painfully tight grip. I knew immediately what it was, for I might have got rid of his head but there was still the body. Shivering with terror I glanced down at the wooden hand clasped around my ankle, and let out a blood-curdling scream.

'No, please god no.'

I opened my eyes and shot out of bed, my heart thumping loudly in my chest. For a moment I stood there shivering, trying to take in what had just happened, for although it was common for me to have such nightmares it never got any easier. Clasping my hands together I went and sat on the edge of the bed, staring vacantly ahead. Even though I knew disposing of Gilbert might not stop the nightmares, the awful dummy just *had* to go, for if I didn't do something soon it would be *me* going to that asylum.

'Right.' I mumbled underneath my breath. 'There's no time like the present.

I swiftly put on my dressing, and glancing at the clock I saw it was the early hours of the morning. Shining my torch ahead of me I crept barefoot along the landing and retrieved the key that we kept under the plant pot on the table opposite the entrance to the attic. I unlocked the tiny door and clambered up the twisting stairs. The coldness of the attic hit me immediately as I entered, sending an icy chill through my bones.

'What *am* I doing?' I said in an unsteady voice.

For a second, I almost turned back, deciding to wait until morning. The attic was after all the most frightening room in the house, and here I was searching for the old toy dummy that had just tried to strangle me in my nightmare. It was enough to send anyone insane. Nevertheless, there would never be a good time to do this; I was here now and might as well get on with it.

From outside the oval window the moon shone brightly, illuminating the room in a cheerful glow and highlighting the mountains of clutter. I recall stuffing the dummy in one particular trunk, underneath mounds of musty old clothes in the far corner, however it appeared someone had been up here recently, rummaging about and now everything had been mixed up, including all the items in that corner. Mumbling to myself I strode over and began shifting the endless trunks and boxes away from the corner until at last I found the trunk with beautiful ornate swooping eagles hand crafted lovingly into its wood. Heaven only knows my reason for putting Gilbert in this specific trunk, for it was far too grand a home for such an evil dummy. I knelt down and slowly opened the lid and the hinges creaked ominously. As expected, the contents looked undisturbed, just as I'd left them. Methodically I rummaged through the musty clothes and odd pieces of jewellery, placing them neatly on the floor beside me, until the entire contents had been emptied. I stared in complete bewilderment at the bottom of the empty trunk. Gilbert was nowhere to be seen.

'What...where are you?' I whimpered in disbelief.

Complete panic took over, and frantically I began emptying each box and trunk around me, flinging their contents haphazardly over the floor, not caring about the mess.

'Why are you hiding from me Gilbert?' I uttered, not knowing whether to laugh or cry. 'Has someone come along and moved you or....' I froze for a moment. 'Or...or did you move yourself.' I let out a rather peculiar laugh.

I can't precisely recall how long I spent searching, but there came a point when I obviously must have given up. In a daze I stumbled to my feet, staring at the untidy heaps of clothes and other items that surrounded me. The attic was now in even more of a state. I remember thinking how furious my Aunt would be when she saw it, but as it was already in a shambles maybe she wouldn't notice. Nevertheless, I would try and make the effort to clear it a little, when I was feeling up to it. Overcome with fatigue I staggered out of the attic room, and forgetting to lock the door I made my way wearily back to my room.

With a slow stretch I turned onto my side and blearily glanced out the window to see the morning sun creeping over the horizon. For one blissful moment I was completely oblivious to the events of last night, but then reality hit me, sending with it an acute feeling of alarm and fear. Just the thought of Gilbert made my stomach feel queasy, the odd little dummy that wouldn't go away, and yet had mysteriously vanished into thin air. I had the strange sensation of teetering on the edge of a cliff, believing someone was about to push me over, and then I would plunge into the abyss of madness.

I lay back in bed for a moment and rested my arms behind my head. With an air of resolution, I decided to dispel any negative thoughts of being insane and allowed myself to believe Gideon wasn't just a figment of my overzealous imagination, that maybe there really was another world out there somewhere, and I only had to wait until Friday to find out.

Chapter 7

The morning seemed to come along in no time at all. Having little sleep, I wearily dragged on my dressing gown and made my way downstairs to the kitchen. My Aunt was nowhere to be seen, so I assumed she'd popped out for groceries or some such thing. All of a sudden, the house felt desolate and bleak without her, something that had rarely bothered me before; in fact, I was often quite happy being on my own, and if I wanted complete solitude I would sneak off to the library, a room my Aunt rarely visited. When I was a child, I'd play for hours on end in one room or another without a care in the world; I knew Aunt was never far away and would sooner or later pop her head around the door to check on me.

But that day as I stood by the kitchen table there was something different, I felt on edge, scared of my own shadow and I couldn't shake off the sense of foreboding in the pit of my stomach. I scanned the length of the kitchen, half expecting something or someone to jump out at me. Nervously I sat down on one of the kitchen chairs, facing the door so I was certain to see anyone entering. Whilst eating breakfast I tried to focus my mind on Gideon, and how I was going to explain him to Mace, I began agonizing over the best way to phrase my words but it all just sounded like some poor excuse. Giving up, I switched my attention to the chores instead. My Aunt would frequently scribble down a list of household duties for me to carry out and leave it on the kitchen table. Today however it seemed she'd forgotten, but instead there was a lovely pile of washing up in the sink and I assumed it was for me to tackle.

My mind was elsewhere when it happened. I was gazing out the window waiting for the kettle to boil when I suddenly noticed a movement in the reflection of the window. Flinching, I swung round and dropped the milk bottle, shattering glass all over the kitchen floor. Standing there beside the table was a woman in a grey dress, young like myself but a little taller. Just like Gideon her figure appeared almost transparent and ghost like. I suppose she was quite beautiful with her dark striking eyes and raven coloured hair that flowed down her back like a veil. But then I realised she was glaring at me rather nastily, like I was her enemy that must be destroyed. For one brief, silly moment I tried to make myself believe it was Mace playing some childish prank, as it was the sort of thing he *would* do, but as I continued gazing at the apparition, I realised that it was far too an elaborate illusion for him to have created, or anyone else for that matter. On the other hand, Rawlings was supposed to be haunted, so perhaps the woman before me was an angry spirit who had suddenly decided to descend upon my home. As a child my Aunt had told me many tales about the supernatural and they had always terrified me, but I imagine none of them made me feel as scared as I was now.

Her mouth moved. 'And so, we finally meet.'

I gulped nervously. 'Who…who are you?'

She glared at me unsmiling, and as she moved her hand slightly, I realised she was holding a bow.

'It doesn't really matter who I am.' She said, positioning an arrow in the bow and aiming it in my direction.

'Please…please don't shoot.' I said with a whimper.

'Be silent.' she answered abruptly, as if in deep concentration.

'Why are you doing this?' I said, trying to distract her.

'Because *you* are all that stands between Gideon and I, so your life must come to an end.'

The proclamation that she wanted to kill me should have been my main concern but it was overshadowed by the knowledge that she *really* was an acquaintance of Gideon. Of course, it had already dawned on me that this was the woman who was after me, the one Gideon had warned me about, but I was suddenly intrigued to know what they were to one another.

'Do you know Gideon well?'

She pulled back the bow in readiness. 'I've no wish to talk with you. I just want you to die.' With a cruel laugh she released the arrow.

There was no time for a delay in my reaction, my gut instinct took over and I quickly ducked and collapsed on the floor with a cry, narrowly missing the arrow. I stared up at the woman, my eyes wide with alarm. With a shriek of frustration, she strode towards my slumped frame. I tried to move away but found my legs slipping on the wet floor, and onto the broken shards of glass. With a sense of urgency, she swiftly positioned another arrow in the bow and aimed it at my head. In despair I shielded my face with my hands and shut my eyes, waiting for the end, but nothing happened. I'm not really sure how long I lay, unable to move or look up. It was only when my left leg had become rather numb that I eventually plucked up enough courage to shift my position and open my eyes. Tense and scared I nervously looked around the kitchen, and to my utter relief it seemed the awful woman had gone. Perhaps she had evaporated, just like Gideon, before having another chance to kill me. Whatever the reason I was just thankful the scary ordeal was over, and I had come out of it unscathed. However, it was only when I went to move my leg that I noticed the blood trailing down my calf, and saw that there was a deep cut on my kneecap and tiny nicks down my left leg. I cried out in sudden agony, as if the pain had only become apparent when I'd noticed I was injured.

The kitchen door suddenly swung open and I saw my Aunt standing in the doorframe looking completely aghast.

'Oh, my Lord Effie, what on earth happened?' Her eyes were wide with shock. 'Look at all the mess. And you're bleeding.'

I was unable to speak, and for one moment I wondered if the shock of what had just happened had rendered me mute. After all it wasn't every day I had a visitation from a peculiar woman brandishing a bow and arrow, with the sole intention of murdering me. I gulped hard when I thought of what might have happened if my Aunt had been in the kitchen at the time, how easily she could have got hurt, or worse still received a fatal wound, for although I was the intended target, my instincts told me that this woman wouldn't spare the life of a sweet old lady, not if she got in her way.

'Effie?'

'I ah... I'm fine Aunt. It was just a small accident.' My voice sounded odd as I spoke. 'The milk bottle slipped from my hand and I fell and cut myself on the broken glass.'

'Oh Effie, you can be so clumsy at times' She said, helping me up from the floor and into a chair. With an angry sigh she went about cleaning and bandaging my wound. 'There, all mended. Thankfully it's just a graze, so no harm done. You really should be more careful you know Effie. One of these days you'll do yourself a real injury and I might not be here to fix it.' She furrowed her brow as she looked at me then began placing the unused bandages back in the first aid box.

'I know Aunt, I'm sorry. I'll clean up the floor.' I said in a half-hearted fashion, glancing down at the bloodied mess of glass and milk.

'You'll do no such thing child, stay where you are and rest for a while.' She eyed me dubiously. 'You really do look pale, are you sure you're ok?'

'I'll live.' I smiled weakly at her. For another day at least, I thought gloomily.

My Aunt began to clear up the floor, muttering to me again about being more careful around the house. She then went on to remind me of the various chores that needed doing. It was comforting to hear her voice, and to know that everything was back to normal, for a while at least.

'There, I can't see any more glass, can you? She said, peering forward at the stone floor. 'I'll pack it away in a box and put it outside for the binmen. Now, we don't want any further accidents do we Effie?'

I smiled at her softly. 'No Aunt, I'll leave them to Mace.'

'Yes, he does seem to have more than his fair share of mishaps. Isaiah always says one of these days it will be a fatal one.' She paused, staring at my face. 'Well don't look so surprised Effie he said it out of concern for Mace's welfare. Talking of that friend of yours, isn't he coming over today?'

'Yes, yes he is.'

As she glanced down at my bloodied dressing gown, she suddenly began to shake her head in despair. 'Oh lord Effie, look at the state of you. Go upstairs and change immediately before Mace sees you.' With an impatient look in her eye, she glanced at the clock. 'It's far too late to still be in your nightwear.'

Even though it was still morning, the very fact that I was still slouching around in my pyjamas was not acceptable in her eyes. I should be up and dressed, doing some work. I would usually have protested and moaned a little, and she would narrow her eyes at me until I gave in. However, on this occasion I was extremely eager to get changed and take a shower, hoping that by doing so it would wash away the haunting memory of the woman.

'Yes Aunt.' I replied wearily. Rather shakily I rose up from the chair and stumbled unsteadily across the kitchen.

Just as my Aunt was busying herself, clearing away my breakfast dish from the table and carefully removing a stray piece of glass, we heard a loud rap from the front door.

'Oh, I bet that's Mace. She said in a distressed voice. 'The one time we don't want him to be here early, he is.' With a huff she rushed out the room to answer the door.

It was at that point I happened to notice the fridge door, and the arrow that had deeply embedded itself right through '*Effie's chores*', with the task '*Clear out the attic room.*' written underneath. I scoffed to myself, wondering if this was a coincidence, or my Aunt already knew about the fresh lot of mess up there, surely not I thought. It was lucky she'd not spotted the arrow otherwise I would have to try and explain where it came from, and make up some silly farfetched story, which would be preferable to the ridiculous truth. With a chuckle I pulled out the arrow and hid it within the folds of my dressing gown, thinking myself lucky that it had dented the fridge rather than my head. It's strange how some occurrences can seem amusing in the aftermath of such terror.

Without warning the kitchen door was flung open wide and Mace came strolling in. He stood there looking soaked through, his dark tousled hair flattened by the rain. When he saw me, his eyes became wide with amusement and he started to laugh hysterically.

'Look at you E, whatever happened?'

I stood there glaring at him. 'Just a minor accident.'

My Aunt hurried into the room. 'Effie stumbled onto a broken milk bottle and hurt her leg. It's just a few tiny cuts, nothing to fret about Mace.'

He put his hand over his mouth in an attempt to stop laughing.

'Does he look like his fretting Aunt?' I said crossly.

Ignoring my comment, she ushered me out of the kitchen. 'Effie's just going upstairs to freshen up Mace,' she said throwing him a glance before looking back at me. 'Do watch your bandage in the shower dear.' She muttered, shoving me in the direction of the stairs as if I was a visitor and didn't know the way.

'Hurry up E.' he said, still laughing. 'Try and not fall down the stairs, won't you?'

I glanced back at him. 'Ha, ha, very amusing.'

My Aunt turned round and scolded him for making silly comments. 'It doesn't do to joke about such things.' She exclaimed. 'A dear gentleman friend of mine died from a broken neck a few years back when he accidentally stumbled down a staircase, so please be careful what you say.'

Mace looked suddenly sheepish. 'Sorry Connie, I forgot. You were very fond of old Mr Jeffries, weren't you?'

She lowered her head, looking grave. 'Well yes, Isaiah believed he was on the verge of asking for my hand in marriage.' Her eyes drifted off for a moment. 'Oh well, such is life.'

After a shower I got dressed and then slowly wandered down the stairs, still unable to forget the peculiar woman. I made my way to the living room where Mace was warming himself by the fire.

Ordinarily it would have been a good day to stay inside, as the rain was thrashing against the panes almost as if it wanted to enter the property, and there were gale force winds howling violently through the trees. But my instincts were warning me to go and spend some time away from Rawlings, just in case that strange woman made another unwelcome appearance, and besides I felt the need for some bracing air to clear my head.

My Aunt had already left as she needed to go and see her friend Mrs Wainwright, who was another committee member, and I had no doubt they would be discussing the sad demise of poor Lydia Davenport, which meant she would be gone for most of the day. Isaiah wouldn't be visiting until late, and so we didn't need to worry about him poking his nose in where it didn't belong.

Feeling rather guilty, I asked Mace if he'd mind very much if we went down towards the seafront for a walk. After he'd stopped moaning about how he'd only just managed to get dry he reluctantly followed me outside, mumbling to me how it was still raining. I tried to reassure him by saying how it was brightening up, but he just scowled at me. It was a misty sort of rain that left freshness in the air and the lingering smell of wet earth. I already felt better.

We strolled along the deserted promenade, gazing across at the vast expanse of sea, where several boats were bobbing about on the horizon and immense waves were crashing angrily into one another, and as they smashed up against the sea wall it almost seemed they were trying to escape their only home. Seagulls hovered overhead, spasmodically darting towards us, on the lookout for scraps of food. The rain had become worse now and was lashing against our faces as we struggled to walk forward in the strong winds. Poor Mace, I thought, he must be cursing me. I grabbed his arm and we ran towards one of the many shelters dotted along the promenade, and there we sat huddled together. I reached in my rucksack and pulled out a thermos of hot chocolate, pouring him a hot, steaming cup. He looked at me rather grumpily and for a while we just sat in complete silence, looking out at the sea.

I was still pondering on how best to tell Mace about Gideon, as it would just be mean and selfish to expect him to travel on our trip without him being aware of the truth. I scolded myself for not informing him sooner, and now it would look like I was only telling him because I had to.

I looked at him out of the corner of my eye.

'See, I'm not entirely merciless, am I?

'What?'

'The hot chocolate, I made it just before we left. Oh, and I brought these too.' I said with a little laugh, gingerly passing him a flapjack from a paper bag in my rucksack. 'Aunt made them.'

He mumbled something under his breath and began to eat.

Yet again we didn't speak, but just sat drinking and eating our flapjacks, watched eagerly by a brave seagull hovering directly in front of us waiting for us to feed him.

'Okay, I suppose you're forgiven for dragging me out in this horrendous weather.' He said rather belligerently. 'If you give me another flapjack, I might be able to manage a smile?'

We both looked at one another and laughed.

'You can have the rest if you like.' I said, passing him over the bag.

For a while we chattered about topics of no importance, and this brief interlude was a much-needed distraction before I had to face discussing the matter in hand. For despite our differences, I knew Mace was the only person on this earth who would understand what I was going through. All of my other friends, probably including Clarice, would give me that look, the look you would bestow upon someone who had just said or done something a little abnormal, and after that there wasn't really any going back, and those so- called friends would become distant and cold. My Aunt would certainly not understand, in her eyes everything had a logical explanation and anything illogical just didn't exist.

'Mace?'

'Huh.' He replied, still munching on a flapjack.

'I ah...well before we take our trip, I have something I'd like to tell you, and as you're my best friend I know you'll understand.'

He turned to stare at me, raising his left eyebrow. 'Spit it out E.'

Strangely enough, once I began it all came gushing out. I told him all about my life with Gideon, and how he was the real reason for wanting to go through the gateway. 'That was him yesterday Mace, standing in the rain outside Hudson's café, he.... he was trying to warn me about this woman, and.... and today she materialised in my kitchen and tried to murder me.' With a gulp my eyes momentarily flicked to his. 'Mace, Mace are you listening?'

His face looked reticent. 'Yes E. Is that it or is there another revelation you've been keeping from me.'

I looked down at my hands and began wringing them together. 'That's basically it, apart....'

'Apart from what?'

'Well, you see we have an old wooden dummy at home, a family heirloom I believe.' I gulped again. 'His name is Gilbert, and since a young girl he's regularly appeared in my nightmares.'

Apart from the crashing of the waves, there was a deathly silence.

'Mace, please say something.'

I sneaked a glimpse at him and saw he was staring pensively out to sea. His large eyes seemed to be focusing on one particular spot far away, as if he'd seen something that had put him into a trance.

I laughed nervously. 'Have I finally succeeded in rendering you speechless?'

He turned to look at me. 'No E, even you can't do that.' His eyes travelled over my face. 'Oh E, what are we going to do with you eh? I already knew you were slightly bonkers but now I'm a tad concerned about your sanity.'

Although sarcasm was undeniably typical of him, I was slightly concerned at the bitterness in his tone.

'Well Mace, I'm sure there's a little madness in both of us, and that's why we get along so well.'

He glowered at me. 'If you really believe that then you're more deranged than I thought you were.'

'All I ask is for your help, even if you think me a little mad. I can't go through the gateway without you Mace, and I'm so dreadfully worried that the woman will return and finish me off. I'm scared Mace, really scared.'

He was looking out to sea again, his eyes lost in the depths of the ocean.

'Mace I'm so sorry I didn't let you know about all this before, it…it was wrong of me.'

He eyes darted angrily to mine. 'Yes, yes it was. You should have trusted me E, I'm supposed to be your best friend for god's sake.'

I let out a deep sigh. 'Will you still help me Mace?' I said beseechingly.

He picked up a pebble that had strayed from the shore and tossed it back where it belonged.

'Effie, I know you can't do this without me, you crazy woman. That's why Mace, the intellectual one of us is here to guide you on your quest. 'He grinned at me and reached over, planting a kiss on my forehead. 'No more secrets?'

'Never again Mace.' I spoke sincerely. 'I promise.' I moved an inch closer to him in an attempt to keep warm. 'So, you're sure you've found the right location?' I asked, deciding to change the subject.

He raised his eyebrows. 'Well, actually yes. Like I said yesterday I think it's in a place called Browning's Wood, which isn't very far away, and has the two beech trees you mentioned about. We also need to look out for a fork in the road, a stone statue, and an elephant.' A broad grin appeared across his face. 'Okay I'm only kidding about the elephant, I just thought it would be fun to add it.'

I giggled.

'If my deductions are correct.' He winked at me. 'Which they usually are, then we can safely say *I've* located the wood.'

I clapped my hands together in glee. 'Mace, you're incredible. But how did you discover its whereabouts?'

He averted his gaze. 'Oh ah…I have a vague recollection of visiting the woods when I was a child, and what with the tree clue you provided me with, well it took me a while but eventually it all just slotted into place.' With a short laugh he tossed the remainder of his flapjack to the awaiting seagull.

I studied his face as he continued to stare out to sea. Something in his tone seemed wrong, as if he wasn't telling me the entire truth. I couldn't understand how he could suddenly recollect the woods, a place he'd never mentioned before. Nevertheless, I decided not to question him about it, not when it seemed so unimportant; what mattered was we had found the location, and he now knew about Gideon, the woman, and the dummy, and most importantly he was happy to travel with me.

'Go and bother someone else, you vulture.' Said Mace as he shooed away a seagull that had landed by his feet. 'You've bled me dry of food.'

A surge of eagerness took over me and I grabbed his arm.

'Let's take the trip to the woods this afternoon Mace. If we leave now, we can be there in a few hours.' I hesitated. 'I would've waited until tomorrow but under the circumstances....'

'You mean the incident with that potty woman this morning.'

'Well, yes.'

'But what if she's ready and waiting for you at the other end of the gateway?'

'Mace, I have Gideon at the other end, he'll know what to do.'

'Good old Gideon eh.'

I gave him a weak smile. 'Please Mace, we could at least *try* and find it today, and if we have a wasted trip then so be it.' I looked at him, trying to read his thoughts. He was staring out to sea again, a lost look in his eyes. 'What do you think?'

He nodded silently, looking dispassionately ahead.

'You'd better go home and pack then, we'll leave this afternoon.'

'Oh Mace, thank you.' I flung my arms around him in pure joy.

I practically ran back to Rawlings in a dreamlike state, full of nervous excitement. Every so often I'd find myself glancing over my shoulder just in case a woman dressed in grey was skulking somewhere in the shadows. Is this how it's going to be? I asked myself. Will I have to live my life in constant fear, jumping at every sound and scared of my own shadow? For I sensed if I stayed and did nothing she would sooner or later reappear, and this time I wouldn't be so lucky.

Haphazardly, I threw a few items of clothing and toiletries into my rucksack, not really thinking straight. After all, I had no idea what to expect. For instance, it wasn't as if I was travelling to another country and needed my passport.

I couldn't bring myself to tell my Aunt, she wouldn't believe me anyway. Besides, I thought to myself, why worry her needlessly. If we couldn't find the gateway we'd be back in a matter of hours, and she'd be none the wiser. If we *were* successful, I'd visit Gideon and sort out this business with the woman, and probably be back home in a few days, as I didn't plan on staying very long. It all sounded so simple when I said it in my head, but as we all know reality is often somewhat more complicated.

'I should pack a torch.' I mumbled.'

Reaching across the bed I grabbed the torch from my bedside table and stuffed it into my already crammed rucksack. I began to wonder if my Aunt would enquire as to why I'd packed so much for a night at Clarice's. She had peered at me rather suspiciously when I told her, as she knew I hardly ever spent the night at a friend's house. Over the years it had always been them that had come to Rawlings, although many I suspected only visited out of curiosity, thinking that because I lived in a big old house it *had* to be haunted. This idea seemed to appeal to them and on one occasion we had practically the entire class sleeping over in various spare rooms, including a nasty little boy who had a habit of pinching me and tugging my hair; I remember making a wish one night that he'd magically disappear and never return, and to my utter astonishment it appeared to come true, for soon after he went missing, and was never seen again. How I tortured myself over his absence, praying night after night for god to take my wish back, and that I didn't really mean this boy any harm; for years I blamed myself and even to this day I still feel a little guilty.

Rather slowly I carried my rucksack downstairs then went and stood in the grand hallway. A sudden attack of melancholy crept over my heart at the thought of leaving my dear old house, for despite only going away for a short time, I felt incredibly sad, almost as sad at having to leave my Aunt. Laughing to myself at being so silly I went outside and stood on the front step.

Mace arrived, surprisingly on time and nearly drove his car into one of the pillars.

My Aunt muttered something under her breath and shook her head at him in puzzlement. 'Whatever possessed you to use your car again Mace, I didn't think you were driving anymore?'

'Change of heart Connie.' He said, clambering out. 'Don't worry, it's all fixed and perfectly safe.' Slamming the door, he turned and grinned at me. 'You know how much Effie hates taking her car on....'

Before he had a chance to finish his sentence, I rather swiftly raised my voice. 'Any journey, I hate taking my car on any journey.' I said with a nervous laugh. 'Even if it is just to Clarice's house.'

'Yep, that's E for you.'

My Aunt looked mystified. 'Why don't the two of you just cycle over, it's hardly very far.'

Mace and I exchanged glances.

'I wanted to give the old thing a bit of a spin. Giles says if I don't start using it again soon, he's going to sell it.'

'Well, your father Giles is right you know Mace.' She smiled graciously then looked at me. 'Effie, are you sure about this. Why doesn't Clarice come over here, it would make much more sense.'

What my Aunt really meant was that she lived in a much smaller house than us. And also, since the death of her father, Clarice and her mother, Mrs Lapworth, were struggling to hold onto their home, as money was tight. I know Mrs Lapworth got easily stressed over this and wasn't always in the best of moods. A while back there was an incident in the greengrocers involving Mrs Lapworth and a shop assistant, who accused her of trying to leave the store without paying. Apparently, Mrs Lapworth had lashed out and hit her. Being such a small community, this news got round Abercrombie in less than a day. I overheard Isaiah discussing the matter with my Aunt, and he was saying some really unkind things about Clarice's mother.

'Well.' I said, trying to think of the right words. 'I thought it would make a change to spend the night at Clarice's house, and her mother is looking forward to seeing Mace and I.'

Aunt tried to conjure up a slight smile but couldn't help but look worried.

'Very well then.' She said quietly, turning her attention to Mace. 'Well do drive carefully, my niece means a great deal to me.'

Mace gave her an odd look. 'Of course, Connie, I promise. And anyway, we'll be back before you know it.'

Suddenly I had the urge to fling my arms around her and tell her I loved her. Looking back, I wished I had.

Isaiah's car was making its way up the driveway.

How very typical of him to arrive now, I thought. If only he'd been later like he'd said and we could have avoided him altogether.

He stared down at my rucksack as he awkwardly clambered out his car.

'Going somewhere Effelia?' he said curiously.

Mace answered before I had a chance to reply. 'Yes, Effie and I are going on a little trip.'

Isaiah looked suddenly startled. He gave Mace a fleeting glance before looking at me and narrowing his eyes.

'Effelia, what is he talking about?'

My eyes darted to Mace in annoyance then back to Isaiah. 'He means we're taking a trip to Clarice's house, to...to spend the night.'

He stood there, looking deep in thought. 'Well, I shall be only too pleased to give you both a lift.' He paused, mulling over his words. 'Perhaps I could stay at Clarice's for a little while and chat with you all.'

'Thank you, Isaiah but that really won't be necessary, Mace is happy to drive. Besides, I'm sure my Aunt would love it if you kept her company for a while, wouldn't you Aunt?' My eyes rested on her.

Ordinarily I wouldn't have suggested such a thing, as I loathed Isaiah being at Rawlings, but at that precise moment it seemed the best idea to suggest. I looked at her, waiting for her to reply.

'Well, that sounds a most agreeable idea.' My Aunt uttered, smoothing down her hair.

Isaiah's face clouded over. He nodded slowly at my Aunt. 'Of course, Constance, whatever you say.' As his eyes crossed over from me to Mace, I saw the way he glared at us morosely. 'Let's allow the children to have their bit of fun.'

Mace rolled his eyes and glanced at his watch, looking impatient.

'Time to leave Effie, Clarice will be wondering where on earth we've got to.' He said, raising his eyebrows at me.

'Yes, you're right.' I muttered in a low tone.

I gave my Aunt a hug, trying to hold back the tears. 'See you soon.' Drawing back a little I kissed her lightly on the cheek. 'You look after yourself Aunt.' I gave her another hug.

'Oh, Effie dear, anyone would think you're going to be away for ages.' She said with a quizzical laugh. 'You'll be back tomorrow.'

I smiled poignantly at her. 'Yes Aunt, I shall.'

Chapter 8

The afternoon sun shone brightly as Mace and I drove down the long driveway. I watched as my Aunt and Isaiah became distant figures in the background, standing like statues guarding my beloved Rawlings.

Mace had made a thermos of coffee, and in the glove compartment there were a selection of sweets which I had to keep passing to him.

'There should be a toffee in there somewhere E.' he mumbled in between chewing. 'Be a pal and have a look.'

With a sigh I began to search through the sweets. 'Oh, here we are.' I declared, unwrapping it and popping it into his open mouth.'

For a while we sat in silence.

'So, where do you keep that dummy of yours, Gilbert isn't it?'

I looked at him in amazement. In my haste I'd forgotten to ask my Aunt if she knew where the old toy had disappeared to. With any luck she'd given him away to charity or the church jumble sale. I pictured him propped up amongst old teddy bears and dolls, waiting for some poor unsuspected child to come and purchase him; either that or they would recoil in horror. Did I really want to risk unleashing his evil onto others, for if last night's nightmare was anything to go on then the answer would most certainly be no. Besides, he was probably still lurking somewhere in the attic, watching and waiting.

'Effie? Earth to Effie.'

'Ah, well…. Gilbert usually lives in the attic.'

Laughing, he shook his head frantically. 'And does he *usually* live with all the other nightmarish old toys in the trunks. Perhaps they have a gang of them up there that all come to life in the night, ready to scare people.'

With a frown I glared at him. 'It's no laughing matter Mace, believe me.' As he continued to laugh, I was almost tempted to pick up the remainder of the sweets and throw them out the window.

'*This* is why I never mentioned him before, because I knew you'd make fun of me.'

'Sorry E, I was only trying to make you laugh, not poke fun at you. I'm sorry, it was insensitive of me.'

I smiled gently at him. 'Apology accepted.' With a harrowing sigh I turned to face him. 'The thing is I was up there last night searching for him and well.... well, he's gone missing.'

'Don't worry E, Connie's probably moved him somewhere.'

As he momentarily stared onto the back seat the car veered very slightly to the right. 'Either that or he's hitched a lift with us.'

I shuddered. 'Perish the thought.'

For a while I allowed my mind to be distracted by the scenery, which was mainly fields, splashed with mustard yellow and the odd animal grazing in the distance. With the soothing hum of the engine in the background I put my head back and closed my eyes, letting the breeze from the open window gently caress my face.

'I'm so glad you're here to keep me company Mace.' I said looking appreciatively at him.

'Thank you, Effie.' He gave me a cheerful look and tilted his head towards me as he spoke. 'You've got to admit I'm your ideal travelling companion. I'm amiable, funny and witty, with enthralling conversation and spasmodic spouts of silences just so you don't think I talk too much. And if that wasn't enough, I'm also an excellent reader of road maps.' He began to hum to himself. 'You even get coffee and sweets thrown in too. I'm irreplaceable, don't you think?' he spoke with his mouth full of a chewy sweet.

I smiled and gazed out the window again. 'Yes Mace, you certainly are, and so modest too.' I sipped my coffee, which was far too sweet for my liking but I drank it anyway, not wishing to offend him.

Mace scratched his head. 'Read out the directions again, will you E.'

I took the map and glanced at the route Mace had highlighted in bright green. 'According to this we need to take a left turning and go through Mayberry, which should then lead us to a village called Damson Oak?'

'Yes, yes go on.'

'Once we've passed the village we travel on for a few miles, and somewhere up ahead should be Browning's Wood.' I said, tapping the map. 'We should be there in less than an hour.'

'Well, that's super Effie, but then I *did* mark our route out, so I'm sure it's correct. All you need to do is look at my directions.' He took one hand off the steering wheel and scratched his head again, smiling at me. 'What would you do without me to show you the way?'

'I'd find a way to manage, I'm sure.' I said in a droll voice.

'Really?' He raised his eyes at me. 'You'd be lost without me, and you certainly wouldn't have found the magic gateway thingy.'

I glanced at him. 'Are you telling me that you already *know* where the portal will be in the woods?'

'Well...no, but how difficult can it be. And wait a minute, why are you suddenly calling it a portal rather than a gateway, they mean the same don't they?'

I shrugged my shoulders. 'Yes, I've just decided that portal sounds a little more exciting, like we really are going on a mysterious adventure to some distant world.'

'Portal it is then E.' he grinned from ear to ear. 'I suppose you could call me your saviour. The great Mace saved the day. He's going to find the magical land, and then protect his best friend from any dangerous creatures, that might be lurking in this strange new world.'

The implication that I was some fragile female, incapable of doing things for myself was somewhat aggravating, but I suppose I should give him credit for discovering the location and sorting out the directions, even so, he didn't have to boast so blatantly about it. However, I hardly had the energy to argue with him, not that there was much point, Mace would always win an argument whether he was right or wrong, and I was always the one to back down and admit defeat, usually because I was too tired to carry on our little spat or couldn't come up with a suitable reply.

He began to jabber on about a variety of subjects, one of them being Clarice and how much he seemed to think she liked him. Apparently, she'd tried contacting him several times yesterday, which I thought was rather odd. Perhaps I should have told him about the flat and how Clarice couldn't make it, but decided it could wait.

I glanced at the junction ahead thinking how it looked vaguely familiar, and then I realised it was a road sign for Mayberry, the exact same one we'd passed just a while ago.

'Mace, we've already been along this road, you must have taken the wrong turning whilst you were talking, and somehow doubled back.' I uttered feeling both amused and aggravated at the same time.

'What?' he said in a surprised voice. Furiously he snatched the map from my hands. 'No, we can't have. I'm sure we were going in the right direction.' He yelled, looking at the map intently.

'Mace, please keep your eyes on the road.'

He glanced up fleetingly and his lack of concentration caused the car to swerve across the road, sending the contents of his cup to spill all over the map.

'Be careful.' I shrieked at him. Luckily the road was deserted.

He threw the coffee-stained map over his head and onto the back seat.

'We don't need that stupid thing anyway.'

This was so typical of Mace he was always so impetuous that it very often got him into trouble.

'But we *do* still need it.' I shouted, watching the map blow up against the open window and go flying out into the air. 'Well, that does it.' I exclaimed furiously. 'Why don't we just use our senses to guide us there?'

'You know E that's not a bad idea of yours.' Mace said, laughing. 'You are slightly deranged at the moment, so maybe if you close your eyes you can visualise where the portal thingy is, or even better conjure up what's his name- Gideon? He can be our guide.'

I gave him a furious glare, thinking how very tiresome he was beginning to become. 'Please don't joke about Gideon it really isn't helping. Can't you be serious for a minute? In fact, just be completely silent. I know that's not easy for you Mace but I'm sure you'll find a way.' I said with a deep sigh.

He muttered something underneath his breath.

I *was* going to ask him to stop the car so I could retrieve the map but we'd already travelled some way, and besides I think we knew roughly where we were headed.

'We'll have to go through Mayberry again then left instead. Let's keep focused this time.' He said, snapping at me.

I glanced in his direction as he sat staring indignantly straight ahead. The quietness that followed was welcoming for a while but my conscience got the better of me, and I knew it would have to be me to back down, just like always.

'Look Mace, I didn't mean to shout at you. It was just as much my fault that we took a wrong turning as yours. I...I should have been paying more attention to the road.' With a sigh I glanced into his face, trying to work out what was going through his mind.

Another stony silence followed, until suddenly he pulled a chocolate bar from a bag down beside him.

'Want one?' He said in a quiet voice, handing me the bar.

'You have chocolate bars as well?' I exclaimed, hoping that this meant he was speaking to me.

'Oh yes. I can always find room for chocolate.' He turned and smiled gently at me. 'Oh, and E? I'll promise not to joke about Gideon.'

'Thank you, Mace.'

I smiled at him, trying to imagine how he would react when he came face to face with Gideon, and as much as I tried, I couldn't visualise it; both of them came from different worlds, and under normal circumstances their paths would never cross, but then there wasn't anything normal about what we were doing

We soon found Damson Oak, and just on the outskirts of the village we suddenly spotted the statue. It was a tall imposing figure made of granite, which had a plaque displaying the name Cornelius Underwood, the founder of the village, and just as Mace had predicted, a fork in the road lay ahead with a signpost for Browning's Wood on the right. Having travelled a little further, we came upon the two large beech trees, and beyond them were a mass of dense oaks.

My heart did a leap.

'That must be Browning's Wood.'

'Oh yes E, it most certainly is.'

As we approached the woods, Mace parked the car just in front of some tall iron gates, which were partially covered with branches. We got out the car, and placing our rucksacks on our backs strolled towards the gates, which had thick heavy chains wrapped around them, secured with a padlock.

'Do you think it's private property?' I asked, glancing at an old rusty sign displaying the words '*Keep Out*' which was lying on the ground beside the gate. 'Perhaps the woods belong to the Browning family.'

'Who cares E, and even if it does, we wouldn't let a minor detail like that stop us, would we? He kicked the sign across the gravel. 'We've come this far -I'm not turning back now.'

I gazed up at the solid looking oak trees, tightly bunched together along the entire perimeter of the woods.

'I have the distinct feeling we aren't meant to enter.'

'Effie, you always have a feeling about something or other.' Whistling he stared at the gate. 'Wait here E, I'm going to clamber up.'

'Be careful.' I said, biting my lip.

'Worry not Effie, I'll be fine.'

I watched as Mace got a foot holding in the bars, and being so tall and flexible he easily managed to grab hold of one of the overhanging branches and pull himself up into the tree.

'Your turn E.' he yelled. 'Just climb up and take my hand.'

'You make it sound so easy Mace.'

'That's because it is, you should have more faith in yourself E.'

Apprehensively I glanced around to check no one was about then began the difficult task of clambering up the bars, and it took several failed attempts before I successfully managed to reach the top. Mace grabbed my hand and hoisted me up beside him, and then we carefully edged ourselves around the tree so we were away from the gates, and after stepping onto the branch directly below us, we jumped to the ground.

I always think there's an air of mystery about a wood, a certain enchantment; the way the trees cluster together, preventing the eye from seeing too far into the distance, and the shadows that flicker intermittently with the sunshine; a silent calmness envelops you, almost lulling you to sleep. My Aunt always used to tell me that the woods is the sort of place where faeries made their homes, and if you remained there long enough, they would make themselves known to you; for one nonsensical moment I imagined one would suddenly dart in front of us and show us the way to the portal, the magical portal that I hoped was nearby. But this was merely a foolish fancy, for in reality we would have to locate it ourselves, and we really didn't have a clue what direction to take.

We were in the heart of the woods now and Mace was trailing behind me. He seemed unusually quiet, as if something was on his mind.

'Tired?' I asked, glancing round at him.

'Whatever gave you that idea E?'

I chuckled. 'I know you're not a walker Mace.'

He scoffed. 'Well, I wouldn't mind, but we're just aimlessly hiking across the woods looking for something that probably doesn't even exist.' With a deep sigh he threw his rucksack down on the ground. 'We didn't really think this through, did we E? Perhaps we should turn back.'

'No.' I exclaimed in alarm. 'We can't just give in. The portal is around here somewhere, I can just sense it.'

He rolled his eyes. 'Well, I think we should rest - my legs are aching.'

Looking sulky he wearily trudged over and sat on a nearby log.

I flopped down beside him.

For a while we both sat there in silence, listening to the distant sound of birdsong and the gentle swaying of the trees. It was so lovely and peaceful, but too peaceful for Mace, something must be *really* wrong, I thought.

A sudden noise came from the trees up ahead and sounded like a bird frantically flapping its wings. I got up and took a closer look, whilst Mace sat there looking dejected. Initially I couldn't see anything but as I kept looking, I suddenly spotted an owl peering out from amongst the branches, watching us with its vivid yellow eyes. I stared at it curiously and jumped when, quite unexpectedly, it swooped down in our direction, so low its talons almost touched the top of my head. Instinctively we both ducked and watched in awe as it passed over and perched in a nearby tree. And there it waited, still looking at the both of us with its inquisitive eyes.

'How strange.' I commented. 'Do you think it's going to attack us?'

'How should I know?'

I was just about to ask what was bothering him when, without warning, the bird started to hoot rather loudly and flutter its wings. In bewilderment I watched as it suddenly flew off in a southerly direction, towards a narrow stream, and sat there perched on a tree stump.

'This may sound odd Mace, but I do believe the owl wants us to follow him.' I whispered over to him.

'Why are you whispering, the owl can't understand what we're saying E.'

I laughed 'I've no idea.'

With a groan Mace rose up from the log, and dragging his rucksack along on the ground he made his way over to where I was standing.

'Well, it looks like we're lost anyway, so what have we got to lose.' He remarked slightly mockingly, tugging me forward. 'Come on then E, let's follow the sweet little owl.'

I frowned at him.

We ambled onwards along the riverbank, trailing behind the owl. It squawked noisily as it flew along the route of the stream, which twisted and turned its way deep into the woods. The trees were thicker now, darkening the whole area.

'Any sign of Gilbert, your friendly dummy.' Mace said grinning from ear to ear.

A vision of the dummy's contorted face suddenly popped into my head. I read somewhere that speaking about your nightmares with another person would put a stop to them, or perhaps cause them to seem less frightening, however I had serious doubts about this theory and wondered if it would've been wiser to keep them to myself.

'You've cheered up.' I stopped for a moment and glared at him. 'However, I now wish you hadn't. Why have you yet again mentioned Gilbert, when you can clearly see I find the subject distressing? And I'm sorry, but making a joke of it isn't helping, it…. it just reminds me of the nightmares.'

'Apologies Effie.' He sighed. 'Can't we take a short break - my feet are killing me.' He moaned.

'Well, I'm not sure, what about the owl?'

'Maybe we just need to follow the stream, not the owl' Mace uttered, slumping down against a nearby tree trunk.

Feeling frustrated I threw down my rucksack and sat down beside him.

'You've not got as much stamina as me.' I said, chuckling.

Mace looked at me and pulled a face. 'I think you'll find it's the other way round.'

We both smiled at one another and then glanced over at the owl, which seemed to be watching us again. The bird remained still for a while, staring at us with its big eyes. Then, with a flap of its wings it flew over and landed in my lap and started tugging at my jacket with its beak.

I laughed. 'Hello owl, is it time to carry on our journey, is that what you're trying to tell us?'

The owl squawked.

'Unbelievable.' Mace muttered, widening his eyes at the owl. 'What an intelligent little creature you are. Tell me, did Gideon send you.' he laughed. 'Or *are* you Gideon, in bird form?' Shaking with laughter he continued to stare at the owl before lowering his eyes.

With another squawk the bird left my lap and began flying up ahead.

'Come on.' I said, trying to ignore what Mace had just said. 'It's beginning to get dark. We should keep moving.'

The journey was becoming far too arduous. Mace had become silent again and had considerably slackened his pace, and my feet were developing blisters. I was just contemplating stopping to see if I'd remembered to pack some plasters when the owl came to a sudden halt, resting on a brick like structure beside the brook, which now flowed into a larger stream containing an ancient stone ruin.

I stared at it in wonder. 'What do you suppose that used to be?'

Without answering, Mace shrugged his shoulders.

The ruin was partially covered in water, and tiny waterfalls were cascading over the numerous sections of crumbling low-bricked walls, which were dotted up and down the stream at different levels. It was then I noticed a series of large stepping-stones, just poking above the stream, leading all the way to the centre of the ruin, where several large trees were clustered together in a large circle, their branches hanging down like great dark curtains.

As I gazed ahead, I observed the owl sitting amongst the branches, obviously expecting us to follow. I went to smile at Mace but to my surprise he'd rushed forward and was already leaping across the stepping-stones, two at a time. With a sigh I followed after him. Once we'd reached the trees, he mumbled something under his breath then forced his way between them and disappeared. In eager anticipation, I moved forward amongst the overhanging branches. A tingle of excitement ran through me, similar to when I was a child on the night before Christmas at Rawlings, only this time it was mixed with nerves. Having passed through the trees I came out into a small clearing, where there appeared to be a strange well- type structure in the centre. I briefly glanced at Mace who was sitting down beside the trees, his head bowed.

'Well, haven't you taken a look?'

He grunted and muttered something I couldn't quite hear.

I went and crouched beside the well and tentatively peered down inside, instantly hearing the strange swishing noise from within. At first, I wasn't able to see anything at all, but as I carried on staring intently into its depths, I could just make out a dark blue mist, swirling around at a tremendous rate like a whirlwind. This had to be it, I thought. At long last we'd found the entranceway to another world. Only now we'd found it I was having great difficulty comprehending that we had.

'It's amazing, isn't it, Mace.' I exclaimed as I stared wide-eyed into the well.

There was no answer.

'Mace? I rose up and looked around. 'Mace?' I returned to the other side of the trees to see him sitting there, staring into space. 'There you are.' I laughed nervously. 'Did you see what was in the well?'

'Yes,' he said glumly. 'Apparently we've *finally* found the portal.'

I glanced at his disgruntled face. 'Is something wrong Mace?'

He sighed deeply. 'Oh, it's nothing. It's just that ...part of me wished we hadn't found it. Now everything will change.'

'We don't know that.'

'What about Gideon?' He paused. 'I'll be in the way. He wants to see you, not me.'

'Oh, Mace I'm sure that's not true. He's looking forward to meeting you.' I said, pulling him up by the hand. 'Now come on, let's go and look at the well again, and pluck up the courage to jump in.'

On reflection, I should have paid more attention to what Mace had just been saying, but as I hovered over the entrance to the portal, my thoughts were entirely consumed with the thrill of meeting Gideon for the very first time, and also the fear of becoming trapped somewhere, far away from home, and unable to return.

'Mace, what if it's dangerous.' I gulped, turning round to face him. 'I'm scared, aren't you?'

He grabbed me and tenderly kissed the top of my head.

'I'll be seeing you, Effie.' He said in a low voice.

I was just about to ask him what he meant when I felt myself being swung round and pushed, and down I toppled, headfirst into the well.

Chapter 9

A high-pitched scream escaped my lips as I found myself plummeting into the murky depths of the whirlwind, and almost instantly I came into contact with veracious winds that threw me about like a rag doll; the strength of its force took my breath away and I placed my hands over my ears to try and lessen the deafening noise of the swirling winds. Daring not to look I scrunched my eyes shut in fear of what I might see. An idea crossed my mind that it must be a similar to being sucked into the heart of a tornado, not a very pleasant thought in the circumstances, and one that just added to my overwhelming feeling of panic. It seemed like an eternity before the winds gradually began to subside, and I allowed myself a tiny glimmer of hope. A sudden jolt catapulted me through the air and I landed face down on the ground. I lay there for a moment, whimpering, too scared to look up.

'Mace, Mace are you there?'

There was silence.

With a sigh, I carefully moved my head, and my cheek brushed against what seemed to be soft moss. The force of the land must have caused me to injure my temple and a sharp pain shot through my head. Disorientated by the thumping coming from my temple, I gradually lifted myself and tried to stand, but my legs were so shaky they gave way. Pain enveloped my left ankle and I collapsed to the ground, shivering with cold. I felt dazed and bewildered, not just from the pain coming from my head, but from the whole events of the last few moments.

'Mace?' I yelled again, but with more urgency. I began looking around frantically for him. Surely he jumped in after me, but then why did he push me? I half expected him to come bounding up to me. 'Is this one of your silly jokes Mace, because it's really not very funny.'

Yet again there was no response.

Doubt started to creep through my mind. I took a nervous gulp and sat there for a moment in a complete daze.

'It seems I'm on my own.' I muttered rather loudly.

Taking a proper look at my surroundings I wasn't exactly sure where I was, it looked similar to the woods I'd just come from, but looking closer I noticed how the trees seemed much taller and were bunched together in a solid mass, rather like a forest. There was an eerie silence that lurked around me, and it felt like the trees were watching me, waiting for something to happen. It then occurred to me that this could be the very forest where I had my dreams. Only somehow it didn't have the same feel about it, none of the trees were familiar and I couldn't see the great oak where Gideon and I had carved our initials.

As my thoughts turned to Mace, I felt myself growing angry. It's true to say he had seemed rather downcast on the journey through the woods, and perhaps he had changed his mind about going into the portal. Nevertheless, even if he did have a justifiable reason, it didn't excuse why he inexplicably pushed me into the well and cruelly abandoned his best friend in a strange world. Such was my fury that I didn't believe I would ever forgive him.

Deciding it would be best to make a move I heaved myself up from the ground and blindly stumbled along, without a clue where I was heading. Miraculously I somehow managed to escape the darkness of the trees and found myself right on the edge of the forest with a meadow directly ahead. The bright sunlight hurt my eyes as I limped my way across the soft grass, however the warmth of the sun seemed to be soothing my aching body as it crept over me like a blanket, and all of a sudden, I seemed to have regained my strength. The meadow was large and circular, and was truly beautiful with its delicate white daisies and shimmering buttercups, poking their heads through the long emerald grass. I threw my rucksack to the ground and sat down, gazing at the interlaced branches of the forest trees in the distance, amazed at how far they reached over, almost like arms beckoning me to come towards them.

It's strange as although the area seemed unfamiliar, I suddenly had a sense of being somewhere near Browning's Wood, maybe it was wishful thinking, I wasn't sure, but as I continued to sit there a dreadful realisation came to me- the meadow was bathed in sun, but when Mace and I had reached the portal by the waterfalls it had almost been dark, and would have been pitch black by now.

With a harrowing sigh I buried my face in my hands.

'Oh Gideon, If I'm truly in your world then where are you?' For one silly minute I thought of shouting out his name, just in case he was nearby, after all he was supposed to meet me by the portal, wasn't he? 'Oh.' I began laughing rather hysterically as I realised my only option was to return to the dark foreboding forest I'd just left, and go and wait by the portal that had catapulted me into this world.

Reluctantly I got to my feet, slung my rucksack over my back and slowly ambled back towards the forest. As I approached it, I pondered over how my injuries had suddenly got better, it almost seemed like the sun had healed them, either that or they weren't as bad as I'd first thought. It wasn't long before I was surrounded by the denseness of the towering trees. Glancing up I tried to work out their species, they didn't seem to resemble the great oaks of my dreams, and in fact I couldn't quite establish *what* they were, for they were of an unknown kind, and belonged in another world, this world. As I walked along further into the heart of the forest, the closeness of the trees made it dark and gloomy, and as the branches made threatening shadows on the ground; they reminded me of giant hands, ready to reach out and snatch you away. It was at this point I began hearing strange creaking sounds and long deep groans from above me, almost as if the trees were in pain.

I still half expected, or hoped that Mace would jump out from behind one of the trees. Yes, I would be mad with him, furious in fact, but more than anything, I would be immensely relieved. At this point I would even contemplate kissing him passionately on the lips, but then I would slap him.

My mind tried not to dwell on the woman with the bow and arrow, and how she was probably stalking me this very moment, ready to put an arrow through me; I was in *her* homeland now, and because of that I'd just made it extremely easy for her to kill me.

Some time passed before I realised, or rather had to accept that I'd become completely lost. I gulped with nerves, trying urgently to repress the feeling of fear that was galloping towards me with every breath I took. It was so dark now I could barely see where I was going, and had no idea if it was morning or night, for being this deep in the forest it was hard to tell; it had still been daylight in the meadow, but that seemed hours ago. Thick bracken covered much of the area, and I had to fight my way through with difficulty. All of a sudden, my eyes were drawn to a soft light that seemed to be illuminating from around the base of one of the trees. Going closer I realised that they were flowers, beautiful yellow flowers that glowed wondrously, almost as if a ray of sun had escaped from the sky and landed on their delicate leaves. Feeling comforted by their light I sat down and leant against the tree, staring dreamily at the tiny flowers, praying they were a beacon of hope.

It was decidedly chillier now and I did the buttons up on my jacket and pulled the hood over my head. What a peculiar outcome, I thought, for I hadn't expected to be stranded in a forest, alone and scared, in a strange world. Of course, I was naturally worried about the journey through the portal, who wouldn't be, but I didn't think I'd be taking the trip on my own, and I truly believed Gideon would be here waiting for me.

The sudden snapping of a twig made me jump.

Hello…. is that you Gideon?' I sat there, listening intently, but there was nothing.

With a deep sigh I reached for my rucksack, trying to remember if I'd actually packed any food. I'd been in such a hurry to stuff everything in there it was quite possible I thrown in a chocolate bar. Impatiently I rummaged through its contents, thinking it odd that there was so much in it, for I had no recollection of packing half this stuff. Perhaps Mace had sneaked the items into my rucksack when I wasn't looking, but unfortunately forgot the food, he most likely would have eaten it anyway. Thankfully a bottle of water was buried right at the bottom of the rucksack and I quickly drank the entire contents, not realising just how thirsty I actually was. On the off chance of finding food in my jacket pockets, I searched through them hoping that I'd come across a forgotten sweet or some such thing, and to my joy I discovered a chocolate bar. After finishing it I wrapped my arms around me in a vain attempt to keep warm, and then sat there mesmerised by the flowers, trying to forget where I was. My eyes were heavy now and before long tiredness got the better of me and I fell asleep.

I felt strong arms enveloping me from every angle, pulling me in and keeping me in their vice. It made me feel so happy and relaxed, almost like I was being blanketed in great warmth. Nothing else mattered now. I never wished to wake from this dream. I could stay this way forever.

'Effie?'

I *knew* Gideon would come and find me. I couldn't see him yet but I could hear the unmistakeable sound of his voice, drifting softly through the forest.

His voice sounded urgent.

'Effie, Effie, where are you?'

I wanted to call to him and tell him to leave me alone, to let me have my own dream. All around me I could smell the scent of the bark, deliciously invading my senses, and making me feel giddy. How I wished for this unique sensation of contentment to continue.

Gideon's voice was louder now, and all of sudden I knew he was with me. Wearily I half opened my eyes and could just make out his blurred figure, standing beside me. When he spoke, his voice seemed strangely apprehensive and cautious.

'I'm going to get you out of here Effie.'

'Please Gideon.' I mumbled. 'Don't wake me.' My eyes closed and I snuggled up against the tree trunk, which seemed to have become a soft pillow. I could feel myself falling into its depths. 'Is it really you, or am I dreaming.' I said sleepily.

'I shall answer all your questions later but we must leave this place now.'

'I'm fine Gideon.' I uttered, deliriously happy.

Long thin tendrils of warmth were gently caressing my face and wrapping around it.

'Effie wake up.' Gideon cried, trying to pull me away.

I never wanted to wake; didn't he understand? It seemed he was hacking at the branches around me, breaking them away. Then he was lifting me up and I felt his warmth up against me. I was so angry with him but too weary to speak. I wasn't sure how long he carried me but sleep soon took over. I dreamt I was back at Rawlings, sitting on a chair in the front porch, and when I turned to look at the person sitting beside me it wasn't Aunt or Mace it was Gideon.

Invariably the thoughts that enter our heads when we first awake are full of peace and restfulness, but then that feeling is lost and reality takes over. Sometimes it brings kind feelings, such as happiness, excitement or anticipation. Other times it can be cruel, bringing on sadness, anger or dread.

That particular morning my first thoughts after the initial moment of ignorant bliss were of confusion. I could hear singing from a little way off in the distance, and it certainly didn't sound like my Aunt. It was a man's voice, a man familiar to me, and then I remembered. Suddenly I felt a surge of anxiety wash over me on the realisation that Gideon was actually here with me now, and no longer just part of a dream. I was reluctant to open my eyes, scared of what I might see, and a big part of me wished to be in the sanctuary of my room at home. Realising how foolish I was being I opened my eyes and looked around. The tall trees of the forest that had seemed so threatening last night were now far off in the distance, and I was back in the meadow. A figure, not far off was gently humming a tune and was leaning over a crackling fire, busily preparing something over a large pot. The smell wafting my way was a delicious aroma and I realised how hungry I was. I knew before he'd even turned my way that it was Gideon, he was unmistakably familiar.

'Effie?' he said with a smile, beckoning me over to the fire.

As if in a trance I rose and slowly walked towards him. Usually, I was so at ease in his company that I seldom had difficulty in knowing what to say. Today however was completely different, and at that precise moment I was unable to utter one solitary word. It was as if he was a stranger to me, and I was overcome with shyness, my old enemy that seemed to blight my life. I tried telling myself that he was the same old Gideon and everything would be fine, but at the back of my mind I couldn't help but wonder if it would be different now, for I no longer had a dream to hide behind.

I could feel his eyes upon me, watching as I momentarily lost my footing and stumbled forward, but thankfully I managed to regain myself. I wondered what he must think of me as I staggered towards him so clumsily, how completely dishevelled I must look and quite plain looking in the flesh. I visualised him pondering over me with deep regret at his error in judgement in asking me here. He would be too kind and polite to tell me that it was a mistake, but I would be able to tell by the look of pity on his face that he wanted me to go home. I tried to tell myself that this was a ridiculous conclusion to come to, and as usual my self-doubt was attempting to take over.

'Effie, are you unwell, you look a deathly pale?'

The sound of his voice startled me, catapulting me back from my daydream. I watched as he hurried over and took my arm, guiding me to towards the fire.

'You must rest, travelling through portals is weary on the body.' He paused and smiled. 'That's what I've been told anyway. It will take a while for you to adjust.'

I gulped and lowered my eyes.

He reached for my chin, lifting it up so my eyes were level with his. He looked so real, so captivating and medieval looking, in some strange sort of way. For the first time in my life, I was really looking at him. His whole face seemed more defined. The dark curls that framed his face glistened in the sunlight; his sable eyes had tiny specks of blue I hadn't noticed before that lit up his face when he smiled, displaying his perfect white teeth. The dreams had not done him justice.

'I'm so glad you're finally here Effie.' He hugged me in a firm embrace, drawing back almost immediately. 'Please, come and sit down. You really need to eat to build up your strength.' He looked concerned. 'You'll feel better then.'

I detected a hint of awkwardness in his voice, as if he was slightly unsure of himself. It hadn't occurred to me before that he too would feel nervous at our meeting. I suddenly felt a little relieved.

His mouth broke into a huge grin. 'I do hope leak and potato stew is agreeable with you?' He emptied some of the stew into a bowl and gently placed it on my lap. 'I made it myself.'

I managed a faint smile but still found myself dumbstruck in his presence, my face blushing profusely.

We sat in silence whilst we ate, very occasionally sneaking a look at one another. Once I'd completely cleared my bowl, I glanced up to see him gazing at me. With a gulp I averted my eyes.

'I'm glad you enjoyed my cooking.' He laughed. 'Would you like some more?'

Finally, I managed to speak. 'No, no thank you, it was delicious but I'm quite full now.' My voice sounded polite and cold.

He stared at me for a moment then smiled. 'Well, I'm glad you enjoyed it, Effie.'

Frantically I tried to think what to say to him but my mind was a complete blank. How absurd, I thought to myself: Gideon and I had many subjects to discuss but at the moment it seemed I was incapable of even opening my mouth, let alone talking to him. Perhaps the journey through the portal had addled my brain. I looked ahead at the forest, trying to remember what had happened last night.

'Here, drink this, you must be thirsty.' He passed me a mug.

'What is it?' I asked

'Oh, just tea, I can assure you it's perfectly safe.'

'Thank you.' I cupped my hands around the mug.

The thought of stew and tea were comforting. Maybe this meant there'd be many similarities to home. A dull ache suddenly passed over my heart, as I imagined my Aunt sitting there in one of the big old armchairs, worried sick about me. What had I done, why on earth didn't I leave a note, telling her I'd be away for a while, what kind of niece was I?

Out of the corner of my eye I could see him staring at me again as I sipped my tea. I'm sure he was aghast and disappointed at how different I was in real life.

'Forgive me for staring. I just can't quite believe you're here.' He said, shaking his head in disbelief.

'Me either, I keep thinking I'll wake up any moment and find myself at home in bed.' I said, drinking the rest of the tea.

Gideon looked worried. 'I do hope you're not homesick.'

I pictured Rawlings and suddenly wished I could be there now, safe and sound in my beautiful familiar home instead of full of uncertainty in a strange land. Gideon was my one saving grace; all this was worth it to be with him.

'No, no, I really can't tell you how glad I am to be here.' My face broke into a smile. 'I keep trying to convince myself it's not a dream.'

A look of relief crossed over Gideon's face. 'I'm so glad you feel that way. And, believe me Effie, this is not a dream. You really are here, in my land.' He said, looking intently at me.

I met his gaze, feeling my face turning scarlet. If he moved his face slightly closer it would take very little movement for our lips to meet. I looked away, unable to cope with his penetrating stare.

There was a long pause and we both sat there for a while in silence.

He smiled gently at me. 'It must have been so tiresome for you, seeing me night after night. I feared you'd grow weary of my visits.'

'No, not at all.'

'Really?'

'My dreams of you are always so lovely.' I said, pulling an annoying strand of hair away from my face. 'You know how much I look forward to seeing you each night.' I blushed, suddenly feeling embarrassed at what I'd said.

'I feel exactly the same way Effie.'

We both gazed at one another.

With a sigh Gideon glanced up at the storm clouds hovering intermittently over the sun. 'We should make a move, as we've a long journey ahead of us.' He said, rising up and taking my hand. 'I do hope you want to see my home.'

A rapid wave of panic and excitement swept over me.

'Yes, I'd love to.'

The words tumbled out of my mouth before I'd actually had a chance to make a logical decision. Did I really know what I was doing? No, not really. But it didn't matter, as long as I was with Gideon.

Whilst freshening up I pondered over Mace. He was often erratic at the best of times but his actions of yesterday had completely shocked me. There was something more going on, something he wasn't telling me, and on my return, I intended to find out what it was. However, in the meantime I had pleasanter matters to contend with. Smiling at Gideon I reached for my rucksack and went over to join him.

'Ready?' He asked, putting out the fire.

'Yes.'

As he gathered up his belongings into a sack, I noticed an axe poking up amongst the various pots and food, and assumed it was for chopping firewood. He secured the bag with some rope and slung it over his shoulder.

'We must remain vigilant, as these parts can be fraught with danger. Stay close by my side Effie.' With a tentative smile he reached for my hand and held it firmly within his.

I felt rather dumbstruck again and nodded silently at him. I imagined I was in a dream and we were drifting along without a care in the world. I couldn't even begin to envisage the hazardous terrain that lay before us, and neither did I wish to. The less I knew the better.

Chapter 10

We left the meadow and made our way up a steep hill. I felt the long grass, which was still damp from the early morning dew, brush against my legs. There was no need for words as we strolled happily along together, and the warmth of Gideon's hand was comforting and reassuring. Before long we had reached the top of the hill and I glanced back and saw the iridescent shades of colour shimmering their way over the landscape as the sun's rays reached over, slowly spreading its gentle glow over the both of us. For a moment I closed my eyes and let myself bathe in its glory.

'We have a way to travel yet.' Gideon said, pointing ahead. 'My home is over that mountain in the distance.'

Below us lay a deep valley, where rich green landscape was engulfed in a patchwork of colourful flowers that were illuminated in ribbons of sparkling hues, and beyond I gazed upon golden cornfields gently embraced by the exquisite glow of the sun. Vast crystal blue lakes ran below the mountains, glistening like diamonds.

'Gideon it's truly breath-taking.'

'Yes, yes, it is.'

For a moment I had the urge to rummage in my rucksack to see if Mace had sneaked in a camera, as this would certainly be the time to take a picture, but then I decided a mere photo wouldn't do the scenery justice.

I continued to gaze down into the valley.

'I can't imagine what dangers would lurk in such a beautiful place.' With a contented sigh my eyes turned to Gideon.

'Oh, you'd be surprised Effie.'

For a moment I studied his face, waiting for him to elaborate, but he just remained silent.

'But doesn't anyone live around here?'

'No, not in these parts, as I said the landscape is unpredictable. We like to maintain our life much like our ancestors, and we decided long ago to keep the land as it's always been. Most folk are content to remain in our home of Briarwood, and it's very rare for anyone to venture too far into the wilderness.'

'Surely not everyone lives in your village. There must be more dwellings elsewhere?' I asked, perplexed.

Gideon looked down into the valley and sadness filled his eyes.

'Let's rest for a while.' He took my arm and pulled me down. 'There are others yes, but not near these parts. There's another land located southwards.' His voice sounded odd. 'A long time ago some travelling monks stumbled upon the place, quite by accident. Back then the land was full of promise, as it was covered in rich arable farmland and dense woodlands, spread with rare flowers and herbs. Rivers and streams were plentiful and masses of wild deer, also known as Hart's, roamed freely. So, the monks took it upon themselves to name it Hartland.'

'It sounds like a wonderful place. Have you visited it?' I asked, innocently.

Gideon looked immediately alarmed.

'No of course not, why would I.' He said, snapping at me.

The sudden coldness in his voice startled me and I tried to think of what I'd said wrong.

'I...I was only asking.'

'No sane person would go there willingly and any villager foolish enough to venture in that direction will hardly ever return to Briarwood.'

I looked searchingly at him, not understanding his sudden anger. It was like a dark cloak of fury had descended upon him. But I couldn't stop now I had to learn more.

'But why don't they return, are they unable?'

'Usually yes, on arriving in Hartland, folk are persuaded to make it their new home. Also, the good people of Briarwood frown upon anyone leaving their little community, for any reason whatever, so even if you *did* return to our village one day you wouldn't be made welcome.' He tore a blade of grass and tossed it in the air.

'What about you, you've left the village.'

'Ah, but I'm merely journeying to collect you. We shall be back before you know it.'

'Surely this Hartland can't be so bad.' I said with a nervous laugh.

Gideon stared ahead, looking pensive. 'Yes, I'm afraid it is. Back in Briarwood we all call it Harshland, as it seems a more fitting name than Hartland.' He smirked. 'Of course, to reach the place you need to travel beyond the borders of our land and across the wilderness, which is practically impossible without being....'

'Eaten alive?' I said, half joking.

Ordinarily Gideon would have found this amusing but I could see by his face that his mood had not lifted.

'Maybe, yes. But I would rather take my chances fighting the hazards of the wilds than dare enter that place.'

'Why Gideon, what's so awful about it?'

I looked at him as he stared down into the valley, and when he spoke his voice was completely dispassionate.

'The once beautiful landscape is now perpetually covered in a thick blanket of ice; leafless woods barely stir in the desolate chilly air. Still rivers lay silent and frozen in their tomb of death without a hope of sun. The quivering winds whistle about like a shrill voice of death, and will blow harsh upon your face, filling your heart with sorrow. If you listen hard enough you can hear the haunting sound of the birds as they cry in the coldness. The night sky is devoid of stars and casts a dark gloomy shadow across the land. It is a forlorn, desolate place that will destroy you, grind you down until you are a shadow of your former self.

I gazed at him in amazement, noticing how his eyes had a dark lost look that I'd not seen before.

'But what happened there, why did it become such a horrendous place to live?'

'No one is really sure. Some folk say that when the founders disturbed the woodlands, they awoke a dark presence, that was so evil and strong it cast a mysterious spell over the land and its inhabitant's.'

'Well then, I can't imagine who would wish to live there as it is now.' I said, with a faint laugh.

'Oh, you'd be surprised. Inquisitiveness can be a rather unfortunate trait in many ways. Travellers have entered the borders of Hartland just to satisfy their curiosity, others are foolhardy and arrogant individuals who believe the rumours to be purely myth.'

'What happened to them all, how were they persuaded to stay?'

Gideon was staring at the ground as if in a little world of his own. 'Once they'd arrived, they would have no choice but to stay. Almost immediately they would be changed.'

'Changed, what do you mean?' I asked anxiously.

He paused. 'Let's just say that the evil magic will keep you there and will gradually make its way into every crevice of your mind. It will consume you, destroying any feeling of love you may have had, until all that's left is emptiness and sorrow. You will have lost all control over your life and will live an endless existence, trapped in a prison of misery.'

I stared at him open mouthed, and for several moments we both sat in silence. In bewilderment I pondered over what he'd told me about the place, how awful it sounded, but I was more mystified at *how* he spoke about Hartland as if he'd been there before. However, in the end I decided not to push the matter.

'Oh, well I'm glad we're not heading southwards then.' I said with a little laugh.

He finally turned his head and looked at me, a gentle smile appearing on his face.

'That's enough depressing talk. Come on, let's get moving, we've a way to go before nightfall.'

We made our way down the other side of the hill, crossing over golden cornfields and passing down twisting lanes with high hedges closing above us, and then we were in the open countryside again.

A thought suddenly occurred to me. Since I'd arrived Gideon hadn't mentioned the woman who had tried to kill me. I wondered if she was lurking somewhere in the shadows, waiting to make her attack. I decided to come right out and ask him.

'The woman you warned me about, who is she?'

His eyes grew wide for a moment.

'I was wondering when you'd ask me. Her name is Verity and she lives in the village with her brother. I've known her all my life.' He laughed. 'Many folk believe her to be perfectly amicable.' He was silent for a moment. 'But she has a dark side to her character, and at times she is slightly unhinged.'

'So, she *is* a little mad.'

He glanced at me and nodded. 'Well...yes I suppose she is a little.' With a nervous laugh he lowered his eyes. 'Anyway, for some reason Verity is fixated on me and has been for a long time. She became incensed when she learnt about your existence, and informed me she was going to pay you a visit. I'm so sorry Effie for scaring you that day in the rain, by saying that she's coming after you. It's just that even though, deep down, I knew she wouldn't have the ability to visit you in person, I thought it only right to warn you.

I stared at him open mouthed.

'But Gideon she *did* pay me a visit.'

'What... how?'

'Verity materialised in my kitchen and almost killed me with an arrow.' I said rather sternly. 'If she'd arrived a little later my poor Aunt would have been there too.'

He looked completely taken aback.

'No, surely not, I mean Verity wouldn't be capable of doing such a thing. She was probably just trying to frighten you, that's all.'

'No, no.' I said shaking my head vehemently. 'She wanted me dead.'

For a moment he just stared at me in disbelief. 'Effie I'm...'

I interrupted him, my voice sounding strangely high-pitched.

'And what do you mean she wouldn't have the ability to visit me in person, she must have used that power of the mind method, just like you.'

'But Effie, Verity would've had to focus all her concentration on you and your home in order for her to materialise in your world, but how could she when she's never met you, or seen what you look like, or visited your home. I don't understand it.'

I scoffed. 'Neither do I, and yet somehow she managed to find a way.' Narrowing my eyes, I studied his face carefully. 'And I presume you were the one that told her about me, why *did* you do that Gideon?'

His face was suddenly full of anguish. 'It...it slipped out. You see, by telling Verity about your existence Effie, I hoped it would make her less obsessed with me.'

I laughed. 'Well, it didn't work.' With a sigh I lowered my gaze. 'And did you tell her I'm on my way to Briarwood?'

'No, he said, shaking his head. 'But she'll soon find out when we're back in the village.' He looked thoughtful for a minute. 'Do not be concerned I can assure you I shall deal with the matter as soon as we reach home.'

I looked at him dubiously. 'I do hope so Gideon. The woman needs locking away.'

He took my hand. 'Let's not think of Verity anymore.' He said in a soft voice. 'Do not allow her to spoil our journey.'

'I'll try, but I can't promise.' I uttered.

Gideon grabbed my hand. 'Come on, just a little further and we can make a camp for the night.'

The sky had become overcast now, so changed from the morning and the rain began to pour down, steady and insistent. We clambered down a grass bank and came to a wooded area, where the trees grew very close together. The mass of bracken and tangled undergrowth seemed to have taken over, and Gideon found a large broken branch to help us fight our way through. The ground was covered with dank rich moss and scattered with twigs, which snapped as we trod upon them. But all of a sudden, we were away from the dark trees and had come out into a tiny cove with an array of pale coloured flowers growing out from amongst the rocks. The air was full of their scent, sweet and heady and tiny droplets of water fell onto me as we brushed passed their soaked petals. A deep pool of shimmering green and blue water lay at the heart of the cove, as still as the night. I could feel the pure moist air of the water on my face and I stood there, breathing in its freshness. I could not imagine a more tranquil place to rest.

'It's so unexpected, isn't it?'

The sound of Gideon's voice startled me, bringing me back to reality.

'What is this place?' I said in wonder.

'It's an ancient cove that's been here for centuries. Some folk believe that if you stare into the pool for too long you will see your fate, and others think it to be the entrance to a magical other world.'

'You mean a portal.' I said, excitedly.

'Yes, I suppose so, but this portal won't take you home.' He looked at me thoughtfully. 'In the heart of nature there exists many other worlds, all cleverly hidden away from inquisitive travellers. These places possess a powerful magic, and can take on an elusive appearance. Since time began, we have all been led to believe in such tales.' He chuckled. 'But I fear there are many who will scoff at such stories, and say they are purely myth.'

He took my hand and led me over to some rocks.

'For instance, a gateway to another world could be concealed in the trunk of a towering tree, or in a single flower.' He looked down into the pool. 'Or perhaps we will discover one here.'

I stood there in silence, mesmerised by the glistening water.

'Of course, the only way to find out is to dive into the pool.' He extended his arm out towards the water. 'You can go in first Effie.'

I looked at him in shock for a moment then realised he was joking. As his face broke into a broad grin, I smiled back at him.

'Very funny.'

Perching on a rock I watched as he began to prepare supper.

Suddenly I was reminded of Mace, my dear friend who had so callously pushed me through the portal; for he too would have made a joke, one of many. He also would have complained about the lack of food, and the arduous journey.

'It looks so tempting, doesn't it?' Gideon said, gazing into the water.

I glanced at the clear blue water. It did look inviting and I'm sure it wouldn't take much for me to plunge in.

'Yes, very, but I shall refrain from going in the water.' I said, laughing. 'I really don't think I'm ready to travel through another portal, not yet anyway.'

He smiled gently at me. 'I'm glad to hear it.'

We ate supper and Gideon draped the blankets over us. We both lay there in silence, looking up at the brightness of the moon. Out of the corner of my eye I could see Gideon staring at me.

'What's wrong? I said, thinking that I had something on my face.

'Nothing's wrong.' He said in a quiet voice. 'It's just that your face is so entrancing. So much like...' He paused.

I raised my head and looked at him 'Like whom?'

'So much like you, only real.' He laughed. 'Does that make sense?'

'Yes, yes it does Gideon.'

I knew exactly what he meant. Strange as it may sound, both of us had always believed we'd seen one another clearly in our dreams, but it wasn't until we had finally met in person that we *really* saw one another, properly.

My final thought before I drifted off to sleep was of Rawlings. I was racking my brains trying to recall the last time I'd been in the library reading one of the musty old books, but I couldn't recall when it was. Thinking about it, I felt unable to even visualise the room. For the life of me I just couldn't remember it.

In my dream I wondered over towards the pool in a trance and sat down beside it, plucking one of the delicate flowers from the ground. I closed my eyes and breathed in its potent aroma and gently caressed my cheek with the petals. A sudden splash caused me to open my eyes and look down into the water. There was a shape forming within it. I sat there staring into its depths, mesmerised by its beauty and overwhelmed with curiosity. It was then I realised it was just my reflection staring back at me. I smiled to myself thinking how silly I was. But something was wrong, my reflection in the pool wasn't smiling back at me, and my face was stern and deathly white. Unable to stop myself I leant forward over the water. It was silent and still and I could feel the coldness rising up from within it. And there I waited until my reflection reached up and grasped my arms, dragging me down into the pool, forcing me through the doorway to a terrifying world.

I let out a small cry and awoke with a start. Gideon, was still fast asleep. Shivering, I pulled the blanket back up around me. For a split second I was tempted to go over to the pool and gaze down into it, but instead I shut my eyes, willing myself to sleep.

The following morning, we journeyed east and came upon moorland. In contrast to the beautiful woodland areas and fields, the landscape of the moors was stern and bleak. It was mostly flat to look upon but deceptively hilly in parts.

By now I'd completely lost track of the days. Gideon seemed to think we'd been travelling for quite a few but told me how impossible it was to judge.

'Time is something of a mystery to us all. Here in my land, it has a way of creeping past you without you knowing.' He said, taking my arm.

'But why don't you use clocks or watches?'

'We have no need for them here. The only timekeeping used is by the sun setting at dusk and rising at dawn.'

The wind had gathered speed and was blowing coldly into our faces.

He stopped for a moment and turned to me.

'But I have no doubt that the rate of time here differs greatly from where you come from.' His face looked full of sorrow. 'That is why you will have to decide soon whether to remain here or go home.'

I stared at him. 'But I do have time don't I Gideon, time to see your home?'

There was a silence.

'Yes, of that I am sure.' His voice sounded sincere but there was a hint of sadness in his eyes.

I looked at him, wishing I could comfort him with reassuring words and tell him I was staying here forever, but it wouldn't be fair to give him hope then snatch it away. I tried to imagine never again seeing my Aunt or looking upon my beloved Rawlings, or to meet Mace in Hudson's café. There was a dull ache in my stomach, a feeling of sickness. I gasped and bent forward.

'Effie what's wrong?'

I looked up into his face, which was now etched with concern. How could I tell him I was homesick; how could I say to him that I wanted to go home. But then I remembered how we'd revert back to only seeing one another in our dreams.

I straightened up.

'Nothing, I'm absolutely fine.' I forced a smile. 'Come on then, time is at the essence.' I said, taking his hand in mine and trying to ignore the ache. 'I'm eager to see this home of yours.'

We must have walked miles before we came to some grey stone slabs that looked like huge stepping-stones. Half joking, I asked Gideon if a giant had placed them there to jump from one to another. He answered me in an amused voice, telling me giants didn't exist in these parts and that the stones marked the graves of ancient folk. Having passed the stones, we sat and rested for a while, watching the small birds darting between us and flying up into the darkening sky. He pointed to a hill in the distance and told me that once we'd crossed over the slight hill we could then rest at the other side. He knew of a sheltered spot where we could set up camp for the night. Dejectedly I glanced at the hill and sighed. It seemed Gideon's definition of slight hill was somewhat different from mine. It was definitely a steep hill. No, actually it was a mountain.

He surged forward with a sudden spurt of energy.

'Here, take my hand.'

Reaching out he gently dragged me up behind him. My legs were already tired and the last thing I wanted to do was struggle up this mountainous hill. But Gideon strolled up effortlessly and before long we'd reached the top and were heading downwards. And there at the bottom of the hill, nestled away out of sight, was a tiny grove. I breathed a sigh of relief. Never before had I'd been so pleased to arrive at a destination. My legs were so heavy I felt ready to collapse, and although Gideon didn't say, I could tell that he too was feeling weary.

We set up camp, ate and prepared the bed.

'It wouldn't be wise to wander from camp, as dangerous bogs are close by.' He said, laying emphasis on his words. He yawned and pulled the blanket over himself and carefully arranged it so it covered me too.

'I'm too exhausted to take one more step.' I laughed, looking at his face, which was rather pale and drawn.

'Good, sweet dreams Effie.'

He gently kissed my forehead and looked intently into my eyes for a moment. It seemed to me he wanted to say something but then changed his mind. He smiled softly then closed his eyes.

I stared up at the sky, it was so clear tonight and the moon shone down like a pure beam of light flooding over us. I moved my head over to look at Gideon, who by now was fast asleep. It never ceased to amaze me just how handsome he was, even now with his eyes shut and his dark curls falling across his face, he still looked perfect. I had the sudden desire to reach out and stroke his hair but then thought better of it. I would feel awful if I woke him, so instead I lay there. For some reason I couldn't seem to rest. My body was tired but I felt restless and unsettled. I tried to think of Rawlings and of my Aunt but their memory seemed so far off in the distance now, little more than a lingering shadow.

I heaved myself up, resting on my elbows and marvelled at how the moon cast a subdued silvery blue on the whole of the landscape. Just beyond the grove lay a mass of trees. I stared in wonder at how they were bathed in the soft glow of the moonlight. It was then I noticed the pathway leading invitingly onwards, through the middle of the trees. It seemed endless, reaching all the way to the moon. Captivated by its beauty and forgetting Gideon's words of warning, I felt unable to stop myself from entering the pathway. As if in a trance I rose and began to creep silently towards it, feeling the damp softness of the grass beneath my boots. As I journeyed down the path, I gazed in awe at the tree trunks that stood silver against the darkness, their great branches casting strange shadows on the ground. Having walked a little further I suddenly noticed an eerie thick mist, which was swiftly rolling along the path, enveloping me in its folds. Slightly worried, I stopped for a moment, deliberating if I should turn back. The creepiest feeling descended over me, making me shiver, and it was at that precise moment I thought it best to return to the camp. Only now the fog had become denser, and even the moon had disappeared. I began to panic, frantically feeling around with my arms and hands, with no idea of what way would lead me back to the campsite. The deadly silence was unnerving me and I became rigid with fear. Beginning to despair I was just about to call for Gideon when I spotted a shimmering movement ahead. Intrigued I stumbled closer to the flickering light and then I heard the most unexpected voice in the distance.

'Effie, Effie it's me dear – come closer.'

I was utterly perplexed.

'Aunt, is that really you?' I said in a voice little more than a whisper.

I could hear the loud thumping of my heart as I stood there.

'Yes dear, you must keep walking towards me.'

My mind was spinning with confusion. My head told me to ignore the voice, after all how could my Aunt be here, she knew nothing of the portal, and even if she did, I was certain she'd think it all a preposterous notion. My heart however was in turmoil, as hearing the sound of her voice suddenly made me realise just how much I was missing her.

Her voice was clearer now 'Effie, I've been looking for you everywhere.' She cried. 'Please come to me.'

'Aunt, don't worry, I'm coming over to you.'

I didn't care about logic, I only cared about my Aunt, and if she truly was here with me now, I had to go and see her.

Taking a deep breath, I began to move forward. I could feel the mist upon my lips now, putrid and sour; covering me like an icy blanket. If only the fog would lift, I could at least see where I was going. I gulped and took a few more steps.

'Come nearer my dear.' She beckoned.

I hastened my pace towards the light. Staggering blindly ahead I suddenly felt a cushiony softness beneath my feet and to my horror I found myself gradually sinking. Frantically I tried wrenching myself free but it had me in a vice like grip.

'Oh no, no, no.' I cried out in anguish.

I was going down now at an alarming rate, and before I knew it, I was up to my waist in the soft mud. I struggled in vain, reaching out with my arms to grab hold of something but it was too strong. I was being sucked down into the black, deep bog. I screamed as loud as I could, calling out for Gideon, but my voice was weak, and I knew he'd never hear me. From somewhere in the distance I heard a faint cackling noise, which sounded like a cruel wicked laugh. I realised then how stupid I'd been, for Aunt hadn't been here at all; she was still safe and sound at Rawlings, unlike me who regretfully was just about to be preserved in a tomb of mud for all eternity. I clung to a tiny ray of hope that all this was some ghastly dream, but then why hadn't I awoken yet?

Suddenly I was vaguely aware of someone shouting my name, and hoped with all my heart it was Gideon and not the creature that'd lured me here, to ensure I perished.

'Effie, where are you?'

There it was again, only this time it was clearer, and it sounded like Gideon. I wanted to answer but the mud was now entering my mouth, causing me to choke. 'Gideon?' I spluttered his name, coughing and choking on the mud. 'Help...help me.' I mumbled. A beam of light was approaching, and with great relief I saw him.

'Don't panic, I'll get you out.' He said, swiftly putting down his lantern and bending forward over towards me. Clasping my hands tightly he very gradually heaved me out of the bog. 'It's alright Effie, you're safe now.' He leant me forward as I coughed and spat out some of the congealed mud, then firmly put his arm about me and helped me up. 'Come on, we should leave this place quickly.' He spoke in an angry whisper. 'Whatever possessed you to wander off?

'I…I couldn't help it. The moonlight….' I coughed. 'And…and the trees were so lovely I just had to go along the path. Then I saw a beam of light.'

He frowned and gave me fleeting glance.

'You're lucky I awoke, otherwise the mire would have claimed you for its own.'

A shiver ran through me.

'What was it Gideon? I was certain I heard my Aunt's voice.'

He was silent for a moment, concentrating on the way ahead, and it was only when the camp was in clear view that he spoke.

'It was a trap Effie, to lure you into the mire.' He whispered, loosening his arm from around my waist. 'An evil presence lurks within these parts, and no one is exactly sure what or who it is, but ancient folklore tells of pixies.'

I looked at his face trying to decide if he was humouring me, but as he carried on explaining he looked deadly serious.

'These tiny pixies are so angered by the continual stream of travellers passing through their lands that they lead them to their deaths; many a terrified traveller has been lost in this lonely place after dark. The fog envelopes them, causing the traveller to become disorientated.' He glanced at me. 'Just like you they are irresistibly led to a beautiful beam of light and are deceived into believing they hear the voice of a loved one calling for them.' He paused for a second. 'Stray too far into the fog and it's easy to lose contact with this world. Some say they see images of the past or future, others have said that a gap appears in the fog which is an entrance to another world, and some, not as lucky as you, simply disappear into the mire. That's why we must take great care whilst travelling in these parts.'

I started to laugh. 'But pixies, I really can't believe they'd be responsible.' The very idea of it seemed ludicrous, I thought. 'An evil dummy maybe, but not pixies.'

'Why would you think an evil dummy was responsible Effie?'

A sickness rose in my throat. 'Oh…no reason.' I bit my lip.

Without thinking I wiped my sleeve across my mouth, transferring even more mud to my face.

'Gideon looked at me and chuckled. 'You should see yourself. You *really* are caked in mud.'

I peered at him out the corner of my eye, deliberating whether to fling some at him. 'You shouldn't make fun of me you know. I could very easily smear it over you.'

He laughed. 'Sorry.' Reaching for my arm he pulled us to a stop. 'Look Effie, I blame myself for what happened. From now on I promise to explain in detail the particular dangers we could face.' He grinned cheekily. 'After all I wouldn't want you to become covered in mud again.'

'Wouldn't you? I said, reaching out and smearing his face with mud.

We both stood there laughing at one another.

The mist had all but diminished now and we were back safely at the campsite. As luck would have it, we'd set up camp near a stream, enabling me to wash and change into fresh clothing from my rucksack, and also clean my muddy clothes, which I hung to dry over a branch of a nearby tree. Gideon had assured me that there wasn't anything lurking in the water, which was reassuring, although I kept thinking that a tiny pixie would reach out and grab my ankle, and pull me down into the murky depths of the water.

Afterwards I crept back over to Gideon, who appeared to be fast asleep, his face still smeared with mud. With a smile I curled up next to him and carefully dragged the blanket a little over my way.

'Feeling better?' His voice sounded weary.

'Yes, thanks.' I said in a soft voice. 'I'm just a little cold.'

Gideon moved closer and tucked the blanket around me.

We were silent for a while, laying there in the dark. Clouds had now floated over the moon swamping us in blackness.

'Do you really believe in these pixies?' I asked, curiously.

Gideon stifled a yawn.

'Well, I've never seen one myself but that doesn't mean they're not real. The dangers that lurk out here can manifest themselves in many ways and have the ability to appear differently to each individual.'

'Has it always been this way?'

'Well yes, you may have been led to believe that all these tales are merely fables, but you must understand Effie our world hasn't changed much over time. Most of our land is still covered in forests, with all the great wisdom of the ages embodied in each tree, and the fields, meadows, moors, lakes and mountains have all remained preserved in time, along with the folklore.'

'Our worlds are very different, aren't they Gideon.'

'From what you have told me then yes, for your minds have become closed to such possibilities. However, I imagine if you travelled back to the past of your world, you would see that the landscape was very much like ours, and people still believed in folklore.'

I pondered over this for a moment but decided not to question him further on the matter. Gideon had warned me that there were dangers in this world but I hadn't really taken him seriously until now. It had taken me nearly losing my life in the mire to come to my senses. Maybe my mind *had* been closed, but it wasn't anymore.

'Well, it's all very fascinating.' I said, shifting my rucksack so it was in a comfortable position to lay my head on. My eyes were suddenly heavy with sleep. 'Gideon, I know you're tired but just one more thing before we go to sleep.'

'Yes', he said sleepily.

'Thank you for saving my life tonight.'

'You're welcome Effie.' He reached over and kissed my forehead. 'Goodnight.'

'Good night Gideon.'

As I stared up at the sky I mulled over the peculiar happenings of the night: how close I had come to losing my life, and how foolish I felt for believing my Aunt was in this land. For one brief moment I tried to picture her pruning the roses at Rawlings, but her face was indistinct. However, when I finally went to sleep, she was in my dream, and her face was vividly clear to me. She was standing in the mist holding a flickering lantern and calling out to me for help, but I couldn't reach her and had no wish to.

Chapter 11

Despite last night's events I awoke feeling happy and relaxed. Gideon's presence obviously contributed greatly to my state of mind, however I was beginning to believe that this land possessed a magical quality, a strength so powerful that it had the ability to affect my state of mind, for it appeared all my worries were gradually being drawn out of me, as if they were poison, as if I didn't require them anymore. But they were *my* worries and my worries to keep, and I wasn't sure if I'd be quite the same without them.

We ate breakfast and Gideon freshened up in the stream and changed his clothes. In no time at all we'd packed up our things and were on our way. I couldn't help but take one more glimpse at the grove, which in the brightness of the day had lost its beauty and enchantment. A fleeting feeling of melancholy came over me as I thought of all the poor unsuspecting souls that had been lured into the clutches of the mire in the dead of night, and become forever lost in its depths.

I hummed to myself as we passed over several fields, which were swathed in an abundance of waving lavender that stretched faraway across the hillside into the distance.

'It won't be long now Effie, only a little further. Can you see the mountain peak just over the trees?'

Even standing on tip- toe I could scarcely see the peek over the tall tress ahead of us.

I sighed. 'Gideon that will take forever' I said, not overly happy with the prospect of hiking up a mountain.

He smiled cheekily at me and placed his hand on my shoulder.

'I didn't say we were walking all the way, did I?'

I threw him a curious glance. 'What do you mean?'

'You'll have to wait and see Effie.'

We crossed over into woodland spread with a carpet of wild flowers. The soft lush grass lay against a blaze of flower masses of white, pale blue, faint purples and soft reds. It was truly a wonderful sight. I ran my hand through the flowers as we walked amongst them, breathing in their glorious fragrance.

I asked Gideon if there were any hidden dangers lurking amongst the flowers. After the grove I would never again doubt such terror could exist in such a beautiful place. But he assured me that the woods were harmless. We sat and rested for a while and he asked me if I knew about the story of the bluebell woods. According to legend the bluebell flower, also known as wild hyacinth, is blossomed from grief. Children are warned never to remain alone in such a place, for if they were to pick a bluebell it would anger the faeries and the child would never find their way home. He also told me of the importance of plants to his people. How every tree, flower or herb has a specific magical value, and once prepared their unique life force has the power to transform one's life.

As we carried on our journey I gazed back at the faded blur of blues, purples and greys, wishing I could go back there and paint the delicate shades of perfection. When we'd reached the edge of the woodland, we were able to see the mountain in clear view, which was surrounded by a crystal blue lake that shimmered in the sun.

'So, are we going to swim across the lake?'

He laughed. 'Well, we are going to travel across it.' He drummed his fingers across his lips. 'But that's not a bad idea of yours Effie.'

I gently smacked him with my hand. 'No, please tell me you're not seriously considering swimming.' I exclaimed with a giggle.

'Effie, I do consider myself a good swimmer but not even I could make it all the way across that water.' He said with a crooked grin spreading across his face. 'Besides I'm anxious for you to see my home, and meet my father.'

My stomach did a sudden lurch.

'Oh. Yes...yes of course.'

Sensing my trepidation, he took my face in his hands 'Look Effie, please don't worry everything will be fine. Just you wait and see.' he said reassuringly, eyeing me carefully.

I reddened and laughed awkwardly. 'I know.'

For a moment we stood there gazing at one another.

How I wished his words could put me at ease but all I felt was a sense of foreboding, looming ahead of me across the horizon where Gideon lived. It seemed my worries and niggling little doubts hadn't completely deserted me.

All of a sudden, his eyes left mine and glanced over my head and into the distance. 'Ah, here comes Croft.'

'Who's Croft?' I asked curiously.

'He's my old friend and will kindly carry us the rest of the journey.'

'Oh' I said, none the wiser.

Whomever this Croft was it must mean we would reach the village soon, a prospect that filled me with panic. But on the other hand, it also meant no more walking, and that was certainly a good thing.

'Here he is now.' he said pointing up to the sky.

I looked up, and just a way in the distance I could make out a shape gradually flying towards us. It glided gracefully through the air, and as it neared us, I saw it was a huge bird, similar to an eagle but considerably larger. It was swooping towards us at a tremendous speed, so much so that for a moment I was sure it would crash right into us. But then it came to an abrupt halt before us, shuffling and wriggling its huge body until it was lying down on the soft grass, its great wings spread wide on the ground. It brought its great head forward until it rested on Gideon's feet. I gawped in amazement at its size and beauty. Its whole body was covered in soft brown fur that shimmered like golden caramel, and its bright orange eyes were extraordinary, but it was the endearing way he looked at Gideon that seemed so incredible.

'This is Croft my loyal companion of many years.' The bird nuzzled up to Gideon and he tenderly stroked his head. 'It's good to see you Croft.'

The bird answered with a loud screeching noise.

'Can I stroke him, he won't bite, will he?' I said nervously.

By the size of the bird, I was sure he could devour me in one go.

'Any friend of mine is a friend of Croft's. He very intelligent and can sense you mean him no harm. Go on Effie, don't be afraid.'

I timidly reached out my hand and Croft bent forward, sniffing it for a while before giving it a lick with his sandpaper like tongue.

'See, he likes you.' Gideon said triumphantly.

I smiled. 'It seems he does.'

We mounted the bird and I placed my arms tightly round Gideon's waist. Almost immediately we were flying across the landscape, over the trees and lakes, high up over the mountains. It was exhilarating but scary, and with every swoop I clung to Gideon, ever so often taking a tiny peak at the view.

'We're here, we're home' Gideon said with a joyful shout.

Nerves were fluttering through my body like an infestation of butterflies, and I took deep breaths in a vain attempt to calm myself. Trying to be brave I opened my eyes and saw we'd reached the other side of the mountain and were flying down low into a valley. I saw a winding river amidst the deeply coloured clover hills, and towering trees as far as the eye could see. We then passed over flower filled meadows and golden cornfields, until finally we came upon a group of great beech trees surrounding and sheltering a small village.

Croft lowered us gently to the ground and landed by a long shadowy hedgerow that grew either side of a narrow footpath. Gideon gently patted Croft on the head and we watched as he took off. The hedge was intertwined with garlands of wild rose and honeysuckle. Gradually, we made our way along the path, which winded and twisted downwards for some time, and when it finally came to an end a stab of panic shot through me and I began to feel nauseous.

'Is everything alright Effie?'

I nodded and forced a smile, in an attempt to reassure him.

How I wished we were still on our journey, just the two of us. He obviously didn't realise how much I was dreading this moment, and I couldn't possibly tell him how I felt. Foolishly I wished that something would occur to delay our arrival, although I couldn't imagine what. However, just thinking of this suddenly reminded me of a similar experience, but rather annoyingly I couldn't for the life of me remember what it was.

With a sigh I felt for his hand and held it tightly, leaning close to him. As he smiled at me, I thought how easy it was for him, going home, for unlike me he appeared not to have a care in the world.

We came out by a large circular area, which I presumed was the village square. It was surrounded by a large number of trees with outstretched branches that intermingled with each other, forming a leafy wall around the perimeter and shrouding it in shade. In the middle of the square stood a huge sprawling blossom tree like no other I had ever seen before, for its gnarled branches curled in every direction and reminded me of twisted hands reaching up to the sky. Built around the tree was a wooden circular seat, and several benches and tables were laid out nearby.

'That's an odd-looking tree.'

'Yes, it's very ancient.' He said laughing. 'There's a very romantic story behind it, one that I shall save for another day, for I fear you've had more than your fair share of tales for a while.'

'Well, yes that is true.'

Looking ahead I saw a winding, cobbled street with various mismatched stone-built cottages with thatched roofs, and another gravel path with more dwellings beyond.

I can remember thinking how odd it was that we'd not come across any of the villagers yet, and I thought perhaps they were hiding away in their tiny cottages, peeking through the curtains to catch a glimpse of the strange woman that passed their way. All of a sudden, I was quite relieved and my heart became steadier, for *if* this was true then that would mean Gideon and I could sneak through the village without being seen. After all, I could meet the villagers another time, when I was more prepared.

'If you're wondering why it's unusually quiet that's because it must be market day and nearly all the folks are in the village green.'

My heart did a flip. 'Ah. What way is that?' I said in a shaky voice, hoping it wasn't in the direction we were heading for.

He smiled charmingly at me. 'This way Effie.'

I followed alongside him as he made a sharp left then unlatched a gate and confidently strolled into an open field full of people, and market stalls. He seemed oblivious to the way in which I sauntered slowly along next to him, dragging my legs. He greeted several villagers, nodding at them as we passed. Many of them stopped what they were doing and stared at me. Some gasped in amazement and others looked with disbelief and puzzlement. I returned their gaze, trying to figure out what was wrong.

'Don't worry. Soon we'll be able to rest at home.' Gideon said.

I nodded without saying a word. I'm sure he took my silence for fatigue but I felt unable to speak, stunned into silence. For once it wasn't the curse of shyness that was preventing me from talking but the strange shocking looks I seemed to be receiving from all these people.

We trundled on pass the stalls, where people appeared to be busily buying and selling vegetables, fruit and other such things. Their chatter seemed to cease as we went by, and was replaced with whispers.

Gideon looked at me rather apprehensively. 'I hope this isn't all too overwhelming for you Effie.'

I remained quiet, still trying to comprehend what was wrong with everyone. Surely the villagers had seen visitors before. My face was burning up with embarrassment and I suddenly had the urge to run, to get away from the glare of their prying eyes.

Finally, I found my voice. 'Gideon, why are all the villagers staring at me?'

He took a sideways glance at me as we carried on walking.

'Oh, they're not used to strangers, that's all. Give them time, they'll come around' He said, looking at me with a somewhat uneasy smile.

'But they seem shocked to see me, disturbed almost.' I looked up at him, eager for an answer.

He seemed taken aback, unable to think of an immediate reply. When he finally spoke, it was to make a remark that was utterly futile.

'They are almost certainly completely dumbfounded by the vision of loveliness that just glided past them.' He grinned at me with his broad smile.

'Oh, Gideon please, that's not the reason.' I replied feeling rather irritated. 'Now come on, do tell me.'

For a fleeting moment I saw a slight hint of uncertainty in his eyes but it was rapidly replaced with his usual look of composure.

'Effie, you're just tired. The folk here are just curious that's all and have little else to occupy their day. I'm sorry, I shouldn't have taken you across the village green, it's just a much quicker way to get home, that's all.'

I glanced at him but it was hard to gage his expression. Reluctantly, I decided not to continue quizzing him over the strange behaviour of the villagers as I had a feeling by the way he glossed over the subject, that I wouldn't receive any other explanation.

Having reached the end of the green we crossed over into a narrow avenue with low hedges either side and then a wider one which was profusely scattered with oaks and appeared like a woodland scene. Tiny thatched cottages and farmhouses peeped out irregularly amongst the trees. There was something undeniably homely about the thatched roofs, and the way they seemed to cover the cottages in a cosy blanket of snugness. I couldn't help but marvel at the peculiar charm of the village, as it was like stepping back into a bygone era. We passed down yet another shady lane, bordered with elms, and scattered on the ground was the most brilliant splash of yellow from their fallen leaves. At the end of the lane we came out upon open countryside with cornfields and meadows.

Suddenly Gideon pulled me to one side, his face looking solemn.

'Effie, you must promise to let me know if you wish to go home.'

'What's brought this on?' I said laughing.

'More than anything I want you to be happy here in Briarwood and for us to be together, but I will understand if you choose to return to your world.' A faraway look appeared in his eyes. 'It's...it's not easy for an outsider to adapt to our way of life. But I shall help you in any way I can.'

As he stared into my eyes I was lost, transfixed by his gaze. The mere thought of being parted from him filled me with anguish. I'm not sure how or why but the more time I spent in this world the less I thought of my own, and any homesickness had all but disappeared now.

'Gideon you're worrying unnecessary. I'm perfectly happy here and have no intentions of going home.' I hesitated. 'Unless you come back with me, and I know that's not possible. So, it looks like you're stuck with me.' I smiled at him reassuringly and took his hand in mine, swinging it from side to side.

His face softened.

'Well, let's go home then Effie.' He bent down and tenderly kissed my cheek.

Chapter 12

Holding hands, we crossed over into a cornfield and made our way in the direction of a small church, which had a sloping churchyard and a low white steeple, peeking out from amongst some magnificent looking yew trees. I stared at the little church as we passed, curious as to the secrets that may lie there. A sudden left turn led us down a dirt path, shaded by trees that overhung one another. And there, almost hidden from sight, was a charming red brick cottage, with smoke billowing out of the chimney and a thatched roof that seemed to be so commonplace for this part of the country. The front of the dwelling was entirely smothered in wild honeysuckle, and its sweet scent immediately filled my senses. However, it was rather a sickly aroma that caused my stomach to churn slightly, but my nerves could have attributed to this, in fact I was certain they had.

A man was leaning across the gate to the cottage, almost as if he was expecting us. Immediately I saw the likeness to Gideon, for the outline of his face was exactly the same but with less softness, and he too had large eyes and the mane of dark wavy hair, only his was noticeably tinged with grey. As he straightened up, I saw he was tall like his son although somewhat stockier.

Gideon squeezed my hand. 'There's my father.'

I nodded without saying a word.

My heart was beating high in my throat now and my knees had suddenly become weak and shaky.

Gideon's father's eyes widened with surprise when he saw us. He came out the gate and strolled towards us. 'So, you've finally decided to come back have you son.' His eyes flickered to mine then back to Gideon. 'I was becoming concerned.' He embraced him then pulled back slightly, a concerned look on his face. 'You know I don't like you travelling across country, you should have got Croft to bring you all the way there and back.'

'Father, you know why. I told you in the note.' Gideon inclined his head in my direction. 'This is Effie.'

His father turned his attention towards me and I felt the full impact of his stare. It was an intense stare, a stare that made my cheeks flush with discomfort. But to my dismay he didn't smile, and when he spoke his voice sounded distant.

'Ah yes, Effie.' He extended his hand. I'm pleased to meet you.'

'Likewise, Mr Thoroughgood.' I uttered in a quiet voice as I shook his hand.

'Please call me Caleb. Mr Thoroughgood sounds so formal.'

I smiled warmly at him and nodded.

As we entered the cottage, I was immediately aware of the various smells within the house: there was a strong scent of herbs, flowers and wood smoke, mixed with a distinct musty smell that often lingers in old properties, none of which were unpleasant. However, the aroma and the cottage itself had a strange feel to it, and I couldn't quite fathom out what it was.

We went through to the living room, a cosy area that seemed rather overcrowded with furniture. Underneath the tiny window there was a table and chairs, flanked by various other seats. A large oak bench filled with old cushions was situated directly opposite a blazing log fire with a grey- bricked surround. Although the glow from the flames gave the room a much-needed cheery feel, for some odd reason I came over a little sad. Trying to shrug it off I turned and smiled at Gideon. He took my hand and we both sat on the bench, whilst Caleb sat opposite us in a high- backed chair, glaring at his son, and every so often his eyes flickered to me and he sighed. For a few uncomfortable moments we all remained silent.

Gideon cleared his throat.

'Look father, I know you're not pleased with me.' He said, sheepishly.

Caleb hesitated for a moment before rising from his chair and shaking his head, looking decidedly stern.

'I'm glad to have my son back that much is true.' He glowered at me before turning away. 'Firstly, you must both be in need of refreshment. 'As it so happens, I've just made a fresh pot of tea, and I think there's some cake left in the pantry.'

As he went out the room and slammed the door, Gideon and I exchanged glances.

'Your father doesn't seem too happy.' I said in a low voice.'

He slowly shrugged his shoulders but didn't comment. For a while we both sat there quietly waiting for Caleb to return. Gideon kept giving me reassuring smiles as well as squeezing my hand, but it didn't really help calm my nerves, for nothing could do that at the moment. I jolted suddenly as the door swung open and Caleb re-entered with a tray, and there we all sat in yet another silence. The tea tasted awful and when I enquired about the type Caleb informed me it was made from dried lavender flowers, and was especially beneficial for a restful sleep. I smiled back at him, and politely carried on sipping it.

'Well, the cake is delicious Mr…. I mean Caleb, did you bake it yourself?'

'No, a friend of mine made it.' Caleb said coldly, folding his arms. 'Do you really think I have time to bake?' He looked at me carefully for several minutes and then abruptly leant forward 'Why are you here, what do you want?'

'Father, please.' exclaimed Gideon angrily. 'You know why.'

'Do I? You've been rather secretive recently son, and I put it down to this young lady.

Feeling rather awkward I pulled myself up from the bench.

'Perhaps it would be better if I leave you two alone, to have a chat. Shall I go outside in the garden? I mumbled, eager to escape the tension.

I could feel Caleb's eyes boring into me. 'Yes, you should do that Effie.'

Throwing his father a disgruntled look, Gideon rose and took my hand, leading me out into the hallway.

'I'm so sorry Effie, just give me a moment with my father.' With a weak smile he escorted me through the kitchen and out the back door. 'I hope you find the scenery satisfactory.'

I gave a short laugh. 'I'm sure it's perfectly lovely.'

The garden was mainly grass with a scattering of wild flowers that stretched all the way down to a small riverbank, where the only sound was the gentle trickle of the stream below. Beyond the river lay yellow cornfields, as far as the eye could see. In normal instances I would have found such a view completely mesmerising, but at this precise moment I was too distracted by Caleb's odd behaviour. It seemed it wasn't just the village folk that were unhappy at my arrival.

'Gideon, is everything alright?'

He looked at me reassuringly. 'Yes, yes Effie. Once I've spoken to my father he will calm down. Take a seat and relax, I shan't be long.'

Gideon turned away and swiftly vanished through the back door.

With a deep sigh I leant back in an old wooden chair and tried to relax. The sun was just disappearing and the narrow, soft clouds curled into strange shapes, creating streaks along the horizon, lighting up the sky with a golden splendour. I breathed in the fresh early evening air and tried to ignore the raised voices from inside the cottage. But after a while the temptation to listen was too much for me and I found myself moving the chair nearer to the property. I could hear Gideon's father telling him how foolish he'd been in bringing me here, how I can't remain in the village for very long and that Gideon should be well aware of the consequences if I stayed.

I tried to imagine what possible repercussions my being here would cause, but for the life of me I could think of none. It was almost as if I'd upset the natural balance of life here in Briarwood, by my mere presence. A small part of me revelled in the fact that I could cause such a disturbance, but overall, it made me apprehensive and scared, and I wanted to run away and hide somewhere.

As I continued to listen, I heard Gideon pleading with his father to give me a chance, and to allow the villager's time to get to know me. Caleb was shouting back at Gideon, saying how it's not a question of whether they like me or not, it's just not possible.

As the sun vanished over the horizon a sudden chill swept over me. Taking this as a sign to go back inside and confront them, I rose and trudged over to the back door and swung it open. Both of them were standing in the kitchen, and seemed startled into silence by my appearance. But I could see by their faces that they hadn't ended their little discussion.

My shyness was overridden by anger and frustration.

'Excuse me.' I said in a strangely polite voice. 'Do you mind if I join in this conversation, you're having about me?

They stared at me in bewilderment.

'It's all right you know. You really don't have to stop talking just because I've come back in.'

Caleb raised his eyebrows and had a bemused expression on his face.

'I gather you overheard the words I just spoke to my son. Hasn't anyone told you how rude it is to listen in on other people's conversations?'

I stood there for a moment, trying to think of who Caleb suddenly reminded me of, but I couldn't picture their face or recall their name.

'Well?' he snapped.

I glared angrily at him. 'I don't consider it to be rude when your conversation concerns me. Besides, your voices were so loud I couldn't help but overhear them.'

There was a momentary pause and Caleb was looking at me with a steely gaze.

'Well in that case you'll be well aware of my feelings towards you.' His face softened slightly. 'Please don't misunderstand me, I'm sure you're perfectly lovely but I really think it's best you go back home.'

'But...but I've only just arrived, please give me a chance.'

Caleb's voice rose sharply. 'It's not a question of giving you a chance. I'm trying to warn you of what this place will do to you.'

I looked at him blankly. 'Whatever do you mean?' My forehead was beginning to throb and I felt tired and irritable. 'Caleb, please tell me.'

He shrugged very slightly and turned away, striding over to the window.

'Time is irrelevant here Effie. Days can go past, and you'll become oblivious to how much actual time has drifted away.' He let out a short laugh. 'And you won't just lose all comprehension of time, you will also begin not to care where those lost days have gone, or wish to know why.'

I put my hand up to my forehead and stumbled back slightly, but Gideon quickly steadied me and guided me to a chair, telling me I looked worn out. Without removing my eyes from Caleb, I sat down, barely aware of Gideon's hand on my shoulder.

'Do go on.'

Caleb continued staring out the window, looking up at the darkening sky.

'You see Effie this place has a way of clouding your mind. The longer you remain here the less you will think of your home, it will become a distant memory, a forgotten thought. But all the time you will have a strange sense of foreboding that you won't be able to explain, a melancholy feeling, like a sickness that will creep up on you when you least expect it. And then you will suddenly remember, something may trigger it, and you will realise why you feel this way, and all those memories that you hold most dear will come flooding back all at once. They will be so overwhelming that you will yearn to return home immediately.' He swung round to face me. 'Be prepared for that day, for it *will* arrive.'

Frantically I shook my head.

No, it can't be true. It all sounds completely preposterous. I would never forget my home or...or anything connected with it.' I turned to look at Gideon, expecting him to back me up. 'You don't believe your father, do you?'

He remained silent and exchanged glances with Caleb.

'Gideon?'

'Well not completely, father does tend to exaggerate rather.' He took my hand, looking at me with great care. 'I'd like to think that if your memories are strong then they will never fade and the urge to return home will not occur. But if you *do* wish to go home you must tell me Effie. For like I've told you before, the longer you remain in Briarwood the more dangerous it could be for you to return without physical damage.'

Caleb hovered over me.

'Gideon is right. That is why my son can *never* go back with you Effie, you do understand that don't you. He's spent his entire life in these lands and to travel to another world would cause.... well, it would do him irreversible damage. I therefore suggest you go back before it's too late.'

I looked up at Gideon's forlorn expression. How I wanted to reassure him that remaining here was what I truly desired, but now I had a niggling doubt at the back of my mind. If only I possessed the power to flit back home whenever I felt like it, and then I wouldn't have to make such a heart rendering choice.

He grasped my arm. 'Effie?'

'As I told you Gideon, earlier on today, I've no intention of going anywhere, not for the foreseeable future.' With a drawn-out sigh I glanced at Caleb. 'I will however think over what you've told me, and if a desperate need to go home takes hold I shall be sure to inform you both immediately.'

Gideon's face broke into a smile and he came and sat beside me. 'That sounds perfectly acceptable Effie.'

Caleb raised his eyes but didn't comment.

'Have you had many visitors to the village Caleb?' I asked curiously, trying to change the subject.

'Yes.' He ambled slowly towards us and sat down, resting his arms on the table and clasping his hands together. 'Over time we have had many, some from your world and some from other lands.' He looked at me with a deep penetrating stare. 'None have lasted here. All have decided to go home. Whether they successfully arrived at their chosen destination, or became lost along the way, I do not know. And, even if they were to come back to Briarwood, they would not be very welcome. Deserting the village is severely frowned upon, His gaze moved to Gideon. 'Even if it's our own kind.'

'Oh, father please. You are too harsh on the villagers. Many a time I've left the borders of our home, as have others from here, including you. It's a natural urge to go and explore the great lands beyond the village. No one judges us for going on our adventures, no one even notices.'

Caleb glared at Gideon, narrowing his eyes.

'I noticed when I awoke one morning to find my son gone.' He glanced at me. 'Did you know Gideon went on his little trip without even warning me beforehand, he left me a measly note on the kitchen table then sneaked off into the dead of night, placing himself in unnecessary danger to find you. Well, did you Effie?'

'Well, no I....'

Gideon slammed his fist down on the table.

'Father, don't blame Effie. It was my decision to go, she hardly forced me. I'm sorry I didn't inform you in person, but I knew you'd try and stop me.'

'Yes, I would have.' Caleb's voice was adamant.

I suddenly thought of the madwoman with the bow and arrow. Even though Gideon had told me her name was Verity I couldn't bring myself to call her that. Suddenly I decided 'The madwoman' was a much more fitting name for my, would be executioner.

However, I would of course keep this to myself, as they may think me a little strange if they heard me calling her by this.

I faced Caleb.

'What about this Verity woman, did you know she attempted to kill me at my home?'

He roared with laughter. 'And so, in your infinite wisdom you took it upon yourself to come and visit the very place she lives. Pray tell me Effie, what is the sense in that?'

'Father, Verity wouldn't be as foolish as to try anything here. Any crime, such as attempting to take a life, or worst still murder, is punishable by death. By transporting herself to Effie's world she knew she was untouchable.'

Caleb looked at him, thinking over his words. His eyes flitted between us.

'Maybe so, I still find it hard to believe that Verity would do such a thing, she's much too pleasant.' He looked puzzled. 'You've known Verity for a long while Gideon, do you really believe she is capable of such a crime?'

'I believe what Effie told me father.'

'Do you Gideon? Perhaps we should speak to Verity sometime and see what she has to say on the matter. It's always wise to hear both sides of a story.'

Gideon nodded, his eyes flitting warily from me to his father.

I leant forward over the table towards Caleb.

'I can assure you I'm telling the truth. You may not want to believe it Caleb, and I can clearly see you have no wish to. But she *did* try and murder me.'

'Well perhaps she had good reason to.' He snapped back at me.

'Father, how can you say such a thing?'

He shrugged his shoulders and looked dejectedly at Gideon. 'Sorry, it just came out. You see son, I always thought you were just as keen on Verity and she was on you.'

I glared at Gideon. 'Is this true?'

'No, no of course not.' He said bluntly. 'Father you are greatly mistaken.' Frowning he took my hands in his and stared into my eyes. 'Effie, I can assure you; I've *never* had any feelings for Verity, you are the only one I have ever cared about.'

Caleb let out a little laugh. 'That's not what Verity told me.'

'Enough father.' With an angry sigh Gideon rose from the table, pulling me up with him. 'Come Effie, you must be weary. Allow me to show you to your room.' As he led me to the door he turned and glared at Caleb. 'Effie means a great deal to me and I ask that you be civil to her.'

As we left the room I glanced back at Caleb. He was hunched over the table looking decidedly disgruntled. I wondered then if he was right about the madwoman; perhaps Gideon had given her reason to believe there was something between them, and maybe he had a soft spot for her, after all they had grown up together, what if their relationship had blossomed into love? Deep down inside, Gideon could be torn between the two of us, for although he had just told me I was the only one he cared about, I still had a shadow of doubt lurking at the back of my mind.

'Oh Gideon, you father really doesn't want me here, does he?'

'Of course, he does.' He guided me up the stairs. 'He's just sulking because I've been away. But he'll get over it.'

'I do hope so.'

We went along the tiny landing and he opened the door on the left.

'This is your room, Effie.' He stood there and extended his hand. 'It's the guestroom, so the beds already made up.'

'Oh, does the room get used much?'

'No not really, it used to when…when.'

'When what?' I said staring into his glazed eyes.

'Oh nothing.' he smiled sadly, handing me the lantern. 'Here, take this, you don't want to be fumbling about in the dark.'

I went and stood in the doorframe with the lantern.

'Thanks Gideon.' Nervously I leant forward and kissed him on the cheek. 'Goodnight.'

He grabbed me, pulling me towards him for a hug, and for a moment we stood there embracing. I felt his breathe on my neck as he held me tight, and as he spoke his lips lightly brushed against my skin. 'Sorry about tonight Effie, everything will be altogether different in the morning, I promise.' He said hoarsely, drawing back a little and staring into my eyes. 'Now you get a good night's rest.'

I watched as he strolled down the stairs.

The room was pleasant enough and was simply furnished. A distinct aroma of roses hung in the air like the scent of an old memory of long ago, it was somehow soothing and made me feel I could be quite happy in this cosy room. I started humming to myself as I unpacked my rucksack, throwing my dirty clothes on the floor, with the intention of sorting them out later. I hung my jacket in the wardrobe and placed my other possessions in the large teak dressing table, which was situated on the far wall. I noticed how someone had lovingly carved their initials *FH* into one of the draw fronts, and thought how precious it must have been to them, whoever they were.

Feeling extremely fatigued I flopped down onto the bed, which I found to be rather comfortable. With my eyelids flickering, I lay there for a moment staring out the window, watching the dark branches of the trees swaying gently in the night air. I fell asleep almost immediately and dreamt I'd set out for a walk into a very lovely world, a sort of silent fairyland.

Chapter 13

Seldom had I felt so disorientated, for on opening my eyes I initially had no idea where I was. The room had a strange quality about it, that I couldn't quite explain, but it wasn't unpleasant. As I blearily looked around, a thrill of excitement coursed through me as I realised where I was, and with a little smile I climbed out of bed.

There was a gentle tap on the door.

'I ah…I shall be down in a moment Gideon.'

'Actually, it's Caleb.' He cleared his throat. 'I've prepared you some breakfast, if you'd like to come downstairs to the kitchen. Afterwards you may have a bath, if you like. Gideon is preparing it this very minute.'

'Great.' I called out, a little perplexed. 'Thank you, Caleb.'

Maybe Gideon was right when he said things would seem altogether different in the morning. I wondered if the two of them had carried on their discussion after I had gone to bed last night, and managed to resolve the situation, one could only hope.

I strode over to the full- length mirror in the corner of the room. It was a very beautiful mirror with sweet little cherubs, intricately carved into each of the corners, and although it looked rather unique, I sensed it was quite commonplace, in fact I was certain I'd seen one similar, somewhere. I made a strange noise as I saw my reflection, thinking what a sorry sight I looked. My face was smeared with grime and my unruly hair looked like I'd been dragged through a hedge backwards. How embarrassing I thought, Caleb must have believed me to be some kind of wild woman when he first set eyes on me, no wonder he'd peered at me so strangely.

After dragging on my clothes I'd worn yesterday, I crept down the narrow staircase. The thought of having a bath seemed like heaven, for since arriving in this land I'd only been able to wash in the stream. I paused for a moment at the foot of the stairs then apprehensively went into the kitchen where Caleb was busying himself at the stove. He turned around and smiled warmly at me, gesturing for me to take a seat.

'Good morning Effie, please do sit down and eat.'

Taking a seat, I gave him a meek smile and began eating my breakfast. I felt myself watching him as he made the tea, not quite believing how alike he was to Gideon, for although his face was slightly wrinkled, he still appeared relatively young. It was almost as if the clock of life had stood still for him.

'Is the food to your liking?'

Swiftly I lowered my eyes. 'Yes, thanks.'

Do you take honey in your tea Effie? By the way, it's camomile tea, as I sensed you weren't keen on the lavender.' He said, sitting down beside me and pouring out the tea.

'On no really, it's fine. It just tastes somewhat different to the tea I usually have.'

Looking a little disinterested he nodded then sighed, glancing out the window as if his mind was elsewhere.

My cutlery cluttered down onto the plate. 'Thank you, Caleb, it was a lovely breakfast, especially the mushrooms.'

He glanced at my empty plate. 'Good. You have Mrs Brookfield to thank for the eggs and old Mr Clayton for the bacon.' A look of amusement suddenly appeared in his eyes. 'And the mushrooms...well a dear friend of mine provided them.'

'Oh' I said, sipping my tea. 'Did you buy the food from them?'

There was a short silence.

'Well, no not exactly, you see here in Briarwood we believe in exchanging items of use between each other.'

I stared up at the dried herbs that hung in great bunches from the rafters, suddenly remembering what Gideon had explained to me some time ago.

'Gideon mentioned about your remedies, is that what you trade?'

He paused for a few minutes. 'Yes Effie.' That is correct. I'm what you call an herbalist. I can create tonics for many things and can cure or help ease a variety of symptoms.' Glancing at me he poured out some more tea. 'For a long while now I've been successful in providing our village folk with the medicines they require. Whether it's a physical or mental ailment I can usually treat and ease their pain, and they in turn will provide Gideon and I with everything we require.'

I smiled graciously at him. 'Do tell me more.'

'Well, for instance Mrs Abbott suffers from chronic joint pain. So, every week I mix her a special remedy, and she in turn provides us with apples from her orchard.' A glint appeared in his eyes. 'Gideon has become very skilful in making apples pies and crumbles, you really should try one.' He looked thoughtful for a moment, staring ahead. 'It means no one ever needs to go hungry and always has everything they need. Of course, there are the occasional times when certain villagers are incapable of working, for a variety of reasons. In this instance we all come to their aid. It is a very tight knit community.' Eyeing me intently he laughed. 'Even Verity does her bit, she provided the mushrooms you just ate.'

My cup almost dropped from my hand. 'What?'

'Verity likes to go foraging for them in the woods and regularly provides them to the villagers. When she visited the cottage yesterday, not long before you arrived, she very kindly left me a basketful.'

Suddenly I had this picture in my mind of the madwoman cackling with laughter as she searched for poisonous mushrooms for me to devour, and I imagined her delight when I began rolling around in agony, clutching my stomach. A terrible dread came over when I half expected Caleb to say he and Gideon didn't like mushrooms.

'Don't worry Effie, they're not poison ones.' He said chuckling. 'I consumed some last night and I'm perfectly fine, and besides I can tell they're the harmless ones just by looking at them.'

I breathed a sigh of relief.

'It was silly of me to think they were harmful. I mean Verity wasn't even aware I was on my way to Briarwood.'

He looked at me blankly. 'Oh, but she was aware. I er...mentioned it to her a while back. Gideon wrote about it in his note you see, the note about going to collect you. I assumed he had already told Verity you were on your way.'

'No, no he didn't inform her.'

'Ah.' He sat there deliberating for a moment then rose from the table. 'Well, if she wanted to kill you Effie, she's had plenty of opportunities.'

I nodded silently.

'Bath's ready.' Gideon shouted, poking his head round the side door in the kitchen.

The thought of having a nice long soak in a bath seemed like heaven, and I would be glad for the excuse to get away from Caleb. For although he seemed altogether more amiable today, I was conscious that I may say the wrong thing and spoil his seemingly happy mood.

I followed Gideon into the room leading off from the kitchen, and a blast of heat immediately hit me. Along the far side of the wall was a large blazing fire, which had various cauldrons and buckets hanging from above it, all bubbling away. However, it was the large cast iron bathtub full of steaming water that really caught my eye, it stood majestically in the centre of the room, just waiting for me to plunge in.

'Magic, eh?' Gideon exclaimed a huge grin on his face.

'It must be.' I said, going along with his joke.

'All I have to do is click my fingers and a group of dwarfs appear with steaming buckets of hot water, and before you know it, they are able to completely fill a bath.'

I stared at him open mouthed. 'What?'

He looked at me intently for a moment before laughing.

'No, no Effie, I'm afraid there's not really any magical dwarfs, although I wish there were. We use this as a washroom and it's where we have to boil all our water after collecting it in buckets from the stream out the back.'

'Oh Gideon, that must have taken you ages.'

'No not really, and besides you're worth it.'

I reached out and gave him a light hug. 'Thank you, but you're not to do it again. Next time I'll be perfectly happy just having a wash down.'

'No, I won't hear of it Effie. It really doesn't take long to half fill the bath. The first chore we do in the mornings is fill the buckets, that way we're assured lots of hot clean water all through the day. We also dry our clothes in here when it's raining.'

'It all sounds perfectly logical Gideon.'

With a gentle smile he closed the door behind me.

I immediately stripped off my old clothes and clambered into the tub, and it was just as good as it looked. The occasional dip in a cold stream didn't even come close to the luxury of a good warm bath. Lazily I reached across for the bar of soap and a glass bottle that I hoped was a type of shampoo. Slowly I massaged the lotion into my hair and lathered up the soap, smothering myself in its silky softness. Leaning back, I allowed myself to completely relax. When I'd eventually finished, I wrapped myself in a cloth like towel that was draped over a chair beside the bath, and gingerly put my head round the door and into the kitchen. Gideon and Caleb were nowhere to be seen. Taking a deep breath, I darted out of the kitchen and up the stairs to my room. My eyes were immediately drawn to the dress laid out on the bed, along with a note that read -

Dear Effie

Father and I have gone to collect some firewood and will return shortly. Please make yourself at home.

Also, I found this dress and thought you might like to wear it today.

Love

Gideon xxx

I stared dauntingly at the pale lilac dress. The garment was rather long and flowing for my particular taste, in fact I'd never really been one for wearing dresses of any description, but not wishing to upset Gideon's feelings I reluctantly put it on. The material felt smooth against my skin and, as I thought, reached well down to my ankles. I combed my wet hair, allowing it to hang loose over my shoulders. Usually, I would attempt to remove the tangled knots and then give up, tying it back in a bunch. But on this occasion the comb glided through my hair completely effortlessly, right to the ends. Hmm, I thought to myself, perhaps Caleb had put a secret ingredient in the lotion.

After briefly glancing in the mirror, I carefully stepped down the stairs, taking care not to rip my dress, and went into the living room. The fire must have only just been put out as it was still lovely and warm in the room, but it seemed dark and enclosed, with hardly any natural light from the tiny window. For a while I glanced around, noticing how there were hardly any books on the shelves and the ones that were there were faded with age and practically unreadable. Although I knew they didn't possess a library, I wondered if they had anymore tucked away, for how could one survive without any books to read.

With a sigh I decided to sit on the bench and wait for them to return. The whole cottage was silent apart from the dull sound coming from the grandfather clock in the hallway. I was certain if I listened to it much longer it would send me to sleep.

The sudden sound of footsteps jolted me back to reality and I shot up from the bench, quickly smoothing down my dress. Feeling nervous I went and stood by the fireplace and waited for Gideon and Caleb to enter. I heard the sound of laughter and chatter, and then the living room door was flung wide open and both of them entered, carrying firewood in their arms.

'Hello.' I said with a little smile.

For a moment I'd forgotten about my dress, but then I was rapidly reminded by the complete look of amazement in their eyes. They looked me up and down and seemed completely dumbfounded. I was reminded of a similar look in Caleb's eyes yesterday when I'd first met him. As they continued to stare, I couldn't stand it any longer.

I began blushing profusely. 'What's wrong...is it the dress?'

Surely, I didn't look that different, I thought to myself.

Gideon's voice broke up as he spoke. 'There's...there's nothing wrong with the dress Effie, in fact you look completely stunning.'

Caleb looked white, almost like he'd seen a ghost. The firewood he was carrying suddenly dropped to the floor.

'She looks, she looks just like....'

'Father please.' Shouted Gideon, interrupting his father in mid-sentence. 'No.' he said sharply, glaring at him.

I stared at the both of them in complete puzzlement.

'Whatever is it?'

'The dress Effie, you...you look.' Caleb gulped and turned to Gideon as if looking for guidance.

'What my father is trying to tell you Effie is that you look truly radiant in that dress.' He gave him a sly glance. 'Aren't you father?'

Caleb nodded, composing himself. 'Yes, you look very nice Effie.'

I had the sudden urge to burst out laughing. This was ridiculous, did they really think I was that daft. Earlier on when I'd studied myself in the mirror, I was pleasantly surprised with my glossy locks and the prettiness of the dress, but by no means did it justify

134

this peculiar reaction. They were hiding something - I was sure of it. Only for now I would go along with the pretence.

'Thank you, Caleb, you're too kind.' I said, trying to keep composed. Casually I went over and helped Gideon pick up the firewood from the floor.

'I was thinking of going for a stroll to explore the area. What do you think?'

Gideon face broke into a smile.

'Well, yes. That's an excellent idea Effie. I could accompany you if you wish?'

Caleb's strange, startled expression had disappeared now and he looked almost normal again.

'Oh Gideon, I'm sure Effie would value some time on her own, after all you've both been together so long on your journey. And anyway, I require your help to find some herbs, a rare kind.'

'Perhaps I can help.' I piped up. 'If you know where this herb might be found I can go and gather some for you.' I paused. 'Besides, I'd really like some fresh air'

They were both looking at me again.

Caleb scratched his head. 'Well, I don't see why not. I could describe them to you Effie and let you know where they can be found. Gideon can remain here and bake you one of those homemade apple pies I was telling you about.'

'What a wonderful idea, I shall look forward to it.' I smiled at them both.

Gideon looked rather perplexed.

'Are you happy to go alone Effie?'

'Yes, unless there's something nasty lurking nearby, such as a bog.'

He laughed. 'No, there's no bogs…. or pixies.'

'Rest assured Effie, the land surrounding the village is perfectly harmless.' Caleb said, folding his arms.

What about the madwoman, I thought, what if she has a tendency to go on country walks on the outskirts of the village? I imagined bumping into her, the look of horror on her face as our eyes met. Should I be worrying unduly, after all Gideon had told me he would deal with her.

I gulped. 'What about…her?'

'Effie, she has a name.' Replied Caleb, looking irritated.

I felt Gideon's hand on my arm. 'I shall go directly to the village and speak with Verity, and warn her to stay away from you Effie.'

'And if she fails to do so?'

Caleb shook his head and muttered something underneath his breath.

'Let's just see if she heeds the warning first, shall we.' His yes flickered to Gideon. 'In fact, I shall come with you son and we can all discuss the situation together, and try and get to the bottom of it. I'm sure there's a completely reasonable explanation for what Verity did.'

'Oh, come father it really won't be necessary for you to come along. I'm perfectly capable of sorting the matter out without you.'

He frowned and nodded silently.

Shortly after Caleb had provided directions and given me a description of the herbs, I grabbed the basket in the hallway and went out the front door.

Chapter 14

It was a welcome relief to leave the cottage and escape the mysterious behaviour of Gideon and Caleb. I had no doubt in my mind that I was at the centre of it all and I could feel the tension mounting like dark clouds just before a storm.

Breathing in the fresh county air and the heady scent of the honeysuckle I turned and went along the narrow lane and into the fields beyond, swinging the basket I carried from side to side. Caleb had told me to carry on in a northerly direction until I come upon a wood, and that's where I should find the herb. I found myself lifting up the long dress so it wouldn't drag too much in the grass. Not an entirely suitable item of attire for a long walk, I thought to myself.

As I strolled through the fields I thought of Gideon. I'm sure he was keeping secrets from me for my own protection but I wasn't as fragile and weak as he seemed to think I was. How I wished he'd open up and tell me instead of keeping me in the dark, for how could we carry on and lead a normal life with this shadow lurking in the background.

I found the woods without any problem and squeezed my way through thick bracken to enter it. The area was immense but I wandered on, quite regardless of time or distance, admiring the beautiful woodland sorrel and trying to take in the endless assortment of flowers. So far there was no sign of the herb, and I began to wonder if I'd ever find it. Unsurprisingly it didn't take long for me to completely lose my way, so I decided to walk straight ahead, believing that this way I would at least emerge on *one* side of the wood. After having strolled about half a mile I came upon an open grove of colossal oak trees that loomed threateningly above me, and it was only when I'd passed by them that I suddenly realised this must be one of the highest points of the wood, for I was overlooking a scene of incredible beauty: I could see an orchard, bathed in sunshine; several villagers were working in nearby cornfields, whilst further on I could just make out the old church on the edge the village, and just below me cows were grazing in an area of rich meadowland, through which a sparkling stream ran. For some while I stood there, marvelling at the sight, unable to take my eyes away.

As I sat on the bank, gazing down at the views, my mind drifted back to what Caleb had said about this place and how it would take over your life, clouding your judgement and causing you to forget your memories of where you came from. Briarwood maybe verging on the enchanted but surely it didn't have the power to remove all recollections of my past life at my old home. It was funny though, for as I sat there my mind couldn't recall the name of the house where I resided in previously.

Determined not to let this worry me I rose and leisurely wandered along the high bank, and to my delight spotted the herb I was looking for. It was exactly how Caleb described, small and grey with a hint of pale pink on the tip. I gathered as much as I could and placed it in the basket. I decided my best option now would be to skirt round the woods. With any luck, if I headed southwards and went across the fields towards the church, I should find my way back to Gideon's home without having to venture through the village. I was ashamed with myself for being such a coward but I hadn't recovered from the look of wrath and astonishment I'd received from the villagers yesterday. After crossing over, what seemed like endless fields, I finally saw the church up ahead. Quite impressive, I thought, for someone with no sense of direction.

As I approached the church, I spotted a lone figure hunched over on the bench beside the graveyard, and going nearer I saw it was Caleb. I hesitated, wondering if it was too late for me to creep away and pretend I hadn't seen him. Feeling brave I strolled over, trying to think what I was going to say. The noise of my feet on the path must have startled him and he looked up at me in surprise.

I smiled feebly and gave him a little wave.

He smiled back. 'Please Effie, come and sit down.' he said, patting the seat with his hand. 'I'd like to talk with you.'

My eyes widened. 'Very well.' Rather reluctantly I sat down beside him and put the basket on the ground. 'What is it, Caleb?'

'I'd like to apologise for how I spoke to you yesterday Effie.' He clasped his hands together. 'You must understand I have my son's best interests at heart. I should hate for him to get hurt, or even worse, lose him altogether.'

I looked sympathetically at him. 'I understand that Caleb, he's your only son and naturally you're very protective over him. But you have to know I would never intentionally hurt Gideon, he means the world to me.'

Caleb looked suddenly forlorn and when he spoke his voice was but a whisper. 'He's not my only son.'

I stared back at him in astonishment.

'Oh.' In a daze I sat there listening to the birdsong in the nearby trees. 'I...I'm sorry. Gideon never mentioned he has a brother.'

There was an uncomfortable pause.

'*Had* a brother.' Caleb proclaimed with agitation in his voice. 'He was called Noble, and was slightly younger than Gideon.'

'Has your other son...Noble gone, I...I mean did he leave the village?' I asked, not quite sure what to say.

'Yes, I believe he wanted to go travelling and look for....' He paused and for a brief moment his gaze drifted off towards the cornfields. 'To look for other lands, and one night he snuck out the cottage without a word and I never saw him again.'

'It must have been awful for you.'

Caleb was silent for a moment and then sighed deeply. 'Yes, it was rather. Gideon of course went looking for him.' His eyes began misting over. 'He searched for ages, looking everywhere for his brother, but it was too late, Noble was gone, gone forever.'

'But where do you think he went?'

'Who knows, he probably perished in the wilds.' He bent forward and put his head in his hands, weeping silently.

Apprehensively I reached out and placed my arm around Caleb. I could see now, the reason he was so angry with Gideon for leaving, he was frightened he'd lose him too.

'I'm so sorry Caleb. I really had no idea.'

Caleb looked up and pulled a handkerchief from his waistcoat pocket. 'Gideon blames himself and believes if he'd gone after him sooner Noble would be here now.' He sniffed 'He blocks it out by pretending his brother never existed. I suppose it's his way of dealing with it.' He said wiping his eyes with the handkerchief.

'Oh, I see.'

Caleb turned suddenly and inclined his head closer to mine, looking into my eyes. His stare was so intense I had trouble looking at him.

'Please don't speak of this to Gideon it only upsets him. Just pretend I never told you.' He looked pleadingly at me.

Unable to meet his gaze a moment longer I stared down at the ground. 'I'm...I'm not sure, it doesn't seem right. I really wish you'd not mentioned all of this, it places me in rather a dilemma.' I glanced at the pitiful look in Caleb's eyes and sighed. 'Oh, very well, I shall forget this whole conversation. Just promise never to put me in this sort of situation again.'

'Thank you, Effie, I promise I shan't. This will be our little secret' He smiled gently as he spoke, staring at me.

There was something in his look that disturbed me, a gloating look. It was almost like he was pleased that I'd agreed to keep this from Gideon, and by doing so he had proved I wasn't worthy of his son's affections.

'It used to be his room you know.'

'Sorry?'

'The room you're staying in Effie, it used to belong to Noble.'

'Oh, I see. What about FH?'

He looked suddenly bewildered.

'The initials carved into the dressing table?'

'Oh that.' His gaze travelled over to the trees and he smiled rather strangely, then with a sigh he glanced down into the basket. 'Ah, I see you've found my special herbs, excellent.' He exclaimed. 'Come let us return home Effie.'

We rose from the bench and made our way back to the cottage.

I nearly asked Caleb again about the initials FH but had a feeling I wouldn't get an answer. It was just something else to add to the list that he was hiding from me, and I suspect if I asked Gideon, I would get the same response.

We passed a villager on the way. He greeted Caleb and then looked at me blankly. I smiled and said hello. He hesitated for a moment and then managed to muster a weak smile.

'That's Mr Gregory' Caleb whispered as the man went by us. 'Friendly enough sort when you get to know him.'

'Oh' I said, laughing casually.

From what I'd experienced so far, I couldn't imagine any of the villagers being friendly towards me, not even when we came to know one another. I may be new to the village but the way they'd stared at me yesterday just wasn't normal.

'I healed him once when he hurt his leg very badly with a saw. As luck would have it, I happened to have a small amount of the healing flower, a very beautiful yellow plant with a strange glowing light. Its healing qualities are incredibly successful.' His expression darkened for a moment. 'However, it cannot mend everything.'

'I've seen the flower.' I said excitedly. 'My first night in the forest I spotted some by a tree.'

'It's entirely possible Effie, if only you'd known their value and gathered them up.' He laughed lightly.

'Is it really rare?'

'Yes extremely, seldom is it found in Briarwood. How ironic that such a unique plant should only grow in the most dangerous parts of the wilds.

I laughed. 'Surely not, the forest where I saw the flower was perfectly fine, a little scary perhaps, but only because it was becoming dark and I was on my own.'

He stared at me rather oddly then nodded.

Arriving at the cottage he lingered by the front gate and turned to me. 'You find it strange don't you, the villager's reaction to you'

'Well, I would hardly call them a friendly sort. I may be a visitor to these parts, but surely they've had strangers here before.'

Caleb grinned, showering his whole face in softness.

'That is true Effie, but these village folks have lived a certain way for centuries, and such things as ploughing the fields, bringing in the harvest and tending to livestock, are exactly what their ancestors did, and the ones before them, and so on. The same landscape meets their eyes, the same river flows by the mill, the same dwellings. All these things will never change, and they have no wish for them to change. So, seeing an unfamiliar face in the village unsettles them, and they feel threatened.'

'But apparently none of the visitors stay so why do they worry?'

'Ah, well there's a reason for that.' He exclaimed walking up to the door. 'They fear that visitors, such as yourself, *will* decide to settle in Briarwood one day, then others will follow, and gradually, over time, the way of life here will be spoilt.'

I followed behind him as we entered the cottage, and was immediately hit with the same potent smell that wafted through the property, only now it was mixed with the delicious aroma of apple pie. He took the basket of herbs from me and placed them on the tiny table in the hallway, and then we went into the kitchen.

'Do take a seat Effie.'

With a smile I sat down and watched as he begun peeling some potatoes.

'But if visitors such as myself were to stay in Briarwood it wouldn't necessarily mean the village would be ruined, would it?' Perhaps we'll blend into the village life just perfectly, without the need to alter a single thing.'

With a sigh Caleb stopped his peeling and came over and stood by me, placing his hand on my shoulder.

'Effie, it's not just about the visitors, you see the village folk here, including myself, still believe we are all protected by an ancient enchantment that lingers over Briarwood, and it is said that any change will damage the spell and cause the way that we live to become lost, forever.

The door opened and Gideon entered, his face breaking into a smile when he saw me. 'How was your walk, Effie?'

'It was very enjoyable.' I replied, deciding not to add the part where I'd become lost. 'What...what about you?'

He glanced over to the pantry. 'I baked some apple pies and then took a trip into the village.'

'And?' I asked, wanting to know if he'd spoken with the madwoman.

His face looked suddenly agonised. 'Well, I did drop in on Verity and she has promised me not to come near the cottage for the foreseeable future.'

Caleb huffed. 'Poor woman, I hope she wasn't too put out?'

There was an uncomfortable silence.

My eyes remained fixed on Gideon, waiting for him to assure me she wouldn't try and harm me again. But instead, he just lowered his gaze.

'What about that time she tried to kill me in the…. the.' I stopped for a moment, unable to recall where it had occurred. 'Well, you know.'

Gideon exchanged a knowing look with his father before looking at me. 'Effie…. well you see Verity, she completely denies the entire incident, and…. and says you must be mistaken.'

'And you believe her?'

'Well…. no but you have to admit it's all a little strange.'

I laughed incredulously. 'But she's hardly going to admit it now, is she?'

'Effie, there's no need to speak to Gideon in that tone. He's done his part and had a word with Verity, it's hardly his fault if she doesn't know anything about it.'

'Father, naturally Effie is worried.' He went over and knelt beside me, staring beseechingly into my face. 'Whatever occurred between you and Verity that day you must know I am on your side Effie, and will continue to support you and will ensure you don't have to come in contact with her during your stay.' He took my hand and kissed it. 'And if you decide to make Briarwood your home then…then.' He gulped. 'Then I have faith the matter will resolve itself.'

Caleb let out an abrupt laugh. 'How?'

'All in good time father, all in good time.' He smiled endearingly at me then rose to his feet. 'Now I see you've prepared the potatoes father. I have some lovely trout from Mr Clement to go with it.' Crossing over to the stove he turned and gave me a wink. 'And there's apple pie for afters.'

'And did you drop off one of the pies with Verity as I asked son?'

Gideon's eyes darted in my direction before looking sheepishly down at the table. 'Yes, yes I did.'

'Good lad.' Caleb said, wiping his hands on a cloth. Slowly he made his way towards the door. 'I must go and visit her soon and have a chat.' He briefly glanced at me. 'Let's hope she's not too upset about all this.

After dinner both of them insisted I go outside and relax whilst they cleared up. Perhaps it was my imagination but I had a feeling they wanted to discuss something without me being there, some deeply guarded secret that I mustn't know about. So yet again I ventured outside into the garden and sat back in one of the chairs, wondering if I'd suddenly hear raised voices.

I gazed dreamily across at the cornfields, thinking over what Caleb had said about the villagers, trying to fully comprehend it all. These people here were a closely packed community, snug and content with their peaceful existence, where they felt safe from the prying eyes of the outside world. However, I couldn't help but wonder how wearisome it must be, seeing the same old faces day after day, and never giving outsiders a chance to become part of their quaint little village, a village that was not only inexplicably lost in time, it was also stuck in time, and there wasn't anything or anyone that could move it forward.

Gideon soon joined me and we sat together holding hands. I mentioned to him about the breath-taking view I'd stumbled upon whilst on my walk, and he immediately knew where I was talking about, and with some enthusiasm told me how it was his favourite place in the whole of Briarwood, and often he would sit there, contemplating life. We discussed meaningless matters such as dinner and what we were going to do tomorrow. It seemed the madwoman had become a subject neither of us wished to discuss, and I sensed he was now unsure about what to believe in regards to her trying to murder me; it was apparent Caleb thought I was making the whole thing up, and I wondered if he'd urged his son to think the same. However, now I was even starting to doubt myself, for the memory of the incident had become unclear, like a dream that gradually fades away. Perhaps it *had* merely been a nightmare all along, and it was just my overactive imagination thinking she was really after me. Ultimately, I knew sooner or later our paths would cross and then I would discover her true motives.

I lay in bed that night pondering why we all have to conceal certain matters from one another, and I surmised that it's usually to protect someone, to stop them from becoming hurt in some way, but unfortunately these secrets we conceal sometimes have a habit of producing an undesired effect, creating turmoil if the victim is to discover what it is your hiding. I'm certain Gideon and Caleb were both keeping something from me, I could see it in their faces, but as it happened, I wouldn't need to wait long to find out what it was.

Chapter 15

The days to follow went by in a blur and I was barely able to distinguish one from another, just as Caleb had predicted. But this didn't seem to worry me and I happily eased into my life at Briarwood. I would spend my time going for leisurely walks, painting, cooking and of course spending time with Gideon. Together we would often go hand in hand through the beautiful fields and woods beyond, laughing and chatting, not a care in the world, and often I would watch him in his workshop as he carefully crafted intricate wooden figures.

Caleb seemed to warm to me and no longer mentioned that I should leave. However, one day when we were picking blackberries together in the meadow, he briefly mentioned how his wife used to come to this spot and collect the fruit.

'I'm so sorry she passed away Caleb, I said staring emphatically into his face. 'Gideon told me about it ages ago.'

He'd glared back at me, telling me how it was none of my business, and throwing his basket on the grass he had stormed off. I thought it a little peculiar, however his wife must have been very dear to him and perhaps he would never truly stop grieving. In our dreams Gideon had rarely mentioned his mother, only to say she was gone, and if I ever brought up the subject a dark cloud would linger over his face, and he would become silent.

As of yet I had not crossed paths with the madwoman and I began to wonder if they ever would. Maybe she had gone away, disappeared into the wilds and accidentally been dragged into the mire, or perhaps she was merely keeping out of my way after being warned by Gideon. I even began to believe she was perfectly amiable and that we might even become friends, although I thought this unlikely.

The village folk were still in the habit of giving me odd looks, and I noticed how they whispered to one another as I passed them by. I told myself that one-day soon they would actually smile back at me, but I couldn't imagine it being any day soon. But despite this

I really didn't mind, for they only looked at me in this manner because I was an outsider, not because of any other reason. Oh, how I would delight in proving them wrong, I wouldn't leave like all the other visitors, this was my home now and here I would stay.

When I was a child, I used to believe that each and every person was allocated the exact amount of happiness in his or her lifetime, and when it was all used up, that was it. I believe this idea had been inadvertently planted in my head, for I vaguely recall someone who I used to know telling me how happiness never lasted, how we should appreciate it whilst we had it because it wouldn't be around forever. For in the days to follow I remember thinking how right they were.

I awoke that morning feeling exhilarated. I stretched my arms out and leapt out of bed, thinking how content I felt. Gazing out the window I could see the morning sun shining gloriously through the trees. Today I decided to do some sketching of the landscape. It was easy to be inspired in Briarwood, for everywhere you went there was a glorious view just ready and waiting for you. I would find a good place to sit then spend some time on my drawing before perhaps having a brief snooze.

As I dressed, I began humming a tune, I had a feeling it was familiar to me, only I didn't know where from, but then I remembered it must have been at the church service yesterday, for where else would I have heard it, unless it was Caleb or Gideon, or perhaps one of the villagers.

I jumped down the stairs two at a time and ventured into the kitchen. Caleb was out delivering some of his herbal remedies and Gideon was busy in the workshop, so I had the room all to myself. Humming the tune again I began preparing a light lunch to take with me on my walk. Just as I went to the pantry to fetch some milk from the jug I almost slipped and spilt the entire contents, and it was at this moment I had an unexpected vision of a similar occurrence, only then the milk *was* all over the floor and my leg was cut. But *she* was also there, the madwoman, standing over me with her bow and arrow, her cruel eyes glaring hatefully into mine. As a shiver ran through me, I realised that this *had* been a real event, and no matter how hard I tried to believe it wasn't, I knew that this Verity woman had wanted me dead, and probably still did.

Trying not to dwell on the matter I packed the items for my walk then went outside to find Gideon. His workshop was an old shed situated to the side of the cottage, and was full of various bits of wood as well as trays of seedlings and garden equipment. He was very accomplished at carving small animals and there was a boxful of them already completed underneath the workbench; sometimes he would exchange them in the village market or give them away for presents, and a while back he'd left a wooden heart on my pillow, carved with an elaborate E.

Glancing up from his workbench he gave me a broad smile.

'Hello Effie, what a lovely surprise.'

Instinctively I went and gave him a hug, and for a moment we held one another close and I felt his hand gently caressing my waist.

With a laugh I pulled back. 'I'm just off to do a spot of sketching. I promise not to be late back.'

He smiled and took my hand, leaning his head close to mine.

'I can't wait to show you off tonight.'

This evening was the summer festival in the village green, and the entire village would be there. Although it was an excellent opportunity to try and get to know all the villagers, I also felt rather nervous and wondered if I'd end up becoming tongue tied, for from what I could remember I was never very good at social events, and found it easier to go and sit quietly in a corner somewhere or sneak off when no one was looking. It always astonished me how some people had the ability to chatter endlessly on and on without becoming tired or running out of things to say, my theory was that one could only get away with waffling on for a limited amount of time before the person listening would become bored, and fed up. I believe I had known such a person once, but whom it was I really couldn't recall.

'Ah yes.' I sighed. 'The joyous festival.' A sudden thought flashed through my mind. 'Will she be there...Verity?'

'I'm not sure. Father has gone to see her today- he'll probably ask her.'

'Caleb is visiting her again?'

'I think she enjoys the fatherly advice he gives her. With her parents no longer here, it must be hard having to bring up her brother single-handedly.'

I went and put my arms around his neck. 'Well, if she does come tonight perhaps I should avoid her, just to be on the safe side.' I swiftly kissed him on the lips then headed out the workshop.

'Effie?'

I turned and glanced at him. 'Yes?'

'I...ah...I' He gulped apprehensively and gazed into my face. 'I shall miss you.'

'I'll miss you too Gideon.'

I wandered slowly out of the village, up the deep twisting pathway and into the fields beyond. I was so glad I'd brought my sketching equipment along with me from the other place I used to live, but unfortunately it was only a small drawing pad and so I was rather limited. However, Gideon was in the process of making wooden canvases so I could start painting, and he'd already created an easel, which was ready and waiting for me in the back parlour. All I required now were actual paints, but Caleb assured me we could create colours from flower petals and water.

Deciding to avoid the large woodland I'd become lost in a while back, I headed westwards instead and made my way to the cluster of trees up ahead, curious to see what lay the other side. Carefully I made my way through the dense branches and found myself in a beautiful meadow full of long grasses and exquisite looking wild flowers. I breathed in the heady scent surrounding me, half tempted to lie down and close my eyes. However, wishing to sketch a view of the village I casually strolled to the end of the meadow and up the heathery hills, settling down on the damp grass. From where I was resting, I could see the village tucked away in the distance, and the whole landscape was basked in glorious sun. For a moment I gazed up at the pure blue sky, scattered with the faintest puffs of delicate clouds, and wondered if life could get any better than this.

As I reached for my sketching pad a butterfly fluttered idly past in the sunshine and landed on my hand, I watched as it hovered there for a while before flying off. I took the pencils from my rucksack and started to draw, but despite the landscape being laid out before me like a magnificent masterpiece, I only managed to sketch a doodle of Gideon. Laughing to myself I slung the pad down beside me and lay amongst the heather instead, shading my eyes with my hands. My thoughts turned to the dress I was wearing tonight at the festival, and a sudden nervous excitement came over me. A while ago I'd discovered an old dress stuffed at the bottom of the wardrobe, and after altering it slightly then giving it a wash in the stream, the garment had actually looked rather presentable, and would make a welcome change from the lilac gown. Since being here I had actually become accustomed to wearing dresses, for although my other clothes had now been cleaned and were hanging in the wardrobe, they belonged to the old me that came from the other world, a place I no longer existed in.

Realising I just wasn't in the mood for sketching I got up and began to walk back towards the village. As I strolled slowly along, I gazed upon the endless green hills that seemed to meet the cloudless summer sky in the distance. I saw the grandness of the shadowy oaks and the cattle grazing contentedly in the fields, and the faraway figures of workers who hardly interrupted the beauty of the landscape as they went about their work. It was such a romantic way of life, and regardless of the ancient enchantment that supposedly protected the village, the entire land had a bewitching allure all of its own.

The day had become rather hot and humid, and as I made my way down the narrow pathway to the village, I could feel the beads of perspiration forming on my forehead. For a brief moment I stopped to breath in the scent of the wild roses, intoxicated by their delicate fragrance. But just as I did so a distinct feeling of sadness came over me, causing a single tear to roll down my cheek. I stood there in a daze, wondering what on earth was wrong with me.

I was suddenly brought back to reality by a noise behind me, and immediately swung round. Standing there on the pathway was a rather peculiar looking young man, with a narrow bony face, small beady eyes and greasy looking hair that clung to his face in the heat. As we stared at one another I noticed the coat he was wearing swamped his frame and how his trousers weren't quite long enough.

'Hello?' I said with a faint smile.

Looking agitated he shielded his face with his arm.

'You keep away, keep away from me ghost.'

For a few moments I stood there in utter bewilderment then extended my hand out towards him.

'Please don't be alarmed. I can assure you I'm not a ghost.' Very slowly I began to move forward. 'I mean you no harm.'

Trembling with fear he gradually removed his arm and quickly took a look. But just as he did so the sun disappeared underneath a cloud and I observed the light fog rolling in over the hedgerow, creeping over my body and giving me a ghostly appearance.

He shrieked, stumbling backwards, looking completely petrified.

'It's true isn't it…. you've come back from the dead.'

I watched in confusion as he scurried up the lane, screaming in terror. As he disappeared into the distance, I tried to understand what he meant about coming back from the dead- did he really believe me to be a ghost? However, I wasn't too concerned, after all he had seemed a little odd, perhaps he wasn't all there in the head.

Trying to forget about it I passed the village green, smiling and nodding at several of the villagers, who all just gave me blank looks. It was so oppressive now that my dress was clinging uncomfortably to my legs and I just wanted to return to the cottage. Just as I picked up my pace and turned the corner, I almost collided with a small girl.

'Oh, sorry.' I exclaimed 'I didn't see you there.'

The girl giggled at me. 'That's alright.' She said sweetly, standing beside me. 'I've never bumped into someone like you before.'

I grinned at her. 'Well let's hope we bump into one another again soon.'

She giggled again. 'I don't care what the others say, you're not scary at all.'

I gazed at her looking puzzled. 'What…why would I be scary?'

Before the girl could answer a woman had grabbed her by the arm, swiftly dragging her across the cobbled street.

On returning to the cottage, I called out to Gideon and he emerged from the kitchen to greet me, wiping his hands with a cloth.

'I wondered where you'd got to Effie.' He said sternly but with humour in his eyes.

Did you? I answered, rather surprised. 'Surely I haven't been gone that long.'

Without thinking I glanced at the grandfather clock in the corner of the hallway. It always amused me how they would wind it up but not pay any attention to it. Apparently, Caleb liked the continual ticking sound and the chimes, but didn't wish to learn the time. I asked him once where the clock came from but he just shrugged his shoulders and changed the subject. Whether that meant he didn't know where it originated from, or he did but wouldn't tell me, who knows. I was becoming used to his ambiguous behaviour and knew it would be futile trying to discover the truth.

'Well, it's just I missed you.' he said coming over to me, hands outstretched.

I grabbed hold of his hands and held them to my heart.

'I missed you too.' With a smile I pulled his hands up and kissed them gently. 'Gideon?' I said, staring up into his face. 'When I was coming down the path into the village, I spoke to a young man who seemed very strange, not quite all there. He...he thought I was a ghost.'

Gideon looked serious for a moment before smiling at me rather feebly. 'Oh...it sounds as if you met Gilbert.'

'Gilbert'? I asked curiously.

'Yes, he's -well he's rather a strange character.'

A chill rose over me and I let go of his hands and stepped back.

'Yes, yes he seemed it.'

'Don't worry he's completely harmless.' He gazed into my shocked face. 'Come now Effie, there's no need to become distressed.' He came close and wrapped his arms tightly around me.

I told myself he was right, there wasn't any need to let it affect me, and yet there was something about the name Gilbert that I found deeply disturbing.

'Better?' he said.

With a sigh I rested my face into the nape of his neck, breathing in his scent. 'Yes, much thanks, it's just so humid I can't think straight.' I looked up into his face. 'There's a fog making its way across the village.'

'Be careful it doesn't lead you to a deadly bog.' Gideon teased.

'Ha ha, very funny, you know you really remind me of...' I cut my sentence off abruptly, trying in vain to remember the person's name.

'I remind you of whom?' Gideon asked puzzled.

'I'm not sure, no one of any consequence.' I swallowed.

He stood there looking at me, and then with a sigh he gently pulled a stray curl back from my face. 'I've prepared a bath for you.' With an amused smile he kissed the side of my mouth. 'Would you like me to wash your back?'

With a gulp I lowered my gaze.

'No, no thank you.'

Still smiling he threw me a fleeting glance before strolling back to the kitchen.

By early evening, as we made our way down to the village, there were dark clouds hovering ominously overhead, and the fog of earlier still lingered in the air, cooling the temperature ever so slightly. As we strolled through the fields I couldn't help glancing at my new dress, marvelling at how the deep crimson colour of the material stood out brilliantly against the golden corn. The garment was made out of a delicate looking silk that covered most of my frame, it was gathered in at the waist with a belt and the neckline was low but not too revealing, with a full skirt that flowed down to my ankles. Just before leaving for the festival, I'd glanced at my reflection and it seemed like a stranger was staring back at me, for the young woman in the mirror looked truly radiant, with her glowing skin and auburn hair that flowed down her back in gentle waves.

I can only recall certain aspects of the festival, such as the way Gideon stared at me admiringly, his eyes constantly upon me, gazing over my hair and dress. Caleb was surprisingly quiet as if he had something on his mind, and on reaching the green he seemed in a hurry to rush off and leave us. Many tables were set out with an abundance of food and drink, and milling around them were the village folk, laughing and chatting to one another, many were dancing to the music provided by a couple of fiddlers, whilst children were running around everywhere, clapping their hands and squealing with delight. I recognised one of them as the little girl I nearly bumped into earlier on, she looked so sweet with her blond hair and puffy dress. I also remember the sea of faces turning to stare at me as we strolled amongst them. As they greeted Gideon, I noticed how they'd warmly shake his hand and chat away to him, then steal a look in my direction before turning their attention back to him. He did his best of course to introduce me, but they practically pretended I wasn't really there. I vaguely recollect Caleb chatting to an elderly man with a drooping moustache, and whatever he was saying caused Caleb to roar with laughter.

'Is everyone here?' I asked, tightly clenching Gideon's hand.

'It would seem so Effie.' He peered at me endearingly. 'It must be a little daunting for you, as I know you've not had many opportunities to speak with the village folk yet.' He kissed my hand and laughed. 'Too many walks in the country I suspect.'

'And spending time with you.'

He stared intently into my eyes. 'Yes, that's true. I treasure every moment we spend together Effie. And...and.' He laughed nervously. 'Well, there's a matter I must speak to you about in private.'

Before I had a chance to reply my attention was suddenly drawn to the direction of the tables, where some villagers were bawling with laughter.

'Perhaps we should move to somewhere quieter Gideon.' I said laughing. My face dropped when I saw how anxious he seemed. 'Is everything alright?'

'Yes of course Effie.' He looked steadily at me for a while, as if in deep concentration. 'But you're right it is a little too noisy for having a serious discussion.'

'Serious?'

He took my hands in his. 'Yes Effie, extremely serious.' A sudden peel of laughter broke his focus and he peered irritatingly over my shoulder at the commotion. 'Come, let us go somewhere else.'

Suddenly an elderly man began yelling Gideon's name, gesturing for him to come over.

Gideon inclined his head near mine and spoke loudly in my ear. 'There's old Mr Templeton, he most likely wants to discuss the cat figures I'm carving for him.' He looked at me, his eyes full of guilt. 'Will you be alright for a moment Effie? I shall return almost immediately.'

With a smile I nodded at him.

He pecked me on the cheek. 'Why don't you go over and get some cowslip wine, then we can sneak off.' He grinned from ear to ear as he began to walk away. 'It's very strong mind, so just take sips.'

I shut my eyes for a moment, trying to imagine what cowslip wine would taste like, knowing I should venture over to the tables to find out. My eyes travelled to the groups huddled around the tables, deep in conversion, and I suddenly wished it was me there with them, chatting away like an old friend, rather than standing there feeling isolated.

Gideon glanced over and smiled at me as he talked to Mr Templeton and I smiled back.

Taking a deep breath, I ambled slowly towards the tables, and immediately noticed how everyone turned to stare at me. I smiled at them in an attempt to be friendly and reached for the jug of wine on the table, not having a clue if it was cowslip. To my amazement a few of the villagers returned my smile. An elderly woman with a red face and wild looking hair came and stood close beside me, gawping at me.

'Hello.' I uttered.

She grabbed my arm.

'You're real then eh.' She leant in close. 'Tell me, what's your secret? What potion have you been taking to look this good?' The woman gazed fixedly at me, waiting for an answer.

'I really don't know what you mean.' I stared into her lined face, feeling a surge of confusion creep over me. The jug felt heavy in my hand and I clanked it back on the table, spilling some of the contents. 'I've not taken any potion.'

'Huh. I thought you'd been taken by them blighters in the Southern lands; it would explain how you…'

Before the woman had a chance to finish her sentence Caleb was barging himself between us.

'I think you've consumed enough drink, haven't you Millicent? He took a firm grip of my arm and began dragging me away. 'Come Effie.'

'But it's her I tell you Caleb, she's come back.' The woman muttered, stumbling forward.

'Pay no heed to Millicent. She is a wretched woman and a troublemaker.' Caleb said in a low voice.

I looked at him slightly perplexed, but then my expression turned to anger.

'Don't you think it's about time you let me know what's going on Caleb?' I uttered, folding my arms.

He gave a big sigh and an odd strained look appeared on his face. 'It must come from Gideon.'

With a little gasp my hand moved up to my throat. It appeared at long last Caleb was admitting something was wrong.

'Very well then, I shall speak with Gideon now.'

'I understand.' He said quietly. There was sincerity in his eyes that I had not seen before. 'You deserve an explanation.' He hesitated for a second, lowering his eyes to the ground. 'Gideon is waiting for you in the old church. His tone was low, barely audible. 'Go to him Effie, go now.'

I looked amongst the villager's, searching for Gideon's face.

'But I thought he was waiting for me here.' I said, thinking it strange he would leave the festival without me.

Caleb pursed his lips. He lost sight of you and decided to go on ahead. I...I promised to come and find you and send you off after him.'

I shrugged my shoulders 'Very well then, I shall go to the church.'

With a swift smile I turned away from Caleb and headed across the green.

Chapter 16

The fog had lifted now, rising into tiny clouds to the sky above, and the temperature of the night air had become so humid it was almost oppressive. A trickle of perspiration ran down my back as I walked along, and my head felt heavy and rather muzzy. I would have liked to return to the cottage and flop onto the bed, however I literally couldn't rest until I knew what was going on. It did occur to me that I might not like what Gideon had to say, but whatever it was surely it couldn't be that bad, not unless I really was a ghost, that would explain a lot of things; perhaps I hadn't survived the journey to this land and was merely a spirit in denial.

Having reached the cornfield, I could just make out the little church in the distance nestled amongst the trees.

Suddenly I heard a rustle behind me.

'Gideon, Gideon is that you?' I whispered, hoping to hear the familiar sound of his voice.

Everywhere seemed silent and still as if a deathly presence had descended upon the land. A fear came over me and I began running across the field, convinced that someone was following me. By the time I'd made it to the church gate I found myself needing to stop and regain my breath. My terror was increased when I noticed how the huge branches of the yew trees cast shadowy creature like shapes upon the grey stone of the walls. But for some inexplicable reason I was reluctant to enter the church, and instead hovered by the gate as if some unearthly power was keeping me rooted to the spot.

'Why am I being so foolish?' I muttered. 'It's only a church.'

Taking a deep breath, I swiftly went through the gate and swung open the heavy doors to the church, and when they slammed shut behind me my heart leapt in my chest. The interior of the building was cool and surprisingly welcoming with a soft glow emanating from the candles on the altar. I relaxed a little, realising that Gideon must already be here. Slowly I stepped towards the burning candles.

'Gideon, I'm here. Where are you?'

I heard a sudden loud crash coming from behind me and I swiftly looked around at the church doors. Standing in the entrance was a shadowy figure in a dark gown. Although I couldn't see the face, I knew immediately who it was. It was the madwoman. For so long now the thought of her had encroached on my thoughts, and now she was finally here in the flesh, I was completely petrified. As she moved forward her gown swished along the stone floor. I could see her clearly now and noticed she was laughing, but it was a vicious laugh. I observed the dark shadows underneath her eyes and the deathly white of her complexion. As she stood directly in front of me her shrill laughter went through me like an icy wind.

'Well, we meet again.' She said sardonically. 'You really don't need to be alarmed; I won't hurt you.'

I gulped nervously. 'What...what do you want with me?'

Still smiling her eyes bore into mine. 'You'll see soon enough.' As she glanced down at my dress, she stifled a laugh. 'I came here earlier to prepare the church in readiness for you then snuck out and followed you back here to make sure you were alone. *I* wanted to be the one to show you, just me.' Without warning she took my arm and held it in a vice like grip. 'Come along now, before Gideon finds you and spoils my little surprise.'

I had become a prisoner of my own fear, hardly able to move or utter a sound.

'You're a quiet little thing, aren't you?' she hissed. Still clenching my arm, she dragged me over to the far-right side of the church and into a small vestry room where several framed manuscripts and paintings hung on the wall above a display case. 'I can't wait to see the look on your face' she laughed hysterically as she gestured her hand to one particular painting. 'Can you see the family resemblance?' A devious smile spread across her face as she awaited my reaction.

My eyes widened in horror and bewilderment as I gazed up at the painting. I stumbled back, and averted my gaze, unable to comprehend what I was seeing. Suddenly I felt the pressure of the madwoman's hand on the back of my head, shoving me forward so my face was almost pressing against the canvas.

'Look at the picture.' she demanded in an aggressive voice.

With a whimper I opened my eyes and stared at the picture. It was a portrait of a woman who looked exactly like myself. The same oval face, the same unruly auburn curls, the same green eyes and the same pale lilac gown. But what alarmed me most was the thing she was carrying in her arms, it was a small dummy, and embroidered on his jumper was the name... Gilbert.

'Fascinating, isn't it?'

As she let out a cackle I continued to stare at the picture in complete fascination, not wanting to look but unable not to. At the back of my mind I vaguely recalled seeing this dummy before. It was like an old forgotten nightmare returning to haunt me.

The madwoman nudged me to gain my attention.

'You are looking at Florentine Heatherington, your great, great Grandmother. Both of you are so alike, don't you think? You both share the same ghastly auburn hair, all knotted and untidy, and those washed-out green eyes are just like yours, aren't they? With the same dull expression.' She laughed contemptuously. 'Florentine resided in Caleb's cottage for quite some time. You must have seen her initials carved into that piece of furniture in the bedroom.'

I stepped back a little and slowly nodded my head.

'Yes.'

'Some considered her a brilliant portrait painter. This is a self-portrait of course. People loved her and she became a valued member of the community, before she decided to flee and never return.' Her eyes glared wildly into mine. 'Many believed Florentine had become lost in the wilds, whilst others thought she'd gone to Hartland, a place of no return. But despite her cruelly deserting our little village, she still somehow managed to become a figure of worship in this church.' With a snigger she looked at the picture. 'My deranged mother thought it clever to call her son Gilbert after the doll in the portrait, and so my poor brother was named after that hideous dummy. Rather appropriate considering he's simple minded. You've met him haven't you, on the pathway.' She laughed ironically. 'You nearly scared him half to death. He believes you to be the ghost of Florentine Heatherington.'

I finally managed to blurt out a sentence.

'As do the other villagers.'

She nodded. 'They're simple country folk. You are living proof that Florentine didn't perish at all but deserted these lands in favour of yours. Finally, she will be seen for what she really is, a traitor. And I shall take great delight in informing all the villagers that you are no more a ghost than I.' She looked triumphant.

'But why now, why haven't you said anything before?' I said, surprised at how controlled my voice sounded. 'Why didn't Gideon...' my voice trailed off.

She bent in close and wrapped her arm around me.

'Gideon should have been the one to tell you, and it was very cruel of him keeping you in the dark.' She threw me a pitiful glance. 'In the end I thought it only right you should know.' An odd ecstatic smile appeared on her lips, making her appear older. 'And how wicked he is for not informing you of the truth about him and me.' She said, laying emphasis on her words.

I moved away from her.

'What truth?' I exclaimed, studying her face.

'Gideon and I are to be married.' She smirked at me.

I was silent for a moment, trying to digest what she'd just said.

'You're lying' I said, my voice becoming furious. 'Gideon would never marry you.' I began to shake with anger. 'I don't believe a word that comes out of that venomous mouth of yours. You'll say anything to keep us apart.'

She turned on my fiercely. 'How naïve you are, you see Gideon is well aware that you will soon be gone, and then we will finally be together.'

'Why would Gideon take the trouble to bring me here if it was his intention to marry you?' I leant against the display cabinet to steady myself. 'And further more I'm staying in Briarwood and there's nothing you can say or do to change my mind.' I said calmly.

'How dare you speak to me in such a way.' She exclaimed, scowling at me.

I suddenly became acutely aware that I could be in grave danger if I infuriated her too much. She had almost put an arrow in me once before, and she could easily do it again. Should I play safe and lie or should I be strong and honest. Ultimately, I had to be true to myself, it was the only way.

159

'Look, Gideon and I… well, we love one another. I'm sorry this messes up your plans Verity. But this is reality, and you must face the fact that you don't have a future with him. It's time you moved on with your life and….'

She shoved roughly passed me.

'Oh, do stop jabbering on. You have no idea about my life, so please don't lecture me.' She laughed out loud, shaking her head. 'You think you know him *so* well, don't you? Reaching out she prodded me in the shoulder with her finger. 'I know the real Gideon.' Her face turned to me. 'It's *me* he wants to be with.'

'Oh really, well let's go and find Gideon and ask him, shall we?' I said in a brisk voice. 'Let's hear him say what an unhinged and delusional woman you are, and how he feels sorry for you.'

Although I was pleased at how clear and strong my voice sounded an uneasy feeling was creeping over me as I looked at her face, part of me expected her to start raving like the madwoman she was, but to my surprise she didn't appear affected by my words.

She looked at me with contempt.

'I've been watching you from afar, and I've seen how you're nearly always on your own, taking your little hikes. It would have been so easy for me to have….'

'Murdered me?'

She pursed her lips but didn't reply. 'As you're aware Gideon and Caleb asked me to keep away from you, to not interfere with your visit to Briarwood. They said how confused you were and that you had to find out in your own time that you didn't belong here.' She paused for a moment, staring at me with a mocking look in her eyes. 'It's *you* Gideon feels sorry for, but as he's such a kind man he doesn't want to hurt your feelings. Seeing you for real has disappointed him and he's come to realise it's me he truly desires.'

'Really.' I laughed. 'The only words of truth you've spoken tonight is that Gideon is a kind man,'

I caught a glimpse of the dummy in the portrait, and shuddered. Something was stirring at the back of my mind, struggling to become known. I pushed it back, hoping it wouldn't return.

Without warning she came up and gripped the tops of my arms. 'Can you not see, it's *you* that's unhinged and delusional my dear.

And anyway, all this talk is of little consequence now. Your fate has been decided for you.'

I could see the madwoman looking at me impatiently; her dark eyes as black as coal. It seems she was waiting for me to question what she meant about my fate. I decided not to give her the satisfaction, as after all I was in charge of my own destiny. As her grip became tighter, I wrenched myself away from her, wondering what other revelations she had up her sleeve. I told myself I must remain strong and composed, for whatever it was she had to tell me didn't matter anymore; her words were of no interest or relevance. She had no power over me.

'Well? Are you not in the least bit interested?' She said, eyeing me curiously.

I didn't reply, hoping that Gideon would come marching in the door at any moment. If he was here everything would be all right, and we would link arms and stroll out of the church and go home, leaving the madwoman alone with her misery.

'Answer me, damn you.'

I jumped at the sound of her shrill voice.

'No, I think you've said enough.' I said in a stony voice. 'And besides I really have no interest in hearing any more gibberish.'

She scowled. 'Oh, it's hardly gibberish.'

As I stared into her despicable face a little voice inside my head warned me it wasn't wise to linger. Gingerly I stepped back hoping she wouldn't notice.

'Going somewhere, are we?' She went on looking at me with her unwelcoming stare. But I've not finished with you yet and by the time I have you will be begging Gideon to let you go back to Rawlings.'

I staggered back. The word Rawlings filled me with the most peculiar sensation, and far off in the distance I experienced a sudden flash of a distant memory. I could visualise a beautiful house but couldn't remember where I'd seen it.

My eyes grew wide. 'Rawlings?'

'Remember your lovely home, do you?' She laughed hysterically, a hint of madness in her eyes. 'And that lovely mother of yours that deserted you, Freya wasn't it?'

'Stop it, stop it now' I shrieked at her. 'I'm going back to the cottage.' Shaking, I began making my way towards the church door.

'Don't you want to see the note about your Aunt Constance?'

I froze on the spot then turned to face her. 'What...what note?'

'The note I have in my pocket, the note that will cause you to scurry off and pack your bags and leave at first light.'

When I spoke my voice sounded distant and unsure.

'But I'm not leaving, not tomorrow, not ever.'

She roared with laughter. 'Oh, but you are.' She glared at me and pulled a piece of crumpled paper from the pocket of her dress. 'Ambrose Walker frequently ventures out into the lands beyond the village, and by sheer luck he discovered this note discarded in a field. When he returned, he passed it to me and I have been keeping it safe until it seemed the right time to show you.' With a look of smug satisfaction, she passed the note to me.

Nervously I took it from her, and with trembling hands I opened the note and gazed at the untidy handwriting, scrawled across the page.

__Effie__ -please come quickly. Your Aunt has been taken seriously ill and is at Oakland's Hospital.
Love,
__Mace__ x

I stared in wonder at the crumpled piece of paper. The great flood that I had unintentionally been pushing away had finally overcome me, and the torrent of memories that had faded from my mind for so long came crashing over me like a tidal wave, consuming me whole. A momentous feeling of emotion and pain shot through me and I collapsed to my knees, clasping my aching stomach. My mind raced and my heart pounded as I suddenly remembered my poor Aunt. How could she have wandered so far from my thoughts for so long?

'Oh no.' I gasped, trying to hold back the tears.

'Finally.' Said the madwoman, jubilantly. 'Finally, it has happened.' She began to clap her hands. 'Now scurry off and find your darling Gideon and say your farewells. You have precious time left together.'

As I glanced up, I could see her standing there grinning and waving for me to leave. Her face seemed to fade into the background and suddenly everything was a blur. It seemed to me I had just awoken from a wondrous dream of pure bliss, and now I had to come to terms with it being over. I rose unsteadily to my feet and blindly ran towards the door, shaking with cold and confusion. With the tears welling up in my eyes I stumbled over the step and ran right into the arms of Caleb, who stood solemnly in the doorway.

The gentle tone of his voice as he spoke was comforting after the harsh voice of the madwoman.

'I'm so sorry Effie, but it had to be done.'

I looked up at him in alarm. 'You planned this didn't you? You knew she would be here.' I said, trying not to sob. I pushed myself away from Caleb, glaring at him. 'How could you?'

He took my hand but I snatched it away from him.

'Yes Effie, I led you here on purpose, as I believed Verity would be the best person to tell you.' He sighed. 'On many occasions I have warned Gideon that he must show you the portrait.' He looked down at the scrap of paper in my hand. 'But I can promise you I knew nothing about the note until a little while ago.'

The madwoman shrieked loudly across the church.

'But Gideon knows about the note, *he* was the one who threw it away by the portal, hoping no one would discover it.' She yelled. 'Then Ambrose came across it, purely by accident. 'Of course, Gideon soon regretted his actions, when he realised *she* didn't belong in the village.'

'ENOUGH.' Caleb bellowed at the madwoman. 'You have no proof of that Verity. Now leave us and do not utter another word.'

The madwoman's eyes never left my face as she casually strolled up the aisle, her scornful face full of rage. She barged passed me. 'Huh.' she uttered looking me up and down with contempt.

Caleb and I watched as she sauntered out into the night, her shadowy figure disappearing amongst the trees. Momentarily we saw her clearly again as a sudden flash of lightening illuminated the sky like a torch, quickly followed by a loud clap of thunder.

He turned to me and frowned.

'Forgive me Effie, I was wrong to allow Verity here tonight.' He took a handkerchief from his coat pocket and passed it to me. 'Here, wipe your eyes.' He stared out at the graveyard. 'Now you know why Gideon and I looked so shocked when we first saw you in that lilac dress, you looked so much like the portrait it was uncanny.' He shook his head and laughed.

'Yes, it all makes sense now.' I said feeling dazed. 'You should have told me long ago.' I glanced at him then looked down at the crumpled note in my hands. 'Did Gideon know about the note, I wonder?'

He was looking at me with his penetrating stare. 'Do not believe what Verity has told you, the poor thing is hopelessly in love with my son.'

I glared at him. 'So, it would seem.'

It puzzled me how the madwoman seemed to know so much about me, how she knew about Rawlings and my mother. The only conclusion I could come to was that Caleb must have told her, or even Gideon, but it didn't make any sense - why would they tell her such things. A niggling feeling of doubt stirred in my mind as I thought of Caleb. He was the one responsible for bringing the madwoman here tonight, and he was the one who asked her to show me the portrait. I lowered my eyes unable to meet his gaze any longer, watching the heavy rain splattering on the ground by my feet.

'What will you do Effie?'

I closed my eyes and tried to imagine I was standing in the garden at home rather than by a graveyard in a strange land. Just the mere thought of Rawlings caused me to become melancholy, and to think that it had drifted so far from my thoughts filled me with grief. This evening had begun with such promise but had ended in hurt and confusion. That deliriously happy feeling I had in my heart had been snatched away from me now, and had been replaced with a heavy feeling of sorrow.

When I finally answered him, my voice was without feeling.

'I have to go home Caleb, to my true home.'

'I understand Effie, really I do.' His face was filled with sadness.

'And Caleb, you were right about the sudden realisation. That day has finally arrived.'

He looked solemnly at me. 'Yes, yes it has Effie.'

Together Caleb and I made our way back to the cottage. The rain had lessened now but the thunder could still be heard, and the low rumblings echoed around us. I could feel a cold breeze on my face and thought how welcoming it was after the humidity of the day.

As soon as we'd reached the cottage, I immediately ran up the stairs and began to pack, shoving my clothes in the rucksack with no thought to folding them neatly. I checked the dressing table to make sure I had everything, pausing for a moment to glance at the initials *FH* carved so neatly into the wood. As I ran my hand over the initials, I thought it strange that this ancient piece of furniture once belonged to my ancestor, and how peculiar that it was still kept in this very room after all this time. For an instant it brought a smile to my face but then the feeling of melancholy returned with a vengeance and I felt tears run down my cheek. Beside myself with wretchedness I went and sat on the edge of the bed, listening to the groaning thunder overhead and the gentle drumming of the rain on the window.

I jumped suddenly as I heard a loud tapping on my door.

'Effie, can I come in?'

Swiftly I rose to my feet and wiped my eyes, not wishing him to see I'd been crying.

'Yes, yes, come in Gideon.'

As he entered, I saw he was soaked through with his hair clinging strangely to his head in clumps. Under happier circumstances I most likely would have burst out laughing, but instead I just looked reticent. As he went to speak, I saw how his eyes were filled with pain and remorse.

'I've been searching everywhere for you Effie. If I'd known you were going to the church I would have gone there immediately.'

I wanted to run and hug him but something held me back.

'I know that Gideon.'

He stepped close to me, looking pitiful. 'Will you ever forgive me for the wrong I have done you.'

'Forgive? Gideon you have done nothing wrong. You should have showed me the portrait but other than that you have nothing to reproach yourself for.'

He looked glumly down at his feet.

'I feared if you saw the painting too soon it would alarm and confuse you. So, I thought it best to wait until you were settled here in Briarwood, and then you would look upon the painting with a happy acceptance.'

My head felt muzzy and the nagging ache in my heart seemed to be getting worse. Once again, the tears came and I turned away from him and looked out the window.

'You said before I arrived here Gideon that you knew of someone who had already travelled from my home to Briarwood. Was that person Florentine Heatherington?'

'Yes Effie, apparently, she came here when she was a young woman and stayed for a while in this very cottage, but then something made her leave. I knew she'd made it safely back to her true home because the two of you are practically identical and therefore you must surely be her descendant.'

In a fit of rage, I flung round to face him. 'So, you let me risk my life on that one factor. Did it ever occur to you Gideon that it might just be a coincidence that Florentine and I look alike? And if I truly am related to her then why didn't I know about it, why isn't there any family portraits of this great woman hanging from the walls of my home. I can't remember much about…about where I live but surely seeing the painting would have brought it all back.' A chill crept over me. 'The only real proof is the dummy.' My eyes bore into him. 'And I have never ever mentioned Gilbert to you.'

He said nothing for a moment, and I could see by the expression in his eyes that his feelings had been hurt. 'No Effie, it's not the only proof.' His eyes flickered over towards the doorway. 'Wait here, I have to go and fetch something.' Looking serious he marched out the room and I heard him bounding down the stairs.

I perched myself on the edge of the bed again with my hands folded neatly in my lap, trying desperately to compose myself, but it was no good trying to relax, I couldn't do that until I was away from this place, until I knew my Aunt was well. Hearing Gideon's hurried footsteps ascending the stairs I instinctively shot up from the bed and went and stood by the window.

'Here.' he said bursting back into the room. 'Have a look at this.' He handed me a piece of paper. 'Florentine must have left this here when she was living in the cottage. Father found it sometime ago, tucked away between the pages of an old book.'

In wide- eyed wonder I unfolded the piece of paper and stared at the drawing. Although it was extremely faded with age the pencil sketch of the grand looking house was undeniably familiar. Underneath the drawing it read…*my dear home. FH.* An unbearable ache entered my heart and I placed my hand across my chest. 'Rawlings, it's Rawlings.' I gasped.

'Is this evidence enough Effie?'

I looked across at him, surprised by the sharpness of his tone.

'Yes, yes, it is. If only you had told me all this before Gideon.' I said, looking exasperated. 'Then seeing the portrait of Florentine in the church wouldn't have been so much of a shock.'

'Yes, I realise that now Effie, I'm furious with father and Verity for hatching this little plan tonight. If only father had spoken to me about his intentions then none of this would have occurred. I had already made up my mind to show you the portrait after I....' He paused.

'After what?' I asked curiously.

He moved his mouth as if to speak but then thought better of it.

I spotted the crumpled letter on the bed next to my rucksack and handed it to him. 'That woman, Verity seems to think you found this note but threw it away before I had a chance to see it.' I studied his face.

He straightened out the note and read it, his eyes narrowing.

'Effie no, I've never seen it.' He shook his head and sighed. 'If I had found it, I would have most certainly passed it to you. I may have delayed in showing you the portrait but this is different, never would I keep this type of information to myself.' He reached out and touched my shoulder. 'You do believe me, don't you?'

I watched as a spasm of pain crossed over his face.

'Yes, yes of course I believe you.' I said softly.

Staring into my face Gideon grabbed both my hands in his.

'I'm so sorry Effie, sorry for bringing you to Briarwood. It was selfish of me to expect you to give up your old life. I *knew* what would happen when you arrived here, I *knew* that our world would make you forget your memories of home, yet still I let you become caught up in the mysterious spell that haunts this land.'

My eyes grew wide with shock. 'No Gideon, no you're not to blame. I was well aware of the consequences of being here. Both you and your father warned me of the dangers, and yet I still remained. Yes, I was sad at leaving home but being with you was paramount. It was entirely my decision; don't you see that?' My eyes felt weepy but I was determined to keep my composure.

167

'Nothing can alter my feelings for you Gideon, not even that friend of yours Verity.'

A slight smile showed on this face.

'Speaking of Verity, I passed her in the lane when I was looking for you. She seemed to take great delight in explaining the events in the church. Apparently, you didn't think it true that she and I are to be married.'

For a split second my heart sank, but then I realised he wasn't being serious.

'Well.... no.'

His broad mouth broke into a grin. 'And you would be totally correct in that assumption. I have never felt inclined to ask her. Verity's mind works in a strange way, and somehow she has this belief that we are destined to be together.' He winked at me. 'But now I'm sure she has had a change of heart.'

I laughed. 'I cannot see how that could happen.'

'Oh, but it has.' He let go of my hands and reached up, gently cupping my face so I looked directly into his eyes. 'You're the best thing to happen to me Effie.'

The colour rose in my cheeks, as I looked deep into his eyes.

'You're the best thing to ever happen to me too.' I said softly, my voice thick with emotion.

Drawing nearer he bent his head forward towards me and gently kissed me on the lips. For a second, he pulled back but then reached for me once more, this time his kiss was more powerful. My head felt giddy as I clung to him, wishing I could remain this way forever, lost in the moment. We stumbled back, still holding onto one another. But then I felt the pain again, in the pit of my stomach. The feel of it took me back across the years to when I was a child at Rawlings, confined to my bed with a stomach bug. I remembered how lovingly my Aunt had cared for me. A feeling of acute sadness suddenly engulfed me and my eyes were watering once more. I moved my face to his shoulder.

'Oh Gideon, you know I can't stay, please take me back to the portal' I sobbed in his arms, unable to contain my tears any longer. 'I must see my Aunt, I'm so worried about her.'

His hand caressed my hair. 'I know Effie. I understand. But this time you don't have to go through the gateway alone...I'm coming with you.'

I drew back from him. 'No Gideon, it's far too risky.'

'I don't care. Father seems to believe that it will affect my health, but the truth is no one truly knows. If we sneak out at first dawn, without telling him, we can just go.'

I looked suddenly angry. 'No, I won't allow it. If Caleb is right about his theory, then…then I've deprived him of his son, and he will never see you again.'

'But I may never see *you* again.'

'Gideon, I intend to return as soon as my Aunt is well.' I kissed him on the lips. 'I belong here with you.'

'Then I shall hold you to that.' His voice became faint. I shall call for Croft and we shall leave at first light.'

Gideon walked from the room with his head lowered and gently closed the door behind him. I wanted to run after him and tell him I was staying, but it was too late, for I had awoken from my mysterious enchantment, it was no more.

Chapter 17

My dreams took me to a garden, containing an array of beautiful flowers, the colours of which glowed softly in the fading light, as if an inner candle was burning within them. I could hear the rustling leaves in the trees, and as they whispered soothingly to one another, I wondered if they were telling secrets, secrets only they could understand. My Aunt was there, wearing her large sunhat that flapped in the wind. She was kneeling down with her back to me, busily tending to the plants and singing a tune. Suddenly I noticed the flowers were growing at a tremendous rate, shooting up from the earth, wild and out of control. I watched as she staggered back looking flustered.

'Effie, Effie help me.' She cried as she turned her head towards me.

It was at that moment I realised it wasn't my Aunt peering at me from underneath her sunhat, but someone with a deadly coldness in her eyes, someone with long straight hair and a vicious scowl. It was the madwoman.

'What have you done with my Aunt?' I screamed at her.

She began cackling then pointed up towards the sky. 'Constance is in heaven Florentine, and it seems the flowers in her garden are putting up a protest.'

I looked incensed. 'I'm not the ghost of Florentine. I'm Effie, Effie Farraday.'

With a devious smile her eyes travelled down to my dress.

'Of course, you are, but you're still about to become a ghost.'

Looking down at myself I saw an arrow protruding from my chest, and as my lilac dress rapidly begun turning crimson, I stared at it in morbid fascination.

The madwoman's cackling became louder.

'Just to be sure I should remove your head from your shoulders.'

With a cry I dropped to my knees and watched in horror as she approached me with an axe. Weak from loss of blood I remained there, trying my best not to full forward onto the grass. My head was spinning now, and as the madwoman's face became a blur in front of me, I felt the axe make contact with my neck.

I awoke in a cold sweat with my heart pounding. Shivering, I pulled the blanket up around me and glanced over to the window, hoping to see daylight, but to my dismay it was still pitch black. With a harrowing sigh I lay back against the pillow, trying to convince myself that the nightmare was merely nonsense: it didn't mean Aunt had really passed away, and that I was soon to join her. However, the madwoman still wished me dead, I saw it in her eyes tonight, and I couldn't imagine she'd had a change of heart as Gideon had suggested, for she didn't possess a heart.

The knowing pain had returned, the pain I now knew to be of acute homesickness, and the only way to dispel it was to go back home, where my true world was waiting for me. This evening I had assured Gideon I *would* be returning to Briarwood, but even though I truly meant what I said, there was a terrible fear lurking in my mind that once I reached home this enchanted place would become little more than a forgotten memory, along with Gideon.

As my eyelids flickered, I noticed the thunder had now diminished to little more than a distant murmur far off in the distance. The potent scent of roses hung in the air, soothing and familiar, lulling me back into slumber, a dreamless slumber.

By morning the air had cooled considerably. I said my goodbyes to Caleb, who on the face of it appeared to be disappointed to see me leave. I wondered if he truly believed that just like all the other visitors, I would never return. He gave me a light hug before turning to Gideon.

'Promise me you'll not do anything foolish son. If you go through that portal you've as good as had it.' His eyes darted to mine. 'I'm sure Effie here wouldn't like your death on her conscience.'

With a frown I shook my head in acknowledgement.

After Gideon reassured his father that he'd be back in the village shortly, we finally went on our way.

The pain of leaving was immense, but in my heart, I knew it was the right thing to do. This sweet little village wasn't going to change, the villagers would make sure of that, and on my return, it would be so easy to slip back into the quaint way of life here.

Croft was waiting for Gideon and I just outside the village. He looked as magnificent as ever with his gleaming coat of fur. Unlike before I bravely kept my eyes open as we glided through the sky, taking in all of the landmarks as we passed over. The return journey was so much quicker, and I was rather saddened when I realised we'd reached our destination so quickly. The bird very gently placed us down by the edge of the forest.

Gideon whispered something in his ear, causing Croft to utter a low mournful sound. 'It won't be for long boy.' He said soothingly to the animal, burying his face into his fur and planting an affectionate kiss on the top of his head. 'You are a foolish beast. You act like we are saying our last farewells. I shall see you in no time at all.'

I threw Gideon a quizzical look. 'Wouldn't it be wiser for Croft to stay here whilst you see me to the portal, as surely you'll be going straight home afterwards?'

He paused for thought, his gaze still directed at Croft.

'I'm staying around these parts for a while Effie.'

I looked at him in amazement. 'What? But Gideon it would be safer for you to return to Briarwood.' I hesitated for a moment. 'If you're remaining here because of me, then you may have a long wait.'

He laughed rather casually. 'Effie, I really don't mind.'

'Gideon please, I can't bear the thought of you lingering around this place. What if something happens?' I suddenly pictured him sinking into the mire or being dragged away by some creature of the night and devoured. 'I'd feel much happier if you returned home.'

He turned to stare at me, his huge eyes showing a glint of humour and tenderness. 'I shall be fine Effie. You seem to forget I'm quite familiar with the perils that lurk around me.' He paused 'And besides, I enjoy being alone sometimes, and away from the confines of the village.'

I looked at him dubiously. 'I know that's a lie Gideon, you're only doing it because of me.' With a feeble smile I went over and placed a hand on his shoulder. '*Please* go home, I shall do my very best to come back to you just as soon as I'm able.'

172

'Very well then Effie.' He said in a quiet voice. 'But I'm still going to spend a little time here, and if there's no sign of you, I promise to go home and wait.'

I could see he was resolute. How I wished to take him in my arms and reassure him that I'd be back through the portal immediately, but that would give him false hope. The pain was back, starting from my heart and gradually spreading over my body. For a moment I wished it were yesterday, when I was wondering happily through the meadow without a care in the world.

'If that's truly what you wish to do Gideon, then so be it.'

'It is Effie.' Looking solemn he turned to Croft and gently stroked his great mane of silky hair. 'Go now boy, go home.'

With a soft moan Croft stared into his master's eyes, looking crestfallen. Gently patting the bird on the head, we said our farewells, then watched as he flapped his great wings before flying high up into the clear sky. He remained poised there a moment, quivering, then disappeared over the great trees and into the shadows.

Once Croft was out of sight, Gideon and I approached the forest. He warned me that we must be on our guard, as the trees could literally smell our fear. I thought how unfortunate it was that the portal was situated in that dreadful place. Supposedly it was for a good reason, to deter people from getting too near. All of a sudden, I felt unnerved at the prospect of stepping into the forest once more, as it dawned on me how close I was to taking the trip back, and doubts about the safety of the portal began to creep their way into my thoughts.

'We must speak in a whisper from here onwards.' He uttered with caution in his voice. Kneeling down he opened the sack he'd been carrying over his shoulder. Various tools were within it, including the scary looking axe from the previous trip, which he took out and placed firmly in his left hand. 'Now be careful where you step Effie, the slightest sound could awaken them. Although they rest in the day, as the sun keeps them sleepy, they can easily be stirred.' He whispered.

'But Gideon today's not really that sunny.'

'The tops of the trees are so tall they catch the sun's rays even through the clouds, and it makes them sleep.' He took my hand in his. 'But yes, you're right, less sun means less sleep.'

I laughed. 'Gideon I'm sorry but how can the trees be harmful, they're just trees after all. Whatever can they do to us?'

'Effie, you've already seen....' He hesitated. 'The trees around these parts are like creatures from your worst nightmares, if you disturb them, they'll snatch you away and...'

'And what?'

Looking grim he shook his head. 'Let's hope you never have to find out.'

Although I took notice of Gideon's warning, I wasn't entirely convinced it was true, and thought it more likely to be one of those fables that folk around these parts seemed to believe in. After all, I had stumbled around for hours in this forest at nightfall, and was still here to tell the tale.

We brushed passed the thick trees and entered the forest, mindful of where we were treading. The denseness of the branches gave the illusion that night had fallen, casting shadows on the ground. There was a chill in the air and the same eerie silence as before.

'Gideon?' I said quietly. 'What if the portal throws me off course and I end up somewhere else, somewhere I can't escape from?'

He attempted to smile but couldn't hide the uncertainty in his eyes. 'Fear not Effie, the portal will carry you safely home. You must have faith.'

I looked searchingly into his face. 'Do you have faith Gideon, faith that I will come back to you?'

'Yes.' He reached out and cupped my face in his hands. 'Fate brought us to one another and fate will reunite us once more.' He reached down and gently kissed me on the lips.

Our brief moment of happiness was snatched away by a noise behind us, very much like the snapping of a twig. Both of us swung round to see the madwoman standing there.

'Well, well, how very touching. It almost brings a tear to my eye.' She said in a mocking voice.

We gaped at her in utter disbelief. I noticed how tired she looked with the deep shadows around her eyes. When I saw the bow slung over her right shoulder and the quiver full of arrows, my heart lurched, and I was instantly taken back to Rawlings, and the day she had attempted to kill me in the kitchen.

'Why are you here Verity?' Gideon said angrily.

The madwoman looked at me with hatred in her eyes, and then with a little smile she gazed intently at Gideon.

'I wanted to see you, my love.'

As I glowered at her a feeling of fury came over me.

'Can't you leave us alone Verity?'

Ignoring me she continued to stare towards Gideon. 'What you told me last night greatly upset me, and now I simply cannot bear *her* presence any longer.' She threw me a fleeting glance of utter dislike, before turning her gaze back to Gideon.

I looked at him in surprise. 'What did you tell her Gideon?'

The madwoman cackled. 'Keeping secrets again are we Gideon. You really must try and be more upfront with your beloved.' She glanced cruelly at me. 'I almost feel sorry for you.' She said, tapping her fingers against her lips. 'Perhaps rather than killing you, I should let you go. It would be the kind thing to do.'

I felt myself begin to shake.

'Gideon?' I asked in a quivering voice. 'Please tell me.'

Sheepishly he lowered his eyes, unable to meet my gaze. 'Last night at the festival I was going to ask you something but your meeting with Verity prevented me.' He shot the madwoman a stern look. 'Then the right moment had passed.'

'*What* were you going to ask me Gideon?' I asked perplexed.

Before he could utter one word the madwoman stepped in. 'He was going to ask for your hand in marriage.' She looked pleased with herself. 'Can you actually believe he was going to ask *you,* the strange looking woman from far away who doesn't belong here?'

Gideon looked infuriated.

'You had no right to say that Verity.'

'Oh, Gideon please, we can't wait all day for you to tell her now, can we? And besides you're obviously unsure about the whole thing or you would have said something before.' She said brazenly.

Looking bereft he gazed into my face. 'I had it all arranged Effie, the proposal. After speaking to old Mr Templeton, I searched everywhere but was unable to find you, then I bumped into Verity and she told me of your meeting in the church and how she had shown you the portrait. I was so incensed that I informed her of my intended proposition to you in the hope it would put an end to her twisted beliefs.' He looked at me tenderly. 'I told her how I loved you Effie, only you.'

I stared into his face in complete adoration, and for a split second I forgot my fears. Gideon wanted to marry me and everything was going to be fine. A brief wave of complete happiness engulfed me as I imagined our life together in Briarwood. I would live out my days in this land and we would see our children grow into adulthood and then our grandchildren. Everything would be perfect and blissful. But then the madwoman moved nearer and the moment was lost.

'Gideon, this woman will break your heart. She's leaving you and you'll *never* see her again.'

As my anger overtook my terror, I glared at her. 'That's not true.'

Glaring at me, she took an arrow from the quiver and clutched it in her hand. 'Oh, do shut up, I wasn't speaking to you.'

'Don't speak to Effie like that Verity.' Yelled Gideon. 'And please, put the arrow way.'

She giggled. 'No, I shan't.'

Discretely I moved back a few paces, treading carefully as I went. I kept my eyes steadily upon her vicious face, apprehensive of her reaching for her bow. As I threw Gideon a worrying look, he came over and stood beside me, taking my hand in his.

'Oh, don't tell me the both of you are scared?'

Gideon cleared his throat. 'Look Verity, stop this foolishness and go home.'

'Oh, how convenient that would be for you wouldn't it Gideon.' She laughed drolly. 'But the problem is I shall forever have a thought festering within my mind, an inkling that she might worm her way back here. So, you must see Gideon how imperative it is for me to put an end to this once and for all. In time, you may even thank me for doing this favour for you.'

'That will *never* happen. What kind of person do you think I am Verity?

She burst into laughter. 'I love it when you're angry Gideon.'

It occurred to me how noisy we were being. I suddenly wished the trees would wake up and take the madwoman away, so I wouldn't have to look upon her detestable face ever again.

Gideon moved forward a little.

'For once in your life Verity please try and do the right thing, I beg of you.' He said desperately. 'Do you not understand what the consequences of your actions shall be? You will be convicted of murder and put to death.' He looked at her steadily, laying emphasis on his words as he spoke. 'I will make sure of it.'

The madwoman seemed undeterred by his words.

'Oh, but the villagers won't know it's murder. They're all simple yokels who think this woman to be the ghost of Florentine Heatherington, and they all believe she's returned to haunt them.' She laughed evilly. 'Well, you cannot kill a ghost, can you? She glared at us expecting a reply and then continued ranting. 'I shall simply tell them that the spirit of Florentine has passed on, and they will be none the wiser.' She paused as if deciding what to say next. 'Failing that I shall inform them the visitor has now gone, just like all the rest.' She glared at me scornfully. 'I *may* choose to tell the villagers who you really are, and shall take much pleasure in informing them that you are a descendant of Florentine Heatherington, the great woman they so admired, the great woman who had deserted Briarwood in favour of her old home.' They shall not look upon her so kindly then, will they? She said, icily. 'And as for you Gideon, well let's just say you won't be in a position to stop me.'

He began laughing at her. 'I most certainly will stop you Verity, and you seem to be forgetting my father. He's hardly going to keep silent.'

'Caleb shan't cause me trouble. He looks upon me as his daughter. I can easily twist him around my little finger. He has lots of sway amongst the dim- witted villager's and together we will easily fool them.'

I suddenly exploded, unable to hold my tongue a moment longer.

'Have you ever stopped to think that perhaps the villagers aren't so daft as you make out, how they might already believe you to be a crazed woman who is eaten up with your overzealous obsession for Gideon and your envy of Florentine.'

'How dare you.' She screamed at me, seething with anger.

An odd creaking noise suddenly reverberated throughout the whole of the forest. The trees were stirring.

'Verity please, you must lower your voice.' Said Gideon, beginning to panic. 'You shall awaken the trees.'

'I don't care about the stupid trees.' She shrieked.

An overwhelming sickness flooded over me as I suddenly realised my little outburst may have cost me my life. But it wasn't the trees that frightened me; it was the woman standing a few feet away who was swiftly positioning an arrow in her bow.

'It's time to end this.'

'Verity no.' Gideon yelled. 'Lower the bow this minute.'

It all happened so quickly then I hardly had a chance to breathe. For the second time in my life, I experienced that strange acceptance that my time was up. I remember standing there in some kind of trance whilst the madwoman took aim and fired, and before I could stop him, Gideon had thrown himself in front of me and taken the full force of the arrow.

There was a moment of stunned silence.

'GIDEON.' I screamed.

With a groan he fell back against me. I noticed the arrow had pierced his left shoulder and blood was already seeping from the wound.

The madwoman let out a long piercing cry. 'No, no what have I done.' She dropped to her knees and began to sob.

'Effie?' he said, mumbling into my neck. 'Are.... are you hurt?' He tried to steady himself only to lose his balance and slump against me once more.

'No Gideon, no I'm fine.' Scarcely able to think straight I carefully held onto him then managed to gently lower him to the ground.

'Gideon?' The madwoman cried in anguish. 'The arrow wasn't meant for you. Please forgive me my love.'

I winced as she began to scream again, knowing she was going to awake the entire forest. Suddenly I heard a movement nearby. Something was coming. For an instant I forgot poor Gideon, lying there wounded, as my attention was drawn to the madwoman as she picked herself up and began making her way over towards us. Quite unexpectedly she was promptly stopped in her tracks as a large talon like root appeared from nowhere and firmly wrapped itself around her ankle. She fell forward, desperately trying to grab onto something, her fingernails clawing into the grass. With a heart-wrenching cry she looked up at me in alarm.

'Help me. Help me' she sobbed.

I stared at her in morbid fascination as the root began pulling her backwards along the ground at a frantic pace, through the ferns.

No, no.' She screamed.

I carried on watching until she disappeared out of sight, not quite believing what had just happened.

Hearing Gideon's voice made me come back to my senses, and I bent down over him. He was grasping the arrow in his bloodied hand.

'Help me pull the arrow out Effie.'

'Are you sure Gideon? I don't want to hurt you.'

'You… you won't.' he said as his face twisted in pain. Grabbing my hand, he placed it around the arrow. 'It'll be all right, just pull.'

I stared frantically at him. 'Ready?' As he nodded, I yanked the arrow from the wound and he let out a low moan. I knelt there for a moment gazing down at the blood gushing from Gideon's shoulder. With a gasp I dropped the arrow and pulled my rucksack from my back and rummaged round for a piece of material to place over the injury. 'Here, this should help.' I began wrapping my scarf around his shoulder and underneath his arm, and when I'd done it a couple of times, I pulled it taut and tied a knot. 'There that should hopefully stop the bleeding.' I said peering into this pale face.

He gave me a weak smile.

I smiled back and began stroking his hair, trying frantically to think what to do. Then suddenly it came to me. The healing plant, the one Caleb had told me about, I was sure it was the same flower that I had seen growing by the tree in this very forest on the night I arrived. Besides, I *had* to believe it to be true, as it maybe my only chance of saving Gideon's life.

'I think there's a plant in this forest that can help you Gideon.' I kissed his clammy forehead. 'Wait here whilst I go and find it.'

His voice was barely audible as he spoke. 'No, no Effie it's too dangerous.' He attempted to grab my arm but wasn't strong enough.

'Don't worry, I shall be back before you know it.'

Before he could put up another protest I got up and headed off on my own, into the depths of the forest. I suddenly thought how ridiculous my comment had been, about asking him to wait here, where else was he going to go in his condition. My heart sank when I thought of the tree's roots and I prayed that he wasn't going to be dragged off like the madwoman. I rapidly directed my thoughts to locating the flower, trying to keep my mind focused. Cautiously I made my way through the forest, taking care not to make a noise. A beam of sunlight had escaped through the trees, shining down like a ray of hope. I don't know why but my inner voice was urging me to run over to the spot where the beam had landed on the ground, and to my utter surprise I immediately found the tree in question with the exquisite pale-yellow flowers, glowing radiantly by the trunk. I smiled to myself and gently gathered up a bunch, hoping they wouldn't suddenly wither and die.

By pure luck I managed to find my way back to Gideon fairly easily and breathed a sigh of relief when I saw he hadn't been dragged away by the trees. As I heard a faint scream in the distance, I thought it must be the madwoman. I remember being glad that the trees had taken her, she deserved it.

'Gideon, I'm back.'

As I knelt down beside him, I saw more blood had seeped from his wound and had completely covered my scarf. He had his eyes closed now and his complexion was a deathly white.

'Effie, Effie is that you?' He said in a rasping voice.

'Yes Gideon, I have the flowers and I'm going to heal you with them.'

Seeing how weak he was I quickly untied the bloodied scarf and carefully pulled the shirt from his shoulder, trying not to focus on the injury. With shaking hands, I took the bunch of flowers and pressed the petals delicately up against his wound and waited, praying that they would work. Almost immediately a powerful light illuminated throughout the flower, and I felt an intense heat radiating from its core. I sat watching in complete fascination, as the petals began melting into his shoulder, glowing like a magical plaster. I could feel the heat travelling from my hand and trickling up my arm like a golden stream of warmth, immersing my entire body in a sense of strength. I closed my eyes for a moment, basking in the glory of it.

The deep richness of Gideon's voice brought me back to reality.

'You *did* find the healing flower Effie.'

With a gasp I opened my eyes and looked down onto his smiling face. The colour had returned to his cheeks and his eyes looked bright and alert.

'Gideon.' I gushed, delighted and amazed at his swift recovery. 'I'm so glad you're better.' Laughing, I flung my arms around him.

He winced 'Best be gentle. I'm on the mend but I'm still a little tender.'

'Sorry.' I said smiling happily, drawing back from him slightly.

I glanced at his shoulder expecting to see the flowers but they had completely disappeared.

'They have dissolved into my wound.' He said, as if knowing what I was thinking.

'Is that normal?' I asked curiously.

'Completely, the flowers can only perform one miracle.' He said peering at his healed skin.

'It's so incredible how swiftly it heals.' I exclaimed looking at his shoulder in disbelief. There was no scar or mark visible, just a slight redness.

'Yes, yes, it is.' He smiled lovingly at me. 'And thank you… thank you for saving my life Effie.' He said sincerely.

I looked serious for a moment. 'Gideon if it wasn't for you, I'd be…. well, it would have been me with the arrow wound.' I lowered my head and kissed him. 'You risked your own life to save me. I can't ever thank you enough.' A look of gratitude spread across my face as I gazed at him.

He reached for my hand, caressing it gently. 'For you Effie, I would do it all again in a heartbeat.' As a cold breeze drifted through the forest, he suddenly looked anxious. 'I believe the clouds are gathering. We must be quick.' He rose rather stiffly, picking up his axe and the sack from the ground. 'Come, we must find Verity, she needs our help.'

I looked at him strangely. 'That flower must have done something to your brain, that woman nearly just killed you.' I snapped at him. 'And now you want to *help* her.' I shouted at him in frustration. 'I never wish to set eyes on her cruel face again.'

'Effie, please keep your voice down.'

'Sorry.' I sighed.

'What Verity did was wrong and she needs help, but I cannot and will not abandon her. It would be on my conscious if I do not try and save her. You understand that don't you Effie?'

No, not at all, I thought to myself, the madwoman is the root of all evil. A surge of panic came over me as I remembered how I'd described a certain someone else with those exact words- Gilbert my wooden companion. It's funny how the memory of him had suddenly come flooding back.

I decided to go along with Gideon's plan.

'Well, I suppose so.' I said reluctantly. 'But even if you succeed in saving her, what then?'

'Father has a particular herb in mind that may ease her condition and he is keen to try it out.' He rubbed his shoulder. 'All Verity's family are a little abnormal, her mother was rather peculiar and her brother, well you've already met Gilbert.'

My heart jumped a beat at the mere mention of that awful name.

'What about the father?'

Gideon's paused for a moment, his face darkening. 'Effie, I really think we should concentrate on finding Verity.'

Puzzled by his avoidance of the question I was about to enquire further, but then decided just to leave the matter alone; perhaps the madwoman's father had met a rather grisly end, or maybe he'd committed such a despicable crime that the villagers weren't allowed to mention his name.

We crept as quietly as we could amongst the trees, being careful not to rustle the ferns. I envisaged us searching ages for the madwoman without any luck; after all the forest was such a wide expanse that she could be anywhere. Gideon would be sorrowful at not being able to save her and I would reassure him that he had done all he could, all the while thinking to myself how glad I was. However, to my dismay we suddenly spotted her, propped up against a large tree. A mass of roots had wrapped themselves around her body like a rope, and even her face was smothered in long thin tendrils, that looked like they were suffocating her, or already had. But what shocked me the most was how she was gradually sinking into the bark itself, as if it was devouring her. Looking at her unmoving frame I believed the madwoman already to be dead, and I instinctively moved forward for a closer look. Although the roots obscured most of her face and she had her eyes closed, I thought she looked serene and happy in her final resting place.

'Don't go any nearer Effie.' He took my arm, pulling me back. 'It's too dangerous.' Gripping the axe firmly in his hands he turned and gave me a grave stare. 'I'm going to free her.'

'But Gideon, I think Verity is already dead.' I whispered, worried that he was going to rescue her for nothing and become hurt in the process. I still couldn't believe he was back to normal so quickly after being mortally injured with an arrow. How ironic it would be if I should lose him now, because he stubbornly wanted to save the madwoman, even though she had almost killed him. 'Perhaps it would be best to leave her in peace.'

'Effie, you may not like Verity very much but I'm not going to just leave her like this. And besides I know she's still alive because...'

'Because what Gideon?'

He gulped. 'The trees tend to keep their victims alive whilst they devour them, and it's only when they've been totally absorbed into the bark that they perish.' With an agonised smile he glanced at me. 'Stay here.' Without another word he briskly crept forward and swung the axe down hard onto the roots situated to the right of the madwoman, completely obliterating them. A peculiar whining sound came from the trunk as if it was shrieking in pain. He continued hacking the tree in various parts in quick succession, being careful not to strike her. The huge tree groaned and creaked with every blow until it was almost silent.

In alarm I watched as he threw down his axe and dropped to his knees with a groan, his hand rubbing his shoulder. Such strenuous activity so shortly after his injury surely couldn't be good, I thought. Suddenly he collapsed face first onto the ground, directly in front of the tree. Without thinking I ran forward and knelt down beside him.

'Are you alright Gideon?'

'Yes... yes I just need to get my breath back.' He said hoarsely. Leaning on my arm he pulled himself up and gave me a weak smile. 'I think the tree is severely weakened.'

'Yes Gideon.' I replied staring at the damage he'd made.

The madwoman seemed to be stirring.

'What.... what's going on?' As her eyes opened, they widened in horror. 'No, no.' She focused on Gideon. 'Don't let it take me Gideon. I...I don't deserve to die.'

Wiping the sweat from his brow Gideon reached forward and began tearing the dead roots away from her body, then he grabbed onto her and began to pull. At first, I didn't think the tree was going to release her but suddenly she fell forward into his arms. Half stumbling he carried her away from the tree and carefully lowered her down on the ground. As he attempted to move away, she clung to him and he awkwardly removed her arms from around his neck, and told her to sit and rest for a while.

'Are you alright Effie?' He said, swiftly coming over towards me.

'Yes, are you?'

With a bashful smile he nodded then lowered his eyes.

I observed how dishevelled the madwoman looked, with her muddied dress and straggly looking hair, so different from her usual appearance. A smile crept over my face as I watched her trying to tidy herself up.

She caught me looking and glared back at me contemptuously.

'What's so funny?'

I shrugged my shoulders but said nothing.

With a huff she turned to Gideon. 'Well, it seems this is becoming rather a habit of yours, isn't it my love. First you save *her* from the trees and now me.'

'What do you mean? I wasn't taken by the trees.' I began to laugh rather nervously. 'You're losing your mind Verity.'

'Oh hardly, you *were* almost tree food.' She laughed cruelly. 'Didn't silly old you realise.'

My eyes darted to Gideon. 'What does she mean?'

He glared angrily at the madwoman then turned to look at me.

'That day I first found you here Effie you'd.... well, you'd almost been devoured by one of the trees. I got to you just in time.' He sighed. 'I didn't tell you because I didn't want to scare you.'

Out the corner of my eye I could see the madwoman watching me with a tolerant smile on her face, waiting for me to react. To my knowledge I had merely fallen asleep against the tree when Gideon had discovered me, and also, I'd just been back there to find the healing flower and nothing had happened; it was all a little odd. However, although I wasn't amused that this was *another* piece of information that Gideon had kept from me, I didn't wish to give the madwoman the satisfaction of seeing me angry.

'It's alright Gideon, you don't need to explain.'

He came over and took my hand. 'I'm sorry Effie, I've just been trying to protect you all this time.'

The madwoman rose from the ground, brushing herself down.

'You were being deceitful Gideon.' She said callously. 'You knew that by telling her the truth about Florentine and the trees she'd not be so keen to stay in Briarwood. If you truly cared for this woman you would have been honest from the very start.'

Before Gideon had a chance to reply I stormed over to her.

'Leave him alone Verity. Gideon almost died because of you and yet you don't seem in the least bit remorseful.' My voice became louder, and I felt unable to control it. '*And* he has literally just saved your miserable life but you haven't had the decency to thank him.'

'Well how simply awful of me.' She turned to Gideon. 'Sorry about the arrow my love, it wasn't meant for you.' Her eyes flickered to mine for a moment before gazing back at him. 'I'm grateful to you for saving my life.'

'It's less than you deserve.' He snapped. 'And if you must know it was out of pity, so please don't read too much into it. If you hadn't followed us here Verity then none of this would have happened. You've disturbed the trees to such an extent that I fear we'll all vanish in this godforsaken place.'

She cackled with laughter. 'Oh, please Gideon. I think we've proved that the trees aren't as dangerous as everyone thought.' With a frown she glanced back at the damaged tree, which was making strange groaning noises.

'It's not wise to be too complacent Verity. In fact, I am perplexed at how lucky we've been.' He sighed as a momentous wail echoed throughout the forest. 'But perhaps our luck has just run out.' With a gulp he turned to me. 'We need to leave Effie.'

The madwoman looked suddenly panicked.

'What about me?'

'If you walk in an easterly direction Verity it should bring you out of the forest. I'm sure this is the quickest route home.'

'I hope so.' With a huff she turned to me. 'Of course, I could always travel home with you…. *Effie.*' She wrinkled her nose up. 'However, the journey may have an adverse effect on my health, so it would be wiser for me to stay here with Gideon, and besides his company is *so* much more enthralling.'

'Verity, please just go.' Said Gideon insistently.

'Very well.' She said, smoothing down her hair. Turning to leave she paused momentarily and glared at me with her cold eyes. 'Have a safe journey home and please don't bother coming back.' Then with a chuckle she looked at Gideon. 'I shall be calling for my eagle when I reach the clearing by the edge of the forest, so if you require a ride home my love, I will wait for you.'

'That really won't be necessary Verity, I have Croft.'

With a look of amusement, she flounced off and headed east.

As she disappeared out of sight another groan reverberated a little way off in the distance. Looking frantic, Gideon put the axe back in the sack then grabbed my hand, and we ran silently through the forest. It seemed darker now and the branches of the trees hovered ominously above us, as if waiting for the right time to make their move. Looking upwards I spotted a mass of rooks circling above the trees, as if they'd been disturbed in some way, or were looking for something. Before long we passed the tree with the healing flowers and then stepped down into a large sunken area surrounded by bracken.

Gideon turned to stare at me. 'This is it. If we remove the ferns, we should find the entrance.'

'Are you sure this is where it's located?' I asked, looking confused.

'Yes.' He said pointing to a nearby tree. 'It's easily recognisable as it's near that tree with the strange carving on the trunk.'

I glanced over at the circular symbol carved into the bark.

'What does it mean?'

'Some people believe it's a warning to stay away, but no one truly knows. When I was a child there was always talk about the carving and the existence of the portal amongst the village folk, and it was always something I wanted to see for myself. After tirelessly mentioning it to my father he eventually agreed to take me on a trip to see it. But when we arrived here, I had to make a promise never to enter the gateway.' He smiled poignantly. 'A promise I have kept up to now, although at times I have been tempted to break it just to see what would happen.' His face clouded over. 'I often wonder if others from our land have taken the trip, and if they survived.'

I took his arm. 'Gideon, what's wrong?'

Suddenly he seemed unreachable, totally immersed in his thoughts. I wondered if he was thinking of his brother Noble, the one he never spoke of, the one who went travelling one day and never returned; how completely awful for Gideon to think he had to carry around the burden of his brother's disappearance, when it really wasn't his fault. I was on the verge of bringing up the subject when a deep groan echoed through the trees.

Gideon's whole body jolted.

'Come Effie, let's get you out of here.'

He knelt down and frantically began removing the large ferns.

I crouched forward to help him.

'How odd it's become so overgrown in such a short space of time.'

'It's been longer than you think Effie.'

With a gulp I stared down into the dark depths of the well- type structure, and my heart began to pound when I heard the familiar sound of swirling wind, ready to whisk me away back home, or at least that's what I hoped.

Gideon turned towards me looking nervous. 'We haven't much time. I don't like the sound the trees are making.' Reaching around his neck he produced an exquisite looking wooden bird charm, attached to a silver chain. 'I want you to have this.' He said, carefully placing it over my head 'See the hole by the beak? Well, it is a calling whistle. When you arrive back here all you need to do is blow on it and Croft will come for you.'

'But Gideon that's yours.' I suddenly had a vision of the madwoman giving him a lift home on her eagle, who I suspected was similar to Croft only rather more vicious looking, with a hooked beak and red eyes. Verity would take great pleasure in wrapping her arms around Gideon's waist as they flew over the landscape, snuggling her face up against his neck. 'If you can't call for Croft then how will you return to Briarwood, will you travel by foot?'

'You just concentrate on getting home to your Aunt.' He smiled tenderly but I could see the pain behind his eyes. 'I love you, Effie. More than you will ever know.'

'And I love you too.' I said looking deep into his eyes. I leant forward and rested my face against his cheek. 'Promise me you'll visit me in my dreams tonight Gideon.' I said tearfully.

'I promise.' He lifted my chin so I was looking into his eyes. 'Effie, I'm sure it will be just like it was before, and we shall see one another every night. And when your Aunt has recovered you can come back to me and we can be together for the rest of our lives.'

I gazed into his eyes, knowing that this moment couldn't last, that the time had now arrived for me to leave. If only I could eradicate my overwhelming feeling of homesickness and go back to my state of oblivion of yesterday morning, but that dream had ended now. With a heavy heart I stepped nearer to the portal, holding Gideon's hand tightly.

'I wish I could come with you Effie.'

I looked upon his entrancing face one last time. 'Another time perhaps, when we know it will be safe for you.' I swallowed, trying not to cry. 'Goodbye Gideon.' I said, releasing my grip on his hand.

'Have a safe trip home Effie. I promise we shall see each other soon.'

'I know Gideon.' I took a tentative step forward. 'Take care of yourself.' I kissed him hard on the mouth then jumped down into the portal and out of his life.

Chapter 18

Once again, I found myself being sucked down into the depths of the whirlwind, being tossed and turned in every direction, as if I were made of paper. But unlike the previous trip I wasn't scared, for my heart was too heavy to care. Before I knew it, I was being flung violently threw the air and I then tumbled awkwardly to the ground. My stomach was churning in such a way that I feared I would be sick, but I wasn't sure if it was due to the way I was feeling or the bumpy ride through the portal. I immediately opened my eyes and looked around at my surroundings. It seemed I'd been thrown through the overhanging trees and had landed by one of the little waterfalls, in some mud. For a moment or two I remained lying there, trying to muster the energy to get up, but it seemed like all my energy had been drained from my body. I should think myself fortunate I'd not been injured in the fall, but I didn't feel lucky at all, I just felt miserable. With some considerable effort I managed to rise to my feet and very slowly limp forward. My whole body ached veraciously and I grimaced as a sharp pain shot through my temple and then my ankle. A strange feeling of melancholy suddenly came upon me like a cold fog, and I had the distinct feeling I would never be happy again. Gideon had warned me of the wear and tear of travelling through the portal and how it affected your mind as well as your body. A lump came to my throat as I thought of him. Remembering I still had some painkillers in my rucksack I managed to retrieve them and pop two into my mouth, but it was so dry and sore that I had to swallow several times before they would go down properly.

Looking back, I'm not entirely sure how I managed to make my way out of the woods, as darkness was descending fast and I could barely see the way ahead. The last thing I wanted was to be stranded in the woods overnight, which was silly really as I was home now and there weren't any scary trees waiting to come and drag me away. Clumsily I stumbled along the bank of the stream, for what seemed an eternity then decided to head straight ahead in the hope it would bring me to the edge. There was no owl to show me the way this time, or a moaning Mace trailing behind me making sarcastic comments, I was on my own, which funnily enough suited me just fine, for unless it was Gideon I didn't wish for any company. In the failing light I could just make out the iron gates up ahead, and as I got nearer, I noticed that someone must have broken the padlock, for the gates were wide open.

For some strange reason I thought Mace might be waiting to greet me but then I realised just how impossible that would be, for how could he possibly know I was back. Whilst I'd been away any thoughts of my best friend had strayed far from my mind, but on my return, I remembered every gory detail, including the way he'd callously pushed me through the portal.

The painkillers had done little to help and my entire body ached to such a degree that I had trouble walking; all I wanted to do was flop down somewhere warm and sleep. Wearily I hobbled past the gates and saw there was a car I didn't recognise by the side of the grass. Perhaps someone had decided to take a stroll in the woods, I thought, although it was rather late in the day for a walk. Moving closer I cautiously peered into the window just to see if someone was asleep on the back seat, but it was empty. Gingerly I tried the door and to my surprise it wasn't locked. Too tired to care at this point I clambered in, telling myself that if the owners of the car were to suddenly return then I would apologise and leave. They may even take pity on me and offer me a lift home. Sleepily I glanced around the car, and spotted a large bottle of water and some car keys on the dashboard. How odd, I thought, that the owner would leave their keys hanging about. Not that it really mattered to me anyhow, I was just glad to rest somewhere warm. I grabbed the bottle of drink and guzzled it back, and although the water was lukewarm it relieved the awful dryness in my mouth. Feeling weepy and unsettled I clambered onto the back seat where there just happened to be a blanket; I draped it over my body and lay back, falling asleep almost instantaneously. I wasn't too sure how long I exactly remained asleep but when I awoke it was bright sunshine. With a groan I stretched and went back into the front of the vehicle. It still puzzled me why someone would leave a car here, but I deduced that it must be abandoned, rather conveniently for me. With a yawn I suddenly caught a glimpse of my reflection in the car mirror and gasped in shock. The sight that stared back at me was shocking: my hair was completely dishevelled and I had smears of dirt across my face and clothing, which made me look like I'd been rolling about in the mud. My bloodshot eyes were puffy and my complexion was so pallid that anyone would think I'd not slept for a month or more. But despite my appearance I felt relatively better this morning, in mind and in body. Just out of curiosity I clambered out of the car and opened the boot, hoping I wouldn't discover a dead body or something else along those lines. To my relief all that it contained was a black holdall. As I took a peek inside the bag I gawped in bewilderment when I saw what it contained: there were toiletries, a change of clothing, food, which consisted of chocolate, another bottle of water and an apple, which unfortunately had turned completely rotten; obviously the person must have left it all here a few weeks ago. It was becoming increasingly obvious that the car had been purposely put here to help me, and there was only one person I could think of who would do such a thing- Mace, it had to be Mace; I managed a little smile, thinking how he must be riddled with guilt for what he did and was trying to make amends. Chuckling to myself I dragged the bag onto the back seat. I freshened up and changed clothing, then sat and ate the chocolate bar, which tasted a little strange but was enjoyable all the same. Once again, I glanced in the mirror and this time I was pleasantly surprised by my reflection, a considerable improvement now that I was mud free. I did however notice a faint scar to the right of my temple, which I didn't remember having before. With renewed strength I inserted the keys in the ignition and to my delight the engine started.

The drive back passed by in hardly any time at all which I was extremely thankful for, as I hated driving, especially in a strange car. How odd it was arriving back in my hometown of Abercrombie, it was almost like a dream, and in reality, I was back in Briarwood watching from afar. Looking around nothing seemed to have altered much. It was the same high street, shops, cinema and park; even Hudson café was still there. This put my mind at ease, knowing that everything was as it should be, and I hadn't landed in an alternate universe.

Apprehension swept over me as I approached Oakland's hospital. I hoped with all my heart that my Aunt was well, as I would never forgive myself if anything had happened to her. I parked in the hospital car park, and taking deep breaths approached the reception area. A slightly built middle-aged lady sat behind the desk looking decidedly stressed as she frantically typed away on a computer.

I cleared my throat.

'Excuse me miss, can you help me?' I said in a rather weak voice.

'Just one moment.' The receptionist answered, barely looking up from the computer.

I nodded silently at her and stood there, waiting patiently.

Whilst I was standing there, I couldn't help but visualise my poor Aunt all wired up and being fed by a drip. Or worse still, there was the distinct possibility I was too late, what if she lying in the cemetery, all cold and alone. How heartbroken she would have been before she died, knowing I had deserted her. And I would never forgive myself and spend each day agonising over what I had done. I don't know why I was always so pessimistic; it was one of those traits I couldn't seem to make go away, no matter how hard I tried. In reality my Aunt was most likely sitting up in bed knitting bed socks and chatting to the other patients; when I entered the ward, she would bestow upon me a beaming smile and in a few days, she would return to Rawlings where I would nurse her back to health.

An ached raged through my heart as I suddenly thought of Gideon. If only he was here with me now to hold my hand and give me a reassuring smile, how much better I would feel. It suddenly occurred to me that I'd not dreamt about him last night; although this was rather a disturbing realisation I tried not to worry unduly, I would most likely see him tonight.

'Name?'

My head jerked towards the receptionist who was peering at me from underneath her glasses.

'What?'

'What's the name of the person you are enquiring about? She said in rather a clipped tone.

I looked at her blankly. 'Oh sorry, Farraday' I said slowly.

'First name.'

I paused. My memory seemed to be working in slow motion; as for the life of me I couldn't recall my Aunt's first name. Out of the corner of my eye I could see the receptionist glaring at me rather impatiently. With a nervous laugh I bit my lip.

'Oh, it's Constance, Constance Farraday.' I said jubilantly, as if I was pleased with myself for having remembered such a simple fact. 'She's my Aunt.'

The receptionist widened her eyes and stared at me for a moment before typing something into the computer. 'No, no there's no one by that name been admitted.'

'Are you sure?' I asked puzzled. 'I...I was told she was seriously ill in hospital.'

She threw me an odd look before lowering her gaze to the keyboard. 'Well Constance Farraday is *not* in this hospital.' With a sigh she looked up into my bewildered face. 'You best check St Victor's Hospital in Moorbury. It's more than likely your Aunt has been admitted there.'

I laughed nervously. 'St Victor's, but...but that's not possible, I distinctly remember building work had only just begun on that hospital before I left.'

Looking rather cross the receptionist glared at me sternly.

'Young lady, I can assure you St Victor's Hospital is very much up and running. It has been for several months now.' With a sigh she reached across the desk for some paper. 'I'll give you their number, and you can call to check on your relative.' She scribbled it down then passed it to me, and then throwing me a suspicious look she returned to her computer screen.

Deciding it would be unwise to press her further on the matter I rang the number from the free payphone opposite the reception desk. A voice answered almost immediately.

'St Victor's Hospital, how may I help you?'

The rest was a blur. I vaguely recall enquiring about my Aunt, and they too hadn't had any admittance under her name. Although it seemed peculiar that the new hospital had been built, I still managed to convince my befuddled brain that I was mistaken, and that somehow, I'd forgotten that the hospital had been built before I'd actually left Abercrombie.

Moving in slow motion away from the payphone I slid down into a nearby chair, feeling nauseous and staring ahead in a trance like state. My Aunt's image suddenly popped into my head and it occurred to me that after the confusion over the hospitals I was still no nearer to finding her. More to the point why did that note say she was in hospital when it was becoming evident, she wasn't. With a groan I hunched forward in the chair and wrapped my arms about my body. As I glanced up, I saw the abrupt receptionist eyeing me peculiarly, she most likely thought I was a little deranged, and who could blame her. I grabbed a nearby book from the table and pretended to read it.

'Effie, Effie Farraday is that really you?'

I looked up to see a man standing in the restaurant doorway, staring at me. At that precise moment the last thing I wanted was any unwelcome distractions. Feeling slightly agitated I half-heartedly returned his look. There was something about him that seemed vaguely familiar. He was a tall man and rather well built with cropped dark blond hair, but it wasn't until he smiled at me with that unmistakable glint in his crystal blue eyes that I remembered who he was. It was Duncan Bartholomew from school, and although I'd not clapped eyes on him for years, he really didn't look that much different. I was aghast with myself for not recognising him straight away, how could I forget that face, the face I'd always thought so appealing and had always admired from afar. Momentarily all my other thoughts disappeared as I gazed into his eyes, my cheeks beginning to turn scarlet with embarrassment. I bit down hard on my lip then stuttered his name. 'Dun...Duncan?'

As he strode forward towards me a look of relief crossed over his face. 'Few, I was beginning to think I'd made a mistake.' He said, wiping his brow with his hand.

I smiled bashfully at him, racking my brains for a witty reply but failing miserably.

'No, it's me.'

He looked bemused. 'For a minute I didn't recognise you.' He paused. 'You look all grown up.' A look of admiration spread across his face.

'Yes I am.' I said, lowering my eyes.

An uncomfortable silence followed and I could see the abrupt receptionist snapping at a man standing at the desk.

'What are you doing here Effie?' He asked.

I looked at him with a blank expression before finally answering. 'Well, it's my Aunt, she was supposed to be at the hospital but I can't find her anywhere.' I blurted out the words before I'd realised how stupid they made me sound. Thankfully I didn't really think he was listening, as he was too engrossed in staring at me.

'That's too bad.' He answered. 'Would you like to grab a cup of coffee?' He indicated towards the direction of restaurant. 'We've got loads to catch up on.'

Had this been a few years ago I was certain my wall of shyness would have prevented him from even speaking to me, as through no fault of my own I had a habit of making myself look completely unapproachable, it was a look that only shy people could relate to, and was very often misinterpreted as being rude or snobbish. However, I now had a newly found confidence and was able to actually smile at him and hold a lucid conversation without falling to pieces. What a terrible shame the timing was wrong.

I looked at him apologetically.

'I'm so sorry Duncan, but I'm in rather a rush. Perhaps another time?'

He stared back at me for a moment looking rather taken aback. Men like Duncan weren't used to being turned down, and as I returned his look I pondered if anyone *had* ever rejected him.

'Oh well, yes perhaps another time?' he said in soft voice.

'Indeed.' I said smiling graciously at him 'That would be lovely.'

'Why don't you give me a call Effie?' He said, jotting down his number and handing it to me. 'I'd love it if we met up.' He looked steadily at me with his penetrating blue eyes.

I smiled as he lingered beside me as if waiting for me to change my mind. Somehow, I don't think he'd be so keen if I told him the truth about what had been going on in my life, in fact he'd most likely run a mile.

'Well, goodbye Duncan.'

With a hesitant look in his eyes, he waved at me. 'Bye for now then Effie.' He threw me a dazzling smile. 'Don't be a stranger.'

I watched as he casually sauntered back into the restaurant. I had a fleeting urge to call after him, but it didn't last. How could I do such a thing when I had Gideon? But still it was nice to know that someone such as Duncan found me attractive. Smiling to myself I slammed the book shut and put it back on the table.

It seemed to me the next logical move would be to go home and see if my Aunt was there. And, if she wasn't, I would go and find Mace and ask him what was going on. Leaving the hospital, I drove down Conway Street and happened to glance in at the window of Hudson's café as I passed. To my utter amazement I caught a glimpse of Mace, or someone extremely similar, sitting in our usual seat by the window. Abruptly I put the brakes on, and screeched to a halt. The car behind hooted me several times and the driver threw me a furious look as he drove around my car. I looked back at him, mouthing that I was sorry. The temptation to see Mace was just too great and I drove on further down the street and parked up. A mixture of nerves and anticipation ran through me as I opened the café door, my heart pounding. As I stepped through the doorway, I noticed how different the place looked. It seemed the whole cafe had been refurbished with rather garish looking wallpaper and cheap looking tables and chairs. A couple of waitresses were milling about but I didn't recognise them, and Mrs Worthington was nowhere to be seen. Tentatively I looked over towards the window and saw the unmistakable figure of Mace hunched over the table. It was almost as if I'd stepped back in time and for a moment, I wished I had, for everything would have been so easy and comfortable. As I approached the table, I saw how his hair was in its usual unkempt state, and how the tatty old sweatshirt he was wearing made him look as scruffy as ever. Despite the fact that Mace had pushed me through the portal I was still pleased to see him, and wanted to run over and fling my arms around him. But then I noticed he had company, and as I got closer, I saw it was one of his college friends. I wasn't entirely sure of her name but I had inkling it was Moira. They seemed to be in deep conversation and didn't notice me until I was standing right beside them.

'Hello Mace.' I said in a quiet voice.

He glanced up slowly and when he realised it was me his eyes widened with disbelief and bewilderment, and for a short while he sat there gawping at me, but then his look changed to one of disinterest and he lowered his gaze and began stirring his coffee.

'Oh, it's you.' he said nonchalantly. 'You're back then.'

His reaction to seeing me wasn't exactly the one I'd expected and I felt myself faltering over my words. 'Mace I ...well you could sound a little more pleased to see me.' I said, confused at his unfriendly welcome.

Still not meeting my gaze he reached for his friend's arm.

'Moira, I need to chat to Effie in private. It won't take long.'

I was startled by his strange behaviour and couldn't seem to comprehend what was going on. How could he say it wouldn't take long to speak with me, when we had so much to discuss.

'Oh ok.' Moira said in a high voice.

They both exchanged a peculiar knowing look and she rose from her chair. Looking briefly at me she then leant close to Mace, whispering something in his ear. It was done in such an intimate way that it made me feel awkward. She threw me a sullen look before slowly wandering over towards the door. I glanced back at her with a faint smile on my lips. Almost immediately I grabbed her seat and sat down opposite Mace, hoping that it was one of his annoying little jokes and that now Moira was gone his behaviour would go back to normal.

'I've so much to tell you Mace.'

He was looking at me now in a slightly belligerent, school boyish kind of way.

'Have you?'

I watched as he continued stirring his coffee.

'Aren't you in the least bit interested in what happened to me?'

'Not really.' He sighed and took a slurp of his drink. 'You see Effie when you first left, I *was* hurt and angry with you, wondering if you'd ever return, but after a while I decided to get on with my life and discovered I was perfectly happy without you. And with Moira things became ever better.' He said, taking a large bite of cake from his plate.

I looked flabbergasted. 'But Mace how can you say that. You shoved me into the portal and left me. We were supposed to go together, remember?' I yelled at him, slamming my fists down on the table.

'Effie for God's sake, please keep your voice down, do you want the whole café to hear you?' He whispered crossly looking around at the other customers. He leaned towards me. 'Besides, I didn't push you Effie. You went of your own free will.'

'Liar, you most certainly shoved me.' My voice had risen again. 'What happened Mace, why are you acting this way?'

He narrowed his eyes and smiled, slowly shaking his head. 'Look, it doesn't really matter now does it Effie? Life has moved on, for you, and for me.' He took a long slurp of his coffee. 'I'm surprised you've returned after all this time. You've been gone so long I thought you must be happy there, with what's his face.'

My eyes grew wide with surprise. 'Mace I've only been gone for a short while.' My voice faded as I spoke, and an uneasy feeling crept over me. 'Haven't I?'

He slammed down his cup, almost spilling the contents. 'No Effie, you've been gone a couple of years.'

All of a sudden, I couldn't catch my breath and I bent over the table. I was aware of how time differed from world to world but no, not years. I tried to think, to make sense of the whole thing.

'No, no it's not possible.'

'Sorry Effie, but it is.'

My head was spinning and a distinct feeling of nausea was welling up inside of me. The confusion over the hospital suddenly made sense. I watched as Mace devoured the rest of his cake not understanding why he was apparently unaffected by my distress.

'So why did you bother to come back?' he said indifferently.

I straightened up slightly and tried to fight off the rising wave of emotion that was bringing tears to my eyes. 'After getting your note I realised I had to return home.'

He gave me a blank look. 'Effie, what are you going on about, I didn't send you a note.' He said, screwing up his face.

'Oh yes you did Mace.' I said adamantly. I delved into my pocket and produced the crumpled piece of paper. 'See, it's definitely your handwriting and you've signed your name at the end.'

He picked up the note and examined it intently, then began to laugh. 'Huh. A good forgery, but no, I didn't write it. You see this note is written with an ink pen, and I never write with that type of pen, and it's just a bit too neat for me.' He said, shoving the note across the table towards me. 'Plus, I wouldn't put a kiss at the end, you know that, Effie.'

'But if it wasn't you....'

He shrugged his shoulders but didn't reply.

I sat there speechless, trying to figure out what was going on. The note must have been a lure, a lure to bring me home for no reason. My heart lurched at the realisation of it all: Aunt had never been ill; she was safe and sound at Rawlings, and I hadn't needed to be parted from Gideon at all. It then occurred to me that the culprit could be the madwoman; she had wanted rid of me, and what better way than to make up a story that would force me to go home. But then how would she know the name of the hospital, and how did she forge Mace's handwriting?

'Wake up Effie.'

I stared at Mace. 'Are you sure you didn't write the note?'

He rolled his eyes. 'No, I don't know anything about the note and I don't care who wrote it.'

'Well, thank you for being so supportive Mace.' I shoved the note back into my coat pocket. 'Doesn't our friendship mean anything to you anymore?'

'No, not really.' His eyes looked straight through me in a cold, expressionless way. Suddenly he glanced over my shoulder and his face brightened. 'Oh, here comes Moira.'

'So, that's it then?'

'Pretty much Effie.'

Tears were welling up in my eyes but somehow, I held them back. 'Very well Mace, I shan't bother you again.' I stood up to leave and for a split second I saw a flicker of compassion in his eyes but then it was gone.

Moira removed her coat and brushed passed me to sit down. She slung her coat over the chair and looked directly at Mace.

'Is she leaving now?

Mace paused and widened his eyes at me. 'Yes, Effie and I have finished our little chat.'

Wobbling slightly on my feet I stared at him, then lowering my head I slowly made my way across the café in a daze and stumbled out the door. On reaching the car the wave of emotion I'd been holding in suddenly engulfed me and I bent my head forward and sobbed against the steering wheel. But through the tears I thought of my Aunt and Rawlings, they shone bright and strong like a beacon of light through the darkness, they were all that mattered. I wiped my eyes and started the engine.

Chapter 19

As I approached Rawlings a little smile came upon my face. I saw the afternoon sun dart through the branches, creating an intricate pattern on the ground. With eager anticipation I peered ahead, and when my home came into clear view a feeling of contentment came over me. Being summer, the house was covered in its usual blanket of purple wisteria, and such was its vibrancy that the house looked almost mystical.

I parked the car by the side of the house and took a quick peek in the mirror to check my face. My eyes were still red and puffy from crying but it didn't matter, there wouldn't be any more tears now I was back home, not once I was reunited with Aunt. Unsure of whether or not I still had my front door key and feeling too lazy to rummage through my rucksack looking for it, I clambered out the vehicle and tentatively rapped on the brass knocker. After standing there for what seemed like forever, I decided to wander around the back of the property to see if my Aunt was in the garden, it was summer after all, and she was bound to be pottering about there somewhere. But I'd only taken a few steps when I saw the front door slowly being opened. Suddenly feeling anxious I closed my eyes and took a deep breath, praying that it would be her standing there, looking the picture of health. As I gradually opened my eyes, I gazed in disappointment at the figure standing in the doorway. For a moment we both stood there like statues, staring at one another.

'Oh. Hello Isaiah.' I said in a surprised voice.

I peered at him curiously at he continued staring at me in complete an utter shock. His face had turned so white I wondered if he thought me to be a ghost. Why did he have to be at Rawlings, and what was he doing here; perhaps he'd moved in whilst I'd been away, and taken over the house.

'Isaiah?'

'Effelia, is that really you?'

I laughed nervously. 'Of course, it's me.'

I had an awful thought whirling around in my mind, a feeling that something really terrible had happened to my Aunt. The pain of her loss would be so unbearable that I wasn't sure if I could cope. In the end I decided to come right out and ask him.

'Is...is my Aunt at home?'

He hesitated for a moment, looking decidedly shifty. 'No Effelia, I'm very much afraid she isn't.'

The pain in my stomach had returned, rapidly spreading to my heart with a surging ache. I looked at him, trying to read his thoughts. How could it have slipped my mind how annoyingly aggravating this man was. I'm sure he was taking great pleasure in keeping me in suspense.

'Then...then, where is she?'

His face was more relaxed now and he gave me a devious smile.

'Do you really wish to know Effelia? After all you've been gone so long, I'm surprised you care.'

'Please Isaiah, just tell me, my Aunt is alright, isn't she?'

He stood there with his arms folded, carefully peering at me.

'You look rather worn Effelia. Why don't you come inside and I'll make you a nice cup of tea.' Seeing how infuriated I looked he put his head back and laughed. 'Constance is currently at Miss Piper's house having afternoon tea. She will be home shortly.' He stood back and stretched out his arm, beckoning me in. 'Well come on in Effelia.'

The ache began to gradually subside. 'My Aunt is well then?'

'Quite well, considering the stress and worry you've caused her over the past couple of years.' He looked at me furiously as I dropped my rucksack down on the floor of the hallway. 'How could you Effelia, how could you leave like that and not bother to contact us for so long?'

I stared at him in bewilderment. 'Well, I...look Isaiah it really isn't any of your business.' With a sigh I stepped back towards the door. 'Perhaps I'll go over to see her now at Miss Piper's house.'

'NO' Isaiah roared.' He clenched his fists as if trying to compose himself. 'No, I think it best if you wait for Constance here. I shall go and call her right now.' He attempted to smile.

'Very well then.' I said wearily. 'But please would you tell her to return as soon as possible. I'm eager to explain....' I paused. 'To explain what happened.'

'What *did* happen to you Effelia?'

I averted my eyes from his scrutinizing glare. 'That's for my Aunt to know, not you.' Picking up my rucksack I edged my way passed him. 'Let me ring Miss Piper, what's her number?' I said reaching for the telephone.'

Looking alarmed he snatched my hand away from the receiver. 'Oh no Effelia, that really won't be necessary. You go and rest in the living room and I shall forewarn Constance.' He placed his hand on my arm. 'It will be a terrible shock for her you know.'

I raised my eyebrows. 'Very well Isaiah.'

A simpering smile spread across his face. 'Now go and make yourself comfy.' He watched as I headed for the living room. 'Would you like some cake with your tea?'

I shook my head. 'No thank you.'

Even though I'd hardly eaten since returning to Abercrombie I just couldn't stomach anything at the moment. Isaiah's erratic behaviour was making me sick with nerves. Something was wrong I could feel it in my bones. Perhaps he'd done away with my Aunt and buried her body in the cellar, and after making up a story about her going away he had taken over ownership of Rawlings. For there was no doubt he had made himself at home in a house that didn't belong to him.

I leant back in one of the big old armchairs and stretched my legs out. Despite it being mid-summer, I felt myself shivering, and I suspected I was still suffering from the after effects of my trip, as my body still ached a little and I felt really fatigued, however it was nothing a good night's sleep in my own bed wouldn't cure. If only I could sneak up to my room right this minute and not have to go through the ordeal of having to explain my whereabouts these past few years to my Aunt; she certainly deserved to know where I'd been, but would it be best to tell her the truth or make up a more plausible story. Strangely enough as I sat there contemplating the matter I suddenly became completely muddled about where I had actually travelled to and why.

Isaiah poked his head around the door. 'I've just spoken to Constance, and she's on her way home.'

'That was quick.'

'Well, we didn't need to have a lengthy conversation Effelia. Naturally she was rather speechless when I informed her of your return. You have a lot of grovelling to do young lady, as Constance won't forgive you lightly.' Not waiting for a reply, he disappeared back behind the door, whistling a little tune.

After a few more moments he reappeared laden with a tray, and as he poured out the tea we sat in silence by the unlit fire. Every now and then I caught him peering at me out the corner of his eye, which was very disconcerting.

'That's it drink up Effelia. I'm sure you're tired after your journey, why don't you sleep for a while.'

I rubbed my eyes. 'No, I…I must stay awake for my Aunt.'

As Isaiah began jabbering on his words seemed to be fading into the background. I gazed dreamily into the fireplace, wishing I could see the flames as they danced and leapt in the hearth, but it was cold and still. I was so overcome with tiredness that I felt the cup slipping from my hands, and Isaiah swiftly reached forward and took it from me. Murmuring something, he covered me with a blanket then I saw his blurred figure leaving the room. My head lolled back against the armchair, and I lay there snug and warm. The last thing I noticed before closing my eyes was the painting above the fireplace, the portrait of my mother…it was gone.

I'd no idea how long I slept for, but it was a heavy, dreamless sleep. When I awoke my head felt groggy, and for some reason I could barely manage to keep my eyes open. Initially I believed myself to still be in the armchair by the fireplace at Rawlings, but as I blearily looked around it soon became clear I was somewhere entirely different, somewhere unfamiliar. Apart from the bed, which I was lying on, the room was sparsely furnished with a bedside table, a bookshelf and a wooden chair. As well as the main door I noticed another one situated in the middle of the right wall and wondered if it led to a bathroom. With a sigh I glanced over to the window and noticed it was covered in iron bars, and my heart lurched when I saw a shadowy figure standing in the far corner of the room. Suddenly I couldn't get my breath, and beginning to panic I tried desperately to get up from the bed only to find myself flopping back against the pillow. I gazed in alarm as the figure limped slowly towards me, and as the person came nearer, I saw it was Isaiah.

'How are you feeling Effelia?' He bent over and peered closely at me. 'You gave your Aunt and I quite a scare.'

'What...what happened?' I said in a perplexed tone.

He scratched his forehead. 'You don't remember?'

'No, didn't I just fall asleep in the armchair?'

'You may have slept for a little while Effelia, however when I returned to the living room, I found you pacing the room in an extremely distressed state.' He reached over and dabbed my forehead with a damp towel. 'Whatever happened to you in the last couple of years appears to have had an adverse effect on your mind.' He shifted his spectacles further up over his nose, looking at me steadily. 'And...well it's caused you to have a complete breakdown.'

I stared at him in disbelief. 'No, no that can't be true.'

He began shaking his head. 'I'm afraid it is Effelia. You were quite hysterical, ranting and raving about someone called Gilbert.'

A distinct chill ran through me. My nightmares of the dummy were so real that they always remained startlingly vivid for quite some time, so it was extremely strange that I couldn't recall having the dream. I deduced that Isaiah was making it all but had no idea why; ever since answering the door at Rawlings his behaviour had been odd, and the sooner I found out what was going on the better, in the meantime I decided to play along with his little game.

'Oh, that was nothing but a silly nightmare. I hardly think its cause for concern.'

Isaiah looked surprised at my response, and for a moment or two just stood there staring at me. 'Really?' He half smiled. 'Then how come I had to restrain you whilst your Aunt called the doctor?'

Looking perplexed I shrugged my shoulders.

'Well anyway I'm better now and should be getting back home, Aunt will want to see me.' Once again, I struggled to sit up but my head was spinning and I felt sick. 'Why do I feel so strange?'

Dr Stirling gave you a sedative.'

'Surely there wasn't any need for that. And where am I.... I mean I don't recognise this place.'

'You're at my house Effelia.'

In all the years I'd know Isaiah not once had I ever been to his house, not that I had any wish too. He always gave me the impression that he wasn't keen on visitors, and I always imagined him to have a secret wife hidden away somewhere.

'Why? Surely I'd be better off in my own bed at Rawlings.' I said gruffly. 'It doesn't make any sense.'

'Effelia the doctor has advised us to keep you away from Rawlings for the time being, just until you are well again. After all you did have your breakdown there.' His face suddenly looked grim. 'He was rather keen to have you admitted to The Manor, but I persuaded him otherwise.'

I instinctively burst out laughing. 'The mental institution?'

'It's not to be laughed at Effelia. The Manor is a well-established institution that comes highly recommended. Dr Stirling knows what he's talking about.'

'Does he now? Who exactly *is* this Dr Stirling, I mean I've never heard of him before.'

'Oh, he works at The Manor.' He lowered his eyes and sighed. 'I promised the doctor to see how things go, but if your situation should worsen then I shall have no choice but to go along with his wishes.'

I gulped. 'What about my Aunt, can't I see her?' I said, beginning to feel a little distraught.

'All in good time' He said, humming to himself. 'I've tried to make this room as pleasant as possible. There's plenty of good reading over there.' He pointed over to the bookshelf. 'I know how you love your books.'

Despondently I glanced across at the stack of books.

'I would much prefer to read in the comfort of my own home.'

'Of course, you would Effelia, but you can't.'

I glared at him but said nothing.

Suddenly we heard the faint sound of a doorbell ringing.

'Who the devil can that be?' He said in a moaning voice. 'I'm not expecting anyone.' Looking irritated he began to limp swiftly across to the door. 'I shall return in a while with some refreshments.'

'It's most probably my Aunt.' I said eagerly.

She was bound to come and see me, I thought hopefully, and then I would persuade her to let me go home. Just thinking of this lifted my spirits.

Isaiah stopped at the doorway and turned towards me. 'It won't be your Aunt as I told her to visit in a few days.' He smiled mockingly at me 'Oh, and as for that friend of yours, I wouldn't bank on him dropping in anytime soon.'

'I take it you mean Mace.' I said coldly. 'Why wouldn't he?' I asked, assuming that Isaiah didn't know about our little spat of yesterday in Hudson's cafe.

'Well, I'm sorry to tell you this Effelia but... well I bumped into him the other day and....' His voice trickled out.

'And what?' I exclaimed.

He opened the door and hovered there. 'I don't think I should tell you now. You're in such a fragile state of mind.' He gave me a simpering smile. 'Now get some rest.'

'But Isaiah....'

He slammed the door behind him and I heard the key being turned in the lock, followed by, what sounded like, a bolt being pulled across.

This whole situation was bizarre and I was beginning to wonder if I was dreaming. I had come back to Abercrombie believing everything would be as normal, but as it transpired everything couldn't be more abnormal: Apparently, I'd had a terrible breakdown and was now convalescing in the house of the man I despised, with my Aunt nowhere in sight, and my best friend had disowned me.

I heaved myself out of bed and staggered slowly to the door, just to check it really was locked, and of course it was. In pure frustration I began frantically banging upon it. 'Isaiah, Isaiah?' I yelled croakily. Wearily I crossed over to the window and peered through the bars in the hope of seeing the person who had rang the doorbell, but to my dismay I looked down onto the back garden. The rain was gently drumming against the windowpane. It was such a soothing sound that I stood there for some moments, gazing dreamily outside at the overgrown lawn and rusty old swing. I could feel my eyelids closing and reluctantly I clambered onto the bed and lay my head against the pillow. My thoughts turned to Mace and what it was that Isaiah was going to tell me about him. I was pretty sure it was another one of Isaiah's little mind games, but still I couldn't help but wonder if he really did know what Mace was up to. I had little doubt that Isaiah gloated over keeping me in suspense, it was the sort of thing he'd do. I closed my tired eyes and rather reluctantly drifted off to sleep. I awoke feeling completely disorientated, with no idea how long I'd been resting. Isaiah was skulking by the window with his arms folded. I saw that he had placed a tray with some sandwiches and a cup of tea beside me on the bedside table.

'Did you have a good sleep Effelia?'

'Yes, most satisfactory thank you.' I watched as he strolled over towards me and put the tray on the bed. 'Who was at the door earlier?'

He looked blankly at me. 'What?' He paused. 'Oh, you mean yesterday. It was just a salesperson, no one of any consequence.' He handed me the cup. 'Here, you must be parched.'

'How long was I asleep for?'

'Oh, since early yesterday evening.'

I took a sip of the tea and grimaced when I realised how sugary it was. 'Well, I feel better after my rest.' I said, trying to sound cheerful. Giving him a weak smile, I began to eat a sandwich.

'That's splendid Effelia.'

For a while we both sat in silence as I finished my sandwiches.

'Drink your tea up. I'm sorry it's so sweet but Dr Stirling recommended it for your condition.'

Looking sternly at him I clanked the unfinished cup of tea down on the saucer. 'Isaiah, I haven't got a condition and I hardly think sugary tea is the answer. The best medicine I could possibly have would be to go back to Rawlings and see my Aunt.

'And you shall Effelia. That is precisely what I want for you.' He looked hesitant. 'But I…I have some information I need to divulge.' He turned from me and paced over to the bookshelf 'I feel the time is right.'

'Is it about Mace?'

He looked vexed. 'No, that can wait until later. I have more important matters to discuss.' His face looked stern. 'Now finish your tea. I shall return in half an hour after you've had time to shower.' He pointed over towards the door on the right. 'You'll find several pairs of pyjamas hanging up in the en-suite, along with your toothbrush and toothpaste.' With a nervous laugh he limped towards the door. 'Now hurry Effelia, I shall be back soon.' He stood there in the frame of the door. 'And then I shall enlighten you with my information.

I hadn't the slightest idea what it was he wanted to tell me and I wasn't particularly interested; as long as my Aunt was well, that's all that mattered, and the sooner I returned home to her the better. I drank the remains of the tea then trudged towards the en-suite. Usually, a shower would have been sufficient enough to wake me up, but for some reason I still felt lethargic and weak, as if my entire energy had been drained away. I put on the pyjamas, which I recognised from home, and then cleaned my teeth. How relieved I was to flop down onto the bed, and with a yawn I leant back against the pillow, trying desperately to keep awake.

The key was turned in the lock and Isaiah came strolling in with an anxious expression on his face. He tried to smile, but I could tell it wasn't genuine. Without saying a word, he dragged the chair over to the bed and sat down.

'Still tired are we Effelia?'

'As a matter of fact, yes.

He suddenly looked smug. 'Well, it's to be expected, when a person experiences a breakdown, the mind automatically wants to shut down, and what better way than to sleep.'

I glared at him. 'I've not had a breakdown.'

He laughed. 'They're also in denial.'

With a frustrated sigh I closed my eyes for a second. 'What is it you want to discuss with me Isaiah?' As I peered at him, I noticed the dark shadows underneath his eyes. 'Is there something on your mind?'

'Well yes...but I'm not really sure where to start.'

'The beginning?' I said in a rather sarcastic voice.

He glared at me for a moment then laughed out loud. 'Oh Effelia, you do have a dry sense of humour.' His face became lost in thought.

'It's not my Aunt, is it?' I uttered in a quiet voice. '

'No.' He said dismissively, rising from the chair and going across the room.

Whatever he had to say it was clearly causing him difficulty. I watched as he limped over towards the window.

'Have you ever wondered why I've always been here for you Effelia?' He reached up and placed his hand on the bars. 'Has it ever occurred to you who I am?' His voice was breaking up as he spoke.

Yes, many a time, I thought to myself. Behind that charming façade hides an evil deceitful man, and such is your influence over my Aunt that one day I fear you will succeed in snatching Rawlings from our grasp. You are a fraud, Isaiah.

I cleared my throat. 'No, I've never given the subject much thought.'

He swung round and gazed at me. 'Well perhaps you should have because I'm your father Effelia.'

'What?'

'You heard me, I'm your father.'

There was a hushed silence.

I stared at him, feeling beyond speech. He spoke so casually as though his announcement was of little consequence. Nothing had prepared me for what he'd just said. I felt stunned, but was also seized with a sudden desire to laugh.

'Well say something Effelia.'

I narrowed my eyes suspiciously, suddenly wondering if he was making all this up, just for the fun of it.

'But…. but that's impossible. I wasn't even aware you knew my mother?'

'Your dear mother, oh yes I most certainly knew your lovely mother' He shook his head. 'More about her later' He came striding towards the bed. 'Well, aren't you pleased? Aren't you happy to discover I'm your father?' He looked at me intently.

I bit my lip, deliberating how to reply to such a statement.

'I don't know. It's a lot to take in.' I said, still rather dubious.

Isaiah stared at me blankly and then began to nod. 'Of course, it must be a great shock for you.' He turned away and began strolling up and down the room, clasping his hands together. 'There's something else too, something you may find hard to believe.' He threw me a sideways glance and carried on nervously walking around the room.

I couldn't imagine anything more shocking that what he had just announced.

'What? I asked curiously.

He was hovering by the bookshelf, rearranging the books. 'I didn't used to live in these parts.'

'You come from another town?'

'No, no Effelia.' With a short laugh he carried on tidying the shelves. 'From another world, not another town.'

I stared at him in astonishment. 'Another world?'

'It seems such a long time ago now.' He spoke slowly as if choosing his words carefully. 'I decided many years ago I would rather spend my life here in Abercrombie than in that godforsaken place I used to reside in. When I fled my homeland, I was still a fairly young man but had no idea how old I actually was, as we don't count the years like you do here.' He looked over to me 'Time is a very complex thing that people struggle to understand, it has a mysterious quality and the pace of time differs in a variety of ways, depending on the world you live in.'

A recollection from the depths of my mind suddenly jolted to the forefront: I'd heard a very similar account regarding the enigma of time, but it seemed my brain wouldn't allow me further access to such information.

I gulped. 'Do go on.'

'I took a chance and travelled to your land, and as luck would have it, I only aged a little and caused minimal damage to my body.' He laughed ironically. 'Unfortunately, my limp returned from when I'd fallen from a tree as a young lad. But I was glad, as it reminds me that I'm really living instead of just existing.'

'But, but didn't you get homesick?' I asked, thinking of the first thing that popped into my mind.

'No, not one bit. The place I used to live was pure hell.' A look of torment appeared on his face. 'Besides, if I returned, I would almost certainly be put to death. Crossing over to another world is forbidden.'

'You must have had family there; don't you miss them?'

He suddenly roared with laughter and shook his head 'If you had a family like mine you would do anything to get away from them. When you came along, I felt god had granted me a second chance.' He stared fixedly at me. 'A new life with my darling daughter, and never once have I regretted my decision.' He came over and gently cupped my cheek with his hand. Tears were welling up in his eyes. 'So now you know why I've wished to be near you all these years.

I've only your very best interest at heart Effelia. Please have some faith in me.'

I stared at him and gulped. 'I'll try.' I said in a low voice.

There was a long a pause.

'You look tired Effelia. We shall talk some more a little later.'

I was dumbfounded by everything he had just told me, and couldn't seem to digest any of it, especially the part about me being his daughter. It seemed I had stepped into a strange dream, a dream where everything is muddled and wrong, and only on awaking would it all slot back into place. For now, I chose to put it to the back of my mind and concentrate on Mace instead.

'I need to know one more thing before you leave.'

'Certainly.' he replied, seeming pleased I was taking such an interest.

'You were going to tell me about Mace?'

His face dropped. 'Is that *boy* all you're bothered about after what I've just told you?' Going over towards the door he turned slightly towards me and snarled. 'You'll have to wait until tomorrow.'

I stared after him as he abruptly left the room.

Chapter 20

For a long while all I could do was lay there staring up at the ceiling in complete an utter bewilderment. I felt like a patient in The Manor who was stuck in a perpetual state of disorientation, incapable of accepting what was happening in the real world, as the real world was suddenly too difficult to cope with.

All these long years I had believed there was something odd about Isaiah, the way he hung about Rawlings all the time, taking an avid interest in everything I did, creeping around my Aunt with that smarmy smile upon his face. And now he had finally revealed the reason why...because he was my father. It all made perfect sense now, and yet I couldn't bring myself to accept it.

Suddenly I heard the doorbell being persistently rung, and then there were raised voices. I didn't bother to get up from the bed, what was the point when I wouldn't be able to see who was there, and I didn't have the energy to go and eavesdrop; there was little chance of hearing anything anyway. Isaiah must have slammed the door shut as I heard a loud bang and then someone started hammering upon the door and shouting. Deciding just to ignore it I closed my eyes and snuggled my face up against the pillow. My poor brain was muddled to such an extent that I embraced sleep gladly like an old friend, for it blocked out everything.

Isaiah returned one more time that day with some sandwiches and tea but seeing that I was still half asleep he didn't linger or say very much, for this I was glad about, as I wasn't ready for another of his odd revelations.

That following morning the sunlight streamed in through the window, escaping through the bars, and making shadowy patterns on the wall opposite. Dragging myself out of bed I walked slowly over to the en-suite and locked the door. Yet again the surge of water from the shower did little to eliminate my weariness. Afterward I dressed in my pyjamas and sat on the bed, combing my hair and trying without success to remove the mass of tangles. In a moment of madness, I had a strong desire to cut it short, just so it would be easier to manage, and besides it would be nice to have a different hairstyle for a change. Maybe Isaiah would lend me some scissors, I thought, laughing to myself, however in my mental state I had a feeling he wouldn't trust me with that type of weapon.

I heard movement at the door and Isaiah entered carrying a tray.

'Good morning Effelia, I trust you slept well?'

I stared at the wall of books in front of me. 'Not really.' I murmured, not wishing to appease him by answering yes.

'Well never mind eh, you have all the time in the world to rest.' Isaiah said, smiling.

I wondered what he meant by that remark. How much longer did he intend keeping me here like a prisoner.

'I think it would be wise of you to call the doctor so he can come and see that I'm well. I'm sure he and Aunt wouldn't be happy to know you've been locking me in this room Isaiah.'

He placed the tray down on the bedside table.

'Effelia, as I explained before, they are both more than aware of your situation and totally in agreement with this particular course of treatment.' He smiled wryly at me.

Without seeing Aunt or this Dr Stirling I had no way of verifying if what Isaiah said was true but my gut feeling told me it wasn't, as it seemed extremely peculiar they'd not yet come for a visit, and what kind of doctor would agree with locking someone in a room, it wasn't as if I was dangerous.

'Come on, eat up' He said, picking up the tray and laying it down beside me on the crumpled bed.

With little interest I stared at the food and drink in front of me.

'You were going to tell me about Mace.'

Isaiah didn't answer for a moment. He drew in his breath. 'Oh that.' he said sharply. 'I might have known that would interest you more than the fact I'm your father.' He sat down beside me and placed his clammy hand over mine. 'I'm sorry Effelia, but he's left town with that fiancée of his Moira, such a lovely, sweet girl. She has family east and they've bought a house together in that area, which they'll move into after they get married next month. He told me how he wishes you well.'

I felt severe stabs of pain shoot through me like a thousand arrows piercing my body.

Isaiah glanced at me sympathetically, waiting for my response.

'Oh, that all happened quick.' I said, my voice breaking up with emotion.

'Effelia, don't forget you were gone for two whole years, surely you didn't expect the boy to wait around for you to return home?'

'Well, no, but...'

Isaiah cut me off abruptly. 'After all, you were only just good friends with him.'

I stared nonplussed at the tray. 'Yes.'

Isaiah sat there looking at me as if trying to read my face. Patting my hand, he rose and walked over to the window.

'I think it's worked out rather well, don't you? He was peering out between the bars as if something had caught his attention. 'Good riddance, if you ask me.'

Suddenly I was furious with him. 'You've never liked Mace, have you? Why, I don't understand?'

Isaiah drew back from the window. 'Let's just say your life will be so much happier without him, believe me.'

'No, no it won't. Mace will always be my best friend and nothing will ever change that.' I yelled at him.

An evil laugh escaped Isaiah's lips. 'Oh, but it will. Now he's out the way nothing can hinder you.'

I could feel my face burning up with anger. 'It's Mace. Not *him* or *boy*, why can't you ever use his proper name?' I screamed at him.

He laughed again and swiftly made his way over to the door. He turned and glared at me. 'Because he's nothing to me, and is of no importance to our life.' 'Now get some rest. I shall return later and we can discuss more pressing issues.'

I sensed he was in a rush, and preoccupied with something he'd just seen out the window. As he left the room, I heard him lock the door behind him and hurry down the stairs. With difficulty I heaved myself off the bed and staggered across to the window. I could hear the murmur of voices from somewhere down in the garden, but couldn't see anyone as the shrubbery around the back door obscured my view. Isaiah's thundering voice came into earshot and it sounded like he was telling someone off, and at one point I thought I heard a woman but wasn't really sure. If only I could find a way to remove the bars and open the window, I thought. I could shout for help or even go so far as to jump out.

With any luck the bushes and shrubbery would cushion my fall. For one idiotic moment I examined the bars to see if there was any way I could remove them, but they looked completely new and extremely strong. With a deep sigh I gave up and flung myself down on the bed, nibbling on a piece of toast from the tray and drinking the lukewarm sugary tea.

I tried to take in what Isaiah had said but none of it made sense. Mace wouldn't just leave Abercrombie without saying goodbye, would he? However, then I thought back to the other day in the café, when I'd last spoken to him, how indifferent he'd acted towards me, it was like he was a stranger not the old Mace I had so loved. My eyes started to well up at the thought of never seeing him again. Everything in my life seemed to be becoming worse with every minute that ticked by. It was bad enough not seeing my Aunt, but now I also had to deal with Isaiah being my father, the loss of my best friend, and there was something else, something important, only I couldn't think what it was. A dull pain shot through my heart, and without warning tears started to flow down my face.

I was awoken by the sound of the key in the lock. With great difficulty I pulled myself up to a sitting position and stared blearily at Isaiah, who was carrying another tray of food.

With a look of concern, he came over towards the bed.

'I thought you may be hungry. I do hope you like fish?'

I positioned my pillow behind me so I was comfortable. The smell of the food wafted across the room, making me hungry.

'What time is it?'

'It's early evening Effelia.'

I stared at him in astonishment. 'But…. but I couldn't have been asleep all that time.'

'Well, you must have been tired.' He narrowed his eyes as he spotted the half-eaten piece of toast and untouched bowl of cereal on the bedside table. 'You must eat to keep your strength up Effelia.' With a huff he placed the dinner tray down on my lap. 'There's fish, buttered new potatoes, peas and a steaming cup of hot tea.' He pulled up the chair and sat next to me. 'I shall remain here until you've eaten every morsel and drank every drop of the delicious tea.' He smiled warmly at me as I began to eat.

'So, who was that you were speaking to earlier outside in the back garden?'

He looked suddenly shifty. 'Oh ah...no one of any consequence.' With a nervous laugh he gestured for me to carry on eating, and when he spoke again it was in a rushed voice, as if he was eager to change the subject. 'I have good news Effelia, your Aunt Constance is visiting you tomorrow.' He paused. 'Just for a little while.'

'Really?' I exclaimed happily.

'Yes. Now finish your food and drink your tea.' He smiled gently at me. 'You want to be well for when you see her, don't you?'

I suddenly wondered if he'd ever smiled at my mother like that. Sensing he wanted to talk more I decided now would be a good time to ask him about her. Knowing that Isaiah was my father and that he'd once known my mother, and loved her was an extremely peculiar feeling. Nevertheless, this man sitting before me could be the key to discovering my mother's whereabouts, and hopefully he could enlighten me on what she was really like. However, I was also frightened of what I might hear, as for years now I had held this imaginary picture of my ideal mother in my head: a strong, capable and courageous type of woman who was known for her kindness and sincerity. I would lay in bed at night successfully convincing myself of how she longed to be reunited with me and how she would spend days brooding over what might have been, bereft that we were parted from one another. Of course, this was all complete conjecture, the rambling thoughts of a young girl missing her mother, but it helped keep me sane through all those motherless years, and gave me faith. Therefore, if I were to suddenly hear something to the contrary, my ideal picture would be slashed to pieces, along with my heart.

'Would you tell me about my mother?' I blurted out the words in haste, and was unable to meet his gaze.

An uncomfortable silence followed.

Isaiah sighed and slowly walked over to the window. When he spoke, his voice was barely audible. 'I first met her in a dream.' He shook his head. 'Please don't ask me to explain as I'm not sure I can. I had no control over the invisible hand that guided me to your mother. All I had to do was fall asleep and there she would be, waiting patiently for me in our dream. We always met in the same garden, a garden not unlike the one at Rawlings, only this one went

216

on forever. I recall how we tried to reach the end of it but we never succeeded. This form of meeting carried on for a long while.' He paused, gently tapping on the bars of the window. 'She was so beautiful and vibrant it took my breath away. I'd never experienced such love and kindness in a person, and her laughter.' He lowered his eyes. 'She was always laughing.'

I sat there quietly, carefully taking in every single word he spoke, not wishing to interrupt just in case he stopped.

'As hard as we tried, we were unable to stop ourselves from falling in love with one another, and it wasn't long before we wished to meet in person. Had I known then that it was possible to travel to your world then I would have gladly done so.' He sighed deeply. 'But your mother was so eager to come and join me in my land, and foolishly I allowed her to.' He still faced the window, staring out at the rainy day, and when he spoke again his voice sounded sorrowful. 'She gave up everything to be with me, bravely travelling to my home and living amongst my people. We married, and for a while we were happy.' He bowed his head. 'But I knew there was a dark shadow lingering in the background. I knew what was coming and what was expected of her.' He turned and glanced at me. 'Please drink up your tea Effelia.'

'I gulped down the sickly-sweet tea in one go.

'What *was* expected of her?'

He started to briskly pace up and down the room. 'They insisted she take the tonic, just like everyone else and began badgering her relentlessly. I pleaded with them to wait until your mother had at least given birth before starting the medicine, and finally they reluctantly agreed.'

'What does the tonic do?' I asked curiously.

He looked over towards me dispassionately. 'It supposedly benefits our wellbeing, strengthening our minds and bodies. It is also thought to prolong our lives considerably. But what they don't tell you is that it has a dramatic side effect, for it destroys the spirit and dulls the senses until you become a shadow of your former self. By that time, it's too late and you're unaware of the changes. From then on you will be content to live your days in a pitiful existence.'

I looked at him in puzzlement. 'But what about you, didn't you have to take this tonic.'

He laughed quietly. 'Oh yes, but rare cases have shown the tonic to be ineffective. Luckily for me it didn't make any change to how I felt whatsoever, I was completely immune. Of course, I kept this fact to myself, because if the council members had known I'm sure they would have given me double doses, or some such thing.'

'So, then what happened?' I asked, trying to stifle a yawn.

His voice sank so low I had trouble understanding what he was saying.

'It was then I felt we had no choice but to leave and escape the misery before it was too late, as I couldn't bear the thought of your mother becoming one of them.' He hesitated, removing a piece of flick from his jumper. 'However, although I was eager to leave your mother was rather reluctant. Then I began to notice minor changes in her personality; she'd flare up at the slightest thing, becoming constantly sullen and irritable for no reason. First of all, I put it down to her pregnancy, but later I discovered she'd already been taking the cursed medicine.' His eyes shot to my half-eaten meal. 'For heaven's sake Effelia, finish your food.'

'I'm actually rather full.'

He looked infuriated. 'I won't tell you another word about your mother until your plate is cleared. You are under my care Effelia, and it's down to me to see you take care of yourself.'

Rather reluctantly I ate the last piece of fish, and then the potatoes.

'There.... happy?' I said with my mouthful. 'So, you were saying about my mother's odd behaviour after taking the tonic. Was this a normal side effect?'

He paused for a moment, looking deep in thought. 'No, not at all, I can only ascertain the tonic had an adverse reaction on her because she was carrying you at the time. All the other tonic takers behaved as expected, apart from the ones who...'

I stared at him. 'The ones who what?'

'Oh, it's nothing.'

'So, my mother *was* forced to take the tonic early? I asked, confused.

'No, no.' He said abruptly. 'Apparently your mother asked to start the course of medicine, believing it would be beneficial to the pregnancy. You see they'd already got to her and corrupted her mind.'

I stared at him in disbelief. 'But.... but then why did she return to Rawlings?'

He scratched his head, looking deep in concentration. 'Well, you see it all came about because of that cursed book.'

'Book, what book?'

'It's rumoured that there is a book in existence, an ancient book that has fully detailed accounts on gateways to other worlds. Your mother got it into her sweet little head that it was hidden away somewhere in the depths of Rawlings, and took it upon herself to seek it out. Without given a thought to her condition she left in the dead of night and travelled back home.'

Suddenly my head began to spin. 'Did she travel home through a gateway?'

He narrowed his eyes at me then chuckled. 'Why yes Effelia, of course. How do you suppose one can reach other worlds, by train?' His whole body began to shake with laughter, and for while he was unable to continue speaking. 'Some people call them portals, or magical doorways, but ultimately all of them mean the same thing.'

I gazed over to the window, lost in thought. 'So...so did you go after my mother?'

'Yes of course, but unfortunately I was delayed. The committee members were furious when they discovered your mother had left, so I had to wait for the right moment.'

With a blank stare I nodded at him.

I couldn't help but find it odd how the conversation we were having seemed to carry on quite naturally as if we were discussing an everyday topic, something mundane like the weather. However, although I was a little shocked by his words, I was not completely astonished. Surely, he must find it peculiar how I seemed to be taking all of this in my stride and why I hadn't laughed out loud at his preposterous story. Suddenly I was sorely tempted to ask him the name of this place he and my mother had fled from, as for some unknown reason I sensed it was the same place someone else had mentioned, someone I couldn't remember the name of.

'Effelia?'

I'd been so immersed in my thoughts that for a moment I'd forgotten he was there. My eyes flickered to his.

'Yes?'

'Would you like me to stop, you look so weary.'

'No, no please carry on.'

He sighed heavily. 'Well, when I arrived at your home your mother had already given birth. Afterwards, she cruelly abandoned you and returned through the gateway. Thankfully you were safe and well and in the care of your Aunt.'

I watched as he rather hurriedly began clearing away the breakfast things from the bedside table, clattering them loudly onto the tray with the other crockery.

'What about the book, do you think my mother ever located it?'

'For some time, I greatly feared she had. But as the years passed by, I became less fretful.' He lowered his eyes. 'If that book had reached Hartland, I'm certain we would know about it by now.'

My eyes glazed over. Hartland that was it, that was the name I was trying to think of. But who else had spoken about it?

'That's enough for now.' He slowly limped towards the door with the tray. 'I shall let you sleep Effelia.'

'Wait a moment, what about this book, is it dangerous or something?'

Without looking at me, he stopped for a moment and spoke in a low voice. 'If the book really exists then it *is* a danger to us all, for if the people of Hartland were to obtain it then pure evil would undoubtedly cross over into this world.'

For an instant I imagined the whole of Abercrombie being taken over by a dark presence, forced into taken a potion that would destroy their minds. I thought how incredibly farcical this sounded, so unreal. But then everything Isaiah had just said about my mother seemed absurd, and my heart told me it was all lies, perhaps even the part about him being my father was untrue.

I leant forward on the bed. 'If you truly loved my mother then why didn't you warn her about this dreadful tonic before she travelled to Hartland and married you?'

He swung round to face me. 'Just like you Effelia, your mother could be very stubborn when she wished to be.' With a deep sigh he stared gloomily down at the tray. 'Despite mentioning the effects of the tonic on numerous occasions she was still adamant on joining me. Perhaps in my foolishness I believed it wouldn't change her, or that the council members would leave her alone because she was an outsider. And well you see...'

'Yes?'

'Well, I wasn't going to mention this but your mother felt stifled and unhappy at Rawlings, she detested her childhood home and would frequently say how it should be torn down. She wanted to spread her wings, not fester in the same big old house for the rest of her life.' His eyes looked pitifully into mine. 'I'm afraid your mother was also desperate to get away from your Aunt. She told me how needy Constance could be, and far too irritating.'

'No, no it's all lies.' I said shaking my head vehemently.

'My dear Effelia, I can assure you it is not. It would be prudent of you to accept the truth, as to dwell on the matter will only cause you heartache, and will certainly not aid your recovery. Your mother is of no consequence to either of us now, and you should just forget about her.' Yet again he limped towards the door. 'Now if you'll excuse me, I have work to do.'

'You can say what you like Isaiah, but I can't forget about her, she's my mother.'

He turned to face me again, his eyes blazing with anger. 'Well suit yourself Effelia, but you'll never see her again. And please don't take me for a fool. I know where you've been these last two years. I know everything, and there's no way you're going back. If it means locking you in this room for the rest of your life, so be it. You're not leaving again, not this time.'

I stared at him in complete horror. 'What...what do you mean?' I lifted myself off the bed and stumbled across the room, screaming at him. 'Isaiah?'

Ignoring me he reached for the doorknob and nearly dropped the tray. Cursing underneath his breath he awkwardly opened the door and stomped out, slamming it shut with his foot. Just as my shaking hand touched the doorknob, I heard the key being turned in the lock, and then the bolt was pulled across.

Chapter 21

For some time, I lay on the bed, dazed and confused, my eyes smarting with tears, tears over not knowing where I'd been for the past two years, tears over the loss of Mace and tears over my seemingly heartless mother. To hear Isaiah speak of her in such a way unnerved me. I wondered if she was completely emotionless, and incapable of thinking of me, or if perhaps there were moments when she'd be sitting somewhere and quite unexpectedly, I would pop into her head. I suddenly pictured her stepping through the frame of her portrait, the portrait I had painted depicting a loving mother, but there would no tenderness in her eyes; instead, they would be cold eyes, cold and dead.

Since arriving at Isaiah's house all this new information was becoming far too disturbing and complicated for me to handle; it felt like a seed of turmoil was growing slow and steadily at the back of my mind, and soon it would overwhelm me and send me into the realms of madness. They would cart me off then, to The Manor, and I would never be seen again.

As the waves of tiredness washed over me, I heard the distance sound of a bell, the front doorbell again, I think, and then there was a loud rapping. I closed my eyes and slept.

In my dream I was lying on some soft grass and gazing up at a pure azure sky. Bright yellow butterflies fluttered around me like petals torn from buttercups by a sudden gust of wind, and like a trail of gold they flew past and up over a hill. Curious as to their destination I rose from the ground, and with ease I bounded after them. Within just a few short leaps I found myself in the middle of a mushroom field. A potent aroma filled my nostrils and my head began to swim. Somewhere at the back of my mind I had a vague notion that I shouldn't be here, that I'd been warned, but it was too late to run away now and too soon to leave. I had to find those butterflies even if my life depended on it, they would not evade me. I tiptoed gently amongst the dome- capped mushrooms that stretched out before me like an endless sea of mottled brown and crimson. A flash of vivid yellow caught my eye and I let out a squeal as I realised my little butterfly friends were now hovering in front of me like a curtain swaying in the breeze. Reaching out I glided my hand in between them and they flittered away.

'Don't leave.' I cried. 'I never meant to frighten you.'

But the butterflies had gone and with them they took my joy and replaced it with a feeling of melancholy. A cold wind swept my hair and suddenly the ground was shaking. I tumbled down and looked aghast at the sight before me. The mushrooms were growing at a tremendous rate and were soon as tall as trees. A dank fog was moving in from the north and the stench of earthy moss hung in the air, making me more forlorn than ever. There was a shadowy figure emerging from the thick mist, no larger than a child; I noticed a pair of little wooden feet pattering along the ground towards me, then I saw the smile, the crooked grin that sent the fear of god into me.

'Greetings Miss Farraday, have you missed me?' He growled.

'Gilbert.' I whispered.

Just as I was about to turn and run something caught my arm, a woman with a face almost identical to my own was clutching me. When she spoke, her voice was soft and calming.

'Don't be afraid.' She smiled gently. 'It's me, Florentine.'

For a moment I stood there transfixed, staring into her face in utter shock and bewilderment. Then I came to my senses and wrenched my arm from her hold and started to run for my life, but my legs seemed heavy and I had to drag myself along. I could hear Gilbert's gruff tone from a distance away, and prayed he or the strange woman weren't chasing after me.

'You can run but you can't hide. I shall find you mistress Farraday.'

My nerves were in tatters as panic took over, and I whimpered with fear as I stumbled blindly forward in the fog. An eerie silence descended upon the field, as if the entire world around me had ceased to exist. The giant mushroom came from nowhere, swooping down to capture me within its folds, then very slowly it began to devour me, until I'd been completely absorbed into its stem.

I jerked awake, drenched in sweat.

'It was only a dream, just a stupid dream.' I muttered, trying to calm myself.

Reaching over I switched on the bedside lamp and took a gulp of water from the glass on the table. It was then I noticed something out the corner of my eye sitting at the foot of the bed. Tentatively I turned towards it and screamed at the top of my voice. It was Gilbert. He was sitting there gawping at me with his grotesque wide eyes. Dropping the glass, I shot out of bed and stumbled across the room.

'No, keep away from. Leave me alone.' I yelled.

Rushing to the en-suite, I entered and slammed the door behind me, locking myself in. I crouched on the floor, shaking uncontrollably. It must have been some time before I heard the handle being turned.

'Effelia? It's me Isaiah. Is everything alright?'

I sat there in a trance like state, and when I spoke my voice sounded strangled. 'On...on my bed, there's something on my bed.' I gulped. 'The dummy...Gilbert.'

For a while Isaiah didn't reply. I put my ear up against the door.

'Isaiah?' I whispered in a croaky voice.

The sudden sound of his bellowing voice startled me and I jumped in fright.

'There's nothing here Effelia, nothing at all.'

'Are, are you sure?'

'Yes, it was just an awful nightmare. Do come out.'

Slowly unlocking the door, I shakily went back into the bedroom and peered in disbelief at the bed. The dummy had gone.

'See, nothing to worry about.' Isaiah said with a smirk. 'Now hop back into bed and get some sleep. Don't forget you have a special visitor tomorrow.' He said, picking up the glass from the floor. Whistling to himself he limped to the doorway. 'Sweet dreams dear daughter.'

I could hear him chuckling to himself as he left the room. What a twisted individual he was, I thought to myself angrily, to laugh at me like that when I'd just been scared out of my wits. Perhaps the trip here all those years ago had done permanent damage to his brain.

Rather nervously I clambered back into bed and tried to relax. For a moment I pondered over the dummy, trying to work out what had just happened; maybe my eyes had been playing tricks on me in the dark. As a child I recollect being scared by the shadowy branches of the trees from outside my bedroom window, I imagined them to be the gnarled claws of a vile creature trying to reach me. My Aunt would come in and reassure me and say it was all merely in my imagination. Dear Aunt, I thought, how wonderful it will be to see her tomorrow. I literally couldn't wait.

Isaiah flung the door open.

'Good morning Effelia, I trust you slept well?' he sniggered. Here, drink your tea it will wake you up.' He held out the cup. 'Come on, do take it.'

I eyed him dubiously and heaved myself up into a sitting position.

'So, what time will my Aunt be arriving?' Reluctantly I took the cup. 'She *is* still coming, isn't she?'

'Well of course, Constance is on her way here now.' He said gleefully, clapping his hands together. 'It will just be a short visit. After last night's shenanigans my concerns for your health have escalated, and I may have to call Dr Stirling out.'

My cup clattered loudly onto the saucer.

'No, no please don't.' I forced a smile at him. 'It was nothing really.' I took a gulp of my tea. 'I'm feeling so much better now, and will discuss with Aunt about returning to Rawlings.' My gaze held his. 'I'm sure she'll eagerly agree with me that home is the best medicine.'

'Indeed.' He said coolly, looking intently out the window. 'Now drink up before it gets cold.'

With a sigh I drank the sickly-sweet tea.

He limped over and snatched the cup from my hand, and then made his way towards the door, where he hovered for a moment.

'Oh, and Effelia, I wouldn't advise you to say anything to your dear Aunt about me being your father, not yet anyway. In fact, you mustn't breathe a word to her about anything we've discussed. It's best to leave your Aunt Constance in the dark about such matters. Don't you think?'

'Well, I...I don't know.' I said, hesitantly.

He paused, his hand on the door handle and then spoke words that chilled me to the bone.

'I've always thought how treacherous that staircase at Rawlings could be, haven't you Effelia? I mean if a person were to fall down and break their neck...well it would be a most unfortunate accident, wouldn't it? He sneered and left the room.

I sat there staring into space, processing the realisation of Isaiah's words. Would he really harm my poor Aunt or was it just an empty threat; either way I had no choice but to keep silent. With a yawn I leant back against the pillows. Perhaps I should have got up and taken a shower before Aunt arrived but my body felt so heavy with fatigue that I just wanted to rest.

The sweet smell of marigolds filled my nostrils and I blearily opened my eyes and looked up to see my Aunt sitting beside me on a chair. Her face looked gaunt and her eyes were full of anguish.

'Oh Effie, you poor thing.' She bent over the bed and gently hugged me. 'Did I awaken you?'

'Oh Aunt, I'm so happy to see you.' I said tearfully, clinging to her. 'How I've missed you.'

She drew back and patted me on the hand. 'My dear, I've been so worried. When Isaiah told me you'd returned from your little trip overseas I was so relieved, as all this time I...I thought something terrible had happened to you.' Her face became rather stern. 'Two long years Effie without a single word, no phone call, or letter. Have you any idea what you put me through young lady.'

I stared at her and gulped. 'I'm so sorry Aunt, but for some inexplicable reason I must have completely lost track of the time.' I uttered rather croakily. 'Had I realised how long I'd been away I would have found a way to reach you.'

'Where exactly did you go overseas Effie? I did ask Mace but he didn't have a clue.'

Stifling a yawn, I looked beseechingly at her, not knowing how to respond. I wanted to elaborate but how could I explain where I'd been when I didn't even know myself. Isaiah knew, he'd told me so yesterday in a fit of temper, before storming out the room.

'Please Aunt, but do you mind awfully if we don't discuss it?'

Her eyes widened as she stared at me, then slowly she nodded her head.

'No dear, if you'd rather not, I understand. Isaiah says you're doing brilliantly and should be able to come home in a couple of days. Isn't that the best news?' She uttered, gently stroking my hair. 'He told me you've been having hallucinations about that old dummy.' She shook her head. 'I can't tell you the havoc it's caused over the years. Your poor mother had many a nightmare over Gilbert.'

I looked at her in amazement. 'My mother used to dream about the dummy?'

'Oh yes, quite frequently. I suppose it would have been wise of me to mention it before, but...but for some reason it happened to slip my mind.'

I studied her face as a lost look came about her, as if she was suddenly in a world of her own.

'Are you alright Aunt?'

'What...oh yes dear.' She smiled at me and sighed heavily. 'Sorry dear, it was all such a long time ago, I have trouble remembering anything connected with your mother. Lord only knows where the dummy went, he's probably tucked away somewhere in the attic.'

'No, I don't think so Aunt.' I lifted my head off the pillow and stared into her face. ''I...I saw Gilbert in this very room, last night. He was perched at the end of the bed.' I said in a low voice. 'I've tried to tell myself it wasn't real, but it was real Aunt, the dummy was really here.'

We gazed at one another in an uncomfortable silence.

'Effie really, if only you could hear yourself. What you're saying is quite preposterous.'

As I rested my head back against the pillow, I observed how oddly she was peering at me, the way one looks at someone who is a little insane. I recall her displaying a similar expression when she looked at Edgar Mitford, a rather peculiar, but harmless old gentlemen, whom Aunt befriended about five years ago, after she took pity on him. He was soon following her about at all the church functions and would tell everyone he was living at Rawlings with her. In the end she had to have a quiet word with him and soon after he threw himself off Abercrombie Bridge and drowned; my Aunt always blamed herself for his death, and no matter how much we tried to tell her it wasn't her fault she just wouldn't have it. Evidently, according to Isaiah, it was common knowledge that poor Edgar had suicidal tendencies, and he'd already attempted to take his life, several times in the past.

'Aunt I swear it's the truth.'

'Balderdash.' She chuckled. 'How could Gilbert possibly have got over to Isaiah's house?'

'Perhaps he escaped from the attic and sneaked over here to torment me. Or...or maybe Isaiah brought the dummy here.'

Now that's enough of this foolish talk Effie.' She said sternly. 'You're not yourself my dear.' Reaching out she straightened the blanket. 'I do recall your mother grew out of the nightmares, or rather found a way of dealing with the problem. Somehow, she was able to turn the nightmares into happy dreams. And, in the end Gilbert became her friend. So, you see dear, there's no need to be afraid of him. Gilbert is just a silly old dummy.' She patted me on the arm. 'And I know you can overcome this, just like your mother.' She smiled lovingly at me.

'Dear Aunt, you always make me feel better.' I said, looking warmly at her.

The mere fact that my mother had also been plagued with the same night terrors cheered me up considerably. I didn't feel isolated anymore, and if it wasn't just me having the nightmares that also meant I wasn't going insane after all.

'But I do wish you'd told me ages ago about my mother and Gil...Gilbert.' I stuttered. Even just saying his name sent a shiver down my spine. 'It would have helped me.'

She squeezed my hand. 'I know dear, I should have. But you should have confided in me too. Anyway, I promise to go into the attic and have a search for the dummy, just to put your mind at ease.' Her voice suddenly sounded faint and a haunted look appeared in her eyes. 'I'm sure your mother would know where the old toy is located, if she was here.'

For one second, I was tempted to tell her about my mother, how she was far away and how her mind had been possessed by a dreadful tonic. But it sounded so utterly ridiculous I was certain Aunt would never believe me anyway. Besides, I couldn't risk it, not with Isaiah. He probably had his ear up against the door.

'So, how are you keeping Aunt?' I asked, changing the subject.

'Oh, you know, the usual aches and pains, but on the whole I can't complain.' She smiled meekly at me. 'All the better for having my niece home.'

I lay there frantically trying to keep awake, and for a brief moment my eyelids closed up.

'Oh, dear Effie you look so worn.' She reached over to the bedside table. 'Here, I almost forgot about this.' She held the cup to my lips. 'Isaiah made you another tea, he says it's imperative you keep your fluids up.'

I took a gulp from the cup.

'I shall leave you in peace dear, so you can get some rest.'

'No Aunt, please don't go yet.' I pleaded with her. 'Can't you take me home with you?'

She looked at me and sighed 'Oh Effie, I would love to but Isaiah and Dr Stirling think it best you remain here for at least a few more days.'

I grabbed her arm. 'No, no Aunt, please. I know what's best for me, not them. And anyway, have you actually met this Dr Stirling, does he really exist?' My voice sounded flustered.

'Well, no, I haven't actually met him but Isaiah says he's an excellent doctor and…'

I interrupted abruptly. 'Why do you always have to take Isaiah's side, have you any idea how irritating it is?'

My Aunt looked suddenly distressed. 'Effie really, Isaiah's right about your mood swings.' She rose from the chair. 'You should be thanking Isaiah for all he's done for you. I certainly don't know where I'd be without him. He's been my saviour these past few years why you've been flitting about overseas, without a care in the world, and without a thought for me.'

I watched as she stood there, swaying slightly. Suddenly I was full of remorse, and looking at her I realised just how frail and vulnerable she was looking. I wanted to wrap my arms around her.

'I'm sorry Aunt.' I paused. 'Please forgive me, I'm not myself.'

She looked coldly at me for a moment. 'No, you're not. The Effie I know wouldn't have sold her mother's portrait.'

I cast my mind back to that day at Rawlings when I'd fallen asleep by the unlit fire. The portrait had been missing.

'But…but Aunt I didn't sell it, I would *never* do such a thing.'

'Hush, don't fret over it Effie. You can always paint another one.' Her face broke into a smile. 'You're excellent at capturing a subject's likeness from memory.'

I tried to heave myself up a little but just didn't have the strength.

'When exactly did I decide to sell the painting?' I asked, looking rather perplexed.

Her hand rested on my shoulder. 'Isaiah and I have had a long time to mull over what's happened to you Effie and we've both come to the conclusion that your breakdown begun just after your art exhibition. It explains why you suddenly left home, the home you love and would never dream of leaving under normal circumstances.' She sighed despairingly. 'Obviously you can't remember but on the day you went away you had a quiet word with Isaiah and told him you'd changed your mind about your mother's portrait, and wanted to be rid of it. A few days later he got in touch with that lovely gentleman from the exhibition and sold it to him.'

I stared at her blankly. Of course, I thought to myself, it had to be Isaiah. I was beginning to think that man was to blame for everything.

'But...but Aunt you should have stopped Isaiah.'

'Isaiah assured me it's what you wished for. Perhaps I should have stopped him but as you were missing at the time, I was too distraught to argue.'

I lowered my eyes dejectedly. 'I see.'

She smiled sadly then reached into her handbag. 'It's water under the bridge now Effie, so put it to the back of your mind.' Leaning over she passed me something. 'Here, Isaiah told me not to give you anything sweet as you're on a specific food programme.' She said in a low tone. 'But what harm can one bar of your favourite chocolate do.' With a giggle she glanced towards the door and then back to me. 'Best hide it under the covers.' She whispered.

'Thank you, Aunt.' I said sleepily, putting the bar under the blanket. I gave her a weak smile as she bent over and hugged me tightly.

The door creaked open and Isaiah came limping in. It was then I observed he'd not locked it. I suppose Aunt would have found it rather odd if he had.

'Nap time Effelia.' He said in a loud irritating voice. 'You must be extremely tired.'

My Aunt pulled back from me and looked at Isaiah. 'Yes, Effie can hardly keep her eyes open, and she looks so pale.'

'Indeed. Her complexion is a little sallow. Unlike yourself Constance, you look absolutely radiant.' Isaiah said, with a glint in his eye.

A school girlish laugh erupted from her mouth. 'Oh Isaiah, you're such a flatterer.'

I turned away in disgust. It always astonished me that my Aunt couldn't see through the absurd pretence. Maybe if I told her he was my father she may change her tune, but I very much doubt it, in fact if anything it might make matters worse; I imagine she would accept his claim without any proof and would ask that he moved into Rawlings, so we could be one big happy family. His constant visits were bad enough and I shuddered at the mere thought of him actually living at the house.

'Well goodbye Effie.' She kissed me on the forehead.

'Must you go Aunt?'

'You'll be home soon dear, very soon indeed.' Her eyes turned to him. 'Won't she Isaiah?'

'Yes, yes.' He said abruptly. With a forced laugh he took my Aunt's arm and gently guided her away from me. 'I'll see you out Constance.'

'Bye Aunt.'

She turned and smiled tentatively at me.

Isaiah gave her a gentle nudge out the door. 'See you in one moment Constance. Oh, and watch your step, we don't want you careering down the stairs now do we?' With a short laugh he turned and stared at me then limped back towards the bed, peering at the cup on my bedside table. 'Please drink the remainder of your tea Effelia. Mr Sandman is waiting for you to slip off to dreamland.' He stood there and smiled slyly whilst I finished the drink. 'You never know you may see your precious Gideon.' Roaring with laughter he left the room and locked the door.

A sharp pain rocketed through my body. Gideon? Why did that name sound so familiar, and why did I have the sudden urge to weep? In a fit of despair, I buried my face into the pillow.

From downstairs I could hear the faint murmur of voices but I couldn't catch what was being said. No doubt it was my Aunt and Isaiah discussing my health. The front door shut and then a while later the telephone rang, and I heard him yelling down the phone at someone.

My eyes were so heavy with tiredness that I knew in a few moments I would be fast asleep. However, I was also extremely hungry, and decided to eat the chocolate my Aunt had given me. Before I knew it, I had devoured the entire bar. After disposing of the wrapper underneath the bed, I lay back ready for my nap, expecting to fall asleep without any trouble, however for some reason an acute feeling of nausea was rising up inside of me. I must have tossed and turned for some time before dragging myself out of bed and stumbling like a sleepwalker to the bathroom, where I immediately vomited down the toilet. I sat on the bathmat, my head leaning up against the side of the basin, then after being sick once more I crawled on my hands and knees back to bed. Perhaps the combination of sugary tea and rich dark chocolate was too much, I thought to myself, as apparently, I *was* on a special diet. Whatever the reason it soon became clear that I was no longer tired; my head felt a little heavy but the awful lethargy had diminished considerably. After a shower I cleaned my teeth and put on a fresh pair of pyjamas, then went and gazed out the barred window.

My thoughts turned to my Aunt, and how lovely it was to see her. In a few short days I'd be back with her at Rawlings, and my life would return to normal. I could put all the unpleasantness of the past few days behind me, and no longer would I have to constantly see the odious face of Isaiah. Oh, he would visit as usual, of that I had little doubt, but I would make myself conspicuous. There would be no more preposterous discussions about him being my father, and if he dared mention it to my Aunt I would do my utmost to make her see it wasn't true, after all there was no real proof.

My eyes were drawn to the empty cup on the bedside table and that's when it dawned on me: It was the tea that had been making me so tired, that sickly sweet tea; Isaiah must have been slipping some type of sleeping draught into my drinks and then disguising the taste with heaps of sugar; that would explain why I kept dropping off to sleep all the time. It seemed so obvious now, and I cursed myself for being so slow to realise. He must have drugged me that day at Rawlings as well, and that's how he brought me here so easily. I suddenly wondered just how dangerous he really was, and what he expected to gain from keeping me here. A chill swept over my body as I recall him threatening to lock me away in this room for the rest of my life. What was this mysterious place he didn't want me returning to?'

Isaiah didn't come and see me again for the rest of the day. I imagine he thought I'd be in a deep slumber till morning. The urge to bang on the door and yell was very tempting but I knew it would give the game away. So instead, I tiptoed quietly across the room to the bookshelf. I was dismayed to find mostly children's books, along with slushy romance novels, but eventually I found a half decent thriller. After clambering back into bed, I got comfy and read for a long while before eventually drifting off to sleep.

In my dream the trees were so tall I'm sure they reached the sky. I craned my neck and stared in wonder at them. Suddenly the ground beneath my feet began to shake and I fell back onto the grass. My mouth fell open as I spotted a pair of tree trunks a little way in front of me, moving forward like two gigantic legs, and attached to the legs was a wooden body, which had an abnormally large head. It was Gilbert, and he was singing. With one of his almighty branchlike hands, he scooped me up and elevated me so I was level with his grinning face.

'Greeting Miss Farraday, I'm so glad you're finally home.
You shouldn't go a wandering in places unsafe to roam.
Pay attention now, I don't mean to be unkind, for in my mind
there lies a clue to something you must find.
So, wake up, wake up you weary child, your hair's untidy and
extremely wild.
If my grasp grows loose, you'll tumble to the ground and you will
be in misery now that you have been found.'

His mouth creaked as it opened wide and to my alarm, I saw he was about to devour me. I could smell his rancid breath, and observed his fang like teeth, and as he moved me nearer. I let out a piercing scream. I shut my eyes, waiting for death. Without warning I began falling, down and down, for what seemed like an eternity, until finally I landed on something soft. Gasping I opened my eyes and realised it was the mattress. I leapt out of the bed and ran across the room, my heart thumping violently in my chest. Almost immediately my eyes darted to the foot of the bed, fearing that my dummy friend would be sitting there with his atrocious grin, but to my absolute relief there was nothing there.

Despite the nightmare of last night, I still awoke that morning feeling invigorated, and ready to face the world. The knowledge that I was returning home in a day or two made everything bearable, however I still had a niggling doubt in my mind that it was all too good to be true, and the reality was that Isaiah had no intention of setting me free from this room. Trying not to dwell on these negative thoughts I clambered swiftly out of bed and went to peer through the barred window. My gaze travelled to the fields in the distance where cattle were grazing. Suddenly I saw the sun emerge through a gap in the clouds, and I stood there transfixed as it highlighted the scenery in different shades, slowly moving across the landscape like a hand of beaming brightness. It filled me with a strange sense of longing, an instinctive urge to be one with nature, and lose myself in all of its grandeur.

Hearing a loud tap on the door I quickly leapt back into bed and pulled the covers over me. Isaiah entered humming a tune, and carrying a tray, just like always.

'Good morning Effelia.' He stopped and stared at me. 'How alert you look today, less pale.' Still looking at me he placed the tray of scrambled eggs and a cup of tea down on the bedside table. 'So, are you feeling better?'

'Yes, less tired.' My eyes widened in alarm as I realised what I'd just said. Allowing him to think I was *less tired* would make him wonder why the drugged tea was no longer affecting me. My face grew red as I spotted him studying me closely. 'But...but I'm still extremely lethargic and just want to sleep all the time.'

His eyes travelled to the cup on the tray. 'Yes, well that is to be expected Effelia.' With a smile he handed me the tea. 'Here, drink up.'

My face became grim as I eyed the cup of tea, wondering how I could avoid drinking it. I could feel his eyes upon me, waiting for me to take a sip. I was just about to accidentally let the cup slip from my grasp when we heard the chime of the doorbell.

Isaiah mumbled something underneath his breath as he walked away from the bed, and then paused by the window. 'Oh, whoever it is they can go away.' He grumbled, glaring at the cup of tea in my hand. 'Well come on Effelia drink up, it's not poison.'

The doorbell sounded again, persistently.

'You really should go and see who it is Isaiah, it maybe urgent. It could be something to do with my Aunt.'

He stood there for a while, staring at me morosely. 'Indeed.' Turning on his heel he marched to the door. 'I'll be back in a few moments.'

As soon as he exited the room and locked the door I darted out of bed, went to the bathroom and swiftly poured the tea down the basin. As I made my way back to the bedroom, I heard him shouting at someone again, and then the front door was slammed. Swiftly I placed the empty cup back on the tray and got back into bed. It wasn't long before I heard him stomping back up the stairs.

'Bothersome people.' He exclaimed loudly as he came back into the room, holding another cup. 'Salesmen again Effelia, of the most irritating kind.' Almost immediately he spotted the empty cup on the tray. 'I had an inkling you might drink the tea whilst I was gone, so I took the liberty of bringing you a refill.' Without waiting for a reply, he handed me the cup. 'Well, what do you say?'

'Thanks.' I said rather sullenly.

'Oh, do cheer up and please try to be civil.' He said, looking agitated. 'Were you troubled by another nightmare last night, I did hear you screaming at one point. Was it about that ghastly dummy friend of yours? Your mother used to experience very similar dreams; you know.' He limped over and locked the door, placing the key into his trouser pocket. 'What a pest that Gilbert is.'

I glowered at him but said nothing.

He drew up the chair and sat down. 'I understand if you don't wish to talk about it. On a brighter note, you must have been overjoyed at seeing your Aunt yesterday.'

'Yes, yes I was rather. I'm greatly looking forward to joining her at Rawlings, so we can get back to normal.'

'Yes, I understand completely. A couple more months and you'll be as right as rain and back at your beloved home.'

I looked at him in horror. 'You mean a few days, not months.' I exclaimed as a rising sense of dread began creeping over me.

'No Effelia, I never said it would be days, and besides you need more time to recuperate' He reached for the tray and placed it on my lap. 'Now eat up, and drink the delicious tea.'

'No, no it was definitely days. That's what you told my Aunt.'

He laughed. 'Well obviously Constance misheard, her hearing's not what it used to be, you know. Either that or you have become confused, it's a very common occurrence during a breakdown.'

In a daze I shakily placed the cup down onto the tray. '*Please* stop telling me I've had a breakdown.' Suddenly something inside of me snapped and I got hold of the tray and hurled it across the room, where it hit the wall underneath the window with a loud crash before falling onto the carpet. 'I know you're lying to me Isaiah, that's all you *ever* do.' I shrieked. 'You're a horrid man who takes pleasure in tormenting people.' I bent forward and covered my face with my hands.'

There was a silence for a moment and I very slowly glanced up at him. I was surprised to see how composed he appeared.

'Feeling better now are we Effelia.' He said in a stern voice. 'This behaviour really won't do you know. You're obviously full of anger and confusion, and that's totally understandable.' He lowered his eyes. 'But I am your father, so please treat me with some respect.'

I shook my head. 'You don't deserve respect.'

'Oh, I do young lady.' He frowned. 'Never mind, all this upset will soon be over Effelia, believe me, and then we can all get back to our normal life at Rawlings.'

'*We*? Isaiah, you don't live at Rawlings, you live here.'

'Slip of the tongue.' He said looking shifty. 'Anyway, I was just about to tell you about my trip.'

'What trip?' I snapped at him.

'This very Sunday I will administer the next stage of your recovery, which will involve me journeying to a certain destination.'

'Whatever are you blabbering on about?' I said fed up with the way he twisted his words.

He paused for a short while, as if preparing himself for what he was about to say.

'I'm going to destroy the gateway. The link will be severed once and for all.' He rubbed his hands together in glee, looking jubilant.

'The, the gateway' I said in a distant voice. 'What gateway?'

'It may surprise you to learn Effelia that it hasn't just been your mother and I who've used this means of transportation, you also have travelled through a gateway, when you went to the other world.'

I pulled back the covers and walked unsteadily across to the bookshelf. Somewhere locked away in my head was a faded memory trying to escape, a memory of another time and place.

'Don't worry it's perfectly natural you can't remember, in fact it's rather incredible how one so swiftly forgets.' He laughed. 'I was prepared for it, and on the day I arrived here in this world I wrote down all the relevant facts of my past life, as well as my potion recipes. Failing to do so would have resulted in my entire memories of my old home vanishing within as little as a few days.' He paused, picking up the thriller novel that must have dropped onto the floor. 'Been reading have we Effelia?'

I gulped. 'Well...yes, I managed to read one paragraph before falling asleep, if you must know.'

He eyed me suspiciously. 'I'm surprised you have the energy to read at all Effelia. This breakdown would have made you extremely fatigued. In fact, you should be resting in bed this very second.'

Pretending to be exhausted I nodded at him then hobbled back to the bed, slowly clambering under the bedcovers. 'You were saying about your memories vanishing.'

He glared at me without speaking for a second before limping over to the bookshelf and placing the thriller novel back amongst the other books.

'Yes, I have to refer to my notes nearly every day so I don't forget, although sometimes I wonder why I bother, as I've no plans to ever return to that rotten life.' Suddenly he seemed pensive and rather sad. 'You see Effelia, whilst you were in the other world you would have forgotten everything about your Aunt Constance and Rawlings, and me, but now you're back in your rightful home you've forgotten everything about the other place. Although it's a cruel irony, it does prove that we're not meant to travel from world to world.' With a sigh he began picking up the broken crockery from the floor and putting it on the tray. 'What a dreadful mess you've made.'

'Surely I didn't really go to this other world, it all sounds too nonsensical to be true.'

'Oh, but it is true Effelia.'

'How do you know?'

Widening his eyes in amusement he chuckled. 'Let's just say someone I'm acquainted with provided me with the information.'

I didn't see the point of asking him who, as I'm sure he wouldn't let me know, and I couldn't for the life of me think who it could be.

But what about this Gideon, I still remember him a little.' I muttered.

'You only remember him because I mentioned him to you yesterday, and it triggered your memory, but by tomorrow you will have forgotten his very existence, and he will fade from your mind's eye forever.'

'I...I think I used to dream about him. But since being back home they seemed to have stopped.' I stared at him. 'Why do you suppose that is?'

'I really can't say Effelia.' He scratched his head. 'Perhaps the dreams have stopped because he is no longer with us.'

'What...what do you mean?'

'I *mean* Gideon is dead.'

I stared into his smug looking face. 'You don't know that, you're only guessing.'

'Well yes, but that would explain why he never visits you anymore in your dreams. Or maybe he just no longer wishes you in his life.' With a casual laugh he shrugged his shoulders. 'It's for the best anyway, because you'll never see him again.'

On impulse I sprang out of bed and rushed over to the door, frantically trying the handle.

'I locked the door when I came back in Effelia, didn't you notice? Now, get back into bed.' He frowned. 'I shall return soon to finish cleaning up the mess you've made, it will be most unfortunate if the tea has stained the carpet.' With a huff he headed for the door with the tray of broken crockery. 'Then because I am such a kind man, I shall bring up more food and a fresh cup of tea.' He looked coldly at me. 'However, if you throw the food on the floor again you won't get any more today.'

Feeling dejected I sat on the bed. 'Couldn't I have a glass of orange juice instead? I asked hopefully. 'I'm becoming rather sick of sugary tea.'

He threw me another suspicious look. 'The sugary tea is good for shock. Besides you've been drinking it up until now.'

'Please, please Isaiah allow me to leave this room. I've been cooped up here for days now, and could really do with a change of scenery.'

As he unlocked the door, he turned to glare at me. 'Very well Effelia, does tomorrow suit you?'

I furrowed my brow, not really believing what I was hearing.

'Yes, yes it does. But are you really allowing me to leave?'

'Why yes of course. I've already contacted Dr Stirling and made arrangements for you to spend some time at The Manor. They have a room prepared, and it has a tiny window that looks out onto the graveyard. All the staff there really are wonderful Effelia, they'll watch over you like hawks and keep you constantly sedated, and you'll even be allowed to mingle with all the other troubled patients.' He looked at me with a devious smile. 'You'll be collected first thing tomorrow morning.' Without another word he left the room and locked the door.

Chapter 22

What a strange turn of events, I thought to myself as I lay on the bed. I never really expected much from my life, not really. Maybe I would make a modest income from selling my paintings, maybe I would meet someone, settle down, and have a few children, or perhaps I wouldn't meet anyone and stay with my Aunt at Rawlings and get a cat, and maybe, just maybe I *would* be content with my life, because whatever happened it wouldn't turn out to be that bad. But now it seemed I was wrong, for it hadn't only turned out to be bad, it was catastrophically bad.

Consumed with panic I rose from the bed and began pacing restlessly up and down the room. I couldn't let this beat me, I had to somehow keep a clear head and be strong. There's a way out of everything if you think about it hard enough. I'm sure my Aunt had told me that once, or something along those lines, she was very keen on her little words of wisdom. Dear Aunt, I thought, how would she react on discovering I was at The Manor, or perhaps she already knew I was going. During her visit yesterday I had displayed symptoms of paranoia when I had mentioned about seeing Gilbert at the foot of my bed, and its entirely feasible Isaiah persuaded her what a good idea it would be to have me committed, he was very skilled in his ability to make people see things his way, especially in the case of my Aunt. I visualised her visiting me in my padded room, feeding me my favourite chocolate bar and combing my wild hair as I stared vacantly into thin air. As the years passed her visits would gradually decrease until one day they would cease altogether, for she would want to forget about me, just as I would want to forget about myself.

With a groan of frustration, I banged my fist against the barred window. Why oh why did I have to possess such an overactive imagination, because in moments such as these it was completely detrimental to my mental health. A glint suddenly caught my eye, and I noticed something silver poking out from underneath the bed, bending down I picked it up, and to my surprise I saw it was a cutlery knife. It must have been from when I'd thrown the breakfast tray across the room, I thought. Sadly, it wasn't very sharp, but it would have to make do for what I had in mind. Frantically I started to saw away with the knife on one of the bars of the window, but my enthusiasm soon lessened as my hand began to ache and when it became blatantly obvious that it wasn't going to work, for there was barely a mark on the iron, let alone a cut. In a fit of anger, I threw the knife across the room.

Later on in the day Isaiah returned to clean up the carpet and give me some more food. To my astonishment I saw a glass of orange juice on the tray, instead of the usual tea, whether this was an attempt at being nice I wasn't sure. The only time I spoke was to pathetically plead with him to contact Dr Stirling and cancel the arrangements for tomorrow, however he just glared at me and said no, absolutely not. I should have tried to grab the key from his back pocket and rush over to the door, which although risky, did give me a slim chance to escape, but instead I just remained sitting on the bed, like an imbecile, telling myself that trying to flee would be futile and could make the situation worse, when in truth I was just too cowardly to act. After complaining bitterly that he couldn't remove the stain from the carpet he gathered the cleaning equipment and marched towards the door, informing me that he would provide a dressing gown and slippers for me to wear when Dr Stirling and a nurse came to collect me tomorrow morning.

After he left, I sat there staring at the glass of orange juice, wondering if it was safe to drink, or if it was laced with the same sleeping draught; in the end I just couldn't risk it and poured it down the basin. After drinking some tap water, I sat on the bed and ate the food. Whatever happened I needed to keep my strength up.

My next idea was to clout Isaiah over the head when he next entered the room; the only heavy item I could think to use was the lamp on the bedside table, so I pulled it from the socket and went and crouched beside the door, so when it was opened I could hide behind it and then attack him, either that or I would just dart out the room, before he could stop me; although the thought of striking him with the lamp was rather appealing, and if he was unconscious it would allow me more time to get away. I saw this as my last opportunity to flee before they came for me tomorrow morning, and carted me off to that horrid place, kicking and screaming, because I wouldn't be leaving quietly. The mere thought of this spurred me on, providing me with a much-needed dose of courage, in addition to the desperation and fear that was bubbling up inside of me.

By early evening there was a cold chill in the room, and I found myself shivering. I pulled the blanket off the bed, wrapped the cover around myself and went and sat in the same spot by the door. I'm not sure at what point that night I realised Isaiah wasn't going to make another appearance, but I stayed in position all the same, foolishly trying to convince myself that my little plan could still work, even if I did have to wait until morning; Isaiah was bound to visit me before Dr Stirling arrived.

The dream I had was most disturbing: I was languishing in the mental institution and was diagnosed as being completely insane by Dr Stirling, only he wasn't a doctor at all, he was Gilbert. After Isaiah signed the paperwork to have me kept in there indefinitely, my Aunt's life came to a tragic end when she *accidentally* became entangled in some rather vicious bindweed in the garden, which slowly strangled her to death. In her last will and testament she left our home to Isaiah, along with a vast amount of money that she'd apparently been saving for years. With his newly acquired fortune he completely renovated the house to suit his taste, furnishing it with ostentatious furniture and gaudy wallpaper; a portrait of him hung from every wall in the house, each one painted to show a different supercilious pose. In the garden, amongst the flowers was a giant-sized carving of a grinning Gilbert. A sparrow flew over and perched upon his head, squawking mockingly to him about what a shame he was just a dummy and couldn't move his joints. 'Oh, but I can little creature.' Exclaimed Gilbert as he moved his creaking mouth. With lightning speed, he reached up and grasped the poor unexpected bird in his wooden hand, then devoured him whole. 'Little birds make tasty grub.' He began to shuffle forward.

'Now to the house I go to cause Isaiah woe. I'll throw him into a pot of boiling water, because he's been so nasty to his daughter. He's an awful beast and I deserve a feast, so at suppertime I shall eat him up, washed down with sugary tea from Effie's cup.'

I awoke with a start to the sound of a strange beeping noise. Feeling disorientated I instinctively grabbed the lamp, which was lying beside me on the floor, and staggered to my feet. At first, I couldn't make out the noise but then I realised it was the sound of a car horn being continuously pressed. A sense of foreboding washed over me, as I realised how close it was. It was their car, the car they were going to use to take me away in. As the front door slammed, I suddenly heard footsteps hurrying up the stairs, whoever it was they were far too quick and light for Isaiah, with his limp he was much slower, but if it was someone from The Manor, then why were they in such a rush? Unless of course they were late in collecting me, only I hardly thought it would matter. I lifted the lamp in the air and my hands tightened around the base, in readiness to strike whomever opened the door. My heart leapt in my chest as I heard the key being turned in the lock. As the bolt was pulled back the door flew open and I swiftly put my foot out to stop it hitting me. A figure came bounding into the room.

'Effie, Effie, where are you?' The person whispered urgently.

At first, I thought I was hallucinating, for although I could only see the back of the figure it looked exactly like Mace. It couldn't be him, I told myself. He had moved on with his life and was now living in another town with his fiancée.

Suddenly he swung round and gaped at me with his big eyes.

'There you are E.' Looking puzzled he stared at the lamp that I was still holding above my head. 'Why are you hiding behind the door brandishing a lamp as if it was a weapon? I know you probably don't like me very much at the moment but there's no need to attack me.' Seeing that I wasn't responding he cautiously stepped towards me, holding out his hand. 'Effie it's alright, I've come to take you home.' His face broke into a broad grin. 'Now lay down your weapon soldier before someone gets hurt.'

Still dumfounded I just stood there, peering at him. He had the usual messy look about him, the same ruffled hair, and the same familiar smile, and he was certainly acting like my friend.

I dropped the lamp onto the carpet. 'Mace, oh Mace is that really you?' I uttered, still not able to comprehend he was really standing there.'

'Well yes, I haven't changed that much, have I?' Raising his left eyebrow, he studied my face. 'You're as pale as a ghost E.'

'Well yes, I haven't been outside this room in a while.' My expression became confused. 'I thought you'd gone away.'

'Gone away where?' He chuckled. 'No E, I've not been anywhere, apart from Abercrombie.' With a whistle he took my hand. 'We'll chat later but at this precise moment we need to get out of here before Isaiah returns.'

In a daze I nodded slowly at him, trying to digest what he had just told me. 'Where's he gone?'

'Not far, that's why we need to leave now.' He began to pull me forward. 'Oh.' He exclaimed when he saw the figure of Isaiah blocking the entranceway. 'You're back.'

With a look of fury Isaiah stared intently at Mace. 'You'll pay for what you've done boy.' He snarled at him. 'And as for your constant interfering...well you've pushed me too far this time.' His eyes darted to mine. 'Don't worry Effelia; I'll deal with this. You go and rest.'

Instinctively I moved further back into the room, half expecting to see Dr Stirling and a nurse standing behind Isaiah, but as far as I could see he was alone.

'I've rested enough Isaiah. I'm...I'm leaving now with Mace, so I suggest you move out the way.'

'Oh, the boy will be leaving, but not you Effelia.'

Without warning Isaiah lunged forward and grabbed Mace's hair, and dragged him out the door, but Mace managed to wrench himself free and stagger back into the room, holding his hands up in clenched fists in readiness to punch Isaiah.

'Oh please.' Exclaimed Isaiah laughing. 'Do you really think you can fight me?'

As Mace lashed out with his fist, Isaiah quickly dodged out the way then swiftly grasped him by the neck and shoved Mace roughly backward, so his head slammed against the wall. He held him there in a vice like grip, his eyes boring into his. 'Don't try and struggle boy, I'm much stronger than you are.' His hands tightened around his throat. 'If you don't leave quietly then perhaps I'll wring your scrawny little neck, it will be so easy and immensely satisfying.'

'No, no please.' Gasped Mace.

Suddenly I spotted the cutlery knife on the floor in the corner of the room. I ran over and picked it up then plunged it violently into

Isaiah's left leg. He cried out in agony, and released his hold on Mace. Staggering backwards he suddenly lost his balance and fell, striking the side of his head against the edge of the windowsill. And there he lay sprawled at our feet, as still as anything, with a trickle of blood running down his face.

There was a hushed silence.

'Oh my god Mace, is he dead?' I said feeling panicked.

He bent over him. 'No, unfortunately he's still breathing.' With a frown he began looking around the room. 'We need to tie him up before he wakes. You stay here E and I'll go and find some rope.'

'What? No Mace, no you can't leave him with me. What if he regains consciousness?'

With a grimace he rubbed his neck. 'Well, I don't know, use your initiative E.' He said in a frustrated voice as he sped out the door. 'Be back in a mo.'

Just as a precaution I went and fetched the lamp, however in Isaiah's present state he wasn't going anywhere, and I hardly wanted to strike him over the head now, not after what had just happened. My eyes travelled down to the knife protruding from his leg, and I noticed blood slowly seeping from the wound onto his precious carpet. With a harrowing sigh I knelt over him, closely watching for any signs of life, but I couldn't even see him breathing. What if Mace was wrong and Isaiah really was dead, it would be my entire fault, as I was the one who had stabbed him which had caused him to fall and bang his head; I could go to prison for his murder, or even worse they would lock me away in The Manor. This reminded me of Dr Stirling, and how he was supposed to be collecting me this morning, what if he arrived now and saw me crouching over an unconscious Isaiah, things wouldn't look good for me.

'Found some rope E.'

I turned to see Mace stumbling clumsily back into the room, dragging two lengths of rope along the floor.

'That's good.' I said still staring at Isaiah. To my relief I suddenly saw his eyelids flickering. 'We should be quick, he's waking up, you bind his hands and I'll tie his ankles together.'

'Yes, okay Effie, there's no need to be so bossy, now is there.' He looked fleetingly at me and grinned. 'You've obviously been spending far too much time in the company of this man. You know how much he enjoys ordering people about.'

With a smile I took a piece of the rope. 'Sorry. It's just that I think we should rush before...before Dr Stirling arrives.'

'Who the hell is Dr Stirling?'

'Oh, it doesn't matter.' With a nervous laugh I glanced down at Isaiah's leg. 'What about the knife, shouldn't we remove it?'

'If *you* want to E, then be my guest.'

Giving Mace a sombre look I placed my shaking hands around the knife's handle, and swiftly yanked it from Isaiah's leg. I jumped a little as he let out a groan and begun muttering something inaudible. For a minute I almost said sorry, then coming to my senses I dropped the knife and began binding his ankles together.

'All done.' Said Mace, examining his handy work. 'Although I say it myself, Isaiah's wrists are expertly bound.' He glanced at me as I tied my second knot to secure the rope. 'Not bad E, not bad at all.' He rose up from the ground and began looking around the room. 'Now, we just need to gag him with something.'

I suddenly felt a pang of guilt. 'Surely there's no need for a gag, and perhaps we should move him onto the bed. It's unfair to keep him here on the floor.'

Mace glanced at me, screwing up his eyes. 'Effie, he's kept you locked in this room for a week. I'm surprised you care.'

'I don't care. I just think it's cruel leaving him here on the floor like some kind of wild animal. He... he could die.'

'Effie, Isaiah is as strong as an ox.' He retorted in a rather irritated voice. 'But, very well, we won't use a gag.' He rolled his eyes at me. 'And we'll lift his bulky frame onto the bed, and if you like we can tuck him in too, *and* sing him a lullaby.'

'Mace please, this isn't the time for joking.'

'No, no I suppose it isn't. Come on then E, you take his legs.'

With great difficulty we heaved Isaiah onto the bed. He was silent again now and appeared to have slipped back into unconsciousness.

I wrung my hands together.

'We can't leave Isaiah in this state. His wounds need attention and he really should be admitted to hospital. And...and we should contact the police as well.'

He grasped my shoulders and peered steadily into my face. 'Stop it Effie, you're too soft for your own good, and you're not thinking straight. Our main priority is getting out this house.' He glanced at Isaiah as he let out another groan. 'We'll think about contacting the hospital and police later.'

As Isaiah struggled to open his eyes, he called out my name.

Mace patted him on the head. 'There, there Isaiah you have a nice little sleep. Effie and I are leaving now.'

As we left the room I watched as Mace locked the door and pulled the bolt across.

'Is that really necessary?'

Narrowing his eyes, he peered at me. 'Don't underestimate him, Effie. Knowing Isaiah, he's probably faking his concussion and will be more than capable of undoing those pitiful knots we tied in next to no time.' He grabbed my arm. 'Come on, let's go.'

As we ran down the stairs, I felt strange and nervous. Being cooped up in that room for so many days made me scared to go outside into the real world, but it was also thrilling to be finally escaping. On reaching the hallway I began curiously peering about the place, for although I was desperate to leave, it would have been interesting to explore the rooms, just to see what secrets Isaiah had hidden away. As we went passed the room on the right something suddenly caught my eye, it was a flash of colour, a distinctive red and green.

A sudden fear gripped me.

'Mace, just a minute I need to check something.' I said in an unsteady voice.

'Hurry E, I'll be waiting by the door.'

Cautiously I went into, what appeared to be, the living room. It was silent apart from the rhythmic ticking of the clock on the mantelpiece. I glanced across at the armchair in the corner, and sitting amongst the cushions was a little figure, staring back at me. In alarm my hand went over my mouth as I stared at Gilbert. Suddenly it all made sense: Isaiah had stolen the dummy from the attic at Rawlings, and he was the one who'd placed him on the bed that night to frighten me, to make me believe I was really going mad. Shaking my head in disbelief I tentatively extended my hand forward to grab the dummy, half imagining he would suddenly come to life and kill me, but as I scooped him up from the armchair,

I saw him for what he really was- a harmless old ventriloquist dummy, and he belonged to me, not Isaiah. Taking a deep breath, I placed the tatty old toy underneath my arm and left the room.

'Well, it's about time.' Mace said impatiently, peering at the dummy. 'What on earth is that?'

I removed the dummy from underneath my arm and held him up.

'It's Gilbert.'

Mace burst out laughing. 'That poor, sorry looking thing is what's tormented you all your life and kept you awake at night.'

I looked at him indignantly. 'Well, he's rather more menacing in my dreams.'

He chuckled. 'If you say so E. Come on, let's go.'

Just as we opened the front door I jumped as the telephone rung, and I had a nasty feeling it was Dr Stirling. We ignored it and went outside. How wondrous it was stepping out into the cool, crisp morning air, it felt like I was experiencing it for the very first time, and just wanted to revel in all of its glory, and even when the glare of the sun hurt my eyes, I was glad, for it meant I was free.

Chapter 23

Mace ran his eyes over me.

'I think its best you change E.' He looked suddenly worried. 'You do realise you're wearing your pyjamas, don't you?'

I looked startled for a moment and then my face broke into a smile.

'Actually, I forgot. I've been wearing them for so long, you see.' Feeling suddenly embarrassed I folded my arms across my chest, being careful not to damage Gilbert.' 'Oh well, I can change back at home, you have got the car haven't you Mace?'

'Yes, it's a bit further up the road. I didn't want Isaiah spotting it, not that he'd recognise my latest car, as I only purchased it a few months ago.' He took my hand and we strolled passed the row of terraced houses.

'What happened to your other car Mace?'

'The brakes failed and it smashed into a tree. Luckily I jumped out just in time.'

'Oh Mace, that must have been awful. That's the second time now something has seriously gone wrong with your car.'

'Yeah, it really shook me up. Now I only use the car when really necessary, such as saving my best friend.' Nearing the end of the road he stopped beside a rather battered up old car. 'Here it is, handsome beast, isn't it?'

I smiled. 'Yes, yes, it is.'

'Clamber in E, the door's already open.'

Carefully I placed Gilbert on the back seat next to a bag and several sweet wrappers, trying not to look at his scary eyes. Then I went and sat in the front.

'Oh, by the way E, I think you need to take a breather before seeing Constance, so I suggest we go and spend some time in Hudson's café.'

'What about my clothes?' I said, panicking.

'Effie, please have a little faith in me. I grabbed some from your bedroom a while ago, and chucked them on the back seat of the car.' He started up the ignition. 'You can change in the ladies at Hudson's café.

I stared at him in bewilderment. 'Thanks Mace, that's very thoughtful of you.'

'Well, I'm a very thoughtful person E.' He looked at me with amusement. 'You really couldn't do without me you know.'

As we drove passed Isaiah's house I shivered. All that I had discovered and all that had occurred in the past few days meant there was no going back, nothing between Isaiah and I would ever be the same again; finally, it would all be over and even if he wasn't locked away, Aunt and I could still banish him from our lives forever, for I would make sure he never set foot in Rawlings again.

Once I'd changed, we both sat in our usual spot drinking hot chocolate. Mace ordered sandwiches and cake too, telling me how I needed feeding up, although I suspect he was just hungry. We both sat in silence whilst we ate, gazing out the window at the people passing by. I chose to forget about our rather tense meeting last week and instead thought of all the happy times we had spent in this café: Come rain or shine we would meet up and jabber on about meaningless topics, laughing and joking with one another, it was hard to imagine those carefree days ever ending, but now as we sat facing one another I feared they had.

'You're quiet E, are you alright?'

I sipped the hot chocolate. 'Yes, yes I think so. It's just rather strange to be out in the real world again.' With a poignant smile I watched as he took an enormous bite from one of the sandwiches. 'I'd like to say thank you Mace, for what you've done today. You really are a true friend.'

He stopped eating and stared at me rather shiftily. 'Well...thanks Effie, it's very decent of you to say so after... He gulped. 'Anyway, it's the least I could do.'

'How did you get in the house and pass Isaiah?'

'It was a stroke of genius E. You see I got this boy, Ernest from up the road where I live to help me out. I had to pay him a small fortune, but hey ho. I'd already smashed Isaiah car window last night, you see, with a hammer. I actually impressed myself at how quiet it was done, and how easy I managed to unlock the car door.' Pulling a face, he glanced at his left wrist. 'Apart from a minor cut I was unharmed.' He took a cake from the plate and stuffed the entire thing into his mouth.

'So, where does this boy come into it?'

He paused whilst he ate the cake.

'Ernest and I arranged to meet early this morning outside Isaiah's house. I told him to clamber into the car and keep honking the horn until I gave him a signal to stop. I hid in the bushes by the front door, and when Isaiah stormed out and headed for his car, I gave the signal to Ernest to scarper as fast as he could. Meanwhile I sneaked into the house and ran up the stairs, looking for you. I immediately spotted the room with the bolt on the door, and guessed that was where he was keeping you.' He slurped his hot chocolate. 'Luckily Isaiah had kept the key in the lock so it was made easy for me.'

I raised my eyebrows in acknowledgment and nodded slowly.

'Well, I was so glad to see you standing there Mace, I can't tell you. I thought for one moment it was Dr Stirling. You see Isaiah had made arrangements to have me admitted to The Manor, this very morning.' My eyes drifted outside onto the rain-splattered pavement. 'But now I'm wondering if he was just trying to scare me.'

'I wouldn't put anything pass that man.' He sighed heavily. 'Apparently you were very sorry but had finally come to your senses and had no wish to be friends with me anymore.'

'What do you mean?' I asked, nonplussed.

'Well, that's what Isaiah told me the first time I tried to see you.'

'That was you then? I kept hearing someone ringing the doorbell. Isaiah said it was sales people.'

'Oh yes Effie, it was I. Ever since our little confrontation in the café last week I've been trying to contact you. After speaking to your Aunt Connie and finding out what happened I ran over to Isaiah's house, but he wouldn't let me in.' He frowned. 'He droned on and on about how unwell you were and how you didn't want to see me again. Of course, lucky for little old you, I didn't believe a word of it.' He wiped his mouth with the serviette. 'But the more I pestered him the more furious he became, until finally he announced that if I set foot on his doorstep again, he would shoot me through the head and drop my body over Abercrombie Bridge. I threatened him with the police but he just laughed in my face, telling me he had many connections in the force and they would see to it that I was thrown in jail for wasting their time. After that I hatched my ingenious plan and the rest is history.'

'It's strange that Aunt didn't mention that you were trying to reach me. She came to visit me, you know.'

Mace started to munch on the remaining cake crumbs on his plate. 'At a guess I'd say Isaiah made sure Connie kept quiet on the subject. You know how he wraps her around his little finger.'

'Yes, yes I do. I said softly.

For a moment I drifted off into my own thoughts, thinking of how Isaiah would do anything to prise Mace and I apart, and it was easy to see how Aunt would believe all of Isaiah's drivel. I could picture him now, standing there with his smiling, sympathetic eyes, telling her how much damage it would do to my recovery if I was to see Mace, how distraught I was on learning of his forthcoming marriage, and how I would burst into a flood of tears at the mere mention of his name.

Effie? Effie, are you okay?'

I gaped at Mace. 'Oh yes, sorry. I was miles away. How's Moira?'

He shot me a look of surprise and then a flicker of amusement crossed over his face. 'Moira?' I've not seen her since that day here in the café, when you made your grand entrance and then left in a huff.' He shrugged his shoulders. 'Why do you ask?'

I thought of how cosy they'd looked together. As I began to speak a hesitant smile crept over my face. 'So, I suppose the story I heard about the two of you moving away and getting married was entirely fictional?'

He gave me an odd kind of look and then suddenly appeared mournful, reaching for his serviette and dabbing his eyes. 'Moira left me Effie. She walked out of my life and left me broken hearted.' He began making sobbing sounds.

Other customers looked over towards us, muttering under their breath. I felt the colour rise in my cheeks with embarrassment.

'Mace, please.' I whispered.

He slouched forward, placing his head down by his plate, and then with a cry he began banging his fists onto the table. 'It's not fair, why did she have to leave me.'

There was a stony silence around the café, and the waitress had stopped in her tracks with a plate of food in her hands, staring over at us apprehensively. I half expected Mrs Worthington to appear from nowhere and come over to see what was wrong. How lovely it would be to see her again. I do hope she was still about, I thought, suddenly pensive.

'Mace please, I know you're messing about.' I looked at him closely, gritting my teeth. 'You are, aren't you?' I said, starting to believe that he was telling me the truth and was actually distraught.

'No, Effie.' He sobbed. 'How can you think such a thing?' Raising his head from the table he exploded into fits of laughter. 'Oh, okay maybe I am messing about.'

I was incensed, so much so that I wanted to strike him, but as I stared into his grinning face my anger disappeared and I too burst into laughter.

The waitress rolled her eyes then carried on working.

'Admit it. I fooled you that time E.'

'Yes, yes you did.' My face became serious. 'So, what *is* going on with you and Moira, why were you acting so strange when I saw you with her last week?'

'Moira's extremely keen on me and would marry me tomorrow if I asked her.' He declared with a grin, 'but unfortunately for her the feeling isn't mutual. She just happened to be there with me that day, and when I saw you standing there, after being absent for two long years, I couldn't help but be angry with you.'

My head started to ache as I suddenly remembered our journey to Browning's Wood, and what had occurred there.

I stared down at my half-eaten sandwich.

'Wait a moment.' I said, shaking my head in confusion. 'I don't understand why it had slipped my mind for the past week; it must be something to do with the tea Isaiah gave me.'

Mace gave me an odd look. 'Tea?'

I slammed my fist down onto the table. 'You...you pushed me through that portal thing, didn't you Mace.' I glared at him. 'I take back what I just said about you being a true friend, because what kind of friend would do something like that.'

Mace began nervously tapping his fingers against the side of his mug, looking sheepishly at me. 'Effie, you're absolutely right, I did push you, but you *were* going to travel through the portal anyway.'

'But you were supposed to come with me Mace.'

'Yeah, well I had a change of heart, and besides you had a friend waiting for you at the other end.'

'Friend, what friend?' A spark of pain flared through my heart. 'Who are you talking about Mace?'

He reached across the table and took my hand. 'Don't worry about it now Effie.'

I snatched my hand away. 'Is that why you pushed me, because I was meeting someone?'

'Oh, I don't know. I suppose so, yes.' He paused. 'I'm sure I mentioned to you at the time how I'd get in the way. Anyway, afterwards I bitterly regretted pushing you in. Many a day I went back to the woods and stood by the portal, trying to pluck up the courage to jump.' He avoided my eye. 'But I couldn't do it.'

'So, you had the courage to shove me into the portal but not to jump yourself.'

'Yes, ok, yes.' He yelled at me. 'I'm a poor pathetic coward, is that what you want to hear Effie.' Without warning he rose to his feet and came over and crouched beside me. 'I acted totally irresponsibly that day in the woods, and I'm truly sorry Effie for pushing you. Will you forgive me for being such a foolish idiot?'

The customers began to look our way again.

Mace leant in close and lowered his voice. 'I promise from this day forth I shall make up for what I did Effie. I've suffered in total misery these past two years, not knowing if I'd ever see you again and if...if you were still alive.' He took my hand in his. 'So, am I forgiven?'

Despite his faults I could never be cross with Mace for long that much was sure. I was so relieved that the friend I knew and loved had come back to me, and was no longer the cold, distant stranger of last week, for at one point I believed I had completely lost his friendship, and true friendships are difficult to come by.

I stared into the warmth of his eyes and smiled.

'Yes Mace, you're forgiven.' I squeezed his hand tightly in mine.

'Phew.' He exclaimed. 'For a minute there E, I had serious doubts.' He rose to his feet and went to sit back down. 'The customers in here today are extremely nosey, don't you think? Anyone would think we'd caused a scene and were being too rowdy.'

I giggled. 'Where's Mrs Worthington, I was hoping to see her.'

'Oh, she only works part time now.' He sniffed then blew his nose with a serviette. 'She asks about you all the time Effie, I just said you were away with your new man, which she did seem a little surprised about, but finally she's realised that you and I are not an item.'

My new man?'

'Yeah, well technically you were with him, weren't you?'

I gave him a blank look then stared out the window.

As we left Hudson's café it was drizzling with rain so Mace removed his jacket and draped it over our heads. I didn't mind that the weather was grey and miserable; it was refreshing to feel the rain upon my face.

'There's something I think you need to see before I take you home Effie.' His voice sounded solemn. 'It shouldn't take long.'

'Very well.' I answered feeling intrigued.

He led me down the street, passed the shops and stopped by the entrance to the church where there was a notice board advertising various church services and functions.

'Take a look.' said Mace, inclining his head to the board.

At first all I could see was a Ladies Committee coffee morning poster, but as I peered closer, I noticed it was partially covering a black and white photo. I pulled the poster away and let out a gasp. The photo was of two young women, myself and someone else with long flaxen hair. In big bold letters above our heads were the words MISSING.

I covered my mouth with my hand. 'I...I don't understand.

'Clarice disappeared a few days after you left E.' Mace said, in a grim voice. 'No one has seen or heard from her since.'

'But, but where do you think she's gone. It's rather odd it happened just after I went, don't you think?'

'Well yeah, it does seem strange. That's why everyone thought you were together.' He frowned. 'There was a full-scale search but they found nothing.'

'Her poor mother, she must be devastated.' I turned away from the notice board. 'I must go and see her.'

Mace grabbed my arm 'No, no Effie. Can you imagine how Mrs Lapworth will react when she knows you're back in Abercrombie, all safe and sound, but her daughter is still out there somewhere. All this time she believed you were with Clarice - how will you explain it to her?'

I thought over his words carefully.

'Yes, I suppose you're right.' I said stepping away from the notice board and looking towards the park.

I stared at the people walking their dogs; all living their normal lives without having to worry about portals, evil dummies and friends going missing. Oh, how I envied them.

'You, you don't think she's.... dead?'

Mace butted in. 'Dear god I hope not.'

I closed my eyes and shook my head.

'That day when Clarice didn't turn up to view the flat, I knew something was wrong when I spoke to her, as she didn't sound herself.' My voice sounded thick with emotion. 'I was going to call on her but... but everything else got in the way, and I forgot.' I started to cry. 'What kind of friend am I?'

Mace pulled me into his arms. 'Don't blame yourself Effie. You weren't to know that she was going to disappear.'

I looked up into his face. 'It was almost as if somebody had persuaded her not to view the flat.' A face popped into my head, the face of Isaiah, and suddenly it all became crystal clear. 'It's him, I'm sure of it.' I shouted, dragging myself away from him and hurrying back up the street.

'Who?' Mace yelled after me.'

'It's got to be Isaiah.' I said looking vexed. As much as it would torment me to go back to that house, I had to know what happened to Clarice, and if Isaiah was the key, then so be it. I would extract the truth from him. 'Mace I'm sorry but we must go back to his house.'

'What now?'

'Yes, we can be there in a few minutes by car.'

With a look of determination, I marched up the street with a bewildered Mace following close behind.

On reaching Isaiah's house we made our way around the back of the property, and luckily discovered an open window. Mace went through first, knocking over a china vase in the process which shattered noisily on the tiled floor. Once we were safely in, we hurried up the stairs to the bedroom where I'd been kept locked away. We both came to a sudden halt at the entrance. The door was ajar.

My eyes widened in shock.

'Why...how can the door be open?'

Without replying Mace barged passed me into the room.

'Be careful, Isaiah may still be in there Mace.' I whispered in a trembling voice. I glanced over at the empty bed and saw the lengths of rope and some bloodstains on the blanket. A wave of panic swept over me and for a moment I couldn't breathe properly. 'How could he have escaped?' I said, trying to steady my breathing.

Mace scratched his head. 'I don't know. It's not possible for him to have got away. Someone helped him, it's the only logical explanation.'

A feeling of foreboding crept over me as I thought of Dr Stirling. Perhaps he really was collecting me this morning, what if he had a key to the house; that would explain how quickly Isaiah managed to escape; the doctor could have set him free and then...then they would come after me and put me away in my new home. For the sake of my sanity, I put this dreadful thought to the back of my mind.

'He's most likely gone over to Rawlings.' I clenched my hands together tightly. 'He might harm my Aunt. We should go over there now.' I said, urgently.

Mace looked at me and gave me a reassuring smile. 'Calm down Effie, he's got no reason to harm your Aunt Connie. She's just an innocent old lady.'

I thought of my Aunt lying in a heap at the bottom of the grand staircase at Rawlings, blood pouring from her head.

'You don't know what he's capable of Mace.' I bit my lip. 'He's truly evil and vindictive.'

Mace screwed his face up. 'Actually, I do. He's already tried to kill me on three separate occasions.'

I stood looking at him. 'He has?'

'I'm almost certain it was Isaiah who pushed me into the railway tracks and sabotaged my car those two times.'

'Of course, that would explain it.' I exclaimed, staring into space. 'I mean who else would it have been. But even though Isaiah detests you, surely he doesn't want you dead?'

He laughed rather ironically. 'Actually, he does. He has a very good reason for wanting to bump me off.'

'What reason?'

He didn't answer but stared over to the window with the same lost, distant look from that day on the promenade, just before we left for our trip to Browning's Wood.

'Mace?'

With a deep sigh he faced me. 'Because Isaiah knows who I really am.'

We were both silent for a moment.

'What.... what do you mean Mace?' I said, in a quiet voice, scared of his answer.

There was a momentarily pause and then he smiled poignantly at me. 'Look E, I promise to explain all later. But right now, we should get to Rawlings.'

I stood there like a statue whilst he ran towards the door, then in a daze I followed on behind him.

Chapter 24

Once again, I found myself travelling down that familiar driveway to my home. As we saw the house ahead in all its splendour, I thought how I would never grow weary of gazing upon its beauty. I could live forever and still not tire of Rawlings.

'Glad to be home?' Mace asked, turning to me.

'I caught his eye and smiled. 'Yes, yes I am. I do hope Aunt is all right.'

'Connie's more than capable of taking care of herself.' Mace answered in a warm voice.

'What if Isaiah's here, what shall we do?'

'Don't worry, knowing that man he'll probably act like nothing's happened.'

We pulled up beside the house and clambered out the car. The weather was still grim, with a steady drizzle of rain, which made everything seem all the more sinister. And although there was no sign of Isaiah's vehicle, a distinct feeling of unease was creeping over me, and the situation only got worse when I realised the front door wasn't shut properly.

'Aunt, Aunt?' I shouted rather loudly as we entered the house. 'Aunt it's me, Effie.' As my voice echoed throughout the vast hallway, I could remember my relief at not seeing a body lying at the bottom of the stairs. 'Perhaps she went out and accidentally left the front door open.'

'Yes, yes that is a possibility E.' He murmured as he automatically headed to the kitchen. 'I'm going to see if there's any homemade cake lying about.'

I paused in the hallway, plucking up the courage to search the rooms. In my mind I imagined My Aunt, Isaiah and Dr Stirling hiding away somewhere in the house, they would probably have brought nurses with them as back up, and when I entered the room in which they were waiting for me, they would pounce. Mace would be taken as well; Isaiah would make sure of that.

I nearly jumped out of my skin when the kitchen door was flung open and Mace appeared looking rather sombre.

'E, I think you'd better join me in the kitchen.'

'What is it?' I uttered apprehensively, not liking the tone of his voice.

'Come and see for yourself Effie.'

As he disappeared back behind the door I nervously ran over and went into the room. My heart sank when I spotted the broken crockery on the floor.

'Oh no.' I said becoming fearful. 'Something must be wrong.'

'Connie could've accidentally dropped the crockery and just not cleared it up yet.' Mace said, trying to sound optimistic.

'No, Aunt wouldn't just leave a mess on the floor.' I started to shiver. 'We need to search the whole house -she must be somewhere.'

Mace nodded in agreement. 'You check downstairs and I'll check up. I'll holler if I find her.'

'Yes, please do Mace.' I said in a shaky voice. Trying to compose myself I began taking deep breaths. 'Oh, and Mace, be careful. It might not be my Aunt you find.'

He scoffed at me. 'Effie, please.' Striding over to the worktop he grabbed the rolling pin from the jar of kitchen utensils and grasped it tightly in his hand. 'I'll be prepared for whatever attacks me.' He gave me a crooked grin. 'Unless of course it's Connie, then I'll lay down my rolling pin.' Narrowing his eyes, he glanced around the kitchen. 'I'm not sure where she keeps her carving knives, but maybe you should take one E, just in case.'

I gave him a weak smile. 'No, I'm sure that won't be necessary.

Whistling he paced towards the door. 'It's your funeral E.'

In a dreamlike state I wandered from room to room, half expecting someone to leap out at me, but everywhere was silent and still. I was beginning to think Mace was right in taking a weapon, as even though I hated the idea of carrying a knife around with me, it perhaps would have made me feel safer, but I feared that if someone was to unexpectedly jump out in front of me, I may inadvertently stab them in pure fright.

My final room to search was the library, and as I went through the door my senses were immediately filled with the musty odour of my precious old books. Despite the library being in semi darkness I suddenly noticed dust particles floating around in the air, as if the area had recently been disturbed in some way. Rather slowly I crept further into the room and let out a gasp as I observed the empty shelves, and as my gaze travelled downwards, I saw all my beloved books scattered over the floor, as if someone had deliberately thrown them there.

'Why would someone do this?' I mumbled to myself in a weepy voice.

Not thinking to turn on the light, I carefully stepped over the books and made my way to the window to draw back the heavy curtains, but just as my hand reached the cord, I caught sight of a shadowy figure sitting in the corner of the room. A blood- curdling scream escaped my lips and I stumbled backwards onto the books. My initial reaction was to flee the room, however as I peered at the figure once more, my heart lurched in my chest.

'Aunt…Aunt you startled me.'

Mace came crashing into the room with his rolling pin, tripping and falling forwards onto the books. 'What the hell…Effie, Effie what's wrong?' He exclaimed, quickly picking himself up. 'What happened?'

Rather shakily I pointed over towards Aunt, who was sitting there staring straight ahead, as if in a trance. Coughing from the dust, Mace went up to her and waved his hand in front of her face.

'Connie, is everything okay?'

Carefully treading between the books, I went over and knelt beside her. As I peered into her deathly white face, it almost seemed she had aged since our last meeting, as she looked unusually tired and gaunt. However, it was her eyes that alarmed me the most, as they were wide and staring.

'Aunt?' I said, reaching over and placing my arm around her shoulder. 'It's me, Effie. Please Aunt, please speak to me' I said, becoming frantic. I had a sudden vision of her being stuck in The Manor for her remaining years, perpetually lost in a world of her own and unable to acknowledge another living soul. 'Aunt, wake up Aunt.' In desperation I took hold of her shoulders and started to shake her.

'Effie, what are you doing?' Mace yelled.

'I'm waking her up.' My voice was thick with emotion. 'She needs to return to reality.'

Mace came over and pulled me away. 'Stop it Effie, that won't help.'

With a sob I stumbled over to the window, flinging back the velvet curtains, but as the day was so gloomy barely any light entered the room. I stood staring hopelessly out at the garden, watching the branches of the huge oaks swaying violently in the wind. They reminded me of gigantic hands, waving at me. The rain lashed against the window and trickled in patterns down the pane, almost like tears, tears for my Aunt.

'Effie, we should call for an ambulance?' Mace said, hovering behind me.

Just as Mace spoke, I heard a weak voice utter my name and I immediately swung round to look at my Aunt. Her eyes seemed to be normal again and were focused upon me. With a look of joy, I ran over and flung my arms round her.

'Aunt, oh Aunt, I knew you'd be alright.'

'Oh, Effie I was so scared.' She exclaimed in a trembling voice. 'I...I saw her with my own eyes.'

I pulled back from her. 'Who Aunt, who did you see?'

As Mace and I waited eagerly for her to reply she buried her face in her hands.

'I think you're in need of a strong cup of tea Connie, and maybe some cake?' Mace said with a grin all over his face. 'I'll go and make a pot.'

My Aunt moved her hands to her lap and stared at Mace.

'Oh ah...you'll find a fresh pot of tea in the living room - it should still be warm. I had to use the old chipped teapot, as my best one is sadly amongst the broken crockery on the kitchen floor. I...I really must go and clear it up.' She looked suddenly flustered. 'Oh, dear what a truly dreadful day this has been.'

'It's okay Aunt, don't worry, Mace and I will clear the kitchen up later.' I very gently took her hands in mine, and was shocked at how cold they seemed. 'Come on, let's go and sit in the living room. I'll get a lovely cosy fire going.'

As I helped her out the room, I tried not to glance at the books, for it saddened my heart to see them in such a state, and never before had I'd been so glad to leave the library.

The three of us sat huddled around the roaring fire. Mace had already helped himself to cake and had just toasted some crumpets, which he eagerly began to devour. I'd draped a blanket around my Aunt and told her to relax for a while, for even though I was intrigued to know who she had seen, it could wait. She was regaining some colour in her cheeks now, and looked more like her old self.

'So, Connie, who *did* you see, please tell me I'm dying to know?' I scowled at Mace.

She cluttered her cup down into the saucer and with a shaky hand placed it on the table. 'It was a manifestation.' With a gulp she stared into my face. 'The ghost of your mother, Effie.'

I looked at her blankly and then glanced over at Mace. He'd stopped eating and was staring, open mouthed at my Aunt.

'My mother?' I said, not believing what she had just said.

'Yes Effie, I'd just gone into the library when all of a sudden, I saw Freya, she appeared from nowhere, just like a ghost. At first, I thought I was seeing things, but then…. then she spoke to me.'

'What did she say Aunt?'

'Well, you see Effie.' With a sniffle she wiped her nose on her handkerchief. 'Your mother told me she was coming home to Rawlings. I couldn't understand every word Freya spoke as her voice kept fading, but I'm sure she mentioned something about a gateway. And then my dear sister simply vanished into thin air.' She widened her eyes and looked at me. 'Your poor mother must have passed away Effie, and now she wishes to return to Rawlings as a spirit.'

Mace and I looked at one another.

A peculiar feeling swept over me, bringing with it a tiny flicker of a forgotten memory. How Aunt had described seeing the apparition of my mother reminded me of someone else, a woman with a cruel face, standing in the kitchen at Rawlings, scowling at me with a deep hatred in her eyes.

'Oh Connie, come on. You were more than likely hallucinating.' Mace said, with a slight laugh.

Aunt looked disconcerted 'Poppycock, I did no such thing.' She folded her arms in defiance. 'It's just a shame Isaiah wasn't still in the library to witness it too.'

'Isaiah was here?' I asked in a distressed voice.

'Well yes.' Aunt regarded me with surprise. 'He couldn't stay at his house, not after the burglary. I insisted he remains here until he feels happy to return home.' She straightened the blanket over her legs. 'What an awful ordeal for such a lovely man to have to endure.'

I clenched my teeth and threw a knowing glance at Mace.

'What exactly happened to Isaiah, Aunt?' I asked in a low voice.

'Well, when I rang him this morning, I became concerned when no one answered the phone, so I took the very next bus over to his house, only to find the door wide open.'

I suddenly wondered if we hadn't shut the door when we left Isaiah's house, as we did flee in rather a rush, so it was highly likely we could have simply forgotten. I also remembered the phone ringing.

'So, you went inside then Aunt?'

'Yes, and I eventually discovered Isaiah tied up in the bedroom where you'd been staying dear.' She shook her head and frowned at me. 'I can't tell you how relieved I felt when Isaiah told me Mace had already collected you Effie, and that you were going to stay at his house for a few days. She smiled sweetly at Mace. 'Thank you, dear boy.'

'All in a good day's work Connie.' Mace said, winking at her. 'Do carry on.'

'Well, the poor man was in a terrible state when I found him. Some brutes had clouted him over the head, stabbed him in the leg, and then tied him up. I thought he should go to hospital but he assured me he didn't feel that bad, so I insisted on him returning home with me so I could tend to his wounds. I rang Edith Piper and she kindly came and collected us in her car and drove us back to Rawlings.

'Oh, I see.' Mace exclaimed, raising his eyebrows. 'Did you contact the police?'

'I was going to but Isaiah was adamant that it wasn't necessary. Apparently, the burglar's left without taking very much.' She leant forward and narrowed her eyes. 'I suspect I disturbed them when I entered the house and they sneaked past without me noticing and made a run for it.'

Mace placed his hand under his chin and nodded. 'That sounds like a likely theory, doesn't it, Effie?'

'Yes, it all makes perfect sense.' I said in a bemused voice. So where is Isaiah now, Aunt?'

'Well after we arrived at Rawlings, I cleaned and bandaged Isaiah's wounds.' She smoothed her hair over. 'He kept telling me he needed to find a particular book that he seemed to think was in the library, and was most concerned about finding it. I urged him to leave it for another time and insisted we go and sit down, so he could rest for a while. I was just about to carry the tray of tea and cakes through to the living room, when Isaiah foolishly picked it up himself, and that's when the tray accidentally slipped from his grasp, and crashed to the floor. Not that I blame him, he was rather shaky after his nasty experience with the burglars. So, I told him to go and wait for me in the living room, whilst I made a fresh pot, but when I went to take it through, he wasn't in there.'

'Had he already gone to the library Aunt?'

'Well, that's what I thought Effie, however when I went in there he was nowhere to be seen, and I was horrified to find the books in a total state of disarray.' A distressed expression crossed over her face. 'I was just about to go and search for him when...when I saw her, the apparition of your mother.' She grabbed my hands in hers. 'Afterwards I was too petrified to leave the room, so I just sat there in a daze.'

'Oh Aunt, it must have been awful for you. Thank god we came and found you.'

'Yes Effie, indeed yes.'

'But why are the books all over the floor?' I muttered curiously.

'Heaven only knows Effie. I can only assume Isaiah caused the mess whilst he was searching for his book. I think the knock to his head has temporarily muddled his thinking.' She shrugged her shoulders. 'Anyway, I'm sure he'll replace all the books in their rightful place when he has the chance.'

I pondered over whether Isaiah had actually lost a book or just wanted to hurt me by tipping the entire contents of the library onto the floor. The latter seemed likely, as he was obviously seething with anger over Mace and I attacking him, and then leaving him locked up in that room.

'So, where do you think Isaiah's disappeared to Connie?'

'Well, I assume he must have already left for his trip. However, I'm extremely concerned about him, as he really wasn't himself and it's not at all like him to just leave without saying goodbye.'

'Trip, what trip?' I asked urgently.

'Oh, he'd mentioned earlier on that he had some urgent business to attend to, that's all I know Effie.'

A hauntingly unclear memory came to mind, something to do with a trip Isaiah said he was making, only it was too fuzzy to recall.

Mace gave me a swift, peculiar glance and then stood up.

'Effie, come and give me a hand in the kitchen.' He said, picking up our plates and cups.' He smiled broadly at Aunt. 'You stay here and rest Connie.'

'Oh, thank you Mace, I will.' She turned to me. 'With everything that's happened I've forgotten to ask how you are Effie.'

'I'm much better now Aunt, thank you. I can't tell you how happy it makes me to be back home with you.'

'That's wonderful dear, I am glad you're not staying at Mace's. After what's happened, I'm all on edge.'

'That's perfectly understandable Aunt, anyone would be.' I patted her on the hand. 'From now on I shall be here to take care of you. Now you relax whilst I help Mace clean up the kitchen.' Smiling endearingly at her I headed towards the door.'

'Oh Effie. I wonder if you wouldn't mind making up the bed in the large spare bedroom for Isaiah. He may be back by tonight and I'd like his room to be ready.'

I stared back at her, wanting so much to tell her the truth about him, but as I looked into her eyes something told me to hold back, for the last thing I wanted to do was distress her even more. It could wait until tomorrow, when things had settled down a little. However, I couldn't bear the idea of him staying at Rawlings, even for one night.

I clasped my hands together tightly. 'Actually Aunt, I...I really would prefer if Isaiah didn't stay here with us. Surely it would be more sensible if he was to find alternative accommodation, just until he feels able to return to his own home.' Seeing the look of puzzlement in her expression, I lowered my gaze 'If we allow him to stay at Rawlings, he may expect to move in.... permanently.' With a deep sigh I looked directly into her face. 'I'd hate that to happen Aunt.'

She sat rigidly in the armchair, her eyes blazing.

'Effie you should be ashamed of yourself for saying such a thing. Not only has Isaiah been through a very traumatic experience today, he's also gone out his way to help you get better, by taking you in and looking after you, and I really think you should be a little more grateful to the man. He's a dear friend of mine and I will *not* see him staying anywhere other than here, for as long as he so wishes.'

'Aunt please…'

She raised her hand up, gesturing for me to be silent. 'No Effie, no, I do *not* wish to discuss the matter any further.' With a shudder she pulled the blanket further across her lap. 'He could have been killed today in that burglary, and I would have lost my truest friend.'

I suddenly had the urge to shake her again, shake some sense into her, but instead I just lowered my gaze. 'Whatever you say Aunt.' Dejectedly I made my way out the room.

As I lingered in the hallway, my eyes were drawn to one of the oil paintings that hung on the wall adjacent to the kitchen. It was a picture that I had seen many times before; in fact, it had been there ever since I was a small child, however for some reason I was suddenly strangely drawn to it. It was of a woodland scene depicting great leafy elms, with the most beautiful shades of muted greens and browns. The sunlight had escaped between the trees and was beaming down onto the mossy ground, where an abundance of primroses lay in little tufts, their vibrant yellow petals rejoicing in the brightness of the sun. As I continued to stare at the painting it evoked within me an inexplicable yearning that crept over me like a whispering shadow from days gone by, a memory that didn't or shouldn't have belonged to me, and yet somehow our pasts were intertwined.

Mace poked his head around the door.

'Please get your head out the clouds Effie and come into the kitchen. I really need to talk to you.' He said rather impatiently. 'This is not the time to stand there admiring an old painting that's most likely been there since before you were born.'

I reluctantly turned away from the painting and went into the kitchen. To my surprise Mace had already swept up the broken crockery and was helping himself to more cake from the glass container on the dresser.

'Surely you're not having more?'

'One can never have too much cake E.' He exclaimed, placing a rather large slice on a plate and moving towards the table. 'And besides I always eat when I'm nervous.'

Looking concerned I watched as he pulled out a chair and sat down, his face looking grave. 'Why are you nervous Mace, what's wrong.'

'Take a seat Effie, you'll need to sit down.'

With a laugh I sat opposite him. 'You're worrying me Mace, has something dreadful happened?'

'No, not exactly.' He took a bite of cake then sat there quietly as he ate. 'For what I'm about to tell you Effie, please don't be too angry. I was so scared it would spoil our friendship so I've kept silent all these years, it's been like a heavy burden I've had to carry around.' His eyes looked directly into my face. 'But now's the time to lighten that burden.'

I nodded slowly at him. 'Has it something to do with what you said at Isaiah's house?'

With a look of anguish etched across his face he stared at me for a while before answering. 'Yes.' He took a deep breath. 'Let me start from the beginning.' He shovelled a large piece of cake into his mouth. 'Oh, and E, please try and not interrupt.'

I slouched forward over the table, resting my chin in my hands. 'I'll try not to.'

He was silent for a moment whilst he finished his cake, and then taking a deep breath he cleared his throat.

'Do you remember E, how moody I behaved shortly after becoming a teenager, you put it down to my age, but really that had nothing to do with it at all.' He began nervously drumming his fingers on the table. 'I had something serious on my mind, something that took me a long while to come to terms with. You see on my thirteenth birthday a solicitor came to call at our house, with a package, a package my mother Sabina had instructed him to pass to me once I'd reached my teenage years.' With a lost look he stared down at his empty plate. 'My whole outlook on life changed after that day.'

'What was in the package?'

He looked suddenly disgruntled. 'I'm just about to tell you Effie, if you can manage to be quiet for a minute.'

'Sorry.'

'Inside were several sheets of written notes from my mother. On top was a covering letter explaining how she'd deserted her home of Hartland and…. and crossed over to this world when she was heavily pregnant with me.' He bowed his head. 'Apparently it was a difficult birth as my mother was very weak after the journey. But, by a miracle we both survived.' He paused and glanced over at me as I sat there gawping at him. 'She then went onto write that after living in Hartland most of her life, the repercussions of coming here had caused her to become gravely ill. It was hoped that her condition would improve over time, but after visiting a doctor he confirmed that she was dying.'

We sat there in silence, staring at one another.

I found it an astonishing and strange coincidence that both of us should have a connection with someone from another world. It was almost as if the man sitting opposite me had suddenly turned into a stranger, and I half expected his features to change, right before my very eyes. How deeply hurt it made me feel to think he couldn't share any of this with me, that he believed it would spoil our friendship. However, these thoughts were entirely eclipsed by the overwhelming sense of grief I felt for him at having lost his mother, for although we both knew she had died when he was a baby, it must have been truly heart-breaking for him when he discovered the tragic circumstances of her passing.

'Mace I'm so dreadfully sorry. It…it must have been a lot for you to take in.'

He gave me a twitch of a smile.

'Effie, I haven't finished yet.'

'Oh sorry.' I muttered, rather faintly.

With his finger he started pushing the cake crumbs around the plate. 'My mother also mentioned something else in her covering letter, something concerning you.' His large eyes looked directly into mine. 'You see Effie, Sabina didn't journey alone when she travelled here, she…she came with your mother.'

The blood drained from my face.'

'What?'

He turned away from me. 'They were friends Effie. When they arrived here your mother, as you know, went to Rawlings but my mother wanted to be independent and settled in a nearby town. Connie helped her find suitable accommodation.'

'But...but my Aunt has never mentioned anything about it.'

He leant across the table and looked me straight in the eye.

'That's because Isaiah, that evil father of yours, gave her some type of potion so she couldn't remember.' He banged his fists on the table. 'Have you not noticed how Connie can hardly even recall her own sister?'

'That's not true Mace.' I said feeling annoyed. 'Many at time my Aunt has spoken about her. Why only the other day she mentioned my mother's terrible nightmares and how she overcame them.'

'That's probably because Isaiah mentioned to Connie that you'd had a bad dream about Gilbert the dummy, and for a short time that memory was triggered.'

I felt anger bubbling up inside of me.

'So, Mace, you've known *all* this time that Isaiah is my father?'

'Yes Effie.' He placed his hand across his eyes then rubbed his forehead. 'Sorry about telling you, just then, in such a careless manner, it just slipped out, but from your lack of surprise I take it you already knew?'

'Yes, he told me this week.'

Avoiding my eye, he nodded slowly. 'I had a feeling he might have. It was probably best he told you anyway.'

I glowered at him. 'So, did your mother mention Isaiah in her letter?'

Looking rather contrite he peered at me from underneath his unruly fringe.

'No, it was amongst the notes that were with the letter. She simply wrote that Freya was carrying the unborn child of Isaiah. Of course, I didn't realise you were his daughter until I was thirteen, but then it all made sense, the way he's always skulking about Rawlings, and poking his nose in your business. He paused. 'I ah...would have told you Effie, but wasn't sure how to.'

Without saying a word, I rose from my chair and slowly made my way over to the window. It was bleak outside and still raining. I could hear the patter of water dripping down from the drainpipe.

'Say something Effie, please.'

'What *is* there to say Mace?' I said in a cold voice. 'The friend I've known nearly all my life, the friend who I thought told me everything has been concealing his true identity from me.' I wiped away a tear. 'And how could you not have told me that Isaiah was my father, how could you keep something like that from me all these years?'

'Well, I knew you hated his guts E, so finding out you were his daughter surely wouldn't have improved your relationship.'

I swung round and glared at him. 'That wasn't your assumption to make Mace, you should have told me, so I could decide for myself.'

'Sorry E, my mistake.'

I continued staring at him. 'So, what else did your mother mention in her notes?'

'She wrote that Isaiah knew about my existence.'

'But how, did he go and visit your mother after you were born?'

He shrugged his shoulders. 'I don't know, she didn't write anything about that. But she did mention that Isaiah was highly skilled in the making of herbal medicines, just like....' He paused and frowned. 'She wrote another name, but I can't think what it was, not that it's relevant.'

'So, do you think he's using a herbal medicine on my Aunt?'

'Yep. I sure do Effie, one that wipes her memory.' He suddenly looked rather fidgety. 'Apart from that my mother didn't really write much more, just a load of random names, but she didn't explain who they were.' He nervously cleared his throat. 'Gideon was one of them.'

A sharp pain shot through my heart.

'Gideon?'

'Yes Effie.' He smiled sadly at me. 'That day you first mentioned his name, I twigged on that it must be the same Gideon. I mean it's not the sort of name that's very common now, is it?'

'So that's why you acted so strange when I told you about him.' I paused thoughtfully for a moment. 'Did your mother not say anything else about Gideon?'

'No, nothing at all, from studying her notes it seemed she had meant to write more about all these people but then.... well either she'd forgotten or was incapacitated.'

I nodded my head in acknowledgement. 'It seems our minds swiftly forget all about our other lives when we cross over to different worlds. Isaiah told me all about it, just the other day.' I said with a smile. 'It's just a pity my brain can't recall everything he's recently mentioned. I don't suppose the sleeping draught he put in my tea helped.'

'Ah, well that explains why your brain is so muddled. He's a nasty blighter that Isaiah.'

I let out a harrowing sigh. 'Yes, yes he is.'

Mace got up and came over towards me. 'Don't worry about it E, you see, my brain is fully intact but yours...well my theory is your poor little mind can't work out what to remember and what to forget, and it not only removed all your memories from when you were in the other place, but also anything remotely connected with what Isaiah has mentioned in the past few days.' He took me by the shoulders and looked deep into my eyes. 'Am I making any sense E?'

'Yes, I suppose so.' I replied dispassionately.

'But on the bright side, although your brain is desperately forcing you to suppress any thoughts of Gideon and everything that happened to you when you were away, those memories are so powerful that they're struggling to come back to the surface, they won't die.' With a grin he moved my hair away from my face. 'You have to admit E, my explanation is a good one. My science professor would be impressed.'

I did my best to smile. 'Do you think I...I loved Gideon?' I asked in a meek voice.

There was a short silence.

'Yes, I think you did Effie. You mentioned to me about the dreams, and how almost every night he was in them, surely you remember?'

'Yes, yes I do a little.' I said in a vague voice.

'Don't be too disheartened E. Between the both of us, we'll unravel the pieces of the puzzle and fit them back into their rightful place.' He gently pushed my head forward so it was resting upon his chest. 'You can always rely on your best pal Mace.' He wrapped his arms tightly around me.

We both remained quiet for a moment.

Suddenly I withdrew from his arms and stared at him.

'Mace, there's something wrong.'

'What E?'

'I...I don't know, I just have a bad feeling about something.'

Mace began jokingly complaining about how every day I had a sense of foreboding, and that perhaps I should go and speak to someone about it at The Manor, because it was really becoming tiresome.

My heart lurched at the mere mention of that place.

'I fear that won't help Mace.' With a half-smile I began to slowly walk across the kitchen.

I likened my memories to being caught up in a thick, impenetrable fog that was preventing me from seeing certain events, both in this world and the other. I now recalled travelling through the portal but can't remember what had happened at the other end. Maybe all I required was just a tiny glimpse of this forgotten world, and this would be sufficient to create a clear picture of what had occurred.

Stopping in front of the fridge I suddenly had a vision of a scowling woman with callous eyes. 'The woman…. the madwoman, she was here in my kitchen.' I let out a triumphant laugh. 'I remember now, she…she somehow had the ability to transport herself here.' I ran my fingers over the small round dent in the fridge door. My face dropped. 'She tried to kill me.' In a panic I staggered away from the fridge and huddled in the corner of the room, stupidly believing that my memory of nearly being murdered had the ability to automatically replay itself.

Mace swiftly strolled over and touched my arm. 'Effie it's okay.' He gently pulled me forward. 'That woman's long gone.' He gave me a huge grin. 'It's good that you remembered. Maybe you're not such a hopeless case, after all E.'

I stood there, mulling things over.

'I don't really believe my mother has crossed over into the spirit world.' I glanced at Mace. 'Do you?'

He shook his head vehemently. 'To my knowledge ghosts don't contact the living as easily as that.'

'According to Aunt, my mother mentioned something about a gateway, so perhaps that means she's planning on travelling through a portal.' My heart sank. 'It…it could harm her.' I gazed poignantly at Mace. 'Just like your mother.'

'Yes, yes it could E.' He scratched his head. 'But what can we do to stop her?'

With an increasing sense of unease, I began pacing up and down the room, then suddenly I froze on the spot.

'Oh no, no, no.' I gasped.

'What is it E?'

'I'm so stupid for not thinking about it before.' I ran up to Mace and clutched his hands in mine. 'Isaiah told me....' I gulped. 'He told me he was going on a trip to destroy the portal. I think he called it a gateway but it amounts to the same thing.' Shaking my head in panic I stared into his confused face. 'Well don't you see - it could be the same one my mother's going to travel through.'

He narrowed his eyes. 'But Effie, Isaiah doesn't know your mother's travelling home, he left Rawlings beforehand, remember?'

'No Mace, you don't understand. He thinks by destroying the portal it will aid my recovery, but in doing so he could inadvertently kill my mother.' I grasped his shoulders. 'We have to go to Browning's Wood immediately and stop him.'

'Effie, you're gabbling, slow down. 'Did Isaiah actually tell you he was going to the woods?'

'No, but how many portals can there be Mace?'

'Well ...'

I interrupted him abruptly. 'We...we *must* go there Mace.' With a strange whimper I ran towards the door, then turned to glance at him. 'If you don't wish to come with me, then I'll understand, but if there's the slightest chance of saving my mother then I have to take it.'

His face looked grim. 'You're acting completely foolhardy E, and reckless: the trip could be dangerous, it could be an utter waste of time.' He pretended to shiver. 'It'll be dark out there soon, I don't like the dark, it's scary and all sorts of sinister creatures lurk in the woods, including Isaiah.' With a harrowing sigh he buried his face into his hands, pretending to whimper, then as it turned into laughter he looked up and grinned at me. 'Oh, come on then E, I'm not the kind of person to turn down a thrilling adventure.' He leapt towards the door. 'Just let me phone Giles and Marigold to let them know I won't be home tonight.' He gave me a gentle shove out the door. 'I shall say I'm spending the night at Rawlings, with you.'

I turned and gaped at him. 'In separate rooms of course.'

He lightly slapped the top of my head. 'Well of course E, no offence, but they know I can't stand the sight of you in a romantic way. And besides we're not married old thing, so it really won't do.'

I giggled.

My Aunt was fast asleep when we left. I drew the blanket further around her so that it covered her shoulders, then I planted a kiss on her forehead. I scribbled a quick note and placed it next to her on the little coffee table. It explained that something urgent had cropped up, so Mace and I had to go out, and that we would return by tomorrow afternoon, at the very latest. I hated leaving her like this, especially with all that had happened, but under the circumstances it was necessary. Of course, the likelihood of returning home with my mother seemed extremely slim, and yet it *was* possible, anything was possible.

Chapter 25

Due to Mace's frequent visits to Browning's Wood, we were able to reach it without any trouble. He parked his car just outside the entrance and we clambered out and made our way to the front gates. Isaiah's car was nowhere to be seen, which cheered me up a little and gave me real hope that he was somewhere else. Mace placed a torch in each of his jacket pockets, for when we needed them later, as it wouldn't be long before the woods were shrouded in darkness.

'Who do you suppose removed the padlock from the gates?'

'I don't know E.' He replied nonchalantly. 'It wasn't me.'

'When did you discover the gates were opened?'

'Actually, it was the very first time I returned to the woods, after you'd deserted me for another man.' He grinned at me, and then pulled some sweets from the pocket of his jacket. 'I no longer had to clamber over that towering gate.' He shoved the sweets in my face. 'Take a couple Effie you need to keep your sugar levels up.'

'Thanks.' I took two and passed them back. 'How many times did you actually return to the woods Mace?'

'Well,' He said, looking deep in concentration. 'Quite a few as I remember, and I must have been serious about jumping into the portal because on many occasions I even took my rucksack, full of clothes.' He stopped and grabbed my arm. 'Sorry E, for being such a coward, but my intentions were good.' With a grin he popped another sweet into his mouth and continued walking. 'Ah, there's our first arrow, up ahead.'

A while ago Mace had chalked arrow marks on several trees, which according to him gave a direct route to the waterfalls, rather than taking the long way round via the stream. On one occasion, prior to marking the trees, he'd accidentally taken a wrong turning and become hopelessly lost, and for hours he wandered aimlessly through the woods, before eventually finding his bearings. He swears blind he saw an ogre type creature one day, lurking behind a tree, and thought the beast might drag him off and eat him for his supper.

'Did you really visit Browning's Wood as a child Mace?' I asked, suddenly curious. 'Or was there some other way you discovered it?'

'The name of the woods was scribbled in my mother's notes E. It took me a while to find it, because it was jumbled up amongst a load of other things she'd written.' He kicked a stone into the stream. 'Then, on the off chance, I asked Giles if he'd heard of it and to my surprise, he knew the place well, he even mentioned the two beech trees, and how they were directly in front of the woods.' He paused and grabbed my shoulders, peering solemnly into my eyes. 'I'm sorry I lied to you about visiting it as a boy, I'm sorry about everything I lied to you about Effie.'

I studied his face closely, pondering if I'd ever understand him completely, he was such a complex character that sometimes I wondered if even *he* knew what was going on inside his head. Whilst I wished he'd confided in me years ago about the letter and notes his mother had left him, there was little point being cross with him, what good would it do.

'I accept your apology Mace. Lucky for you I'm quite a forgiving person, especially when it comes to my best friend.' Looking perplexed I removed his hands from my shoulders and stepped back. 'Wait a minute, if you didn't know about all this until you were thirteen then how come you made a beeline for me that first day you started at my school? I've always found that odd.'

'E, there's nothing odd about it. My foster mother, Marigold had already suggested I make friends with the little girl with big eyes and wild auburn hair, named Effie. She told me you were the niece of that lovely Constance Farraday and that you were sure to be equally as pleasant.'

'Oh, I never knew that.'

He shrugged his shoulders. 'Well, that's because you never asked.' He gave me a weak smile. 'I don't tell you everything E.'

I widened my eyes. 'Evidently not.'

'It's just a shame Marigold was so wrong about you having a pleasant personality. I actually found you extremely hard to talk to and rather snobbish.' Grinning, he reached out and ruffled my hair. 'How we ever became friends, I'll never know.'

I chuckled. 'I'm in total agreement with you on that Mace.' Taking his hand, I pulled him forward. 'Come on *friend*, let's get going.'

We carried on our journey, going left at the next chalked arrow and away from the stream. We walked for about a mile before joining up with it again. By early evening we'd reached the waterfalls, which I remembered as soon as I saw them. It was strange to be back there again, amongst the quaint little rivers that flowed and trickled over the crumbling walls.

Mace gently took my hand as we approached the stepping-stones.

'Whatever happens E, you've got to remember one thing.'

I caught his eye. 'What's that?'

'I will always be your best friend.'

I smiled softly at him. 'You'll always be mine too.' I answered, looking at the deep warmth within his eyes.

He suddenly tickled me.

'And I'll always be here to get on your nerves, and eat all of your Aunt Connie's cakes.' A broad grin spread across his face.

We stood there and laughed for a little while but then Mace's face changed, and he suddenly looked serious.

'What about Gideon, do you want to see him again?'

A difficult question to answer when I didn't even remember meeting Gideon in the first place, I thought rather amusingly. He was hidden away somewhere out of minds reach, like a distant dream of long ago.

'Yes, I suppose so.' I said, following on behind Mace as he begun leaping from one stone to another. 'But I can't leave home again just yet. I've only been back about a week.'

Mace started jumping two stones at a time.

'Yeah, I don't think your Aunt Connie will be too pleased if you left again, nor would Isaiah; he'd probably come after you and drag you back home.'

The more I pondered over it, the more I managed to make myself believe that Isaiah was in a different location; it was another portal he was going to destroy, and it *wasn't* the one my mother was going to journey through. I prayed that she would arrive home safely, and wouldn't end up lost and alone in a world between worlds, if there was such a thing. But most of all I prayed that Isaiah wasn't in Browning's Woods.

I joined Mace on the other side of the bank, beside the trees that encircled the portal.

'The lights fading, we should start using the torches soon.'

'Yep, but I'm having the blue one.' He smiled at me. 'E, I want you to know that if you do decide to go and see Gideon, then I'm definitely coming with you this time.' He reached over and took me in his arms. 'I promise. That's as long as that infernal man hasn't gone an ...'

Mace stopped in mid-sentence as we suddenly heard the sound of raucous laughter. We both swung round and came face to face with Isaiah.

'Blown it up. Is that what you were going to say boy?'

I had a distinct queasy sensation in my stomach as I stared into Isaiah's bloodshot eyes, not quite believing he was really standing there, but deep down knowing all along that we *would* see him. A neat bandage was wrapped around his forehead and the back of his head, and I observed how his left trouser leg was stained with blood, were I'd stabbed him with the knife.

'You look like hell Isaiah.' Mace exclaimed as he grasped my hand. 'It's just a shame you didn't go to hell, you'd be right at home there.'

'Oh, do shut up boy.'

'No, why should I?'

'Mace, stop it.' I said, fearing for his life.

Without warning Isaiah produced a gun and pointed it directly at Mace's head.

'No sudden movement's boy or you'll die now rather than in a minute.' He snarled at him, pressing his face right up against his. 'How convenient you've made it for me boy, now I can dispose of your body right here in the woods.' For a fleeting moment he glanced at me. 'Step away from him Effelia.'

Although I was bitterly afraid, I knew he wouldn't hurt me.

'No, no I won't step away.' Very slowly I moved closer to Mace. 'Put the gun down Isaiah.'

Smiling, Isaiah wiped the sweat from his brow and lowered the gun. 'Oh Effelia, how brave you've become. It's just a shame it's wasted on this pathetic individual.' He stood there coughing for a moment, his body shaking with laughter. Suddenly he lurched towards me and dragged me away from Mace, gripping my arm tightly. Once again, he aimed the gun at his head. 'Don't move an inch boy.' He bellowed.

Mace's eyes looked wider than ever, as he stared at me in terror. 'Effie?'

'It's okay Mace.'

'Good, I'm glad you both understand me now.' His hand shook a little as he continued to point the gun at Mace's head. 'Any last requests before I pull the trigger?'

'A three-course meal and a glass of wine would be nice.'

It amazed me how Mace could still joke when he was staring death in the face, but I could see from his eyes that he was petrified.

'Joke if you will boy, it won't save you.'

'Please Isaiah, he's my best friend.' I said in a thick voice.

'Friend? Oh Effelia, what friend would allow you to go to a strange world all on your own whilst he carried on his normal life here, without a care in the world. He should have been there by your side.'

Mace gulped. 'Effie understands why I didn't go, and the reason for ...'

'No.' I exclaimed abruptly, before he could finish his sentence. If Isaiah learnt that Mace had pushed me into the portal it would only anger him further. 'There's really no need to go into all of that now, is there Mace.'

Isaiah gave me an odd look. 'Quite.' He continued looking at me for a moment then turned to glare at Mace. 'Because of your interference boy, I was left tied up in that room with a head and leg injury, and if it wasn't for Constance I'd still be festering away in there.' A gloating expression appeared across his face. 'But now everything has turned out surprisingly well.' He moved the gun so it was pointing directly between his eyes. 'You don't know how much I'm going to enjoy this.'

'Father!' I screamed at him.

Although I was loathed to say this word it seemed to have the desired effect, as Isaiah turned and gazed at me. Mace swiftly ducked away from the gun and darted between the trees. I wrenched myself free and gave Isaiah a push, but it wasn't enough to make him lose his balance, and with the gun still in his grip he aimed at Mace and began shooting until all the bullets were spent.

'MACE' I yelled. Although I couldn't see him, I feared the worse. With a whimper I ran towards the trees and brushed passed the overhanging branches. 'Mace, Mace where are you?' I began to smile with relief when I saw him standing near the well. Picking up my pace I ran over to join him.

Isaiah came limping through the trees with a face like thunder.

'You just *won't* die will you boy.' He came and stood in front of us, clenching his fists together, as if ready to strike out.

'Nope, there's no getting rid of me.' He took my hand and we edged away from him. 'Look Isaiah, why don't you just go home? Effie and I will forget what's happened here today.' He looked at me and raised his eyebrows as a signal for me to agree.

'Mace is right, let's just all turn round and go back.' I paused. 'We can all forgive one another. And you and I can have a proper relationship, as father and daughter.'

Isaiah's eyes widened in surprise, then he started to laugh and clap his hands together. 'Oh Effelia, do you really think I'm that gullible?

I lowered my eyes. 'No, not really.'

'My dear daughter, after all that's happened, I know you will never willingly condone my behaviour, but you see it really doesn't matter. When we return home to Rawlings, I shall create a delightful concoction for you, an old family recipe, and you'll have no idea how and when I'll administer it. Afterwards you'll be blissfully unaware of any unpleasantness between us.' He smiled smugly. 'But don't worry, you won't have to drink anymore sickly-sweet tea.'

'You guessed I found out?'

'Well of course, I'm not some simpleton Effelia. I had my suspicions, and was certain when you threw that tray across the room and then asked for orange juice, instead of tea.'

I looked at him and bit my lip. 'It's irrelevant anyway, because you won't be returning to Rawlings Isaiah.'

He stepped closer to where we were standing.

'Oh, I think your dear Aunt Constance will have something to say about that Effelia, especially when I inform her of who I really am. How delighted she'll be, knowing that I'm your father.'

'Mortified, more like it.' exclaimed Mace.

He swiftly lunged for Mace, placing his hands firmly around his neck, a look of determination and rage covered his face as he began to squeeze. 'Now let's finish this.'

Initially I was going to try and pull him away from Mace, or kick him in his wounded leg, but then I came up with a better idea. I ran to the well and teetered there on the edge.

'Stop right now Isaiah, or I'll jump into the portal.' I screamed at him. 'And don't think I won't do it Isaiah. Why do you think I returned to Browning's Wood in the first place? I want to go back and see Gideon.'

Mace's face was turning red from the pressure of Isaiah's hands and small gasping noises were bursting from his mouth.

I dangled my foot over the edge. 'Release him Isaiah, release him this instant, or I *will* jump in.'

Isaiah stared at me in alarm as he continued to grip his throat. 'Oh, very well.' With a sigh he removed his hands and Mace dropped to the ground. 'I don't think you'd really jump in Effelia, but you're still unwell after your breakdown and I really can't take the risk.'

'That's right Isaiah, you cannot.'

To my surprise he took Mace's arm and helped him to his feet, then begun pulling him forward to where I was standing.

'You can move away from the well now Effelia.' He looked pleadingly at me. 'Please Effelia...Gideon can wait.'

I stared at him dubiously.

'Effelia?'

With a gulp, I swiftly removed my foot from the portal and stumbled back a little. For a split second I'd almost been tempted to leap in, but then common sense had prevailed.

I turned my attention to Mace, who was coughing violently. 'Are you alright?'

'Well E.' He said, cupping his throat. 'It's...its touch and go.' He smiled warmly at me. 'But I might just live to see another day.'

I smiled back at him.

With a mocking laugh, Isaiah patted Mace on the back. 'That's right boy.' He gripped him by the shoulder of his jacket and placed his mouth close to his ear. 'You *might* live to see another day, but not in this world.'

A sensation of terror gripped me as I realised what was about to occur, and it all happened so quickly I was powerless to stop it. Isaiah gave Mace an almighty shove forward, sending him toppling headfirst into the well. I heard him scream my name and then there was silence.

'MACE.' I yelled in a desperate voice. Instinctively I peered into the portal, gazing down into the murky blue mist, contemplating whether or not I had the courage to throw myself in after him, but strong arms were clasping mine, gradually pulling me back.

'Effelia, please....'

'How could you?' I shrieked, turning to glare at him. 'I'll never forgive you for this Isaiah, ever.'

'We must leave *now* Effelia.' His said urgently. 'The bomb is due to detonate at any moment.'

'Bomb, what bomb?'

'It's already in the gateway Effelia, I placed it there earlier on.'

'What? How is that even possible?' I twisted my arm in an attempt to get away. 'You're lying to me.'

'No Effelia, I am not. If you're thinking of leaping in after him then it will mean certain death.'

'But what about Mace?' I asked in a panicked voice.

Isaiah glanced at his watch. 'We'll discuss that later.' He frantically tugged my arm. 'Come on Effelia.'

We both ran from the portal and passed through the curtain of trees. Isaiah shone his torch over the stepping- stones, ever so often asking me to quicken my pace. I nearly lost my footing several times, but it didn't matter if I fell in the water, nothing mattered now. Once I'd reached the other side of the bank I crouched down and instinctively wrapped my arms about myself.

'Now remain here Effelia until I know it's safe. I need to go and check on why the bomb hasn't exploded yet.' He placed his hand lightly upon my shoulder. 'Have you not got a torch?'

I suddenly remembered Mace still had them in his jacket pockets.

'No.' I replied bluntly.

'Well, I won't be long. Don't go wandering anywhere in the dark.'

In a daze I watched as he went back over the stepping-stones.

I felt like someone had just come along and switched off all of my emotions, for I felt dead inside. Mace had gone now, and I'd probably never see him again. I just prayed he was still alive.

I jumped suddenly as a huge blast erupted from within the curtain of trees, followed by several more explosions. The sound of it shook the ground where I sat and stung the air, causing squawking birds to fly up from the woods and make an echo with their noise. A dark shadowy figure was coming into view, shining a torch over the stepping-stones as he crossed over towards me. For one deluded moment I believed it to be Mace, but of course it wasn't.

'Phew. I just escaped in time.' Isaiah exclaimed, trying to catch his breath. 'It's done Effelia.'

I gazed at him in bewilderment, not quite grasping what was going on, but realising that something just didn't ring true about the bomb.

'I'd like to go back and see the well.'

He narrowed his eyes and stood there looking down at me. 'Yes, very well, I do believe it will help with your recovery, and give you closure.' Still trying to get his breath back he handed me the torch. 'Here, you go first.'

Without looking at him in the eye, I snatched the torch from his hands and made my way back over the stones. I passed through the trees and rather unsteadily shone the torch over the well, where all I could see was a pile of smoking rubble.

'Don't get too close Effelia, the structure maybe unsafe.'

Disregarding what he said I went closer to the mound of rubble, searching for remnants of the well, but all I spotted were a few fragments of stone from the brickwork surrounding it. I leant forward, listening out for the sound of the swirling wind, but it was silent.

'I can assure you Effelia the gateway has gone. I not only threw a ton of dynamite into the well but also dangled some over the side too.' He laughed. 'I'm rather impressed at how each stick almost exploded at the same time.'

I scrunched up my eyes, trying to think straight. 'Wait a moment, I thought you'd used a bomb?'

'On no, that would have been far too dangerous.' He roared with laughter. 'Do you really think I'd risk our lives with a bomb that could explode whilst we were standing right next to the gateway?' With a sigh he straightened the bandage across his forehead. 'I'd planned to use dynamite all along, but was delayed when you and that meddling boy turned up. I temporarily hid the box of explosives in the branches of one of the trees before disposing of the boy, then returned just now to set it all up, and then all I had to do was light the fuses and run for cover.'

'So, you did lie after all?'

'Oh Effelia, it was a tiny white lie, and told with the very best of intentions.'

I eyed him angrily. 'You realise you could have killed Mace.'

'Yes, yes I do. But knowing that insolent boy he's most likely made it safely through to the other end.' He smiled softly. 'You see Effelia, the boy should never have come to this world in the first place, he never belonged, he never fitted in properly, he's been an exceedingly bad influence on you, and now he's gone I will see to it that you get your head out of the clouds and actually make something of yourself.'

'I can manage perfectly fine, without you Isaiah. You should have been the one thrown into the well, not Mace.'

'Oh, I don't think so Effelia.' He retorted. 'Without me you would have never had the gumption to hold your own art exhibition, and without me you would have disappeared through the gateway, those two years ago, and never come home, leaving your poor Aunt in utter misery.'

I eyed him suspiciously. 'What do you mean, of course I would have come home.'

He closed his eyes for a second. 'Effelia, have you not realised it was me that sent you that note about Constance being seriously ill in hospital. It was so easy to copy the boys scrawling handwriting. A while back I sent twenty of them through the gateway, in the hope that at least one would reach you.'

'Yes, well now it all makes perfect sense.' I replied dryly.

'You'll thank me one day Effelia.' He extended his hand towards me. 'Come let's leave this place.'

'My mother was on her way home - did you know that? I turned away so he couldn't see the tears in my eyes. 'Now because of what you've done today she may never return.'

'How do you know she was on her way home Effelia?'

'She visited my Aunt in the library earlier on today.'

He placed his hand upon my shoulder and slowly turned me round so I was facing him. 'Effelia, Effelia look at me.'

With a harrowing sigh I looked into his eyes.

'Firstly, your mother might have used another doorway to this world, there are many out there you know.' His face clouded over. 'Alas I have no idea where the others are located. Secondly, if your dear mother truly loved you, don't you think she would have found a way to come back to Rawlings years ago, to see you grow up.' Looking compassionately into my face he cupped my cheek with his hand. 'You lost your mother before you were even born Effelia, and I lost her when she decided to take the tonic.'

Shivering I moved away from him. 'Where's Clarice?'

'Ah...dear, sweet Clarice.' He lowered his eyes and began to laugh. 'I'm afraid she was becoming rather a liability.'

'Why?'

'Can we discuss it later Effelia.' He began rubbing his forehead. 'Ever since knocking my head I've had a blasted headache.' Taking my arm, he began limping towards the trees. 'Let's make our way home.'

We walked in silence as we passed through the trees, and it wasn't until the waterfalls were in clear sight that I came to a sudden halt.

'Actually, I'd rather know now.' I decided to come right out and ask him. 'Did you murder Clarice?'

He looked rather taken aback. 'What, no, no of course not Effelia, how could you even suggest such a thing.'

'Well after what happened with Mace, can you blame me?'

For a moment his eyes widened in surprise but then he looked deeply hurt. 'It seems you have a very low opinion of me Effelia. But that will change, over time.' He gazed over at the waterfalls, looking deep in concentration. 'The truth is, if it hadn't been for Lydia Davenport, your friend Clarice would still be safely at home.'

I stared at him, looking perplexed.

'Who's Lydia Davenport?'

'Oh Effelia, that trip through the gateway certainly has damaged your memory.' He chuckled. 'Lydia was that dear sweet old lady on your Aunt's committee.'

I tried to cast my mind back and suddenly had a vague recollection of my Aunt being distraught, around about the time of my art exhibition. Then I remembered - Lydia had just passed away.

'Effelia?'

Very slowly my eyes travelled to his face as a chilling thought crossed through my mind: was Isaiah responsible for the death of Miss Davenport?'

My eyes glazed over. 'Yes.... yes, I remember her now.'

He gave me a slight odd look and raised his eyebrows. 'The evening before your art exhibition, I had a visit from Lydia.' Shining the torch, he gestured for me to go ahead of him over the stepping-stones. 'She was collecting money for some charity. Well, I had to pop upstairs to find my wallet and when I returned to the hallway Lydia was browsing through my photo album. It was so careless of me to leave it there on the bureau, however at the same time it was extremely nosey of her to look through it.'

'Was there something in the album you didn't want Lydia to see?'

'I'm afraid so. It was full of photos of you, growing up through the years.' He paused. 'And I'd written your name under each one...and the words '*my daughter*.'

'Oh, I see.' I said gravely, not liking where this was heading.

'Precisely, so there wasn't much point denying to Lydia that I was your father, not after she saw the album.'

We'd passed the stones now and were walking through the woods. I nearly mentioned to him about Mace's shortcut, but couldn't bring myself to tell him, and besides I had a feeling Isaiah already knew an easier way back.

'So, what happened then?'

'Lydia was very kind and promised not to say a word to you or anyone else.' He grimaced. 'But I just couldn't trust her. I knew she was bound to tell her sister, and you know how little old ladies can gossip. Before long it would've been all around Abercrombie.'

Coming to a standstill, I drew in a deep breath and peered directly into his face. 'So, are you going to deny murdering Lydia as well as Clarice?'

Isaiah stood over me, contemplating what to say next. 'Well no, however I would hardly describe it as murder.' He placed his hand across his eyes and held it there for a moment. 'Don't you see, I didn't have a choice?'

'You did have a choice.' I said curtly. 'All you had to do was tell my Aunt and I your true identity, and then there wouldn't have been the need to do away Miss Davenport.'

'Well, I wished to Effelia, but I wanted to declare it myself, when I felt the time was right, and not have the both of you find out by a third party.' He gave me a pitiful look. 'Lydia was an extremely old lady, she wouldn't have lived for very much longer anyway, and was in constant pain with her arthritis.'

'Are you saying you did her a favour?'

'Well...yes, I suppose so.' He let out a sigh and despondently shook his head. 'Old age is such a curse, don't you think.'

'Perhaps, but that hardly gives you the right to end someone's life.' Feeling rather nauseous I turned away. 'So how...how did it happen?'

'After handing over a rather generous amount of money for this charity of hers, she began complaining about how she wasn't looking forward to walking all the way home. Well, the gentlemanly thing to do was offer her a lift. On arriving at her house, I insisted she went and put her feet up whilst I made her a lovely cup of tea, that unbeknown to her was going to be laced with a rather large quantity of sleeping draught. I knew it was kept on her bedside table upstairs, as prior to that she had mentioned it in conversation. I poured just over half the bottle into her tea and disguised the taste with sugar.'

'Just like my sugary sweet tea.'

He chuckled. 'Well yes, but yours was a sleeping tonic of my very own making, and a much milder version. You are the last person in the world I would wish to harm Effelia.'

We stared at one another.

'Then Lydia simply dropped off to sleep and never woke up. Luckily her sister Agnes was out for the evening so it was all fairly simple. I placed the bottle of sleeping draught on the table beside her body and ah.... well, I suppose it was rather wrong of me but I took back the charity money I'd given to Lydia, and also seized possession of the wad of notes she kept stuffed underneath her mattress.' He sniggered. 'She told me ages ago how she'd left the money there for a rainy day, but there'd be no more rainy days for poor old Lydia, not in heaven.'

Rendered speechless, I stared at him in horror.

'Well don't look so shocked Effelia. I *did* give most of the money to your Aunt Constance, for the upkeep of Rawlings. I told her I'd had a windfall on the horses.' He cleared his throat. 'There was an inquest afterwards and it was concluded that poor Lydia had accidentally taken an overdose.' He glanced at his watch. 'It's getting late, we should carry on moving.'

I followed after him as he began limping awkwardly alongside the stream. How I wished he'd lose his balance and tumble in, because it was only what he deserved, far, far *less* than what he really deserved. Such a man should be locked away and never be aloud free for the rest of his natural life. It scared me how cold and calculating he was, how he spoke so calmly about killing Lydia Davenport, as if it was literally an everyday occurrence, and it greatly disturbed me that he may have committed similar crimes in the past. It was like being stuck in a sinister dream I could never escape from, no matter how desperately hard I tried to wake up. This *was* my reality.

Suddenly I spotted a nearby rock by the stream, a stone that would be most adequate in knocking someone out cold, or even ending a person's life, a person such as Isaiah. I hovered there, seriously contemplating picking it up and striking him over the back of the skull. Surely, in such a small space of time, another blow to the same part of the head could be fatal. But that would make me just like him, a cold bloodied murderer. The mere thought of this made me shudder.

With a groan he turned and glared at me. 'Don't dawdle Effelia.'

Rather reluctantly I quickened my step.

'So, what's the connection between Lydia and Clarice?'

'Oh Effelia, questions, questions.' He grumbled, slowing down. 'You're far too inquisitive, young lady. If you must know I briefly visited Clarice on the evening of your art exhibition and told her quite emphatically how you had no intention of sharing a flat with her, and how you and that idiotic friend of yours had been cruelly laughing behind her back.'

'Why did you have to interfere, what does it matter to you where I live?'

'Effelia, Rawlings is where you belong, where you'll always belong. And besides, I knew you never intended to leave. You should have been honest with Clarice from the start, it was unkind to allow her false hope.'

He was absolutely right of course, but I would never give him the satisfaction of knowing it.

'So how is that relevant to Clarice's disappearance?'

'Don't be impatient Effelia, I'm just coming to that part.' He exclaimed with a frown. 'Before I left Clarice's house she happened to mention how, just that previous night, she'd spotted me leaving the Davenport's, and that because it was the same night Lydia died, she was considering going to the police. I managed to talk her out of it, and hoped that was the end of the matter.'

We'd reached the edge of the woods now and the gates were in clear sight.

'But it wasn't the end of the matter, was it?'

He scratched his head and repositioned the bandage that kept slipping down over his forehead.

'No Effelia, it was not. Two days after you went missing Clarice visited Rawlings, and reminded me of the inquest into Lydia's death in two weeks' time. She insisted on me telling the coroner all about my visit to the old ladies house on the evening of her death.' He held his hands up in despair and groaned. 'Her father used to be just the same –unable to drop a subject, like a dog with a bone.' He mumbled something I couldn't quite make out.

'What?'

'Nothing Effelia. I was just thinking of...' he hesitated. 'Oh look, it really doesn't matter.'

I gulped. 'Where is she Isaiah, what have you done with Clarice?'

'Clarice has gone Effelia, I threw her into the gateway, right here in Browning's Wood.'

Despite what he'd just said I allowed myself a tiny glimmer of hope. For surely that would mean she was still alive. Perhaps she would bump into Mace, and at least that way they'd have each other.

'When?'

'I disposed of her that very same day. Thankfully Constance was outside in the back garden grilling the boy on where he thought you were. He'd made up some nonsense about you taking a trip overseas. So, I ushered Clarice out the front door, and told her how you were secretly hiding out in the woods because you needed to get away from everyone. She was most concerned when I told her you were not eating or sleeping, and spent the entire time roaming about muttering to yourself. I pretended that I was just about to jump in my car and visit you and suggested she accompanied me, and being so gullible she agreed without question.'

I stopped again, trying to digest all that he was telling me.

He looked back and glared at me. 'Oh, do get a move on Effelia, I'm extremely tired and eager to get home.'

'Mace and Clarice could be dead, don't you realise? I screamed at him. 'Have you no conscience?'

'Having a conscience gets you nowhere in life Effelia. My philosophy is - out of sight, out of mind. Besides there's a chance they *might* have made it past all the nasty dangers that lurk in that place.'

I fell silent, lost in the sadness of my thoughts.

Isaiah gently patted my shoulder. 'Come now Effelia, everything will be better when we're back at Rawlings. I shall drive you home. My cars just down the lane, adjacent to the woods.' His voice was low and composed, the voice of a person who had achieved what they'd set out to do, and was now content to go home and carry on with their life. 'I promise you shan't be sad for long.'

Something in his tone unnerved me.

'No.' I murmured glumly, staring forlornly at the vehicle up ahead. It was strange, but I felt almost mournful, like at a funeral, Mace's funeral. I had said my farewells and he was gone. 'I should like to drive Mace's car back myself.'

'But Effelia, what about the car keys?'

I swallowed hard, trying not to cry. 'He...he left the door unlocked and the keys are always in the glove compartment.'

Isaiah stared at me intently for a moment. 'So be it. I shall meet you back at Rawlings. Do drive carefully.' Slowly, he turned to leave but suddenly hesitated. 'Oh, I forgot to say, I bumped into Duncan Bartholomew the other day and he mentioned how the two of you became reacquainted at the hospital, when you were enquiring about your Aunt Constance.'

'You know Duncan?'

'Why of course, his father owns several golf clubs in the surrounding area, and Duncan is quite the regular at the one in Abercrombie, where I play. He comes from a very affluent family, you know Effelia.'

I nodded in acknowledgement, failing to see why any of this was relevant. Without saying goodbye, I made my way over to Mace's car, but suddenly stopped as Isaiah shouted after me.

'Anyway, I've invited Duncan over to Rawlings next week. I thought we could all have afternoon tea together.' He exclaimed jubilantly.

I looked at him in utter astonishment. 'How can you even contemplate such a thing after all that's happened?'

A smirk appeared on his face. 'Life goes on Effelia. It's time to look to the future, and let the past slip away.'

'What about The Manor, did you really speak to Dr Stirling about having me committed?'

'Of course not, I was furious with you for throwing that tray, that's all, and wanted to teach you a lesson. You're well again now Effelia, and can return home to Rawlings, where you belong.' He smiled smugly at me. 'With your Aunt and I.'

Unable to bear his company for a moment longer I hastened my pace towards the car, and clambered inside. I saw him in the rear-view mirror, standing there staring at me, then with a smile he waved, before turning away and limping towards the beech trees. I sighed with relief as he disappeared out of sight into the darkness. In a daze I rested my head against the window, trying to come to terms with all that had happened.

To keep me on the steady path of life, perhaps I should lock away all these people I had lost, in the deepest, darkest room of my mind, where I couldn't reach them, and where they'd be safely tucked away, until the inevitable passing of time caused them to fade forever. But hiding such thoughts as if they never existed, surely this would not be right, all these people didn't deserve to be discarded so thoughtlessly, as if their lives had been meaningless, it was up to me to keep them alive in my mind. Therefore, I came to the conclusion that I would have to endure the overwhelming ache in my heart, that presently seemed as painful as an open wound, a wound that belonged to me and me alone, whether I liked it or not. I once read somewhere that the more heartache a person has to cope with in life the more resilient they became. I'm not sure if this was true, but I would like to think that my pain would gradually lessen, and I would become stronger.

Reaching into the glove compartment I pulled out a handful of sweet wrappers. I smiled poignantly to myself. Mace never did throw away his rubbish; if he ever returned home, I would remind him to try and be a little tidier. After finally finding the keys, I started the engine. Taking a fleeting glance onto the back seat I saw Gilbert sitting there with his crooked grin.

'Let's go home Gilbert.'

Epilogue

I lay awake that night for a very long time, full of apprehension and eager anticipation for the following day, a day that would be like no other, a day that is supposed to be the most important event in a woman's life, or so they say. During the weeks leading up to the wedding I'd been gripped by a strange melancholy; it crept over me like a desolate shadow invading my very soul. Thankfully the shadow had left me now, and I was back to my old self, but as my life was to soon change dramatically, I wondered if my old self would take on an entirely new persona, a vastly improved Effie, who was self- assured, gregarious, and someone who no longer had their head stuck in the clouds, but most importantly I hoped to be happier than I'd ever been before.

It was comforting to listen to the rustling leaves, as they whispered soothingly in the trees, and to feel the warm gentle breeze wafting through the open window, onto my face, lulling me to sleep. In my dream I was on the high seas, relaxing in a little sailing boat that was bobbing gently along on the tide. I could smell the fresh salty air and hear the cries of the gulls as they circled overhead. The boat took me to a mystical forest, where creatures from fairy tales roamed the land, and there were others, like myself, although I could not see their faces. They greeted me as if I was an old friend, and together we all lived in harmony, until the end of our days.

The morning of my wedding I awoke early to the sound of rain thrashing against the windowpane, not a good omen, I thought, but nevertheless I was determined that nothing should spoil this day.

For a second my heart lurched in my chest as, out the corner of my eye, I spotted a ghost-like figure lurking ominously over the other side of the room, however I instantly realised it was merely my wedding gown hanging on the front of the wardrobe door. It was an elegant looking dress, lavishly adorned with handmade lace, which was exquisitely stitched across the bodice. 'It's a most sophisticated dress Effie,' My Aunt had said with a beaming smile.

'And if you can't be extravagant at a time like this, when can you be.' She'd muttered, widening her eyes at the price tag. Yes, it was both expensive and elegant, but was it right for me? After bringing it home I kept imagining the owner of the bridal shop turning up at Rawlings asking if I wouldn't prefer a much plainer, conservative gown, more suited to me, and with a lower price tag. I would coyly smile at her and agree.

With one swift movement I swung my legs out of bed and briskly strode over to my gown, dreamily contemplating the day ahead. As I touched the delicate cream fabric, I cast my mind back to when Duncan had come to tea that afternoon, all those months ago, and asked if he could start courting me. Initially I was uncertain, but as the weeks passed our relationship blossomed, and now here we were about to be married. It had all happened so fast, too fast one might say, only I was overwhelmingly flattered that a man such as Duncan should even like me, let alone love me, so when he'd asked me to become his wife I automatically said yes. But afterwards I begun to question my rash acceptance, and wondered if I should ask for more time. 'He's everything one could wish for in a husband, Effie.' My Aunt had said. 'However, you're the one marrying him my dear, and only you can know if it's truly the right decision.' Isaiah had then stormed into the room to join in the conversation. 'Oh, what twaddle,' he replied gruffly. 'Of course, it's the right decision, Effelia would be a fool not to go through with it, and she'll not find a better match than Duncan.' He took my Aunt's hand in his. 'Surely you want the best for your niece, you're a very astute lady Constance, as well as being stunningly attractive, and you've got the good sense to see what a splendid marriage they'll have together.' She crumbled after that and was putty in his hands, telling me how Isaiah was right and that I should listen to my father. Well of course that's precisely what I didn't wish to do, as the day I took advice from Isaiah would be the day I'd lost my mind. I contemplated the alternative of staying single, I could quite happily live my life without someone to love and be perfectly content, pottering around Rawlings and doing my paintings. Nevertheless, I came to the conclusion that I *had* made the right decision in accepting Duncan's proposal, why shouldn't I marry him, to my knowledge no one else had asked me. And perhaps it was fate, the two of us meeting that day in the hospital, and I did believe in fate, and I believed in Duncan, just as he believed in me.

There was a sudden hammering on the front door.

'Charlotte.' I muttered underneath my breath.

Charlotte was Duncan's sister, and was irritatingly efficient, as well as being beautifully stylish and brimming with confidence, she was the kind of person that would elegantly glide into a room, mingling effortlessly with people from all walks of life, leaving a lasting impression with everyone who met her. However, she was also extremely kind and since the wedding announcement she had gone out her way to help me with the preparations, and insisted on doing my hair and makeup for the big day. And here she was now, half an hour early. As I heard her quick, light step ascending the stairs, I flung on my dressing gown and crossed over to the bedroom door.

'There.' Said Charlotte, securing the last clip in my hair. 'All done.' She giggled excitedly as she stood back and proudly examined her handy work. 'Now you're not to touch your hair or face Effie, in any way shape or form. I must have my future sister-in-law walking down the aisle looking the picture of perfection. Don't fret though, being the natural beauty you are, I'm sure that brother of mine won't be able to take his eyes off you, however you look.'

Smiling bashfully, I lowered my eyes.

'Thank you so much Charlotte, I really don't know what I would have done without you.' I gazed into the mirror, staring at the young woman in the reflection, the woman who looked like me, but whose appearance was now greatly enhanced: my auburn hair now framed my face in soft, glossy waves, and was arranged in a neat bun at the back of my head, held in place with the aid of many combs and clips, and around my neck I wore a pearl and diamond necklace, with earrings to match. My makeup was subtle, accentuating my eyes and lips. And of course, there was the dress I was now wearing, the elegant gown that was meant for someone else. 'Are you sure you can't stay here until the ceremony Charlotte?'

She swiftly glanced at her watch. 'No Effie, I promised Duncan I'd meet him at the chapel, before the wedding.' Rather hurriedly she began packing away the makeup and other items she had brought along with her in a beige leather case. 'And I promised mother I'd see to it that the flowers were all arranged properly.' She suddenly stared up at the ceiling as she heard a creak above our heads. 'What was that?'

I stared into her startled face. 'Oh nothing, Rawlings has a habit of creaking, it's been doing it for years. It's to be expected with such an ancient property.'

'Huh.' She murmured, looking bewildered. 'Well, I still think you should come and live with us when you're married Effie. Father has already suggested that you and Duncan have the east wing; it has more than enough rooms, each one with scenes of the breathtaking gardens at the back of the property. Imagine gazing out at the sweeping lawns with views of the sea beyond.' She let out a contented sigh. 'In the summer months we always go sailing out on the bay, weather permitting of course, and often we take a picnic down to the cove and lay sunning ourselves all day, taking dips in the sea to cool off.'

'It sounds idyllic.'

'It is.' She replied laughing. Snapping her case shut and picking it up, she begun moving towards the door, jumping a little as one of the floorboards she stood upon made an ominous creaking noise. 'Are you sure you wish to stay in this house after the ceremony, Effie?'

'Well yes, this is my home, and Duncan is keen to live at Rawlings too. Isaiah and him have been talking non-stop about the renovations, and what to begin work on first.' Suddenly feeling embarrassed I looked away from her. 'But my Aunt and I have warned them both that we can only spend what we can afford, and also I should hate to lose the character of the house.'

She laughed. 'I wouldn't worry about the cost Effie. Like I mentioned to your father Isaiah, Duncan has more than enough funds to transform Rawlings, and I know you detest the idea of using his money, but as well as having exceedingly rich parents, my brother is also extremely wealthy in his own right, especially after our great aunt left him her entire fortune in her will.' She pulled a face. 'Oh dear, I do hope you don't think I'm being boastful. I really should try and curb my tongue.'

I rose and followed her to the door, taking her hand. 'No, not at all Charlotte, I think you're very sweet. And it would be lovely to stay at your family mansion, and of course you're welcome to stay at Rawlings whenever you feel like it.'

Her eyes widened in alarm. 'Well…. yes, thank you Effie. Perhaps…perhaps I'll stay the odd night or two sometime in the future.' She went out the door and turned to smile at me. 'Well see you soon.' With a giggle she gave me a small hug 'And don't be late.'

I watched as she trotted down the stairs.

Duncan had told me how Charlotte truly believed Rawlings to be haunted, and since making her acquaintance I noticed how she only visited the house when absolutely necessary, and would make up excuses to meet elsewhere. Perhaps, knowing how she felt, it had been thoughtless of me to suggest she could stay. I would speak to her later and apologise.

I quickly made the bed and tidied a few things away in the wardrobe, trying not to look at Gilbert who was propped up on one of the shelves, glaring at me with his usual horrifying eyes. Then, trying to keep composed, I left the room and began the arduous task of handling the stairs without tripping on my gown and plummeting headfirst to the bottom. Thankfully I made it without any harm, breathing a sigh of relief when I stepped into the hallway.

I observed the bouquet on the table, my bouquet. The flowers were arranged in a neat bunch of white roses, orange blossoms and lilies of the valley, tied together with several strands of silk ribbon. My Aunt and Isaiah were standing together by the front entrance.

My Aunt stepped forward and gazed at me. 'Oh Effie, I'm flabbergasted.' She exclaimed, covering her mouth and shaking her head in disbelief. 'I…I don't know what to say. You're a vision, a beautiful vision.'

My cheeks began to blush profusely.

'Splendid, absolutely splendid.' Said Isaiah, striding forward and clapping his hands. 'I knew Charlotte would do wonders with you Effelia.' His eyes bore into mine. 'I shall truly be the proudest father to walk their daughter down the aisle, that there's ever been.' He paused then spoke in a quiet voice. 'In this world or any other.' Beaming he turned to my Aunt. 'And you dear Constance.' He gasped, strolling towards her. 'Well, your beauty and grace know no bounds.' Smiling, his eyes ran over her pale green suit and hat, which was adorned with a single silk flower. He took her hand and kissed it. 'I shall have to beat away your admirers with a stick.'

'Oh Isaiah.' She exclaimed, chortling with laughter. 'You are the kidder.' She placed her hand over her heart and gazed into his eyes. 'Mr Benson will have to be on his guard.'

The smile suddenly dropped from his face. 'Yes, yes he will. Otherwise, he'll be finding something a lot deadlier than foxes visiting him on his allotment.' He began roaring with laughter.

My Aunt started laughing too, playfully slapping him on the arm. 'What a devil you are Isaiah.' She turned and glanced at me as I stood there looking miserable. 'Well cheer up my dear, it's your wedding day.'

'Sorry, last minute jitters.'

'Oh Effie, you'll be fine.' She said with a gentle smile, looking endearingly into my eyes. 'I promise your father and I will be with you every step of the way.'

'Indeed.' Said Isaiah, touching my arm. 'You mean the world to me, dear daughter.'

'I know Isaiah, you tell me every single day.'

'Well, I would hate for you to forget now wouldn't I Effelia?' he uttered, with a wink.

I threw him a strange look.

Isaiah had sold his house some months ago, after declaring he could no longer live in a place where he'd almost perished, and he seemed desperately worried about the burglars, believing they would come back and attack him again. 'What if they return Constance, to finish me off?' He'd uttered shakily. 'I can't bear it… I really can't.' My Aunt had insisted there and then that he moved his belongings into Rawlings. How swiftly he made it his new home, taking possession of the large spare room upstairs, and filling it with his effects. Sometimes I wished he didn't live at our home, as he had a habit of skulking around in corners, watching me closely at all times, as if he half expected me to run away or something along those lines. And since he'd made the announcement that he was my father, my Aunt seemed to dote on him even more. Evidently, she had always known in her heart that there was something special about him, and was deeply disappointed he hadn't confided in her before. 'It was a delicate subject to broach Constance, especially as it involved your sister.'

Isaiah had told her distraughtly. 'She was my dearest love, and...and when she left, I was completely heartbroken.' He begun to sob at that point, and my Aunt had placed her arm about him and said how abysmally my mother had treated him, and how she was over the moon that he was now officially one of the family.

For a second, I lost my balance a little, and had to put my hand out to steady myself.

My Aunt groaned. 'Effie, you really should have eaten breakfast, you know how faint you become without it.' She uttered, looking rather concerned.'

'Aunt I'm really not hungry.' I said, laughing nervously. 'I'm far too excited to think about food at a time like this.'

She looked at me dubiously. 'Yes well, I still think you should at least have a piece of toast. Breakfast sets you up for the day. If Mace was here....'

Isaiah's voice came booming over hers.

'Constance please don't mollycoddle the girl - can't you see she's fine.'

'There's no need to take that tone Isaiah.' I said indignantly. 'My Aunt was only trying to help.'

For a second my Aunt gazed at Isaiah in shock, but then her face relaxed into a smile as she turned to look at me. 'No, no Effie, Isaiah is right. You're not a child anymore, I shouldn't interfere.' Her eyes drifted to the door of the library. 'If...if you mother was here then things would have been different.'

Isaiah made a grunting sound then crossed his arms.

'Well Freya's not here, is she. Like I've told the both of you many times before, that woman decided many years ago to make her life overseas, and now has a new husband and children. She has forsaken us and will *not* be returning.' He made a whimpering sound, placing his hand upon my shoulder. 'I know it's hard, but we must move on, and forget about her.'

My Aunt nodded solemnly.

Ironically it was easy for me to forget her, because without any memories of my mother there was nothing to remember. You couldn't miss a person who had never been there. Once I believed she had been in my dreams, at least I think it was a dream. She had told me she was returning home, only something or someone ended up prevented her from making the trip.

'Well, let's not all stand here like dummies.' Cried Isaiah in a loud voice, staring at me with a smug smile. 'We've got a wedding to get to.'

We walked out into the steadily falling rain, and I remember thinking what awful gloomy weather it was to be getting married in, not at all what I'd envisaged on my wedding day. The midmorning sun should be beaming down upon my face and all the vibrant summer flowers would be in full bloom, filling the garden with their intoxicating aroma. As my Aunt held an umbrella over my head, I carefully lifted my gown to prevent it becoming soaked from the many puddles, and gingerly stepped across the gravel drive towards Isaiah's car, which had a rather flamboyant bow draped across the bonnet.

As we approached the chapel, I could hear the bells ringing. Charlotte was standing at the entrance, greeting last minute guests with a gracious smile, desperately trying to hold onto her umbrella, as the sudden strong winds blew across from the west. Despite the weather she looked exquisite in her pale-yellow bridesmaid dress. She grinned when she saw me and waved.

'Come on dear.' Said my Aunt in a tearful voice as she helped me out the car. Trying to smile she began patting her eyes with a handkerchief. 'They're happy tears Effie, happy tears.'

Isaiah handed me my bouquet then took my arm, beaming from ear to ear as he led me through the chapel doors.

Suddenly the whole significance of the ceremony seemed dauntingly real, so much so that part of me wished it to be an elaborate dream, and dream where I wasn't *really* in this chapel with all these people, and didn't *really* have to face the torment of being stared at by every single guest. No, I was *really* in my bed sleeping, and it was *really* only a dream.

I remember gazing at the beautifully stained-glass windows as we entered the chapel, as if I'd never seen them before. Rather I stare at them than straight ahead I thought, knowing there would be a sea of faces waiting to look at me.

Aunt wished me luck as she went to take her seat, and I vaguely heard Charlotte asking if I was ready, as she stood behind me.

'Effelia, *Effelia*?'

In rather a daze I turned and stared at Isaiah. 'Yes?'

He pulled me gently forward. 'Stop gazing into space.' He whispered urgently, before turning and mumbling something to Charlotte. Then with a pompous smile he began waving to several guests in the pews.

With a nervous gulp I finally faced the congregation. The chapel was full to the brim and everyone *was* staring in my direction. The building was filled with gardenias, lilies of the valley and an abundance of white roses, and small bunches of them hung on the end of each pew, tied with flowing ribbon. Still in a daze, I clung to Isaiah's arm as we gradually made our way forward. My eyes were drawn to the carpet of white rose petals scattered over the crimson rug, covering the entire length of the aisle. I remember seeing a little boy with a mischievous grin, scurrying across the chapel, back to his scowling mother, and a lady with a rather fussy looking hat, full of garish looking feathers. But it was the tall, distinguished looking guest with dark wavy hair that really caught my attention, and despite only seeing the back of his head I was nonetheless suddenly filled with the same sadness I had felt on the days leading up to my wedding, however as he turned to look, I realised his face was completely unknown to me, and the feeling swiftly faded. My eyes focused on Duncan, who was standing directly ahead of me, nervously fiddling with his hair. I reached for his hand as I approached him, and he gave me a dazzling smile. And there we both stood, ready and waiting to say our vows in front of Reverend Cosgrove.

I've always found in life that although we all just chug along with our little lives, with nothing really out the ordinary occurring, we are incapable of controlling the unexpected, and try as we might we cannot predict the events of the immediate future, no matter how meticulously we might plan our day. For me a strange event was about to take place, causing somewhat of a catastrophe, which would turn my special day into an extraordinary day, for all the wrong reasons.

All of a sudden, the chapel doors were flung wide open, and a strong gust of wind blew into the building, scattering the rose petals in every direction. Everyone, including myself, turned to stare at the figure framed in the doorway, and there were gasps of surprise and low murmurs from the pews.

The person stared directly into my eyes, and then shouted so loudly it echoed throughout the chapel.

'Stop the ceremony.'

A hushed silence fell all around us.

I started to fall into the deep, dark depths of unconsciousness.